ABOUT DOLI

Bostonian Dawn McCarthy's life is shattered following a profound double tragedy. Michael, her Irish husband, drowns in a fiery boating accident off the southwest coast of Ireland. Their only child, Jason, who has witnessed his father's death, is diagnosed with traumatic mutism and no longer speaks. Following a series of failed therapies, Dawn believes her son will never talk again.

Rejecting the doctor's advice, Dawn returns with Jason to the remote Irish fishing village of Kilcastle where her husband had lived and died. There, along the rugged Irish Atlantic coastline, she hopes to find a cure for her son. But it is not an easy return for Dawn. She faces daily reminders of what might have been.

The sudden appearance of a wild dolphin delivers newfound hope. In the days that follow, Dawn witnesses a powerful bond grow between Jason and the dolphin as the boy takes his first small steps toward healing. It is only then that she suspects the enigmatic mammal is much more than she had at first supposed.

Dolphin Song is a tale of terrifying tragedy, magical Irish legends and eternal love. Dawn's voyage takes readers on an unforgettable journey where those we have loved and lost are not gone forever. Instead, we need only take a leap of faith to find them again.

What Readers Say

"…spiritually uplifting. A thought-provoking, inspiring and intriguing story. I will recommend *Dolphin Song* to my book club and anyone interested in Ireland." — *Illinois reader*

"If this was a film, I'd describe it as *The Big Blue* meets *Lorenzo's Oil*. A compelling mix of Irish legend, the magic of dolphins, tragedy at sea and a final twist of eternal love." — *London, England reader*

"This is one of those books you never want to end." — *New Mexico reader*

"The seascape of southwest Ireland jumps off the page. A powerful novel about finding courage and hope in the face of tragedy. Today's world needs just such a story." — *Michigan reader*

BY THE SAME AUTHOR

Fiction for young adults
Hotfoot
Hotfoot 2: Lucky's Revenge
The Lost Scrolls of Newgrange
The Den Adventure

Non-fiction
A Survivor's Guide to Living in Ireland

———————————

Dolphin Song is the author's
debut novel for adult readers

Follow Tom on his blog www.survivingireland.blogspot.com/,
on Facebook www.facebook.com/dolphinsongthenovel
or on Goodreads www.goodreads.com/author/show/8048777.Tom_Richards

DOLPHIN SONG

Tom Richards

Storylines
Entertainment Ltd

First published in 2021 by Storylines Entertainment Ltd
Beara, Bantry, County Cork, Ireland P75A342
© Copyright Storylines Entertainment Ltd
and Tom Richards, 2021
All Rights Reserved

Cover by Touqeer Shahid.
Find him on fiverr.com at Touqeershahid95
Editing by Delia Malim-Robinson Set in Garamond

ISBN: 978-0-9550212-1-3

<u>Rights Acquisition</u>: for information on rights acquisition contact
Storylines Entertainment Ltd.:
storylinesentertainmentireland@gmail.com
or the author: tomjrichards@gmail.com

For Carmel Murray and your faith in me,
& in loving memory of Liam O'Neill, my friend

"We can speak without voice to the trees and the clouds and the waves of the sea. Without words they respond through the rustling of leaves and the moving of clouds and the murmuring of the sea."

— Paul Tillich

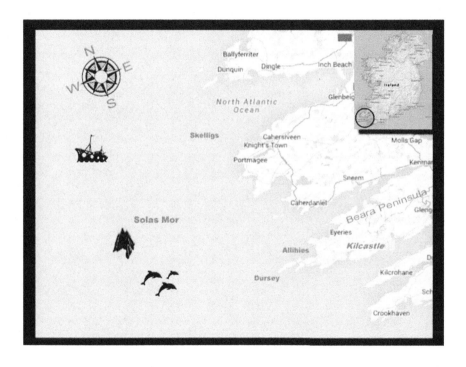

DOLPHIN
SONG

PRELUDE

Michael said to the woman bearing his child: "You carry all that is good in me, all that I hope and pray for. Can I give you a gift in return?"

"What gift is that?" Dawn asked.

"It's a secret. If I show you, will you promise not to tell anyone?"

When she agreed, he took her on his father's fishing boat to the island of Solas Mór and its hidden mystery. For many years she told no one due to the promise she had given and because her love for him was greater than any she had known before.

After a time, Dawn forgot the secret. She would remember it again only when she had lost him and at last understood the song he sang to her from so far away.

PART I

THE SINKING

CHAPTER ONE

On the morning of the accidental sinking, the sixth day of their visit to her husband's Irish home, there was great excitement in the house overlooking the harbor town of Kilcastle. Michael had been swayed to return with his family to the rugged shores of Solas Mór and its hidden secret. Standing in the kitchen sunlight, Dawn helped her mother-in-law prepare lunch and, as they did, answered her son's excited questions.

"Nana, how long will it take to get to the island?" Jason sang in his Boston cadence, eyes sparking like stars.

"Hours," Margaret replied as she used a long knife to cut sandwiches.

"When are we going? Can't we go now?"

"We'll leave as soon as we're finished," Dawn answered as she wrapped them.

"Is it a big island?" Jason persisted, reaching for a square of ham and salad.

"You just ate. These are for lunch," she replied, pulling it away with a wink to her mother-in-law. "The island is huge. Wait 'til you see it."

"Is it as big as Greenland? Greenland is the biggest island in the world."

"How did you know that? I'd never heard of Greenland when I was your age."

"Jason, you're a comical genius," Margaret remarked to her grandson who stood on a chair pulled tight to the table so he could watch. "Where do you learn such things?"

5

"Well, is it big as Greenland?" he asked again, leaning against his nana as she smoothed his curling hair.

"You'll have to ask your father when we get to the boat," Dawn replied, smiling down. "Don't forget Mister Monkey. He's in your bedroom."

Jason leaped off the chair, his laughter filling the room as he scampered out the door. Dawn grinned, hearing his excited footfalls pound up the wooden stairs.

"Comical genius is right," Dawn observed, scanning the pile of sandwiches. "Do you think we have enough?"

"You know how they eat," Margaret answered. "We'll make four more. Now hand me the bread."

When the picnic was ready the family walked from the house, down the steep back steps to the main street. Crossing Kilcastle's busy town square, they made their way to the pier. There, the fleet of trawlers lay tied up between fishing trips, nestled so close together that the protective fenders lashed to their hulls bumped against each other in the swell. When Jason saw his father working on the stern of the blue and white half-decker, he broke from the women, skipping fast along the pier with the sea at his shoulder.

"Jason, be careful! You'll fall in," Margaret called. "Dawn, tell him."

"Jason, listen to your Nana!"

But Jason was already at the boat and she watched as Michael lifted him over the gunwale. Their son whispered to him, eyes slanting to his mother as his father untied the lines that held the vessel fast to the trawlers beside it. She could hear their laughter as Michael coiled in the ropes, stowing them on deck. Finished, he stood tall in the morning sunlight, their boy perched high on his father's shoulder, clasping his monkey. They grinned down at the women who walked toward them across the pier.

"What are you two laughing at?" Dawn called up.

"Mind your own business," Michael replied. "We'll miss the day if you don't get onboard."

"Come on, Mom. Hurry!"

"I'm hurrying," Dawn replied and, handing up the bag of lunch to her husband, noticed her mother-in-law's frown. "You sure you won't come?"

"I'm too old. Just like that boat."

"It's a fine boat," Michael said and, bending over the gunwale, patted the hand-painted name on the trawler's stern. "See? You're coming whether you like it or not."

"The *Margie M*," Margaret sniffed. "Can't you change it? It's not even my name."

"Da' always said 'Margaret' had too many letters in it. What's the bother, anyway? You've complained about it since I was in short pants."

"It's still not right. Just don't be gone long."

"He'll get us back on time," Dawn said. "It's such a pretty day for it. Are you sure you won't come?"

"You know how I worry. Besides, it's Sunday. I have to go to Mass."

"I bet you'll say a prayer for us."

"Give an old woman her comforts," Margaret answered and looked again at her men. "You two. Get down here. I want a picture before you go."

Jason protested at the delay but they clambered off the boat and the family posed beneath the orange, green and white national flag of Ireland. The Tri-color was tied fast to a pole bolted to the pier a dozen yards from the trawler, snapping in the breeze.

"Jason, be still," Margaret insisted as her grandson squirmed. "This is special."

His father wrapped both arms around his son long enough for Margaret to take her pictures. Then the three climbed back onboard and Michael cranked the old diesel engine to life.

"Promise you'll be careful, Michael," Margaret called over the bellowing engine.

"I'm always careful," he shouted back through the open wheelhouse door. "We'll be home by teatime. Dawn, let go the lines."

Dawn untied the stern lines still holding the boat and they were free. She stood with her son on the solid timber deck which trembled as Michael advanced the throttle. The *Margie M* moved out into the calm waters of the harbor toward the tall red buoy that marked the entrance into Bantry Bay.

"Wave to Nana," Dawn said, seeing Margaret waving to them.

"Goodbye, Nana," Jason yelled across the water. "Goodbye!"

They watched Margaret until she was hidden by other trawlers that lined the pier. Then Dawn led her son from the stern to the midship gunwale where they stood as the boat steamed further into the harbor. She looked up at the clear sky, seeing the circling gulls squawking for a meal. Breathing deep, she smelled the sea, the wind rustling through her long wheat-colored hair.

"Let's go find your dad," she said, and took her son's hand.

They made their way into the wheelhouse, standing beside Michael as he steered the trawler into the bay. Dawn watched Bere Island and its green fields slide by. She pointed out to Jason the lighthouse that thrust into the sky at its western end and a family of seals basking on sunlit rocks. The boat steamed past Dursey Island with its cable car then out of the bay into the true Atlantic, beyond.

In the fresh ocean chop, her husband lifted his son so he could grasp the wheel to help with the steering. Jason held tight, pulling at the wheel when his father told him to adjust course.

"What's on the island, Dad?" Jason asked, balancing on the steering chair.

Michael tousled his son's curling hair. "You're going to have to wait to find out."

"Mom, tell me."

"It's a surprise. You don't want us to spoil it, do you?"

He huffed as she placed a hand on the back of his neck. Feeling her son's warm excitement, she steadied herself against the rolling pitch of the trawler. She looked through the forward window at a glittering sea and to a far horizon dotted with clear-weather cumulus. With her other hand she found her husband's broad shoulder.

"Michael, remember the first time?"

"No, I don't," he lied, smiling.

"Oh, yes, you do," she replied to the old joke. "Of course, you do."

"Honest, I don't." When she laughed, he put an arm around her, pulling her in. "Gersha, how could I ever forget the first time?"

She grasped his strong forearm and tightened her grip on Jason. The boy's excited face fueled her anticipation for the gift they would soon share with him. With it came the memory of the first time she had taken this voyage. Out the window, she saw the place at the bow's railing where she had stood when pregnant with her son. She remembered the island's high peak and what lay hidden there, and the promise she had given Michael to keep it a secret because it was too precious to share with anyone else.

Five years earlier, in the final weeks of her pregnancy, Dawn had stood at the bow of this same blue and white trawler. She had worn a slicker two sizes too big against the wet of the sea because it was all Margaret could find for her. They had steamed west through soft weather, the rolling Atlantic waves uninterrupted by anything for thousands of miles. The wind from their passage blew through her hair, watering her eyes that grew as round as the wide ocean. She looked up at a flock of seagulls squawking for their breakfast even though Michael had not rigged the boat for fishing. As the gulls cartwheeled through the misty day, she wondered whether they screamed out of faithful habit or because it was their duty.

She clung to the railing welded fast to the gunwale, relying on it to steady her when the boat ran up a broad swell. When the trawler fell into a deep trough it shook the teeth in her head. She believed it when Michael told her the seas could get much worse. She thought she would not like to experience a storm on these waters.

The island appeared a few hours after they steamed out of the bay which emptied into the sea two miles west of the fishing town of Kilcastle. She watched as the island grew from a speck in the distance to something much more imposing. From a mile out, it consumed a good ten degrees of the horizon, its gigantic form dwarfing everything else.

The island had a single peak which thrust skyward, its craggy tip lost in the torn clouds of mid-morning. Its rocky base reminded her of an ancient fortress, a hulking darkness slung low on the sea. From where she stood, she could make out the furious waves sweeping onto the naked land, covering its desolate shore in whitewater, its voice like thunder. The tumult reminded her of how exposed she was on the rocking deck and, thinking herself a fool, placed a hand on her belly and the unborn child within. She let go of the railing and propelled herself back across the pitching deck, through the open wheelhouse door. She found her husband sitting on the steering chair, one hand to the wheel.

"Are you sure it's safe, Michael?" Dawn asked. Grabbing a steel handhold fixed above the instrument panel, she eyed the surf that crashed on to the island's rocks.

"I'm not planning on surfing her on to shore, if that's what you think," was his teasing reply. "Honest, we'll be safe as houses."

"Like hell we will."

He held out an arm and she slid into it, sheltering in his strength, as with the other hand he turned the wheel. The *Margie M* steamed closer to the island which, he told her, the local people called in the Irish *'Solas Mór'.*

"Solas Mór?" she asked, looking up at him with confused eyes.

"The Place of the Sun," he grinned. "Will you not ever learn your Irish?"

She glanced again at the heaving seas hammering the island's shores. "Place of the devil is more like it."

"There's an old pier on the other side," he laughed, pulling her tight. "With the wind in this direction we'll be safe enough. You'll see."

The clouds parted and sunlight lit the rugged peak in burnished gold. They steamed around a point and in the lee of the island the seas calmed. He turned the boat again, heading for an inlet hidden between tall up-thrusts of rock. Five minutes later they docked at an ancient stone pier. Dawn waited as Michael walked on deck to lash the trawler tight. While he busied himself with the ropes, she clambered down the short steps into the belly of the boat. Within the tight space that held the galley, she changed the slicker for a bright sundress which she pulled over her bulging pregnancy. Then she made her way back up on deck and Michael helped her on to the pier and across the rugged terrain of the island.

He led her up a path of sandstone to a hidden ledge, then along it to its end. He grinned at her then leaped, lost in the shadows beneath her. She could make out his arms reaching high for her.

"Jump," he called up.

"Michael, you can be such a pissa," Dawn frowned, her Boston accent taking an edge. She looked down at him, eyeing the distance. "You gotta be kidding. I'm as big as an elephant. What's down there anyway?"

"Come on and find out."

As he reached higher, she thought, 'He's such an easy target, the clown'. Her face contorting in sudden anger, she swung from him, marching away.

"Dawn!" Michael called, and she caught the note of worry in his voice. Unable to keep up the pretense, she spun back with a wicked smile.

"Don't you do that!" he said, relieved her anger was a tease.

"Don't you mess with a pregnant woman," she scolded.

He reached up again and, taking her at the waist, lifted her down. She wrapped her arms around his strong shoulders, raising her face to be kissed. He took her hand, leading her beyond the shadows into sunlight. She stopped, mesmerized by what she saw beyond.

"Oh my God, look at that. It's beautiful."

The lagoon had no business being there, not within such ruggedness. Sunlight sparkled like jewels off the aquamarine waters, its broad expanse nestled within the arms of raw rock, while a narrow inlet led out to the open sea. She stood on a strand of white sugar sand, finer even than the sands of the Carolina beaches she had visited as a child with her parents.

"How did you find this?"

"I told you. It's a secret. Now it's our secret."

Taking her hand again, he led her toward the water.

"No way, mister. Michael, forget it," she objected when she understood his intent. But she let herself be led on, stopping only to pull off her sandals. When her naked feet touched the sea, she found it had warmed in the sunlight. Then she was up to her waist in it.

"Sit back," he said.

Dawn sat into the waters of the lagoon, and into his arms. He swung her through the gentle sea, the sundress billowing, the lagoon's warmth lapping over her awkward body.

"Don't ever let go," she whispered, holding him tight.

"Not a chance."

She opened her eyes, seeing a streak of bright color fly across a boundless sky.

"What's that?"

"A puffin."

"Puffin," she murmured. Smiling at the name, she put her head back in the water.

"Listen," she said, her lips parting.

With her ears beneath the lagoon's surface, Dawn could hear the heartbeat of their child. Placing his head on her belly, Michael also listened. He heard two heartbeats intertwined, his child's and his wife's, and looked up into her smiling eyes.

"I love you."

"I love you, too," she whispered, holding his head tight against her. "God, how I love you."

They floated together while the double heartbeats reverberated through a sea of life. Though she did not know it, mackerel fry played at her feet. Further away, a group of iridescent disk-shaped jellyfish pulsed through shadows seeking plankton that grew near the surface. Even further, the waters of the lagoon were divided by a curtain of shimmering sealight caused by the refracted sun that streamed freely through it. Beyond that, the inlet led to the sea and the mysteries of the immense Atlantic.

It was up this inlet the pod of dolphins swam. They seldom encountered humans in this deserted part of the sea and, hearing the heartbeats, their curiosity drew them from play to investigate. God-given sonar lodged behind wide liquid eyes probed the waters with bursts of short clicks and squeals. When they desired to talk among themselves, the staccato of clicks was replaced with a song that could echo for miles through the sea.

The lead dolphin, uniquely spotted, a white patch covering its forehead, echolocated again. Finding the source of its curiosity, it led the pod into the shallow lagoon. Breaking through the curtain of sealight, it approached the family that floated near.

"Did you hear that?" Dawn sat up, grasping her husband's forearms.

"What?"

"I heard something."

She scanned the lagoon not knowing what she was looking for.

"There!" Michael said, and she followed his pointing finger. A dark fin sliced toward them through the dappled waters.

"What is that?"

"Shhhhh," Michael said, holding her tight. "Wait."

Dawn backed deeper into his arms as the white-faced dolphin approached. Its broad tail flukes shifted, propelling it closer. Focusing on the source of the heartbeats, it echolocated again. The water around Dawn vibrated to its song.

"It's a Common Dolphin," Michael whispered. "See how dark its back is and the white markings? Don't be afraid. It won't hurt you."

"It tickles. I'm not afraid."

When the dolphin sang again, the baby kicked. She held Michael's hand against her belly so he could feel it, too. "It's as if he wants to swim with it."

She lay back, letting the moment wash over her. The dolphin's head rose above the surface, its dark eye seeming to beckon to her. Transfixed, she reached out, wanting to stroke it.

Thunder crashed. Startled, she looked to the sky. Lightning forked through heavy clouds as a gale swept toward them. Thunder cracked again and the dolphin moved away.

"Come on," Michael said, helping her up. "Let's get back to the boat."

Wading from the water, Dawn watched as the dolphin joined its brethren. The pod turned as one, swimming across the lagoon then down the inlet and out to sea. As they leaped over choppy whitecaps, she thought she would never again experience such a moment of mysterious connectedness.

"Dawn? Look there!"

The memory of their first voyage broke as her husband swung the wheel and Jason strained to see through the salt-spattered window. In the near distance, the base of the island was obscured by a dense curtain of ocean fog. The towering peak punched through it, reflecting brilliant sunshine.

"Is that where we're going?" Jason asked. "Is that Solas Mór?"

"That's it," Michael said, winking at his son. "Ah, but we're close enough, now, aren't we? Don't know about you, Jason, but your dad's kinda sleepy."

"Me too," his son replied, raising both arms in a huge stretch. "I need a nap."

Dawn looked from one to the other. "Jason, you can't be sleepy. Last night you both slept like bricks."

Michael swung the wheel again and the boat turned despite his wife's protests. A yellow sea buoy came into view. It floated, lolling in the swell, its distinctive steel warning bell clanging in a tall metal spire. Dawn cocked an eyebrow.

"What are you two up to? I thought you wanted to get to the island."

"We're early. Thought we'd get some rest and wait for the weather over the island to clear. Isn't that right Jason?"

"That's right, Dad," Jason said with a mischievous look.

"I don't know what's going on but it better be good. Michael, you know how Margaret worries. You promised her we'd be back by teatime."

"And so we will," he said as he reached for the throttle. "Relax for a minute, will ya? Mam will be fine. Jason, give me a hand."

She thought how, if they were late, his mother would be anything but fine. Her men left the wheelhouse, busying themselves with the anchor on the sunlit deck. She heard the splash as it hit the water and the hard chorus of steel chain running out the hawsepipe.

"Dawn?" Michael called, holding up a sunchair. "Come on out. Sit a spell in this, why don't ya?"

"He can be such a Bozo," she said to herself, grinning. Waving to him, she followed them out into the warm sunlight.

CHAPTER TWO

Margaret had waited on the pier until the trawler disappeared around the point and into the bay. When it was gone, she hurried past the RNLI Station where the sleek orange and blue lifeboat lay tied-up waiting to respond to any emergency. As she walked by, she prayed it would not have to be used that day or any day. Then she turned up the main street and into the busy harbor town.

As she passed the open shops, she felt her belly knot. Her unease had grown since the half-decker had made-way, and she thought herself a fool. 'Michael knows what he's at,' she scolded herself. 'He's been at sea since he was Jason's age. You know they'll be safe.' But worry had set like baked cement, causing her heart to race. Seeing the steps rising off the main street, she climbed them to the entrance of the church, entering through the tall arched doors.

Since moving to Kilcastle and marrying the fisherman who had made a life with her, she had often carried her troubles into the town's church, lighting a candle before the statue that was the miraculous patron saint for the lost. She had prayed to him whenever her husband Tomás had gone out fishing. She prayed when her son had moved to America with his new wife. She prayed whenever he transited the Atlantic by airplane with his family, back home to visit her. She also prayed every time Michael took his father's fishing boat to sea, and looked to heaven with gratitude when she saw the blue and white trawler steam back in to tie up again at the pier. Except for the one terrible time when Tomás had failed to return, her prayers had always been answered.

In the church, empty because it was still hours before Mass, she lit a candle and placed it before the saint, eyes fixed on the bouquet of white lilies he held.

"Oh, Saint of miracles, patron of the lost, protect my family and secure their safety. Please, dear Saint, let them find their way home to me." Then she bowed her head in silence.

When she finished, she genuflected and crossed herself, then made her way out of the church to the house she had bought with Tomás when they had first married. She spent the morning mopping the solid oak floors then put on a load of laundry, hanging the clothes out to dry in the back garden with its fine view of the harbor. As she did, her eyes cast sideways. She scanned the pier as well as the small dock just below the house where Tomás had taught Michael to swim when he was a boy. She looked for the boat but saw none.

'It's still early,' she chided herself. 'It isn't even eleven.'

Twenty minutes later, Margaret walked back in to town to attend Mass. When the service ended, and after Father Danny had blessed his flock, she again walked up the hill, back to the house. In the kitchen she made a cup of strong tea, looking at the wall clock to confirm the time. Finished, she got back to work to pass the day.

At teatime the unexpected storm blew in. Standing at the living room window, Margaret watched the harbor waters being blown to white fury. The *Margie M* was not back, its slip at the pier still empty. An hour later and thinking herself a fool, she phoned the Coast Guard. The man at the end of the line gave her worry credence due to the severity of the gale and promised to take action. Because Margaret's house rose at the harbor's edge, she heard the powerful twin engines of the lifeboat as the crew cranked them to life. From the rain-spattered window, she watched the boat beat fast through the twilight into the turbulent bay. Though she made another cup of tea, she worried more when the cup shook in her hand. She tried to find sleep on the couch but could not close her eyes. Instead, she gazed out the darkened window and, hearing the wind whistling through the eves, listened for the phone that refused to ring. By morning, with the storm blown out and the sun rising on calm waters, she let herself into the back garden, searching the harbor below. The lifeboat was not back at its station. Neither was the *Margie M.*

"Oh, holy Saint of miracles, saint of the lost," she pleaded, hands twisting together, "please, dear Saint. Lead my family home to me."

Her prayer was disturbed by a knock at the back gate. Opening it she found Mary, a close friend and local shopkeeper, standing on the step. The old woman's neck was bowed as if carrying too much weight.

"Is there news, Mary?" Margaret asked in a trembling voice.

When Mary raised her head, she knew there would be no reply. The sadness in her friend's eyes said all that needed to be said. Margaret fell to her knees, not able to utter even a single word of loss.

Eighteen miles southwest of Kilcastle Dawn stood on the bow of a boat. This time it was not the *Margie M* but the powerful lifeboat's deck that rolled and pitched beneath her. Wrapped in a silver survival blanket, her injured arm cocooned in bandages, she did not know that the stench of smoke still mingled with the tears on her face and through her tangled hair. Nor was she aware of the lifeboat crew who worked with such diligence around her. She did not see the island rising behind her or her son who stood near, a blanket also thrown over his shoulders, his face gaunt with trauma.

It was only when the orange and white Irish Coast Guard helicopter roared overhead that her eyes focused. She followed it as it swept over the island, pirouetting in the vast expanse of blue sky, circling back toward the lifeboat. She noticed the immense yellow buoy wallowing in the sea near the lifeboat's hull, hearing the hollow clang of its bell. She saw a diver surface in the water near it, a thick hawser in his hand. When he thrust a thumb skyward, the shrill motor of a winch engaged and she watched as the hawser was pulled from the sea.

Dawn's gaze turned to Jason. Staring at the rope as it was being hauled up, his young face turned rigid when the anchor chain came into view. His eyes at first registered hope but that was extinguished when the diver held up the other end of the hawser showing where it had been hacked through. Dawn wanted to rush to her son but her legs refused to obey. Instead, she watched as Jason's hair was blown to fury by the downwash of the helicopter which hovered above them. She turned to the wheelhouse. Through the glass, she could see the RNLI skipper as he talked on the radio with the helicopter pilot. His mouth worked as he signed off and the helicopter streaked east toward the mainland. The crew quieted as the skipper stepped out, making his way across the steel deck to stand at her side.

"Mrs. McCarthy?"

Dawn could only see his lips move because her ears still swam with the wail of horror. "What did you say?" she asked. But courage died in the skipper's eyes and she understood what he was going to say before he said it. "No, no, please, not yet. You have to keep searching."

The skipper looked first at her then to her son. Jason registered the bleak message in the sailor's eyes. He stumbled back against the railing; his small hands clenched into tight fists.

"Jason, come here to me," Dawn called.

Her legs at last obeyed and she rushed to him. But as she stepped closer, he did not move. The only thing he was able to do was open his mouth.

Jason screamed.

She could not stop him as he ran uncontrolled across the deck. He fought when a tall sailor cornered him against the wheelhouse. Avoiding his thrashing fists, the sailor lifted him, carrying her sobbing son below-decks. Then she thought day had become night because she could not see. It was only when the skipper called, "Mrs. McCarthy? Mrs. McCarthy?" and snapped his fingers at her face that she opened her eyes. She scanned the vertical deck and found she was lying on it. The skipper took her by the arms, sitting her up.

"We took your son below. I'll take you to him." As he helped her stand, he asked carefully, "Mrs. McCarthy, do you know where you are?"

When she did not answer he frowned and, tucking the silver blanket closer, led her aft. Dawn realized she had no memory of what day it was or what had happened at the end of her family's voyage. It was only as she was led past a bright orange rib, the rubber boat tied down to its station, that she remembered. She remembered the squall and the thunderous waves, and the fire and stinking smoke. She remembered the frantic eyes of her son when they were forced to abandon his father trapped in the bowels of the sinking *Margie M.*

"What about Michael?" she whispered but the skipper tightened his grip, leading her below-decks like a lost child. He slipped off the survival blanket, replacing it with one of thick wool. After checking her injured arm, he sat her on a narrow bunk within the warm womb of the cabin.

"Let's get you both home. You rest now," he said, then left her.

She startled when the twin engines roared to life. She saw Jason lying asleep in a separate bunk on the other side of the cabin, unmoving except for the rocking of the lifeboat in the falling swells. Slipping from her bunk, she stumbled across the steel deck, brushing the wet hair from his face. She told herself he was safe even if his father was not and, laying down beside him, held on tight. Holding him caused her to remember other things. They blew in on ripping tides of memory for which she had no explanation.

A shimmering curtain of light within the depths of the sea as an immense shadow swam through it. The fathomless eyes that looked at her with such startling clarity. Then the immense light which lit the towering island in the awe of a false dawn and the distant song which was beyond all recognition.

She closed her eyes against the overwhelming memory. Opening them again, looking at her son, she took comfort in the soft sigh of his breathing, feeling the rise and fall of his chest against her breasts. "You'll be fine when we get home to Nana. You'll see," she whispered, and held him even closer.

The idling twin engines wound up to a steady roar, the cabin slanting as the boat accelerated. As they gathered speed, she felt the lifeboat edging away from the island and their failed search. When the engines slowed again and they lost momentum, she thought she must have slept because she did not know how much time had passed. She came fully awake when two paramedics

21

lifted Jason, placing him on a stretcher. With the skipper leading, they maneuvered him out on to the deck.

"Please be careful with him," she said, following, but they did not reply as they carried their injured cargo into the half-light of day.

Her eyes never left him as the stretcher was lifted down the narrow gangway on to the RNLI dock. She did not notice the crowd gathered there, or the small bundled figure of Margaret who stood in the afternoon rain, her face filled with dread. Dawn followed Jason into the ambulance. It rushed them through the coastal town, sirens blaring, to the community hospital which stood on a hill overlooking the eastern end of the harbor. When they arrived, a nurse stripped her of the soaked clothing then re-bandaged her arm. She watched as, on the other side of the emergency room, medical professionals examined Jason. When they were finished, she followed them as they pushed the bed holding her son down a narrow hallway. They turned into a room with wide windows looking out on the harbor, the cloud-cover as thick as her worry. Sitting down on a separate bed, she watched her son asleep in his hospital cot which had been pushed next to the window.

"You should sleep too," a nurse suggested.

"I'll try but I don't think I can."

When she could not, the nurse insisted on medication. Sinking into a drugged stupor, Dawn twisted, dreaming first of the burning boat as she swam through raging seas, searching for her lost son. Then she dreamed of the impossible song she had heard and the images she had seen. Even in sleep she was convinced she was crazy. In the late evening she woke, her cheeks wet with tears.

"You were crying. You were having a nightmare."

Margaret sat on a chair pulled tight to the bed, holding out a wad of tissues. Dawn wiped her eyes then propped herself up on an elbow, peering across the room to Jason.

"How is he?"

"The doctor told me he'll be fine. He needs to rest."

"I want to see him," Dawn said, shifting her blankets.

"No, not yet," the older woman replied, placing a hand on her daughter-in-law's shoulder. "Sleep now. He's safe."

"You promise?"

"That's what they told me." Margaret stood, brushing dry lips against Dawn's cheek. "I'll be back in the morning."

"Don't go."

But Margaret only squeezed her arm and left. As her mother-in-law stepped out, a doctor entered. In the dim light, Dawn watched him attend to her son.

"How's the brave lad today?" the doctor asked, sweeping a small light across her son's eyes. "Jason, do you want to sit up? Do you know what city you live in? Is it Boston, Jason?"

As Dawn again drifted to sleep, it never occurred to her that her son had not answered any of the doctor's questions.

In the morning, Margaret visited again. They breakfasted on a tray pulled up to Dawn's bed. She wouldn't touch her eggs and fried rasher.

"You need to eat," her mother-in-law insisted.

Dawn picked up a piece of toast, nibbling a corner as she watched her son.

"He's still sleeping, isn't he? Did you talk to the doctor this morning?"

"He promised he'll see you later today."

Dawn thought she heard a note of fear in Margaret's voice. She glanced across the room.

"He's sleeping too much. Are you sure he's okay?"

"Don't be troubling yourself. He'll be right as rain when they're done with him."

When she left, Dawn found herself thinking of what Margaret had said and worried at how she had said it. 'I'm thinking nonsense,' she thought to herself as she peered at her sleeping son. 'Jason will be fine, just like they promised.'

She got up and crept to his bed. Though he was still asleep he looked normal in every way. She placed a hand on his chest, feeling its even rise and fall then pulled up a chair, sitting with him until the doctor arrived.

"His vitals are normal," the older man explained when he had finished the examination. "You must remember he's been through a shock. All he needs is rest."

"Are you sure? You promise me he'll be okay?"

"Give him time," the doctor replied, placing a hand to her shoulder. "You need rest, too. Why not get some more sleep?"

"I'm not sleepy. It seems all we do is sleep."

"You'll sleep when you're ready, just like Jason. You'll find you have no choice."

When he left Dawn ignored the worry eating her belly as she crawled back into bed. Seeing Jason's small figure bundled at the window, she decided to pray for him with the prayers she had learned as a schoolgirl. But bowing her head, she found she could not remember a single word. Instead, she rolled over and slept.

The days in hospital rolled on like a dull winter storm. A nurse visited them each hour. The doctor examined Jason twice a day. Margaret came to visit at every meal. On the third day, Dawn woke to find her son sitting up in bed staring out the window.

"Jason?" Dawn asked, striding across the room. "Jase, I'm here. Sweetie, look at me." But when she reached for him, he shrugged her off and would not turn to her.

When Margaret next visited, she found Dawn sitting on the bed, her head bent toward the floor.

"It hurts when Jason pushes me away."

"Give him time," her mother-in-law answered, taking her hand. "He'll be himself soon. Believe what the doctor says."

But Dawn suspected she no longer knew what to believe.

When she was well enough, each morning she walked from the hospital down to the pier to see if there was news of Michael. She had learned that the Coast Guard had decided to continue its search. Every day as she neared the RNLI station, she prodded her hope as if blowing life on to dying embers. "They'll find him," she whispered to herself. "You'll see. It's not too late." But whenever she reached the lifeboat station, she was always met with the drawn faces of volunteer crews who had no news to give her.

Eight days after the accident, and having again walked to the pier, she found the RNLI lifeboat skipper standing near the bow of his boat. He sucked on an empty pipe, deep in thought. When he saw her, she could tell he did not know what to say.

"They've called off the search, haven't they?"

He couldn't look at her. "I'm sorry, Mrs. McCarthy."

"He's alive," Dawn insisted. "I know he is."

She spun on a heel, turning back down the pier. As she walked away the skipper kept an eye on her, realizing the brave young woman could not accept what they, Margaret and the rest of the town already knew. Michael had been taken by the sea. It had no intention of giving him back.

As the days passed, Dawn grew anxious whenever the doctor visited. When he questioned her son, as he did during every examination, Jason still would not answer. As the day of their release from hospital grew closer, Dawn found the courage to ask the question that had been eating her soul. When the doctor made his rounds on a late afternoon, making a fuss over her injured arm, Dawn cornered him.

"Why won't he talk?" Dawn demanded. "Tell me what's wrong with him."

"He'll come out of it. You'll see," the doctor said, studying the deep wound above her wrist. "I'll take the stitches out next week."

"I don't care about the arm," she replied, pulling it away. "Why can't Jason talk?"

"He'll talk. When enough time has passed, when he heals from the trauma, he'll talk."

When they were at last released and returned to Margaret's house, Dawn asked her son simple questions, prompting him to speak.

"Jason, what's your teacher's name? Jason, what's your favorite kind of ice cream? Jason, what's your favorite TV show?" But instead of answering he always turned away.

"He won't talk," Dawn said to her mother-in-law. "What's wrong with him?"

"The doctor told us to give him time," Margaret replied. "He's a good doctor. Jason will get better just as the doctor promised."

At the end of the month Dawn asked to be excused from the memorial service for Michael, with its prayers and hymns in the town church. She would not admit it to herself but she could not cope with the hurt of even the smallest thought of her lost husband. A day later, as a new month began, Dawn decided she had no option but to take her son home to Boston. One morning, in the rain of a dying summer, Margaret drove what remained of her family up to Dublin, walking with them to airport security before being forced to turn back.

"Jason will get well. He'll talk again," Margaret promised. "I'll pray for it."

"Thank you, Margaret. I know you're right."

But Dawn suspected that what she said to her mother-in-law was a lie because she no longer believed anyone's promises. As the aircraft climbed from the runway, and throughout their journey across the Atlantic, she kept watch on Jason who sat in silence beside her. She felt the tumult of a broken heart, her faith in the world shattered like the hull of her husband's fishing boat and the strangled voice of her son.

She realized she had nothing to replace them with.

PART II

BOSTON

CHAPTER THREE

Back in the Boston Harbor cottage that was their American home, Dawn worked hard to rebuild a normal life for Jason because the Irish doctor had explained it would help his recovery. She tried to coax her despondent son to take walks with her along the nearby beach as the family had always done before the accident, or play with the computer games Santa had left the previous Christmas. Always, she was met by a wall of obstinate silence. Despite Michael's loss, she tried to hide her heartache behind a sunny smile while prompting her son to speak.

"Remember school, Jason?" she asked as they sat eating dinner two days after their return from Ireland. "Wouldn't you like to see your friends again? What are their names? I can't remember." She leaned across the kitchen table, studying the drawn face. "How about if we go see them next Monday? What do you say?"

Jason picked up the plate of Chinese food she had brought home from the local takeout. His head rose, meeting her eyes. Then he dumped it in a heap on the kitchen floor. He stood, his body rigid, lips quivering. Without a sound, he stalked from the room.

Jason's nightmares started three days later. Dawn was woken in the early hours of the morning by a scream that shook the house. Scrambling to his bedroom, she found her son holding tight to his rescued stuffed monkey. Though he was asleep, his face contorted in terror. When she rushed to him, he lashed out with balled-up fists, howling like an injured animal. She sat at the foot of his bed until the nightmare passed and he found uneasy sleep.

Her own nightmares started a day later. When she woke, she could not remember the dream. She took a deep breath, attempting to calm her panicked breathing. She tried to get up but the sheets were twisted around her legs, soaked with sweat. Her eyes darted across the darkened room, looking for her husband. When she couldn't find him, she collapsed back on the damp pillow.

"Oh, God, Michael. Oh God," she whispered, then wept in silence, not wanting to disturb her son.

When a week passed and Jason still would not talk, Dawn realized that her worry for him had become obsessive. She could not let him out of her sight. She worried about him even when he went to the bathroom. Concerned that her awkward interventions were causing Jason more harm than good, she decided to take him to the family's GP. At the end of the examination, the doctor led her out to the hallway.

"I've never seen anything like it," the tall professional puzzled, leaning against the wall. "Heartbeat, respiration, core temp, blood pressure. They're all normal."

"He won't talk," Dawn said, peering through the open door. Jason sat on the examination table, exhausted eyes fixed on the floor. "He won't even look at me."

"You say that following the accident you were both treated for hypothermia?"

"We were in the water for a long time."

"And they were certain there was no head trauma?"

"They checked him for that in Ireland." She glanced up at him. "You didn't find anything they missed, did you?"

"I don't think so, no." The doctor looked to the ceiling, pondering the situation. "Dawn, did you ever think he's just grieving? He's gone through hell."

"So have I, but I talk. And don't tell me to give him more time. It's been long enough." She searched the doctor's eyes. "What's wrong with him?"

"I'll be honest. I don't know." He glanced in at Jason's sullen expression. "Let's get him to a specialist. We'll fix this."

"You're sure?"

"Of course, I'm sure," he promised, then turned his attention to her. "Let's see the wrist." He took her arm, examining the even scar. "They did a good job."

"I guess," she muttered.

The doctor studied her exhausted eyes. "How about you? Are you eating anything? Getting enough rest?"

She shrugged. "Don't worry about me. Just phone the specialist, okay?"

The doctor opened his mouth then thought better of it. "Sure. I'll do it now."

When he left, Dawn waited in the hall. Foot tapping an anxious staccato on the floor, she looked in again at her son. He had not moved.

'I don't care what anyone say, this isn't just grief,' Dawn thought to herself. She rubbed her eyes, forcing herself to remember the GP's promise. 'They'll fix this. He'll be okay. He has to be.'

Two days later, Dawn took Jason to a specialist in pediatrics. Her son was put through a battery of tests. All the results came back the same. Jason was as normal and as healthy as any other five-year-old but for one exception: he would not talk. Stumped, the specialist referred her to a neurologist who ordered an MRI and a battery of other tests. Once again, the results came back normal. Also perplexed, the doctor referred Jason to a child psychiatrist. When Dawn led her son into the antiseptic office, the dour woman sat him on a stiff chair. For a half-hour the psychiatrist asked a series of questions, prompting Jason to engage. He refused to look at her. At the end of the session, she took Dawn aside.

"I have treated children with similar issues," the woman observed. "Jason's refusal to connect causes immense concern. For this reason, we will take firm action."

"Thank God," Dawn said, feeling a bubble of hope. "What will you do?"

"We must start," the woman stated, removing her thick horn-rimmed glasses, "by killing Jason's father."

"What did you say?"

The psychiatrist peered at her with unblinking eyes. "Neuroses such as these are the result of deep emotional conflict. By metaphorically killing the parent, the patient is freed."

"Really?" Dawn smiled, studying the woman. "You know what? You're an idiot."

"I beg your pardon?"

"You don't have to kill his father. He's already dead." She turned to her son. "Come on Jason. Let's go."

As they left, Dawn reached for him but Jason would not take her hand.

As the days went on Dawn grew more depressed by the continuing downward spiral in her son's temperament. Her loving, fun-filled, vocal child had been reduced to a silent stranger. He became even more sullen and angry. He had nightmares most nights which meant they both slept little. He cried constantly. When Dawn decided to take him back to kindergarten, hoping that seeing his young friends would spark an improvement, Jason's screaming fits frightened the other children. After frantic consultations with his teacher, Dawn made the decision to withdraw him from school until he recovered.

"But he has to go to school," his teacher pleaded. "Jason is a wonderful student. We'll get him special help. Give me time."

"He can't do it, don't you see? Please, Mrs. Bush. I know what I'm doing."

As Dawn escorted Jason down the hallway, the teacher noted his hurried gait, eyes cast aside to avoid any contact even as his mother reached for him. When they disappeared out the front entrance the teacher, a mother of three boys, was certain of one fact: Dawn did not know at all what she was doing.

Later in the day, sitting in the kitchen of their pretty seaside rental, Dawn glanced at her cellphone. It was after 2AM. She had spent the evening calming Jason after another series of nightmares. Her foot tapped the floor as she eyed a pile of bills lying on the table, realizing that her son was not her only worry. Most of them were for Jason's recent treatments. She calculated in her head, subtracting how much the unbudgeted expenses would eat into her savings. They had never bought life or health insurance because they couldn't afford it. Her financial situation was made worse because she had stopped working when Jason was born. She pulled out the bottom bill, sliding it over. It was the monthly invoice for their seaside rental home.

"Fifteen hundred bucks," she said, reading it. She glanced across the spacious room, noting the solid oak cabinets and top-of-the-range appliances. "Like I need this stuff right now."

Listening for her son, she got up, stepping to the refrigerator, pouring a glass of wine. Sitting again, she recalled why she had insisted they rent the house in the first place. She remembered that the decision was motivated by her own guilt, if nothing else. After they had married in Ireland, and before returning to the United States, the couple had discussed living arrangements. They had recognized they could not live in two places at once, so the choice was simple: either Ireland and Michael's home or Dawn's adopted city of Boston.

"We should do better in Boston than here," Michael had told her as they strolled along the shore of Kilcastle Harbor, considering their options. "It's bigger. It's a bit of craíc to it. Besides, I've always wanted to live in the States."

"Are you sure, Michael?" she had asked, taking his hand. "Won't you miss your home?"

"This place?" he had laughed, eyes lingering on the harbor. "Not a chance. And what about Boston? Wouldn't you miss it if you moved here? It's settled, then. The States it is." But Dawn had never been certain that America was what he really wanted.

Hoping to make Michael's transition to his adopted country more comfortable, she had insisted they rent the pretty seaside cottage near Quincy, right on Boston Harbor's seashore. She reasoned that the ocean had always been a part of her husband's life. She thought that if Michael had to live far from his Irish home, and though the cottage was well outside their budget, he should at least live near the sea which was his other home. They had moved in before Jason was born but even then, she had worried he would never be content.

"Are you happy here, Michael? Are you sure we've made the right decision to move to the States?" she would often ask him.

"What more could I want?" he had always answered, taking her up in his strong arms. "As long as we're together it makes no difference where we live."

Yet, she had always doubted him.

To pay for the higher expense of the seaside rental, Michael had set up a small construction company. Though the local Irish community helped by throwing an occasional job his way, she had realized the going was tough and worried for him. Before they had met, Dawn had completed her first year at a local community college with an eye on a full business degree at Boston University. She had financed the expense with a variety of jobs: from office receptionist, to waitressing, to employment as a sales clerk at a local hardware store. When Jason was born, she had replaced full-time education with night courses and stopped working, but had always planned to get a job when their son was older. As he grew into a playful, energetic one-year-old, and seeing how hard Michael worked to make ends meet, she had realized the life of a stay-at-home mother was a luxury they could not afford. Yet, every time she had told him of her intention to go back to work, he had objected.

"What about college?" he had always asked. "If you're going to go back somewhere, go there."

"But Michael, we need the money. We have to talk about it."

"Ah, ya' worry too much," he had replied. "We'll talk about it later."

But they never did. Whenever she had again brought up the subject it had ended in an argument. She had decided to keep her mouth shut, at least until Jason went to school, but she still worried for her husband. On days when he was on a project Michael had returned to their seaside home tired and hungry, chattering with enthusiasm about the job on hand. But on idle days she had noted the brooding in his eyes. Whenever he carried their infant son as they took walks together along the beach, he often stopped to gaze at the eastern horizon. Seeing his longing look, she had always kicked herself, wishing there was a way to live in two places at once. Her only weapon was their annual trip back to Ireland which she had always insisted on. That, and her ambition to go back to work to help him, were the few issues they had ever fought about.

Sitting at the kitchen table of their expensive Boston cottage, still listening for Jason, she recalled their last fight five months before the accident, one which had led to inconceivable pain however unintentionally.

They had stood together on the windy beach behind the cottage, a winter's surf beating the shoreline to foam. Dawn had scrunched her face into a ball, glaring up at her stubborn husband.

"Michael, stop grousing and listen."

"No, Dawn. We're not going on holiday to Ireland," he fumed. "Not this year. We can't afford it."

"It's only February, for fuck-sake. We're not going for months. Can't we at least discuss it?"

"We don't have the money."

"Which is why I want to go back to work."

"But what about college? Why go to work when you can go back to school? We already talked about it."

"Talked about it? We never talk about it. Michael, there's always time for a degree. We need the money now. We're not saving anything."

"And who's fault is that? We'll save even less if we go home this year." He glanced back at the cottage. "Maybe we should move. This place is too damned expensive. An apartment would do us fine."

"Oh, no you don't. One subject at a time." She took a breath, glowering up at him. "Stop being a tight-ass. We'll get the money for the trip. We go every year."

"Things aren't good right now." Swinging away from her, he refused to meet her eyes. "You know I didn't get that renovation up in Framingham. The cheap fecker got a lower bid. We got Jason's school fees to pay now, remember?"

"Oh, don't be a pissa. Things are always tight. Michael, if it's too expensive Jason can go to public school."

"We decided on Catholic school."

"It's only kindergarten!" But his look told her there would be no argument. "Okay, Catholic school. Things will pick up. Not everyone in Boston is a cheap fecker." When he didn't laugh, she decided to play her Ace. "Oh, Michael, get over it. You'll disappoint Margaret if we don't go back."

"Oh, no you don't. Don't bring Mam into it. She'll understand."

"Like hell she will. It would kill your mother if we don't visit." When her husband didn't respond she turned, seeing her son running down the beach chasing shorebirds. "Then what about Jason? You know he loves it there. What are you going to say to him?"

"You know what? Sometimes you try too damned hard."

He stormed off toward the cottage, strong arms swinging.

"And I love you, too!" she hollered after him, sitting with a thump on the wet sand. "What a fuck of an Irishman. He has to go back. It's important for him."

She knew it was, too. Hearing the waves hit the Boston beach, she recalled why she always insisted they return every year to Kilcastle, no matter what the cost. While he might not say so, she realized that Michael longed for his home. When he was back on the mountainous Beara Peninsula she watched as her husband scooped up new-found energy, as if reconnecting his soul to an endless power supply.

During their annual visits, the family took long walks on the Beara Way and its trail that led along the rocky shoreline. There, her son ran across shale-covered beaches, collecting periwinkle, scallop, and mussel shells the tide kicked in. At night and in the soft evenings, they strolled to the pub to receive a homecoming welcome from friends and neighbors. Jason played with the local children as Dawn watched her husband laugh and joke with his cronies.

On every trip, Michael brought along his Uilleann — his Irish pipes — and in the pub joined his friends in playing and singing the traditional Irish songs of fishing, revolution, legend and love. Dawn watched his strong arms pump at the bag, giving breath to the instrument. As his fingers, thick from manual work, danced across the chanter, the Uilleann came alive. Its background growl blended with its voice of lyrical melody and when he played, he was one with the instrument just as the Uilleann was one with him.

But when he was lost in song, Dawn recognized his longing for home in the sentimental voice of the pipes he played so well.

During each visit Michael always took his family out on his father's fishing boat, the *Margie M.* Years earlier, the thirty-two-foot half-decker had been fitted with an old ninety horsepower diesel tractor engine converted for sea duty, and she steamed solidly but slowly even in poor seas. He often took them up the Kenmare estuary as far as the town itself, teaching Jason to troll for pollock, mackerel and sea bass from the stern, just as his father had taught him when he was a boy. Or they steamed up the other side of the peninsula, along Bantry Bay, stopping at the Glengarriff village harbor. Letting the trawler drift, Michael pointed out the seals to Jason and the mansion of the famous Irish-American Hollywood actress to Dawn, and showed them where the actress's pilot husband had landed the Pan Am trans-Atlantic flying clippers in days gone by.

Often, Michael anchored the boat in some unnamed inlet and, unlashing the small rubber rib from its place behind the wheelhouse, swung it into the water. He taught Dawn to start the stubborn outboard engine and handle the boat among the rocky coves that lined the shore. With lessons done, he showed his family how to squeeze into wetsuits and they played like otters in seas dappled with sunlight. After swimming, Dawn often broke out a picnic lunch she had made earlier with Margaret. They washed the sandwiches down with hot mugs of tea which Dawn prepared in the trawler's small galley. Finished, they laughed as Jason threw leftover scraps to the swooping seagulls.

Whenever they boarded the blue and white trawler, Dawn remembered the long-ago trip to the distant island before Jason was born and, though she asked him to, Michael had never found enough time to journey back to Solas Mór and its hidden secret.

"Ah, Dawn, I forgot. We'll do it next time," he always promised when she asked, but between visits with friends and his mother he never seemed to find time to take her back. Dawn found she did not mind his forgetfulness because she cherished their visits to Kilcastle. Though her city upbringing had not prepared her for small-town living, she found the stunning seaside location and its people likable. She grew used to handling the rubber rib boat and practiced in the town's protected harbor, though some of the locals kidded Michael about it.

"She has a deft hand considering she's both a Gersha and a Yank," Jackie, a local fisherman and Michael's best friend teased as they stood on the deck of the *Margie M*, watching.

In the water below them Dawn knelt in the rib with Jason, both wearing yellow life vests. The men watched as she heaved at the rib's outboard, waving as she cast off from the side of the half-decker, inching her way across the harbor waters.

During their visits, Dawn became caught up in the gentle rhythm of town life so different from the frantic pace of Boston. She came to enjoy morning tea at the small cafés, listening to local people talk over their plans for the coming day. She loved her walks along the pier hand-in-hand with her family. When Michael met Jackie and his fishermen friends, she waited as he helped offload catches of fish from huge trawlers into sky-blue boxes for transport to market.

"Jason! Give us a hand!" Michael would always roar and, as his son ran to help, Jason would look to his mother with laughing eyes.

To Dawn it all looked so uncomplicated. So happy. So safe.

One day, as she walked with Michael and Jason along the pier, she saw the sleek blue and orange RNLI lifeboat tied up at its station. Its solid watertight superstructure and fifty-foot-long hull crouched like a tiger in the harbor's placid waters, and she wondered about the importance of its missions.

"Isn't that like what we have in Boston?" Dawn asked because she had seen something similar back home. "Tell me how it works."

Michael explained that when the radio call came in from a boat in trouble, volunteers took the lifeboat out into any sort of weather to save lives.

"You mean they'll go out even in a hurricane?"

"Even in a hurricane, though we rarely have them here," Michael answered.

She studied the lifeboat with new interest. A thought struck her. "Have many from the town died at sea?"

"Too many. If we had the lifeboat years ago my father might still be alive." His eyes filled with concern she seldom saw. "Dawn, that's nothing for you to worry about. I'd never take you and Jason out if I thought the weather was going to give trouble."

She put a hand on his arm. "I know you wouldn't, Michael."

From then on, she studied the weather reports and wondered how many wives worried when a storm blew in because their fishermen husbands were still at sea.

Their annual visits to Ireland were always too short. They always stayed in Michael's boyhood home, sleeping in his bedroom surrounded by her husband's youthful memories. Margaret was excited when they arrived but always gutted when they had to go. As the days came closer to their departure, Dawn's mother-in-law tried to postpone the inevitable.

"You've days until you have to leave," she'd say. "We've still plenty of time." But the day always came when they had to go home.

When they arrived back in Boston it always seemed their visit to Ireland had been only a dream. Michael went back to work. Dawn busied herself with Jason and her night classes. After every visit, she would catch her husband standing on the porch gazing out to sea and to his home which lay far over the horizon, and she could feel his quiet longing. And though she encouraged him to play the Uilleann, he would always make some excuse, leaving the instrument in its scarred wooden travel box placed in the corner of their bedroom until the next visit to Ireland. Dawn recognized Kilcastle as being the source of Michael's strength because she had seen it. Without it, she worried he would become resentful, perhaps blaming her for imprisoning him in a land so distant from his birth. She was determined never to let that happen.

Sitting on the Boston beach, glaring at the cottage and thinking of their argument, she thought how she'd married a man who didn't know what was good for him. 'He's going home if I have to carry him back,' she thought, then turned as she heard her son calling.

"Mom, what's wrong?"

Jason ran up breathless from his play near the sea. He stood short and stocky, a smaller version of his father, wind whipping through his curling hair.

"Help your mom up."

Dawn grunted as she took his small hand. Standing, she looked across blowing sand to their home on the water's edge. Considering the stubborn man inside, she smiled as a plan bubbled into her head.

"Jason, can you keep a secret?"

"What are you going to do, Mom?" Jason giggled, co-conspiracy in his young voice.

"Here's what, but don't tell Dad."

As Dawn carried Jason back to the house, their heads close together, she whispered the secret surprise. That night when her husband went to bed, she took a look at the household credit card balance. She had just enough to make the online transaction.

Two days later Michael came home from work tired and anxious because of a job that was giving trouble. He was surprised to see his Uilleann's green travel box sitting on the kitchen table. Reading the excitement in his family's eyes, he looked from one to the other.

"What are you two up to? And don't tell me nothing because I won't believe it."

Dawn dropped three Aer Lingus e-tickets on top of the box. "We're going to Ireland this summer. I don't care about the money."

Their son's eyes twinkled. "Please, Dad. Let's go see Nana."

Five months later they boarded the plane at Logan Field, bound for Ireland. The family sat together in the aircraft's middle seats, Dawn between them, holding tight to her men's hands.

"Did you tell Nana we're coming?" Jason asked, leaning close.

"Sure, we did. She can't wait."

"Neither can I," he giggled. "We're going to have a great time!"

"It's going to be a trip to remember," his father laughed. "All thanks to your Mam."

Michael's eyes sought his wife's. Within his gaze she could feel the strength of his gratitude. But when Jason laughed with excitement as the plane was pushed back from the gate, not one of them suspected the consequences of her thoughtful gift or the losses they would suffer.

CHAPTER FOUR

The next morning, with Jason sitting in the adjoining living room where she could keep an eye on him, Dawn brought her laptop in from the bedroom, powering it up on the kitchen table. Before going to bed the previous evening, and having considered her mounting expenses, she had made two decisions. First, she would give up the seaside cottage and find a less expensive place to rent. Second, she would start searching for a job. Dawn suspected it would be a monumental challenge to find fulltime employment because she had been out of the workforce for over five years. After spending an hour hopping from one employment website to another, she turned her frustration to apartment rentals. This time she had more luck.

With little on offer in her price bracket, and based only on a half-dozen photos on a property website, she rented an inexpensive two-bedroom apartment built above a South Boston Italian restaurant. Next, she phoned her landlord to give him notice. When she told him about the accident and her husband's death, he didn't object to the broken lease. She held off telling Jason about the move until that evening. She found him sitting in their living room, gazing out on Boston Harbor.

"Jason, honey, look at me."

When he would not, she crouched at his side thinking how much she hated the message she had to deliver.

"Jase, you know what?" she said with as much enthusiasm as she could muster. "We're going on an adventure. Mom rented us an apartment in the city. What do you think of that?"

Jason swung from the window with an expressionless stare.

"You're going to love it, sweetie. Remember the big park with all the swan boats? It's only a train-ride away," she explained, reaching for him. When he slapped at her outstretched hand, Dawn pulled back. "Jase, don't." When she tried again, he ran screaming from the room. Dawn rushed to his bedroom. She found him standing on the bed, howling like an animal, his face taut with rage.

"Jason calm down. It's going to be okay!" When she approached him, he slapped at her again and again, forcing her to dodge his whirlwind of anger. "Stop it! Jason, I said don't!"

His eyes flashed with defiance. Closing his fists, he jumped from the bed, beating on his forehead with mounting fury.

"Jason, God no!"

She tried grabbing his arms but he pushed her away. Sobbing, he fell to the floor. She stood on the far side of the room not knowing what to do. 'He has to stop. It's going to kill us if he doesn't stop,' she thought, brushing tears from her cheeks.

She did not know how much time had passed until her son's crying subsided and he at last slept. She lifted him to his bed, taking care with the blanket so as not to disturb him. Then she found his stuffed monkey in the corner, the one Michael had given him over a year ago. Jason always insisted on taking it to bed and howled with rage if she could not find it. Picking up the comical figure, she counted it as one of their few blessings. It was the only personal item the Coast Guard had managed to pluck from the sea following the sinking. Gazing at the monkey's crooked smile, Dawn noted the matted hair, its long tail stained with engine oil which she had worked hard to wash out but without much success. The monkey's black eyes looked back with lopsided cheekiness, reflecting the memory of better days. Hoping it would help him settle she lifted the blanket, trying to tuck the stuffed animal in at Jason's side. But even in sleep, he lashed out with closed fists.

She noticed her hands. They trembled as if they were someone else's hands. Fear knotted her belly. She felt like a swimmer lost on a failed rescue. Towing her son, she had run out of strength miles from any harbor.

When she was certain he had settled, Dawn dragged herself to her bedroom. For hours she lay awake in the wide bed she had slept in with Michael since they had first moved to the seaside home. It was now a stranger's bed because he did not sleep there anymore. She caressed the cover of his pillow but the fabric was filled with his absence.

She turned on her side. Within the shadowed room she could make out the silhouette of the closed wooden box that held his Uilleann. The musical instrument sat in the corner, untouched since she had brought it back from Ireland following the accident. Tears welled up when she realized Michael would never play it again.

A week later, Dawn moved them into the small city apartment. There, Jason's sullenness and anger grew more exhausting. He was quiet only when she found him sitting on the floor in her bedroom, the doors to the closet open. He gazed up at his father's work clothes which she could not bring herself to give away, and down at the green box of the Uilleann abandoned on the closet floor. At six o'clock every evening, at the time when Michael had always bounded in from work to lift his son in a bearhug, Dawn discovered Jason standing at the apartment's closed front door. Studying his expectant face, she realized he waited for a father who could never come home.

A few days after the move she took him to the local grocery store. As Jason helped push the shopping cart down the crowded aisle, Dawn's smile held an edge of hope.

"That's it, Jason, keep pushing," she encouraged, hands resting inches from his on the shopping cart handle. She yearned to cover the tiny fingers with her own but resisted the impulse. Instead, she watched her son concentrate on the task they had always enjoyed together before the accident, thinking this could be the positive change for which she had waited.

As they came to the end of an aisle, she stopped. "Sweetie, let's go back. Mom forgot to get eggs." She tried to move the cart but Jason refused to budge. "Jason, we have to turn around," Dawn coaxed, bending to him. Her gaze was met with a brazen stare. "Sweetie, what's wrong?"

Her son's mouth opened. His deafening wail filled the store.

"Jason, please. Not here." She looked up to see other shoppers stop, her scalp prickling beneath their stares.

"Mommy," a little girl across the aisle squealed, "is that little boy having a tantrum?"

"Don't look at them," her mother ordered, glaring at Dawn. "It's not his fault. It's his mother's."

Dawn flushed with embarrassment. Beside her, Jason screamed on in unending rage. When she reached for him, he slapped at her then slumped to the floor, writhing on his back. More shoppers stopped as the store manager rushed over, hovering just outside of Jason's rage.

"Is that your son? Can't you control him?" he whined, plucking at a prissy mustache.

"Get the hell away," Dawn ordered, and turned to her bawling son. "Jason, get up."

"Aren't you going to do something?" the mother of the little girl snapped at the manager. The flustered store official glanced at the group of concerned customers then stepped in. He grabbed Jason by the jacket, lifting him from the floor.

"Don't you dare touch him!" Dawn barked, storming toward the manager.

Jason squirmed in the stranger's hands. Twisting, he glared at the manager's face then hit the surprised man in the mouth. Wriggling from the tight grasp Jason ran to the shelves, pulling down bags of cookies, stomping them beneath the soles of his trainers.

"That's a criminal act!" the manager fumed, holding a handkerchief to his bleeding lip. "You'll pay for those."

"Send me the bill," Dawn blared. "Jason, stop it!"

When Dawn reached for him again, he ran. He saw the tall display before she did: glass spaghetti jars were stacked like a volcano near the checkout area. Dawn tried to grab him but he was too quick. He dashed to the display, arms swinging with the full momentum of his anger. The tower collapsed. Glass exploded all around him. For a moment the store was silent, then Jason erupted in a tortured howl. Dawn rushed up, seeing blood pumping from a deep wound torn into his upper cheek, mixing with red sauce pooling on the tiles. Avoiding his thrashing arms, she applied pressure to stem the blood running down his face. The manager ran up, his anger checked by the sobbing boy who bled all over the floor.

"I'll call an ambulance," the manager barked, then fled between a crowd of startled customers.

Covered in blood and spaghetti sauce Dawn knelt at her son's side, heart pounding. She remembered the words of the little girl's mother. Dawn's bleeding son only confirmed what the woman in the store aisle had said. 'This is my fault,' her thoughts raced. 'I should have been left in the boat, not Michael. Christ, look what I've done.'

When the ambulance came, it rushed them to Children's Hospital. There, Jason was carried into a cubicle, the curtains drawn. A young Emergency Room physician managed to quiet Jason long enough to give him a local anesthetic. She explained to Dawn it was fortunate the glass had not cut a half-inch higher or he would have lost an eye. Too guilty to stand closer, Dawn said nothing as the doctor stitched the wound.

"This won't take long, Jason," the doctor consoled, concentrating on her task. "Does that sting?" When the boy said nothing, she kept stitching. "How about that? Does that one hurt? You bet it hurts, doesn't it?" Again, he said nothing. When she finished by bandaging the injury, the doctor drew Dawn outside into the busy ER.

"Has Jason ever talked?" Dawn nodded, and the doctor crossed her arms. "When did he stop?"

"A few months ago. We were in an accident."

The doctor considered the statement. "Why don't you tell me what happened?" After Dawn told her the doctor asked, "Have you seen a specialist? What have they said about it?" Dawn explained that, too. "I see," the physician said. "Wait here. I'll be right back."

When the doctor left Dawn reentered the cubicle to find Jason sprawled on the bed, napping. She sat in a chair, exhaustion covering her like a storm. Her eyes closed and she slept. She was unaware of the tall male specialist who studied Jason from just beyond the open cubicle curtains. When she woke, rising to stretch her aching limbs, he stepped in.

"Mrs. McCarthy?" the man said, offering a hand. "My name is Doctor Morrison. Can I talk to you?"

"About what?" Dawn asked, surprised by his sudden appearance.

"Have you heard of Post Traumatic Stress Disorder?"

Dawn studied the deep-set eyes which held such sympathetic interest. "Of course, I have. Why?"

"I understand you've taken Jason to a number of specialists. Hasn't anyone screened him for PTSD?"

She felt her stomach knot.

"No," she said, suspicious because she had walked down too many blind alleys. "If that was the problem, I'm sure someone would have said something."

"Even the best of us can miss the obvious."

"You think that's why Jason won't talk? Because he has PTSD?"

"Maybe we should find out."

While Jason slept, she talked to the doctor. After he left, she sobbed with relief because she might have found a key that could bring her son back to her. At Morrison's urging she did not take Jason home that night. Instead, she left him under the doctor's care. As she signed the paperwork for her son's admission, she glanced at the specialist.

"Doctor Morrison, do you have any idea how long he'll be here?"

The doctor smiled. "Until he's better. It takes time."

On the day of the first anniversary of the accident, a day she tried hard to forget, Dawn stood at a plate-glass observation window looking in on a sunny therapy room. Dressed in jeans and the short-sleeved company work-shirt issued by her employer when, after months of searching, she had at last landed a job, she glanced down at her watch.

"Shit," she whispered to herself, seeing that she would be late again for work. Certain that Jason was more important than any job, she stepped closer to the glass, looking in at a handful of young patients undergoing the rigors of trauma therapy. Some of the children sat at tables littered with games and toys as therapists encouraged them to name the various objects. Others stood at white boards covered with bright images of animals. Adult counselors pointed from one picture to another, asking their patients to sound out the names. Dawn studied the tiny faces focused in tight concentration. Mouths worked as they sounded out vowels and consonants, sounds which anxieties of various types had stripped from them and which they now tried to re-learn. All were fully engaged in the process of the therapy, working hard to master the simple notes that make up speech. But not her son. Dawn frowned as she watched him.

Jason stood on the far side of the room. A female therapist stood near, carrying his stuffed monkey as if a precious prize. As she lifted the monkey high, Dawn realized that Michael's gift was being used as a tool to reach her son. Through a speaker hanging on the wall, Dawn could hear the woman's coaxing words as she inched closer to him.

"Do you want to say something to Mister Monkey, Jason? What would you like to tell him?"

Jason eyed the woman. Dawn had seen that look of suspicion before. He swung his head up, his wail startling the other children, then backed against a far wall as if waiting for a firing squad's final volley.

"It's okay, Jason. It's okay!" the therapist responded as she exchanged a silent plea with Doctor Morrison. The doctor stood on the other side of the room, observing. They shared a nod and the therapist tried again, this time whispering into the monkey's ear.

"Mister Monkey, do you want Jason to say something to you?" She placed her ear to its mouth, listening. "Oh, Jason, he misses you so much. Please say hello to him."

Jason's face contorted with rage. Then he rushed her, socking the therapist in the stomach, stripping the monkey from the woman's hands. Screaming again, he spotted his mother at the window. He bolted to her, pounding on the glass, his eyes filled with hatred. On the other side of the window, Dawn stumbled backwards from his rage.

Unable to get to her, Jason turned to the room's only door. Finding it locked, he pulled desperately on the handle. Dawn stepped back to the window. Hands plastered on the glass, she watched as the therapist and Morrison hurried to her son. Avoiding the boy's lashing fists they lifted him, carrying the struggling patient from the room.

When he was gone Dawn fell to her knees, her breathing ragged. 'He does not hate you. He can't hate you. He's your son.' She knew the thoughts were lies because she had seen the naked truth in his face and did not understand why she had not realized it before now. Jason wanted to hurt her for the terrible sin she had committed. A sin for which she would never be forgiven.

Jason hated her because she had killed his father.

She paced the floor of Morrison's small office, sick to her stomach. Swallowing the bile in her throat, she drained the cardboard coffee cup she held not tasting its tepid coldness. Sitting down in a low visitor's chair, she began tearing the empty cup to pieces, her foot tapping a staccato on the carpeted floor. When she could not stop it, she rose, pacing again.

"Dawn! I'm sorry to keep you waiting," Morrison called as he bustled in. "Please, sit down."

Dawn kept pacing as the doctor sat at a desk piled high with paperwork. He located a thick file. Opening it, he rifled through pages crowded with notations.

"That didn't go very well, did it?" Morrison said, continuing to search the file. When she didn't answer, he looked up. "Dawn, are you okay?"

She stopped, her back to him. "What did you say?"

"Hey. Look at me." She turned and he saw tears on her cheeks. "Take a seat. Please."

When she sat, she would not look at him, concentrating instead on the half-destroyed coffee cup. Her foot once more tapped a staccato on the floor. Morrison held out a tissue. She took it, drying her eyes.

"Let's start again," he proposed. "I'm sorry it didn't go well."

"You mean it didn't work."

"Exposure therapy isn't for everyone. But no big deal. We have plenty of options."

"Do we? Nothing works." She put her head in her hands. "He won't ever talk again, will he?"

"Of course, he will," Morrison said, surprised. "Look, it's going to happen this way. At first, he won't talk to anyone. Don't expect him to talk to you because it won't happen. But you wait. As he heals, when he starts to feel safe, he'll pick someone as a test. When you see that happen you know he's starting to recover. Then, it's only a matter of reinforcing progress with the object of his trust."

"Like a stuffed monkey?" she asked, looking to the floor. "What good will that do?"

He studied her bowed head, the lusterless hair, her unwillingness to look at him. He recalled how hard the past months had been. When Morrison had first started treating Jason, Dawn had brimmed with optimism. But as the months of treatment passed, he had witnessed the young woman's spirit ground down beneath the weight of her son's illness. Morrison had long suspected she blamed herself for every failure. The thick file at his fingertips held a long list of those failures. He decided he must do what he could to rekindle her optimism. He tapped the desktop, trying to get her attention.

"Dawn, look at me. Of course, Jason will talk again," he promised and sat back, considering his next words. "Maybe it doesn't seem like it but we really are making progress. Ten months ago, we thought we were dealing with a simple case of PTSD, not that there's anything simple about it. Now we know he's suffering from something much more complex. Acute Traumatic Mutism can be caused by any number of factors."

"Like what? Remind me."

"A change to the brain's chemistry. Perhaps an inability for Jason to process the severity of the trauma. At this point I'm not sure. But we're getting closer. Once we determine the cause we can treat the underlying anxiety."

As Dawn's foot tapped a higher octave, she recalled everything she knew about Acute Traumatic Mutism and its terrible consequences. Following Morrison's latest diagnosis, she had researched the disorder. Much of the literature argued that patients could not or would not talk for reasons that remained for the most part unclear. She had learned that following treatment, many patients suffering from the syndrome talked within five days to three months of the traumatic event. She also remembered that a small percentage of patients who did not regain speech within that period might never talk again. Dawn slumped deeper into the chair as she remembered that outcome, one populating her worst nightmares.

"Dawn?"

She looked up, seeing the doctor study her shuddering leg. She placed a hand on her knee, forcing it to silence.

"All he wants to do is go home," Dawn murmured.

"Of course, he does." The doctor's eyes never left her shattered figure. "You know I've read the Coast Guard report. I understand his father's body was never recovered. Jason never saw it. Which means he has never had closure. He can't understand why his dad never came home." He leaned back. "My suspicion is he thinks his father is alive. If Jason saw him, he would talk again. But of course, that's impossible."

"Jason knows what happened. He saw exactly what I saw."

The doctor leaned in closer. "Is there anything about the accident you haven't told me? Anything you've overlooked? Even the smallest, most insignificant detail might help."

Dawn looked back at the floor, aware that she would never answer the question. When the Coast Guard had interviewed her after the sinking, she had told them everything she could remember, everything that had seemed rational. She had, of course, omitted some of the details. Details that didn't make sense to her at the time. Details that still didn't make sense. For all she knew, what she had experienced that night was a figment of a storm-swept imagination, the result of overwhelming tragedy. Dawn was certain they had no bearing on Jason's condition. If she had not shared her illogical recollections with the Coast Guard, she was not about to share them with the doctor who was treating her son. To do so would make Morrison think her insane.

"No, there's nothing else," she mumbled, then took a ragged breath and wiped her eyes. "You know, Jason blames me for it."

"For what?"

When she didn't respond Morrison rose, stepping around the desk. "Don't think like that. You told me what happened. It was an accident. Accidents happen. You weren't responsible."

When she again refused to reply he stepped back to the folder, turning a page.

"Finally," he said, finding the treatment schedule. "Tomorrow morning. Are you free?"

"For what?"

"Shaping therapy. We've used it with other patients and they're responding well. It's completely up to you, of course."

"Will it help him?"

"That's what I want to find out."

She nodded her consent.

"Good. How about ten?" But the acceptance in Dawn's face turned to anxiety and he suspected this was about more than her son. "How's work? Are they still supportive?" When she only shrugged, he asked, "How's the swimming going? You still getting some exercise?"

"You know me," she said with a faint smile.

He laughed. "You mean stubborn as hell? Good. Then I'll see you tomorrow." The mother of his patient rose, turning to the door. "Dawn, let me take that." Morrison extended an open hand. Dawn still held the torn bits of the destroyed coffee cup. She gave him the pieces. "Chin up. We're going to fix this."

She searched his eyes. "So many people have promised that. Let me tell you something, doctor. If you don't fix it, I will."

CHAPTER FIVE

D awn took the subway from the hospital into the city. Getting off at Park Street Station, she hurried through the jostling mid-morning crowds. Looking into Boston Common, she saw kids with their parents playing in the sunny park just like her family did until a year ago. She couldn't take it. Breaking into a jog, she ran from their laughter.

Stopping, breathless, Dawn glanced at her watch, noting she was two hours late for work. Her boss would be pissed-off yet again. Reaching into her bag she fumbled for her wallet, finding a single fifty-dollar bill. Though she couldn't afford it, she hailed a cab because she couldn't afford not to.

She had worked at the call center for six months. When she had accepted the position, she suspected it wasn't going to be much of a job. But having abandoned the college night courses, her dream of a degree in tatters, she realized she was lucky to have it. She had looked everywhere for a fulltime position. Most companies weren't interested because of the huge hole in her resume. Because she hadn't worked since before Jason was born, Dawn faced a wall of prejudice. Few prospective employers responded to her emails or phone calls. Fewer still offered an interview. When she was contacted by World Connect regarding her application for the tele-sales position, she feared it would be her last chance.

On the day of the interview Dawn had built a fortress around the boiling emotions of loss. At the meeting, Bill Saunders — her prospective employer — had been introduced to an engaging, confident, professional young woman dressed in an attractive ensemble who communicated with intelligent directness. When he questioned her slim employment history, she countered with a willingness to do whatever it took to succeed. When he reminded her that World Connect sold customer relationship computer software and pointed out that she had zero experience within the industry, she argued back with candid bluntness.

"Mister Saunders, give me the product manuals and I'll memorize every word. You need me to perform and I promise — I will." When her argument was met by silence she rose from the chair, gazing at him with forthright honesty. "Bill, I need this job. I promise I'll work my ass off for you. What do you say?" She held out a hand.

He considered the sincere woman standing in front of him, and at last took it. "Okay, Dawn. We'll give it a shot. But I'm going to keep an eye on you, understood?"

While thrilled with the new job she also faced a stark reality. Like all new hires, she started work at the very bottom of the pay scale.

In between visits with Jason, she had worked hard to master her new employer's complicated technology, reading everything she could find. Her studies paid off. While her sales over the first weeks were few, she didn't give up. Within two months, she was selling more than most of her colleagues on the World Connect tele-sales team. Six months after starting the job, Saunders had called her back into his office. Leaning across his desk, he had offered a firm handshake.

"Congratulations."

"For what?" she had asked, thinking he was being sarcastic and that she was in trouble again.

"Last week you tied for highest sales revenues with Steve Jacobs," he said, mentioning Dawn's rival. Saunders sat back in his enormous executive chair, studying her with amusement. "When you walked in here, I didn't think you had it in you. I was wrong."

"I told you I'd do it," she grinned. "Thanks boss."

"Just keep it up, okay?" He rose, escorting her to the door. "I'm thinking of creating a couple of new management positions. They might include you."

"Really?"

"Maybe. But Dawn, I'm going to mark your card," he grumbled and she broke into a sweat, knowing what was coming. "Watch the timekeeping, okay?" he said, referring to the many occasions she had been late. The pressure of Jason's treatments was eating into her life and her boss had pulled her up more than once for walking in the door hours behind schedule. "I need you here every hour you're assigned for duty. Otherwise, I'm going to think again. Understood?"

"Understood."

"Okay, now get out there and keep selling."

"You know it," she had smiled, knowing he was serious. "I'll do my best."

"I expect more than that, Dawn. I expect you to be here. No excuses."

Now, sitting in the cab taking her to a job she depended on, her boss's warning boiled in her head. As the driver fought bumper-to-bumper traffic, Dawn convinced herself she would find the time to do it all: to work the ten-hour days Saunders demanded while also attending Jason's stream of therapies and the daily visits she cherished. She had little choice. She needed the money while Jason needed her presence. Soon, she planned to ask Saunders for a raise but she recognized that a salary increase relied on her continuing performance.

Her foot tapped the car floor as the driver made the final turn. When the cab let her off at the towering office complex, she ignored the elevator and bolted up the seven flights of stairs. She stood at the glass door of the large open plan office, gasping for breath. Through the window she could see the room crowded with World Connect sales reps, all sitting in small cubicles, all wearing Polo shirts like the one she wore, all on the phone, all chatting with feigned enthusiasm.

She crushed her face to the window, straining to see around the corner. On the far side of the room Bill Saunders paced in his glass-enclosed office, also on the phone. She watched as he glowered at his troops like a general allocating scarce military resources. When he turned away, she opened the door and crept in.

She made it to her desk and slipped on the headphones. Plugging them into the terminal, she adjusted the computer display. Above her, a photo of Jason and Michael taken two summers ago on the Cape was pinned to the cubicle wall. They grinned down with reassuring love. She reached out, caressing the smiling faces.

"Give me some luck today, okay?" she whispered, then studied the lit plasma screen with its long prospective customer list allocated for the day. From the next cubicle she overheard her friend, Joyce, finishing a call.

"That's terrific, Mister Garcia," Joyce enthused, leaning back in her chair to catch Dawn's eye. "Our consultant will stop by to give a demonstration. Thank you for calling World Connect, your customer relationship software specialists."

When Joyce hung up, she wheeled her chair across the floor, closing in on Dawn's cubicle. "Where were you?" she whispered, eyes swinging to their boss's glass office. "I told him you were in the powder room. But for two hours? The fucker's going crazy."

She smiled at her friend's outburst. Joyce was younger than her, still lived with her parents, and battled her battles with abrasive passion. Dawn glanced toward Saunders's cage, seeing her boss.

"Tell me something I don't know."

Dawn's phone rang with an inbound call. She took a breath and, striking the blinking call button, plunged into battle. "World Connect, this is Dawn. How can I help?" She put her hand over the mic, swinging back to Joyce. "The doctor wanted to see me."

Joyce leaned in closer. "How's he doing? Is Jason any better?"

"No," she said, and turned back to the business conversation. "Sorry Mister Temple. Thanks for returning my call." She listened intently. "Yes, that's right. A free demonstration." She winked at Joyce, turning to the computer and its scheduling program. "That's wonderful. Let me pencil in a date."

She glanced up seeing Saunders. Still in his cage, her boss's eyes were targeted on her like incoming missiles. Her throat constricted, realizing that at some point today she was going to have to pay the piper for her tardiness. But the words coming through the headset demanded attention.

"Mister Temple, I don't think I caught that right. Can you repeat it, sir?" Her eyes narrowed to slits, her voice rising. "Thank you for saying so, but I don't think my voice sounds sexy."

She glanced at Joyce. Her friend's raised eyebrows were asking, 'what the hell is going on?' Grinning sales reps in other cubicles also listened. Across the aisle, Steve Jacobs — her nemesis and a guy she couldn't stand — leaned over a cubicle wall, his thin chin perched on one hand.

"No, I do *not* give the demonstrations," Dawn blurted, eyes glued on Steve's.

"That's it, sweetie," Steve wheezed, enjoying her discomfort. "Go get 'em."

"Shut up Steve!" she hissed, then to the caller, "I'm sorry. That wasn't meant for you." She listened again and her face flushed, anger rising like a tide. "What? What did you say to me? You Bozo!" She struck the call button, cutting him off.

A spattering of applause and wolf-whistles echoed across the office. Steve clapped, loving the moment. Dawn stared at the computer screen, face red with embarrassment.

"Dawn?"

Her head snapped up. Saunders leaned over the cubicle wall, glaring.

"We need to talk," he fumed, then swung to Steve. "You too, Steve. Right now!"

"He wanted me to demonstrate by, and I quote, 'Sitting on my face.'"

In Saunders's office Dawn perched on a low chair. Her boss sat in his big seat on the other side of the desk, his face locked in what she thought might be a permanent scowl.

"But Bozo?" Saunders countered. "Come on, Dawn. That guy Temple was a potential sale. We've been after him for months."

"Really? Okay, so call him back. *You* sit on his face." Her eyes rounded on Steve, his thin frame leaning against the wall. "Or how about you? I'm sure you'd be thrilled."

"And you want to promote her to supervisor?" Steve sniveled.

"Where did you hear that?" Saunders snapped, rocking back in his chair. "Okay, okay. We're getting off the point." He swiveled to Dawn. "You were late again this morning. That's the fourth time in the last two weeks. This time I'm writing you up."

"I don't believe this. Bill, my son is sick. What do you expect me to do?" She stood up, leaning over his desk. "I shouldn't have said anything about Jason. I was a fool to let you know. I told you months ago I'd be late occasionally."

"Dawn, you're late more than 'occasionally'. Look, I'm glad you told me about your son. But you happen to work here, remember?"

"Jason is in treatment. I have to be there, too."

"Why not try multiple personalities?" Steve grinned. "If you were schizophrenic, you could be in two places at the same time."

"You're an ass, Steve," Dawn growled. "What would you do if he was your child?"

"Come to work now and then?"

"Steve..." Saunders warned. "Look. Both of you know top brass are squeezing hard for more sales. You two are the best I've got. But you," his eyes moved to Steve, "can be a jerk. And as for you," he turned to Dawn, "what the hell is going on? Did you see your sales figures last week?"

"Like a toilet flushing," Steve said in his irritating voice. "It must be humiliating to have to rely on pity to keep your job."

"Why you —", Dawn hissed, and launched herself toward him.

"Dawn, sit down. I said sit!" Saunders barked, then glared at Steve. "You! Get out of here and sell something."

After Steve slunk from the room Saunders sat back, eyes on Dawn. "What the hell is wrong with you? You know that guy isn't worth it."

"I'm sorry."

"I know you are and I am too. I'm sorry about your son. I'm sorry about Mike."

"His name is Michael," she murmured, and he could see the pain in her face. He rocked back, considering.

"Dawn, you're good. Except for last week, your performance has been — well, let's just say I'm more than pleased. But your sales last week weren't just poor. They were terrible."

"I said I was sorry. Jason had some new therapies and it took time, and well...." Her eyes rose. "Bill, I need to be with him. You know that."

"I understand. And we'll work something out. But right now, you need to focus. Maybe Steve is right. Why should I consider you for supervisor if you're never here?"

Dawn sat up ramrod straight. "So, the rumors are right?"

"What rumors? I told you weeks ago I was considering some new positions. I've decided to appoint a supervisor."

"And it might be me?"

"Didn't I just say that?"

"Then do it. Promote me right now."

"You're really something," he said, suppressing a grin. "Your sales are on the floor. You're always late. And you want me to promote you now? Why should I?"

"Because I'm the best you've got. And honestly? I need the money for Jason."

Saunders rocked back again, eyes on the ceiling. At last, he looked at her. "I'll think about it. But first you have to pass a supervisor's exam. I'm going to schedule it for the day after tomorrow, nine in the morning." He cocked his head, studying her. "Dawn, it's going to be a race. Steve will take the exam, too."

"Steve? But Steve doesn't know shit. I tell you what. Give us the exam right now, right here. Best person wins."

This time Saunders couldn't help but chuckle. "You don't even need to crack a book, do you?"

"I know this stuff. You know I do. Look. You want to suck up to the board. I need to take care of Jason. I can only do that if I can pay the bills." Saunders turned away, still doubtful. "Oh, come on Bill. Do you seriously think Steve can do it? Customers hate the little gump."

"Gump?" he laughed. "At least Steve gets in on time."

61

"I'll work my butt off. I promise."

His look softened. "Tell you what. Beat the pants off Jacobs in the exam and it's yours. Now get out of here and sell something before I change my mind."

"Seriously?" she grinned.

"Go on. Go!"

"I'll do it, you'll see," she said, backing to the door. "You'll never regret it."

"Won't I?"

Then she remembered Jason's new therapy. "Bill? I forgot. I have to take tomorrow morning off. But I'll work a hundred hours next week. That's a promise. Now you have a good day," she stated, and strode out the door.

He could only look to the ceiling. "Unbelievable."

"Thank you for your business, Mrs. Long. I'll email a contract to you later today."

Dawn sat in her cubicle, Joyce looking on as she finished her telephone pitch. "Oh, and Mrs. Long? Enjoy your daughter's wedding. And don't worry. We'll have an engineer out next week to set things up. Thank you for calling World Connect, your customer relationship software specialists."

She hung up, swiveling to Joyce with a victorious smile.

"Way to go Dawn!" Joyce squealed and gave her a high-five.

"That's six sales today!"

Across the aisle Steve leaned over the wall of his cubicle, smirking. "Her daughter's wedding?"

Dawn eyed him. "What's wrong, Steve? Let me guess. Steve's total sales for today are zero."

"We're not talking about me," he flushed.

"Aren't we? I thought we always had to talk about Steve."

"Oh, I get it. You resort to stupid small talk because you don't understand the technology."

Dawn studied the sneer on his face. "Like what part? Like our software is cloud based? Like our small business edition allows up to one-hundred users to access it simultaneously? Like it's supported by our virtualized, always replicated flash-drive technology for high availability and resilience? Go fuck yourself, Steve."

"Make that twice, asshole," Joyce added.

They heard a smattering of laughter. Most of the office was listening. Embarrassed, Steve went back to work. With her nemesis in his hole, Dawn glanced toward Saunders's office. He sat in his chair, engrossed in a phone call.

"You ready?" she whispered to Joyce.

"Are you sure? What if Saunders catches you?"

Dawn leaned in closer. "I need you, Joyce. You've got my back. Right?"

"Always. You know that."

Joyce peered over the lip of her cubicle, checking on their boss. He rocked in his chair, still on the phone.

"Okay," she said, waiting. "Ready... set..." Saunders turned away, facing his office wall. "Go!"

Dawn turned to her computer, bringing up Google, typing in SHAPING THERAPY. Hitting the return, she waited until the dense information appeared then started reading. She did not notice the nervous tapping of her foot as she concentrated on the complex treatment which might help her son talk again.

CHAPTER SIX

That night, Dawn swam with long strokes through the waters of the swimming pool. Most days after work, and following the evening visit with Jason at the hospital, she walked to the YMCA. There, she swam laps until the fire in her lungs drove out the fury in her head and heart. On most evenings she swam alone. Tonight, Joyce had offered to join her.

Two sets of arms swam abreast, rising and falling in unison: white then ebony, white then ebony, keeping time to the music of their minds. As they pushed off at the pool's end, Dawn raised her head.

"Last lap."

"Go!" her friend shouted.

Dawn dug into the water, pushing it behind as hard as she could. The effort recalled the clawing memories she always tried to outdistance. Eyes under the surface, her distorted vision became filled with sudden images: wild seas full of smoke and fire; Jason screaming for his father as she pulled him overboard; Michael trapped in a sinking boat, eyes full of love even as she abandoned him.

She stopped swimming as if hitting a wall. Thrashing until her feet found the concrete floor she stood, hands covering her eyes, water pouring from her body.

"Hey Dawn!"

She looked up. Joyce was out of the water, standing on the tiles on the other side of the pool. "You need some help?" she called, her voice echoing across the cavernous hall.

Dawn shook her head then swam to the pool's edge. Joyce offered a hand, pulling her out. After drying off they sat together on plastic chairs. For a long time, Dawn said nothing. When she noticed her friend's questioning look, she swung away, staring at the pool's quiet waters.

"You want to talk about it?" Joyce prodded.

"Talk about what? There's nothing to talk about."

"You always beat me when we swim, so don't give me that. Something's wrong. You going to tell me what's in your head?" Joyce pushed thick wet braids behind her dark shoulders. "Did you see Jason tonight? How is he?"

"The same."

"Is that new therapy still scheduled for tomorrow?"

"Yes."

"You worried about it?"

"No," Dawn lied, drumming her fingers on the chair.

"That's all you got to say? Something's on your mind. Is it Michael?" she guessed. "You never say anything about him. If that's what's bothering you, why not talk about him?"

"Not right now, okay?"

"So, it is Michael," Joyce said, leaning in. "Keeping it bottled up is going to do you no good."

"I wouldn't know where to start."

The younger woman smiled. "How about at the beginning? How did you two meet, anyway? All I got to go on is that picture hanging at your desk. He's got a smile as wide as an ocean. How did you ever marry an Irishman?"

"It was an accident."

"An accident?" Joyce asked, sliding her chair closer. "So, go on. Tell me. How did you meet that strong looking man?"

"He was strong all right," Dawn faltered, "and smart, and funny, and talented." She took a breath. "It started with a trip to England but it all went crazy. After my mom died, I had to get away so I went on vacation. The plan was to shake myself up then get back to college. But it didn't turn out that way." She couldn't help but smile. "With Michael, life was always a voyage."

"Don't stop. Then what happened?"

Gazing at the quiet waters of the pool Dawn decided to tell her.

Dawn was twenty-two when her mother passed away. She had lost her father three years earlier and did her best to replace his practical wisdom with her mom's comforting love. When she died too, Dawn thought the hole in her heart would never be mended. Four months after her mother's death, with the family house sold, the mortgage and other debts paid, and legal affairs tidied, Dawn ran from the horror of doctors, lawyers, probate, funerals and the hell that went with it all. Her plan was to fly to London, using her small inheritance to travel Britain's counties by bus and train. She was determined to hide the pain of her parents' loss within the patchwork of England's rolling countryside. But things didn't go to plan.

When she found herself on the western coast of Wales and encountered the ferry to Ireland, she couldn't stop. A few hours later, having sailed to the other side of the Irish Sea, she landed in the port of Dun Laoghaire. Not knowing whether to go north, south or west, she had shot a confused arrow into the rainswept skies. She guessed someone was listening because her eyes settled on a bus parked near the ferry terminal. When she asked the driver, she was told it would take her to Cork City then onward into the wilds of Ireland's remote southwest.

A day later she washed up in Bantry, at the gates of Beara Peninsula. After she toured the bustling coastal town and its crowded market square and for reasons she could never explain, she took another bus along the rocky spine that pushed west into the Atlantic. It was along the Beara that she first encountered the sunlit coves filled with kelp and flowing tides and felt a magic in the soft breeze she could not define. Having journeyed almost to the tip of the peninsula, she discovered the fishing town of Kilcastle and its snug harbor nestled beneath the rugged Mishkish Mountains. It was in their shadows that the grief thundering in her heart grew still and she could take a breath without fearing she would break.

Having found a place to stay for the night, in the early evening she wandered back into town. Sheltering from the pouring rain beneath a pub's outdoor awning, she heard the tugging rhythm of an Irish traditional reel echoing from inside. Captivated by the music, she couldn't help but enter. As she found a seat and slipped off her coat, she was pulled by song to a man sitting with a group of musicians, playing an instrument she had never before seen.

When the group took a break, she introduced herself, a display of nerve and desire that surprised and confused her. As his bright eyes rose to meet hers, the heat of embarrassment shot up her spine. Mumbling an apology, thinking herself an idiot, she fled back into the crowd hoping he would forget the brash American and her awkward introduction. But when he followed, placing a hand on her shoulder, she found that his wide smile salved her humiliation like a sunrise. Making an excuse to his musician friends, he led her to a quiet corner then turned back to buy her a drink. Waiting at the table, she watched as he leaned across the bar to order. His broad shoulders were crammed into a trim rugby shirt, his dark curling hair flowing like a river over the collar.

When he returned, placing two large glasses on the table and sat within a finger's width of her hip, she heard alarm bells go off that she had not heard since well before her mother's death. He picked up his drink, holding it toward her.

"Sláinte," he said in a deep singsong voice.

"What did you say?" she asked. "Say it again."

"Sláinte. It's 'Cheers' in Irish. Try it."

"Slanda?" she said in her broad New England accent. "That's not right, is it?"

"Close enough," he grinned. "But you're supposed to toast at the same time."

She eyed the pint of beer he had bought her, the jet-black Irish stout topped by a thick collar of creamy white foam. "Is this Guinness? I've never had it before."

He sat back, his eyes filling with laughter. "Where did you say you're from?"

"I didn't. Near Boston."

"You live in Boston and you've never had a pint of Guinness?"

"I guess I've led a sheltered life."

He laughed again, leaning toward her. "Then go on, beauty. They say Guinness is good for you. If you like it there's gallons more to come."

Again, he raised his pint, eyes filled with humor. Held by his gaze, her foot tapping beneath the table, she reached for the heavy glass. But as she did, the shaking of her leg shook the pint's surface in mad vibration.

"What the feck is that?" he asked.

"Indigestion," she lied, placing a hand on her knee to make her foot stop pounding. She grasped the pint with both hands and, lifting it, touched his glass. After she took a careful sip, he erupted in laughter. "What's wrong?" she frowned, putting down the pint. Seeing him study her face, she put a finger to her cheek.

"No, not there," he grinned, and reached toward her with a hand that seemed as big as a baseball glove. "Come here."

Confused, she leaned toward him. Her eyes never left his as he wiped the tip of her nose with a finger. He turned it, showing foam as white as snow. "It's supposed to go in your gob not on your beak."

"Gob?" she asked, confused, and wiped her nose. "I'll try harder next time."

"So, there's going to be a next time?"

Not knowing what to say, her eyes swung to the musical group that played on in the corner of the room without him.

"Shouldn't you be helping?"

"Naw. They get on just fine without me."

She sipped her pint again. "That instrument you were playing. What's it called?"

"It's a Uilleann," he grinned, and she noticed how the smile crept into his eyes, holding her as if it would never let go. "An Irish bagpipe. How about if I teach you to play?"

"Not a chance. I don't have a note in me." She sat back, studying him. "You're a puzzle."

"Am I now?" he said, leaning back into the bench seat they sat on. "And why is that?"

She found she did not want to tell him how a man this big and strong shouldn't be so gentle and talented. Instead, she said, "I don't even know your name."

"But you told me yours. Dawn Reynolds, isn't it? Like the sunrise." He reached for his beer. "It's Michael. Michael McCarthy."

"Michael," she repeated, and thought how much the strong name matched his tall physique.

"So tell me, Dawn Reynolds. How does an American find herself all the way down to our little corner of the world?"

"What do you mean? Don't many Americans come here?"

"Not many. Most can't find the place, not even with a map. So go on. Tell me."

"It's a long story. It's boring."

"Gersha," he said, propping both elbows on the table, "you're never going to be boring. So go on. Out with it."

She had seldom shared her life with people she did not know. Yet, beneath Michael's steady gaze she found she could not stop talking. She told him how she had been born in Connecticut and how her father had been forced to move his family to Boston during the Great Recession. She went on to say how the stress of a poor economy killed him far too young. She described her classwork at the Boston junior college and how she had been forced to take time off when her mother grew ill but how she was going back soon, hoping to earn a degree in business at a prestigious Boston university. She told him why she had decided on traveling to England when her mother had died and how she had ventured to Ireland, then on to Beara, not knowing what she was doing because none of it had been planned.

"I'm sorry about your Mam," Michael said. "I lost my father too but at least I still have my mother. You don't have any brothers or sisters?" When she shook her head, he said, "Neither do I. It sounds like it's been fierce hard on ye."

"It's been a nightmare," Dawn admitted as the old grief stirred her stomach. "You said you lost your father. Do you mind if I ask what happened?"

"It was a dark time," he murmured. "I don't talk about it much."

"You should. I'm not great at it either but talking helps. Talking to you helps me."

"Does it?"

She could see his face work as he considered her comment, then opened his mouth and told her. He recounted how, when his father's trawler had been lost at sea, he had searched for days to find it. He told her the horror he had endured when, after a week and having at last found the boat foundered on an island's rocks, he had discovered that his father was missing. He explained how he had spent more days looking for him and how gutted he had felt when he never found a body, and the grief his mother also suffered. He described how he had repaired the boat because his father would have wanted it and how he took his Da's place fishing off the coast to make ends meet. He explained how hard he had worked but worried all his efforts were futile.

"I just wanted to help Mam," he finished. "I don't think I ever did enough."

"You did your best, Michael. I'm sure of it," Dawn stated and, looking down, realized he had taken her hand.

"How do you know?"

"Because I do. I'm sure your mother is proud of what you've done."

"So she says, not that I believe her."

"Then I'll have to ask her myself," Dawn replied, and saw Michael look at her with an interest far beyond any she had seen from any man before.

"I'll hold you to that," he finally said, and she felt his grip tighten.

When they left the pub just after midnight, Michael insisted on walking her back to the bed and breakfast she had booked on the main street just outside the town. In a soft drizzle, she walked with Michael's hand on the small of her back. Though she did not know this man she realized she had never felt as safe with anyone else except her father. Arriving at the hostelry's front door, she turned to him.

"Thank you for walking me home."

"Anytime you want some company, I'm right here," Michael replied, and hesitated. "Can I ask you…what are your plans for tomorrow?"

She looked up at him. He towered over her yet rather than sensing any fear she felt only comfort. "I'm taking the seven-thirty morning bus to Dublin, then back to London. I have to catch a flight home."

"No, you don't," he smiled.

"Yes, I do."

His hands went around her waist and he lifted her as if her weight meant nothing to him. With her feet off the ground, she could look him in the eye. Then he was kissing her, his lips resting on her mouth, searching its corners, moving to brush her cheek. When he put her down, her breathing came in gasps.

"No, you don't," he whispered. "Not tomorrow. Goodnight, Dawn Reynolds."

He turned, striding back down the hill toward town.

"Yes, I do!" Dawn called when she thought to reply but all he did was raise a hand in farewell.

When she woke early the next day, the rain had stopped. Berating herself for the previous night's adolescent folly, she packed her small bag, ate breakfast, paid the owner, and made her way to the bus stop on the town's square to catch the early morning ride to Dublin. There, she found Michael sitting on a bench waiting for her.

"You told me you weren't leaving," he said with a note of hurt in his voice that made Dawn laugh.

"You know that's not true. What are you doing here?" she asked, and was surprised when he picked up her bag.

"What do you think? Come on." Turning from her, he strode toward the town's main street.

"Michael, I have to go," Dawn called, following in his wake. "Give me the bag. The bus is coming."

"You won't be disappointing my mother, will you? I told her you were coming to breakfast. You said you wanted to meet her."

"That's not what I meant. Slow down! I've already had breakfast."

"Then you'll have to eat twice," he said, turning an eye on her. "About time someone put a bit of meat on those bones. Now come on."

Taking her hand, Michael led her up the main street to a house perched high above the town. Though she was nervous when he escorted her into the living room with its wide window and expansive view of the harbor, she forgot her apprehension when an older woman appeared, arms opened wide in welcome.

"Oh, you poor Gersha," the energetic white-haired woman said, taking both of Dawn's hands in her own. "Michael told me you've lost your mother. We'll talk all about it over breakfast."

"Thank you, Mrs. McCarthy. But please don't go to any trouble."

"Call me Margaret," the older woman replied. "I've already eaten but I'm sure you're starving. Now, get in with you before it gets cold."

As Dawn was led into the kitchen, she caught laughter rising in Michael's eyes. She found herself sitting at the kitchen table before a plate piled high with fried eggs, sausages, pork rasher, black and white pudding, fried potatoes and toast. Michael sat next to her, his plate holding a mountain of food she guessed to be twice her own.

"You'll never eat all that," she whispered to him.

"Watch me," he replied, picking up a fork. "Mam's the best cook in Kilcastle. Go on, eat," he said, pointing at her plate. "God knows you must be hungry, seeing you've not eaten yet this morning." Seeing the laughter in his eyes, she wanted to kick him.

"Leave the poor girl alone, Michael," Margaret warned, and leaned toward her guest. "He eats like a horse, you know. Don't think you'll ever keep up." As Margaret poured tea her blue eyes, so much like Michael's, turned again to her guest. "Tell me about your mother. Michael told me a bit but I'd like to know more. If you'd like to talk about her, of course."

Prodded on by the woman's interest and the careful way she listened, Dawn recounted what she had told Michael. When she explained she had spent the final week with her mom in hospice, holding her hand until the end, Margaret pursed her lips in thought.

"You're a good daughter. Many young'uns your age would have run for the hills. But you stayed at her side."

"It was easy because I loved her," Dawn replied.

Margaret's eyes lit up and she turned to her son. "Michael, that's what you said when you were searching for your father."

"What did I say?" he asked, looking up from his plate.

"Did he tell you we lost his father in a fishing accident?" Margaret said, turning to Dawn.

"Yes, he did. I'm so sorry."

"Did he tell you it took him three weeks to find his father's boat?"

Dawn looked hard at Michael. "You told me it took a week."

"Three," Margaret stated. "When I asked him why he wouldn't give up he told me, 'Mam, it's easy because I love him.' It seems to me," Margaret continued, picking up Michael's empty plate, "you were both taught that love of family is one of God's miracles. It's a gift you both share, one not to be taken lightly."

Dawn glanced at Michael and found him looking back. "I guess it is," Dawn said and felt heat rising in her cheeks.

Having missed the bus to Dublin, Dawn spent the rest of the day strolling around the fishing town with Michael. As they walked along the main street, she found herself reaching for his hand any time he came within range. 'It's almost automatic, as if we're meant to,' she wondered to herself, peering up at the man walking by her side. 'It's like he's held my hand all my life.'

She knew the thought was childish but couldn't let it go, just as she couldn't let go of Michael's hand. After they had wandered through the town, he took her across the town square to the pier with its line of fishing trawlers.

"That's my Da's fishing boat, the *Margie M,*" he said, pointing to the blue and white trawler tied to the pier. "Mind you I guess she's mine, now."

She heard the pride in his voice as they examined the half-decker. "I don't know anything about boats, Michael, but she seems a good one," Dawn said. "I'm glad you found it. I'm glad you didn't give up."

"I have to start repainting her tomorrow. There's always plenty of work to do but you'll work hard if you want something bad enough, won't you?" he asked, and her belly knotted at the question. He took her hands in his. "You hungry yet? What about dinner?"

"But we just had breakfast."

He laughed. "That was hours ago. It's after five."

"Really?" she asked. In Michael's company the day had flown.

The ate at a family restaurant owned by one of his friends, located near the pier. He ordered fresh hake for the two of them, just off one of the town's trawlers. Its battered body was fried golden brown and served with crisp French fries Michael called *chips*.

"Chips are potato chips," Dawn objected, picking up one. "These are French fries."

"They're chips over here," Michael said, smiling. "You Yanks are all eejits. You don't even know the language."

"We aren't all stupid," she replied, knowing he was joking. For some reason she decided to see what would happen if she pushed him. "Michael, that's insulting," she said, making a change of tack. She leaned across the table with a sudden frown. "Americans aren't dumb. At least I'm not."

"Oh, Jaysus, I didn't mean it," he said, and took her hand. "It was a joke, Dawn. You're anything but an eejit. I'm sorry."

They ended up laughing about it. But from then on Dawn realized just how easy it was for Michael to be trapped by her sarcasm and how thin his skin was. She found herself liking him more because of it.

When they finished dinner, he invited her again to the pub. "Just for a pint," he insisted, but Dawn learned that to an Irishman 'a pint' always meant more than just one. The musical group played again but rather than join them with his Uilleann, he invited her out on to the dance floor. Weaving between couples, warmed by his laughter and embrace, Dawn found that time passed too quickly because it seemed only minutes before the publican announced closing time. Michael once more walked her back to the B&B. At the door, Dawn again let him lift her to be kissed. When they finished, her feet still dangling above the porch, she rested her face against his, feeling the warmth of his cheek.

"What are your plans for tomorrow?" he asked as he held her.

"I have to take the bus back then catch the flight home to Boston?" she whispered, knowing what would come next.

"No, you don't."

"Yes, I do."

He kissed her again then put her down.

"No, you don't," he said, cupping her face in both hands.

"I really do, Michael. I have to go home."

She could see him thinking hard then took her hand. "I have work to do in the morning. Meet me tomorrow for lunch at the same place we ate tonight. Promise me. You don't have to go back home. Not yet."

"Yes, I do. You know I do."

But after he kissed her and left, and as she undressed for bed, Dawn discovered that she really didn't want to go at all.

Rising the next day, angered again by her impulsiveness, she decided that enough was enough. "You're an idiot, don't you know that? Out of your mind," she chided herself as she stalked across her room, once again throwing clothes into her bag. "You just met this man. You can't possibly feel anything for him."

But as she closed her luggage her gaze turned to the room's window. The harbor waters beckoned to her with bright morning sunlight. "The least you can do is tell Michael you're leaving. You owe him that much, don't you think?"

She found herself reaching for her makeup. As she fixed her lips and touched up her blonde eyebrows, she knew her words were a lie to let her see him one last time.

When she walked to town, discovering that the bench near the bus stop was empty, she was surprised at the level of her disappointment. But then she remembered. 'He's working this morning, isn't that what he said? He doesn't know I'm leaving.' Then she mentally kicked herself. 'You only wanted to say goodbye to him, remember? Nothing else.' But when the bus came, she made a point of sitting on a high passenger seat. Her eyes roved across the square looking for him though she told herself she was a fool. As the driver turned down the sea road that fronted the pier, she spotted the blue and white trawler. Michael was balanced on a gunwale, a paintbrush in his hand.

"Please stop the bus," Dawn called, climbing out of the seat. "I have to get off."

"There's no other bus to Dublin until tomorrow," the driver warned. "You sure, missus?"

"Absolutely. Please let me off."

After the driver helped her down with the bag, Dawn stood on the pier hearing the cries of gulls wheeling overhead. She looked across a patch of calm water, seeing Michael stepping up on to the boat's railing, reaching high to paint the wheelhouse.

"Michael? Michael, over here," she called.

"What are you doing here?" he called back, pivoting around on the railing to see her. "We're meeting for lunch, remember?"

"I can't. I came to say goodbye."

"You're leaving?" he said, and she could see his disbelief.

She cupped her hands, making a megaphone. "We're fools. We don't know each other. I live in America. You live in Ireland."

"So what? I don't care where we live."

"It's happening too quick. I'm sorry but I can't. I'm going home. Goodbye, Michael."

"No, Dawn. Don't. Stay there!"

Then he yelled, stumbling, his boots skidding. Arms swinging, he slipped over the boat's railing, falling head first into the harbor. She ran to the edge of the pier, searching an empty sea.

"Michael? Michael!" she cried. When he didn't surface, she looked down the line of trawlers for help but the pier was empty. "Michael, stop joking!"

She pulled off her coat. Breathing deep, she launched herself into the harbor, hitting the water in a ball of spray. She surfaced, turning a complete circle.

"Michael, where are you?" she yelled, her voice echoing across the deserted water. She heard a soft splash behind her.

"Here."

She swung around. Treading water, Michael had a huge grin on his face.

"You Bozo!" she shouted, swimming toward him. "I thought you were dead!"

"Guess I'm not," he laughed.

"You scared the shit out of me," she yelled. Finding herself caught up in his strong arms, she pushed away. "You wanted me to dive in, didn't you? You wanted me to look for you. Why did you do that?"

"Because I didn't want you to leave."

"Why not?"

"Because."

"'Because' is not an answer, Michael." She reached out, turning his face to her. "Why don't you want me to go?"

"Because you gotta know something first." He pulled her to him. "You see, it's this way. It turns out I love you."

"You can't love me. We only met two days ago."

"But I do. And you know what else?"

"What?"

"I don't want you to go. Not ever." He looked up, the sun in his eyes. "I don't want to lose you."

She placed a hand tight behind his neck. "Michael, what are you saying? Are you saying you want to marry me?"

"That's exactly what I'm saying, Dawn Reynolds. I'm asking you to marry me. Will you?"

"I don't believe this."

"Remember what Mam said. We've been given a gift. I don't want to lose it and I don't think you do, either. So, I'm asking again. Will you marry me?"

Dawn looked up at the gulls cartwheeling above her, their voices carried in on the breeze. Her gaze moved down to find him again: the wet curls of his hair, the line of his strong jaw, the kindness in his eyes.

"If I say no, I'll never find you again, will I? I don't want to lose you, either. We're both nuts but, yes, Michael," she whispered. "Yes, I'll marry you."

When they kissed, she never wanted to let go.

"I was a fool. I never thought I'd lose him but I did," Dawn murmured, her eyes on the empty pool. She felt sick just as she did whenever she thought of him.

"You still have Margaret, don't you?" Joyce asked, taking her hand. "You still have Jason."

"I guess so. You're right."

Joyce frowned at her friend's sadness. "Don't you know how lucky you are? That's one of the most romantic stories I've ever heard. Tell me again. How long did you know each other before he proposed?"

"Two days."

"Two days. It's like a fairytale."

"It was. But it isn't now."

"No, it isn't," Joyce replied, and studied her friend. "Do you want me to stay with you tonight?"

"It's okay. It's time I got home."

"Dawn, you're not alone."

"I know. Honestly. I'll be fine."

But as Dawn trudged to the shower room, she realized what her friend had promised was dead wrong. She would always be alone.

CHAPTER SEVEN

As she walked out on to the rain-swept street in front of the YMCA, loneliness struck Dawn as it did most nights. She hurried to the subway, boarding the Green Line for the ride back to the apartment. Clutching an overhead strap she traveled at speed beneath the city, swaying as if standing on the deck of an old trawler. Scanning the car, she couldn't help but wonder if she wasn't one of the subway's most frequent travelers. Every day she took the Red Line from Southie to work and back again. Every night the Green Line brought her to the hospital and Jason. Red and green had become a part of her life, managing her day like bullying traffic lights.

She became aware of her image reflected in the dark window of the subway car. The long hair was wet and colorless. Circles of exhaustion hung beneath lifeless green eyes. She frowned, realizing she did not recognize the stranger who frowned back in so much pain.

She looked away, her gaze settling on a woman's bare shoulder, finding herself staring at a colorful tattoo. A dolphin jumped from a sea of cornflower blue, its smile laughing up at her, eyes locked on her own. She glanced at the dolphin's owner. The woman, fast asleep on a seat, was Dawn's age, perhaps a bit older. The boy sleeping on her lap leaned against the shoulder of a man next to them, obviously the child's father. The family looked so normal. So content.

The train lurched over a junction, the interior lights flashing like lightning. The woman stirred, meeting her gaze. Dawn had the sudden urge to talk. To share the horror of loss she lived with every day. Before she could, the train rattled to a stop.

She bolted from the car, leaving behind the family who seemed so much like her own. Bounding up the station's concrete steps she broke into a run, rushing down the streets of South Boston. She passed sports bars and delis packed with customers, laughing behind glass windows. She ran from them all.

She took a left down a main thoroughfare, then slowed. The rain had almost stopped. Outside her apartment she bent double in the fine mist, breathing hard, trying to stifle the memories that careened through her head. As she rummaged through her bag for the key, she heard the lilting notes of song.

On the other side of the street a musician played a set of wind pipes. His music echoed toward her, stirring memories she always tried to bury. The song reminded her of *that* song; the one the dolphins had sung that night. The mammals' enigmatic voices had swept over her as she had struggled toward the surface of a terrifying sea in search of her son. It was a song that never made any sense to her, one she could not have heard within the tempest of the storm; one she dared not tell the Coast Guard or Morrison but a song that still haunted her.

She studied the long-haired Rastafarian who played with all his heart, his image reflected in a puddle of water that lay like a mirror across the street. She found her key, opening the security door. Fleeing inside, she locked it then ran up the shadowed flight of stairs accompanied only by echoing footfalls. At the top, fumbling again, she let herself into the apartment.

She banged shut the heavy fire door, leaning against the wall of the narrow hallway. When she finally exhaled, she reached for the light switch. Envelopes lay scattered across the floor where they had fallen from the mail slot and she bent to retrieve them. Sorting through the pile, she already knew what they contained: a demand from the telecom company. A final demand from the electricity company. A statement from Children's Hospital reminding her of the terms of the Financial Assistance Plan she had agreed to when admitting Jason, highlighting two months' late payments. A letter from her landlord threatening eviction if she did not pay three months' overdue rent. She thought back on the words Michael had used when they were faced with similar financial problems. "Feck it, Dawn. It's only some bills. We'll figure it out."

She threw the bills on the hall table, dismissing her husband's lost voice. Her eyes swept across the tiny living room. She took in the two-seater sofa they had bought when first married then looked to the far wall. The shelving unit was filled with a disorganized library of old CDs, books and her son's computer games. She had taken little from their seaside home. Nothing else would fit. She stripped off her coat, shaking the rain from it. Her eyes moved to the wall above the sofa, covered with family photos. She could not help but study the framed images.

In one, Jason, Michael and Dawn played at the edge of the Duck Pond in Boston's Public Garden. In the next, Michael and Jason visited a construction site, both wearing bright yellow hardhats, their son perched high on his dad's shoulders. Lower, a copy of the photo Margaret had taken before casting off on the *Margie M's* final voyage, the family posed on the Kilcastle pier in front of a fluttering Irish flag.

She swung from the photos. Scanning the apartment, she decided she was not ready for another night when she would reach for her men but find only empty beds. Stalking to the kitchen, she microwaved a late dinner of macaroni and cheese, forcing herself to eat. Then she vacuumed the carpets and mopped the bathroom and kitchen floors. She washed a stack of dishes crusted with a week of rushed meals and opened the window to cool the tiny kitchen. She remembered Bill Saunders and the pending supervisor's exam scheduled for less than two days' time. Leaving behind a sink full of dirty dishwater, she grabbed the thick World Connect training manual from the kitchen counter and walked back into the living room.

Sitting on the couch, one foot tapping a staccato on the floor, she thumbed through the manual. The crammed pages revolved like spinning tops. She tossed the manual aside, eyes roving back across the room, coming to rest on the landline telephone handset. She had not noticed the answering machine's blinking red light. Suspecting it was a message from Doctor

Morrison, she hurried to the hallway table, smacking the button. Instead of the doctor the recorded voice filled the apartment with halting Irish singsong.

"Dawn, it's Margaret. Would you be there, Dawn?" Dawn could see her mother-in-law standing in the house on the hill, her pursed lips working to project her voice across the distance. "I haven't heard from you in so long. And how would Jason be? I hope he's getting proper care. Dawn, we're having a day of remembrance for Michael and other fishermen from the town. It's been a year already. It's so hard to believe."

Dawn pulled up the hall chair, her heart racing at the woman's words.

"Everyone is asking for you. You always felt so much at home here. Won't you please come? Dawn, are you there? That's grand. You must be busy. I'll phone back later. Give Jason my love, won't you? I'll say a pray for you both."

The recording went dead. Dawn sat in rigid stillness, not having the strength to get up. She feared she would collapse due to the invitation and its unwanted anniversary.

She took a breath, steadying herself. She decided not to think about it. Instead, she closed her eyes, remembering the places where she had felt alive and loved when her family was whole, in the days before tragedy had touched them.

A year earlier, on the night before the sinking, even before they had had a chance to discuss returning to the distant island, Michael had taken his family to the pub where she had first met him as they often did during their annual visits.

Kilcastle Public House was thronged that night. Dawn danced close to Michael, skipping across a rough pine floor packed with local townspeople who stepped out with a jig and a reel, the room shaking with their laughter. As they navigated through the maze of people, she saw the traditional group huddled at the far end of the room playing with relish. Fiddler, bodhran, mandolin, squeezebox and tin whistle musicians scratched away at a rendition of *The Mermaid*, their voices booming across the room as they recounted the story of a green-haired mermaid.

"So you're a water nymph, are ya?" Michael yelled over the music, looking down at his wife. "Is that the beauty I caught in my net?"

"Oh, you'd be so lucky," she shouted up, tightening her grip. "Keep dancing!"

Her eyes roved across the pub and the local people out having a night of craic. At the bar fishermen, farmers and tradesmen balanced like spillikins, elbows propped on the long oak counter. Some wore work jeans or oil-stained boiler suits while others dressed in sensible slacks and shirts. All held thick pints of Guinness in massive hands, sipping at the porter's creamy top. She strained to understand the melodic West Cork accents as they discussed the price of fish and cattle or the cost of maintenance on trawler engines. In a corner, a group of old men argued in lilting, indecipherable voices.

"What are they talking about?" Dawn asked.

Michael twisted, peering over the crowd. "Watch!"

An old codger wearing a flat cap sloped across his head banged a heavy fist. His pint rocked on the high table, his neighbor swooping in to catch it. "The Fianna Fáil gobshites haven't a fecking clue!" the old man roared. "Any man who thinks as such is thick as a plank, stupid, or an ignoramus!"

"Forget the tossers, John," his neighbor pleaded. "Just mind the pint!" The group shouted their agreement.

"Politics!" Michael laughed as he swung her again. "Ireland's national pastime. What else would that bunch be jawing on about?"

As they turned, women came into Dawn's view sitting at low tables pushed to the side of the room. They sat together on stools drinking glasses of lager or shorts of spirits and lemonade. She heard snatches of conversation as they discussed homes and children and the shopping excursions they would soon take to Killarney. Hearing shrill laughter, she strained to see through the crowd. She spotted Jason weaving through adults' dancing legs as he played with a group of local children, eyes wide with excitement.

"Jason, slow down!"

"Ah, leave him alone," Michael laughed. "He's only having a bit of fun."

He held her tight until she giggled, then gave her another spin. People twirled into view who were now something more than strangers but, because she did not yet know them well, continued to revolve in her mind like complicated puzzles. She spotted Joan, the town's librarian, dancing with another woman in the middle of the floor. Years earlier, Dawn had asked Michael why women dancing with women was so common in this part of the world. He had laughed at her puzzled look, stating it had nothing to do with sexual orientation but rather the Irish male's reluctance to dance. More to the point, it was also because many of the men had been lost at sea. Dawn had stared up at him with an open mouth. "Have that many died?" she had asked. Michael had only nodded.

She noticed how Joan wore her curling hair tucked beneath a woolen cap that shadowed her eyes in melancholy. Yet, she had heard the librarian's ironic laughter and admired the strong face which hid a sense of humor that could make a turnip cackle. Dawn was certain she would like to get to know Joan better.

She spied Margaret standing at the edge of the crowd, clapping to the music. Her bright blue eyes were glued on Jason as he again ran through the thick ruck of dancers and she could see the woman's easy display of love she held for her grandson. Dawn had been comfortable in her mother-in-law's presence since they had first met six years ago. In Margaret, Dawn recognized that she had found a depth of intimacy she had not encountered in any other woman since her mother's death.

Then there was Carol. Arms folded tight across a tiny stature, she stood close to Margaret and Dawn realized she had still not made up her mind about the woman. Carol always reminded her of a belligerent Jack Russell terrier. She had heard her aggressive bark, certain it had to be less harmful than her bite. During their few encounters she had found Carol to be tightly wound, suspecting she was also high-maintenance. The woman seldom smiled and never engaged in a conversation that did not contain a criticism or command. And yet Dawn had learned that Margaret respected her because Carol was the energetic engine that drove the church social committee who, in turn, scheduled much of the town's activities and events. Dawn had made the decision to give the woman the benefit of the doubt. Besides, Jason enjoyed the company of Carol's five-year-old daughter, Lydia, which was reason enough to get to know her better.

Now Jackie... Jackie was something else all-together. Dawn spotted him standing near the bar, his beer belly falling over stained corduroy trousers belted far too tight. His red face huffed and puffed as he drank a pint while throwing darts at a pockmarked dartboard. Michael had introduced him to her as a close friend and she had learned that their history went back to early childhood. She always laughed when Jackie told her unsuccessful jokes or tried to tease her with his fake American accent. But due to her husband's friendship, she chose to ignore his occasional oafishness and instead looked for the good man she felt must rest inside.

The musicians played faster and Michael spun her to match the tempo. The room whirled as the faces of those she wanted to know better blurred into a funhouse of joy. He wheeled her even faster until the music ended in a roar of applause. She collapsed into his arms, thinking she could not be as content anywhere else in the world. After the music, they made their way to the round tables where the publican had placed baskets brimming with hot cocktail sausages and sandwich halves bursting with savory fillings. Dawn sat with friends and family, letting their conversation cover her like a warm blanket.

"How's it going, Jackie," Michael asked, nursing a pint. "Ya getting on okay? We've been thinking of ya."

"I'm okay, I'm okay," Jackie sighed as he sat down beside them and Dawn remembered how Jackie's wife, Claire, had passed away unexpectedly over a year ago. "To be honest, it's been one feckin' thing after another."

"Yeah, I heard you had the engine in that new tub of yours overhauled," Michael grinned as he took a drink. "Must have cost a fortune."

"Not at all, not at all, Michael," he replied with a red face, stuffing a chicken salad sandwich into his mouth. "But enough of me. How's it in America? You made yer fortune yet?"

"Ask Dawn," Michael laughed, and looked at her. "What d'ya say, wife? Are we rich yet?"

"If a fortune can buy us a Chinese takeout once a month, then we have it made," she grinned back.

"We're getting there," Michael continued, picking up a sausage. "I lost a big job after New Year's but just quoted for some work in Marblehead. If it comes off, we'll be fine."

"Of course, you'll get it," Dawn teased. "I didn't marry you just for your looks you know."

Michael laughed again then turned serious.

"It's been a struggle. I don't know I'd be up for it again. How about you? Now you got your trawler fixed, how's the fishing?"

Jackie's red face flushed darker. "Good and bad. Like you, it's been a struggle. I sure could use you and that boat of yours. It'd be good to have a few more fish go to market."

Disappointment crossed her husband's face. "Jackie, I couldn't help anyway. I'm selling her."

"You're what?" Dawn asked. "You never told me that."

"Yes, I did," Michael replied, trying to lean on the old joke between them.

"No, you didn't. You never said anything. Michael, you can't sell your father's boat."

Across the table, Margaret strained to hear but Carol strode up.

"Has anyone seen Lydia?" Carol interrupted. "She's always running off."

"Carol, they're kids," Dawn observed. "Running off is what kids do."

She scanned the room, finding Jason in the crowd with Lydia and Peter, Jackie's young son. They had their heads together, eyes filled with conspiracy. Dawn pointed out Lydia to Carol but before the woman could lay into her daughter, the three children bolted toward them like small torpedoes. Jason threw himself at his mother, hugging on tight.

"Mom, Mom!" he yelped, his young Boston accent sounding rough and foreign compared to his Irish friends. "Lydia, Peter and me — we want, we want, please Mom?"

"Hey, kiddo, slow down," she laughed. "Now, what is it?"

Jason found himself caught in his father's strong hands. Michael lifted him, holding him upside down like a sack of potatoes. "Okay, monkey. Spit it out." Jason giggled as his father playfully shook him. "Come on, out with it!"

"Ice cream!" Jason managed. The other kids took up the chorus. "Please, Mam!" Lydia squealed. "Da', please! Ice cream! Please?" young Peter pleaded to his father.

Jackie reached for his wallet but Michael beat him to it. He pulled out a fifty-euro bill, handing it to his son. Still upside down, Jason grabbed the valuable brown note. Michael turned his son right side up, standing him on two feet. The kids screeched again, launching themselves toward the door.

"That's too much money, Michael. They'll lose it," Carol grumbled, turning to her daughter. "Lydia, be careful!" But the kids ignored her, disappearing into the crowd. With the children gone, Margaret turned to her son.

"Michael, you're not serious about selling the boat? It was your father's."

Dawn caught the look of resignation in her husband's face as he took his mother's hand.

"Da' would understand. It's sort of stupid keeping the *Margie M* if we're only here once a year. If we were moving back, it would be different."

"I know," his mother hesitated. "You have a new life in America now, don't you?"

Michael smiled at her understanding but Dawn could see how much it cost him.

"You're right to stay in Boston," Carol said in a sharp voice. "There's not much here anyway."

Dawn was caught off guard. She realized Carol was trying to rescue Michael and was surprised at the sudden gratitude she felt for the woman.

"Why do you stay here, Carol?" Dawn asked, hoping to distract the conversation.

Carol thought for a moment. "Well, we have good schools here," she said, reaching out and tapping Dawn's forearm with a sharp index finger. "After my husband Paul was lost, they did a wonderful job helping Lydia," she continued, tapping again. "Then there's the medical system, which is much better than the disaster you have in the States," she tapped. "And the food and drink and friends," she continued, and Dawn's gratitude dissolved as Carol tapped out each word. "Why wouldn't we stay? It's our home."

This time it was Jackie who came to the rescue when he noticed Dawn's discomfort.

"Other than that, Yank, there's nothing to keep us here at all," Jackie said with a twinkle, and Dawn couldn't help but laugh.

A PA crackled and a disembodied voice called across the crowded pub. "Michael McCarthy, where's Michael McCarthy?"

Michael caught the eye of the fiddler. The lanky fellow whose bearded face reminded Dawn of a cheerful fox held tight to a microphone. "Get up here, Michael," the musician challenged. "Give us a song!" The crowd broke into whooping applause.

Dawn reached across the table, gripping her husband's strong forearm. "Go on. You know I love it when you play."

Grinning like a child on Christmas morning, he lifted the green box that contained his Uilleann from where he'd tucked it beneath the table and strode toward the group. Dawn watched as he sat with them, unpacking and assembling the instrument.

"He has that Uilleann since he was a boy," Margaret said to her daughter-in-law. "Does he play it in Boston?"

"He doesn't have time," Dawn lied. Her voice was filled with guilt. She had long suspected that he didn't play because it reminded him of his Irish home. She hoped Margaret would pass no notice.

His Uilleann ready, Michael picked up the microphone, eyes locking on his wife.

"Here's *The Voyage*, a classic Christy Moore tune. Dawn, this one's for you."

The daydream dissolved as she found herself still sitting in the hallway, still staring at the telephone answering machine. She stood up, moving back into the living room. Surrounded by photos of Michael and Jason, she stepped to the stack of CDs. Selecting one, she placed it in the player. Christy Moore sang *The Voyage* with its lyrics of loving journeys.

Turning up the volume, Moore's rough voice boomed across the room. She swayed to its waltzing rhythm; her arms lifted high as if she danced with her family. Tears fell as she remembered how easily her hand had slipped into Michael's as they held Jason between them. As she danced, she wished she could make time disappear and bring them back from the distant places to which they had journeyed; back into her life so she could hold tight to their love.

Someone banged on the other side of the thin wall. "Turn it down!" the man in the adjoining apartment shouted. "Go to sleep!"

Dawn turned off the CD player and sat alone within the silent room. When she finished crying, she switched off the light and went to bed. On the street below the apartment the piper continued to play, his song echoing through the night.

At the Children's Hospital the nurse checked on Jason as she did each hour. Entering his room, and like most nights, she found her young patient held in the grip of a nightmare.

She bent over him, concerned by the contorted face. His arms thrashed in horror; his hair was matted with sweat. He clutched his stuffed monkey, the only passenger to accompany him on his strange voyage. Seeing his distress, the nurse did what she always did. She bathed his face in water, cooling his fevered cheeks. She adjusted his pillow and untangled the blanket. She snuggled the stuffed animal close in his arms. Then she pressed a small cup of water to his quivering lips in case he might rouse and want to drink. On that night he took no water and she placed the full cup on the nightstand beside his bed. For ten minutes she sat with him to make certain the nightmare had passed. When he quieted, she left the room, returning to other duties.

Beside him the cup of water rested unmoving, its surface reflecting the nightlight the nurse had left on in case he woke.

91

Five miles south, Dawn lay in bed also trapped by the closed fist of a nightmare. Held by horror, she swam underwater, struggling toward the raging surface.

Desperate strokes pushed her up through a dark sea, past the detritus of the sinking *Margie M*. A shattered fish box swept by on its way to the bottom, then the heavy wheelhouse door torn from its hinges. She weaved, trying to avoid a web of fishing net descending toward her. She tangled in it, panicking because her lungs were desperate for air. As if by a miracle, the net slipped away and she pushed on.

She swung, startled, as the depths of the ocean were pierced by the song of echoing voices. Twisting, she saw a pod of dolphins speeding toward her, their fins churning the sea to bubbling effervescence. A unique white-faced dolphin led the group and, within her confused mind, she recalled the memory of a sunlit lagoon in the days when she still carried an unborn child. The spotted dolphin paused. Swimming through a curtain of sealight, it gazed at her from unfathomable eyes. Out of air, gripped by dread, she pushed on. Dawn surfaced within heaving seas lit by violent lightning.

Treading within scudding crests, her head swung looking for her son. "Jason!"

Between tall waves she saw the yellow buoy swaying, pounded by whitewater. Her boy clung to it. She shouted again but Jason did not hear. He looked to the horizon and at the sinking boat's raging fire. Above the keening wind she heard his terrorized scream.

"Daddy!"

In his room at the children's hospital, light swept Jason's face. The cup of water on his nightstand vibrated as if disturbed by a gentle breath. Still sleeping, his terrified face relaxed. Jason smiled, clutching his monkey tight.

In her bed, Dawn stirred. Still caught in the nightmare she clung to the base of the buoy, looking up at Jason sheltering high within its steel latticework. He swung around as quick as a dog sensing hidden game. He twisted again and she followed his gaze toward the sinking boat. Dolphins leaped toward the vessel. Then the winds and seas calmed as suddenly as if someone had turned a switch. Light filled the darkness as she again heard the song. Its notes swept to her from across the sea, wrapping her in a soft embrace.

In bed, she twisted. Part of her sleeping mind told her that the music drifted up from the piper who still played on the street below. In the kitchen the melody swept through the open window to the sink and dirty dishwater she had left behind. Its surface glittered like starlight, then vibrated as if disturbed by an invisible breath — or a dolphin's song.

Dawn woke to the sound of rushing water. Leaping out of bed, she ran to the sunlit kitchen. A pool of water covered the floor. She opened the door beneath the sink, finding a broken pipe. She glanced up at the kitchen clock: 9:04AM. Remembering the 10 o'clock session for Jason, she rushed to the closet for a mop.

On the floor behind her the water glittered in the morning light.

CHAPTER EIGHT

Dawn sat at a low table, legs scissored beneath a child-sized chair. Stretching, she turned, surveying the room. Nearby, other children sat with parents and counselors, all engaged in therapy. She noticed a boy a little older than Jason using an orange crayon to draw a dog with bright pointy ears. Completing it with a flourish, he beamed up at his father who was seated next to him. Leaning close, the man smiled with pride.

"What does the dog say, Sam?" his father coaxed. "What does it say?"

Sam screwed up his face, working hard to retrieve the correct sound from his traumatized brain. "Woof!" Sam tried, and knowing he had found it howled with delight. "Woof, woof, woooooo!"

Sam's father laughed, tousling the boy's hair as his son snuggled close. Dawn found herself envying the simple connection. She had learned that this boy suffered just as her son had suffered. In fact, every child in the room had been exposed to an extreme event of some kind. Like Jason, Sam had become mute as a result. Like Jason, he looked just like any normal child. Where her son's journey differed from Sam's was that while Sam was making progress Jason was not.

"Dawn? Are you ready to start again?"

She looked up, seeing their therapist's bright smile. Gripping the legs of her small chair, Dawn turned her attention back to her son. Jason was seated on the other side of the low table, dull eyes focused inward. A box of crayons lay untouched on the tabletop, the pad of drawing paper still blank. Dawn cleared her throat, remembering to inject lightness into her voice just as the therapist had coached.

"Jason, see the other kids drawing? Won't you at least try?" Unable to suppress her frustration she added, "Come on Jase, it's not that hard."

The therapist gave her a look, then prompted, "We'd love to see what you can draw, Jason."

At her son's silence Dawn twisted, hunting across the room. Doctor Morrison stood in a far corner, observing. Their eyes met, his quick nod encouraging her to try again. She slid the pad closer, selecting a blue crayon from the box. She drew a smiling cat and held it up for Jason to see. He studied it, his expression neutral. Dawn leaned in, holding out the crayon.

"I know what the cat says, Jason. You do, too. What does it say? It says *meow, meow, meow*, doesn't it, Jase? Wouldn't you like to draw one?"

The therapist held out another crayon. "We'd love to see you draw a cat, Jason."

Jason switched his focus to the therapist's outstretched hand then back to his mother's.

"Go on, Jason," Dawn urged. "Draw one so we can hear what the cat says."

A growl of anger rose in the boy's throat. He reached out, slashing, striking his mother's face. Crayons clattered to the floor. He glared at her, his eyes filled with loathing.

"Dawn?" She looked up to see Morrison. Standing beside her, his face was flushed with concern.

"This isn't working," Dawn choked. She pushed to her feet, rushing to the door, desperate to escape the perplexed glances of other parents. She looked back. Jason's contemptuous stare followed her as she strode from the room.

Dawn did not know how far she had walked or how she had managed to board the subway, or even when she had stopped crying. She only knew that, somehow, she was in Boston's Public Garden where children's laughter brought her back from whatever distant place her mind had journeyed.

Blinking in the bright sunshine, she discovered she was standing at the edge of a large pond. Swan boats filled with children and their parents glided over the water as the families kicked, sending droplets skyward to sparkle in the sunlight. Gazing at their antics, Dawn remembered how much Jason had loved the sea.

"Do it again, Dad. Higher! Mom, Mom! Look at me!"

In her mind, she was back under Irish skies. She watched Michael roughhouse with Jason in the sea where they had anchored the trawler before the squall had hit. She could picture them as Jason was tossed across the gentle swells, shrieking as he hit the water. She could feel his soaking hair press against her skin when she hauled him back onboard, listening to his excited chatter as she stripped him of the life vest and wetsuit to dry him. She recalled his perfect voice and prefect eyes and perfect face, and in her head the months of tragedy had never happened.

A child's shriek fractured the daydream. Squinting in the sunlight Dawn realized she was alone in the Public Garden, not with Michael and Jason. She realized it was another child who laughed, not her son. Looking down, she studied hands clenched into tight fists, white-knuckled in the light. Thoughts bubbled into her head, her gut heaving as she reached a stark conclusion.

"The doctor doesn't know what he's doing," she whispered. "Despite all his promises. Despite all the work, Jason won't ever talk again." She gasped, bending double at the revelation, pain exploding like a bomb.

Shrill laughter made her look up. A little boy squatted on one of the boats screaming as he and his father drowned each other with pails of water. The boy looked so healthy. So strong. So much like her son.

"I just want my boy back," she uttered. "If Morrison can't do it…"

She couldn't finish the thought. As she turned from the pond, retracing her steps out of the park, her mind waded through the months of failures. "The shaping therapy didn't work. None of the therapies work. Jason isn't happy at the hospital. He needs to come home. He's safe at home."

The word rose like a sunrise, quickly doused by self-criticism. "You want to bring him home? Forget it," she hissed to herself, rejecting the idea. "Jason hates you. Remember how he was before Morrison? Remember what

97

TOM RICHARDS

happened in the grocery store?" Warring thoughts tussled in her head as she reconsidered. "But Jason isn't any better now than he was a year ago. If the doctor can't do it then it's up to me, isn't it?"

She continued battling with herself as she strode through the city's late-afternoon crowds, pounding down the steps to the subway. Sitting on a bench next to a woman also waiting for the train, her foot tapped in time to her argument.

"If you decide to do it, if you try to take him home, Morrison will think you're crazy," she whispered to herself. "He'll try to talk you out of it."

She slumped back, not noticing her seatmate listening to the tense monologue. "He'll call you an idiot. He'll tell you you're a danger to your own son." Clasping her hands tight, Dawn bent double. "But you have to keep fighting for him, don't you? Jason needs you. He needs to come home. Don't you dare give up on him." She slapped the bench, standing, her head swinging toward the ceiling. "Christ! I don't know what to do!"

"Yes, you do."

She looked down, seeing the middle-aged stranger. "What did you say?"

"Yes, you do," the woman repeated, pushing a frayed cap up on her forehead. Worn fingers tapped the bench. Dawn sat again as the woman's eyes narrowed. "You're talking about your son, aren't you? You're worried you're going to make a mistake."

"How did you know?"

"You know how many kids I got?" the woman snorted, sliding closer. "Five. And you know what I've learned?"

"What?"

"No one knows anything but you. You're his mother. You know what's best for your kid. So, your answer is: 'Yes, I do.'"

"No, I don't."

"Oh Christ," the woman scowled, leaning in. "Listen close and repeat after me: 'Yes, I do.' Got it? Remember that and you can tell everyone else to fuck-off."

The words jarred. Dawn stared at the face lined with years of experience.

"That's what my husband would say," Dawn replied. "He'd tell everyone to go fuck themselves. He'd tell me to do what I thought was best for our son."

"Then you know what, sweetie?" the woman said, patting Dawn's hand. "That's exactly what you're going to do."

"Jason?"

Dawn stood at the foot of his hospital bed. Her son lay flat on it, staring at the ceiling. She gripped the steel railing of the footboard, bending over him. "Jason, sweetie, look at me."

He turned away, pressing his face deep into the pillow. When she sat on the bed he shifted to the other side. The stuffed monkey lay at his head. She picked it up, putting its mouth to her ear. Listening, she looked up in surprise.

"Sweetie, do you know what Mister Monkey says? He says he wants to go home. What do you think of that?" She leaned closer, lips to her son's ear. "Would you like that, Jason? Would you like to go home with me and Mister Monkey?"

Jason turned to her. For the first time in months, she saw hope break through his suspicious anger.

"We're going home, Jason. We're going home right now."

"Dawn?"

Doctor Morrison stood at the door. It was clear he had overheard her.

"We need to talk," Dawn stated. "Right now."

"You can't be serious. When did you decide on this?"

They stood outside Jason's room. Doctor Morrison crossed his arms, staring at her.

"It doesn't matter. I'm taking him home."

"Dawn, he's not ready. We both know that."

"Oh, come on. He's as ready as he's ever going to get."

"I know you're upset. I know the therapy didn't go well. But in good conscience I can't release Jason. Not now."

"You're not getting anywhere with him," she bristled. A nurse strode down the hall; Dawn lowered her voice. "You've tried everything there is to try. Jason has been here for months. You're not helping him."

"How is taking him home going to help? Dawn, don't be unreasonable."

"Are you telling me I don't know how to take care of my own son?"

"I didn't say that. You're not thinking this through."

Behind them, Jason gazed at his mother through the observation window. Seeing him, Dawn stood taller. "Doctor, if you don't release him, I'll find someone who will. If I can't do that, I'll just take him. You can call the cops if you want."

"You're making a mistake."

"But it's my mistake. If Michael was here, he'd agree with me. Now do you let him go or do we just walk out?"

Morrison looked at the floor lost in thought then raised his head. "I hear you. But first let me show you something."

"You won't change my mind."

"Please, Dawn. For Jason, okay?"

She didn't understand as he led her to a nearby hospital wing, unlocking a gated security entrance. He escorted her down a wide hallway lined with closed doors and observation windows. At the end of the hall, he stopped.

"What I'm about to do breaches every ethical code I've ever been taught."

"What do you mean?"

"Patient confidentiality." When he turned to her, his smile never touched his eyes. "You could get me fired for this. But Jason comes first."

He unlocked a door. Swinging it open, he stepped inside. She followed him into a hospital room much like her son's. The doctor motioned to a spot behind the bed.

"Dawn, I'd like you to meet Rose."

Dawn had to walk around the bed to see her. Rose crouched on the floor, hiding behind the bed frame. She did not move. She did not blink. She stared unseeing into space. The young girl wore a white dress pulled up to her knees. A yellow rose was pinned in her hair.

"Rose, this is Mrs. McCarthy. She wants to say hello. Would you like that?" He turned to Dawn. "Go on. Say hello."

For a long moment Dawn couldn't open her mouth. She inched toward the bed, squatting.

"Rose? Hi. My name is Dawn." When the little girl said nothing, Dawn smiled and tried again. "You're a beauty did you know that? I love your flower. Can I see it?"

When she reached to touch it, Rose pushed herself flat against the wall, her body shaking. Dawn glanced at Morrison. The doctor crouched, trying to make eye contact with his patient.

"I'll see you later, okay, Rose? Before you go to sleep." He stood, motioning Dawn out of the room. She backed against the hallway wall as he closed the door and locked it.

"How old is she?"

"Ten," Morrison replied.

"What's wrong with her?"

"Catatonia."

"She's catatonic? What happened?"

Morrison leaned against the wall next to her. "Rose was involved in a car crash. She was trapped in the vehicle. Before they pulled her out, she watched her younger sister burn to death. It's a scenario which, as you can imagine, resulted in extreme psychological distress. Following therapy, she made progress. Her mother asked to have her sent home. Which, of course, we agreed to do." He stepped away from the wall, hands clasped behind his back.

"Then what?"

"Then, well —" He shifted, as if wanting to avoid the next part. "Four months after her release, that's two years after the original incident, Rose's life fell apart again. Her mother had been overwhelmed by the horrific death of her youngest child. She had a breakdown. Rose watched her mom pick up a thirty-eight revolver, put it to her head and pull the trigger. Rose was re-traumatized. The girl in there?" Morrison said, pointing to the locked door. "That isn't Rose. That's the result."

"She's been like this for over two years?" Dawn whispered. "You haven't been able to help her in over two years?"

"That's not my point. Of course, we're trying. But that's why we're so careful with Jason. Don't you understand? If you take him out of here, if he experiences additional trauma —"

"Two entire years." Her eyes flicked to his. "You bastard."

She stormed back into the main building. As she dodged past nurses and patients in the hallway Morrison trotted after her.

"Dawn, don't do it."

"Piss off! Leave my son alone."

"Please, I can't recommend this."

Entering Jason's room with Morrison at her heals, she marched past her waiting son. She grabbed his backpack, pushing in his belongings then turned on the doctor.

"I'm glad I met Rose. You did me a favor."

"I only used Rose to show you the risks. It won't come to that for Jason."

"Oh, you used her all right. How many different therapies did you try on Rose? Over two years it must have been a lot. You're not doing that to Jason. Not anymore." She pulled the monkey from her son's arms, shoving it in the backpack. "Come on, Jason. Let's go home."

She opened the door wide. Seeing freedom he rushed from the room, Dawn close behind.

"We'll find something else," Morrison pleaded, following them down the hall. "We have options. Don't you understand what could happen? Dawn, think about what you're doing!"

"Stop it! Just stop!" She turned, taking a shaking breath. "Doctor Morrison, I think about what I'm doing all the time. But I just can't do this anymore. Neither can Jason. You've tried so hard but don't you understand? You can't help him. Maybe nobody can. I'm sorry, I really am. But we're going home."

Morrison broke eye contact, looking away. Finally, he shrugged. "I guess I have to understand. You don't give me much choice." He glanced at her. "Wait here. I want to give you something. I'll be right back."

"Didn't you hear me? I'm not waiting."

"Do whatever you want but stay here. This isn't about you. It's about your son."

She stepped back, letting the doctor pass. As he hurried down the hallway, she glanced at her son. Jason's pensive eyes met hers. "It's going to be great, Jase," she promised. "You're going to love being home."

She looked again down the hall. Morrison was already striding back, a white paper bag clutched in his hand.

"Take this," he said, thrusting the bag at her.

"What is it?"

"Sedatives." When she hesitated, he stepped closer. "If you don't take it, I'll stop you from leaving. I'll call the police. Listen to me. He might need them."

She glanced at the bag. "Won't they hurt him?"

"They only work to calm him. Take them. Just in case." As she grasped the bag the doctor touched her arm. "Dawn, I'm sorry that you're disappointed in me. It's just, well, I honestly give a damn. If you need me, will you phone? Let me know how he's doing?"

She placed a hand on his.

"I'm sorry for what I said. I know how hard you tried. This time you lost, that's all." She glanced down at her son. "But I tell you what. I can't lose. I don't have that choice, do I?"

CHAPTER NINE

Jason pushed open the apartment's front door, dashing in like a tornado. Dawn followed, schooling herself to act like any parent at any normal homecoming.

"It's good to be home, isn't it, Jase?" she said, stripping off her coat, not taking her eyes off him as he ran into the living room. "Let's take off your coat, too."

Ignoring her, he raced to the couch. Finding it empty he looked behind it, searching. Then he rushed to the window, stretching to see on to the street below.

"Jason, come over here," she said, sinking to her knees. "What are you looking for?"

She reached for him but he swept by her, frantic eyes darting around the apartment. He ran past her again as she stood, hesitating, uncertain what to do. Foreboding filled her gut like a steel ball, a hunch she told herself had to be wrong.

She found him in the kitchen staring at the empty chair at the head of the table. She could see panic in his eyes, his breathing coming in gasps. With sudden understanding she realized her instinct had been true and what Doctor Morrison had advised was correct.

"Oh, God. He's looking for his dad," she whispered.

She pulled out another chair, sitting beside him. "Jason, look at me." She reached out, her hands inches from his. "Sweetie, I'm sorry, but your Daddy isn't here. I wish it wasn't true but it is. He's not coming home."

Jason's mouth hinged wide as her words hit him. Then his scream filled the room. He pushed over the empty chair, bolting from the kitchen. Rushing after him, she found him in her bedroom. Jason stood statue-still in the middle of the room and she realized he could not accept its emptiness. She tried on her best smile but realized it no longer fit.

"Jase, let's go play in your room. What do you say, kiddo?"

He would not look at her. Instead, he shuffled to the closet, opening the door. She could not bear it as he peered up at his father's abandoned work clothes. She held her breath as his gaze moved to the floor, latching on to the Uilleann's wooden box. He swung to her; hands clenched in tight fists.

"Oh sweetie. I'm so, so sorry."

She held out clueless arms but he streaked past her, out the room and across the hallway to his bedroom. She followed again, finding him waiting for her. He screamed in outrage then slammed shut the door in her face.

She sat alone at the kitchen table, glancing up at the wall clock. It was almost 9PM. Dawn rubbed her face, looking again at the memo pad open at her elbow and the list that had kept her occupied throughout the exhausting day.

Earlier, when Jason had made his hatred so clear, she had paced the living room warring with herself. One threatening voice screamed that she was wrong to bring him home. That maybe Morrison was right and all she was doing was harming her child. But the other voice fought back, reasoning she had tried every alternative and had no other choice. Breathing deep, she had called a truce. 'I'll take him back to the hospital if it doesn't work,' Dawn rationalized but then thought of the doctor. 'Morrison will be so pissed if I do that. He'll say I was rotten for bringing him home in the first place.'

Her mind still uneasy, she had found the pad of paper and sat down to figure out what she could do to help her son. She concluded that if he had any chance of staying home, if she was to ever find him again, she must first make a life for him and life was mostly filled with the humdrum and mundane. At the top of a blank page, she had written: *Making Life Normal for Jason.* Below it, she had scrawled a bullet-pointed To Do list with a dozen actions she would take. For the rest of the day, she had followed her notes to the letter.

First, she had made Jason a late lunch — a sandwich thick with peanut butter and jam. When she had opened his bedroom door, she had found him sitting on the bed, his monkey held in clenched hands. Her heart turned over at the crust of tears on her son's exhausted face.

"Jase, I'll leave this here," she had said, placing the tray on his small desk. She had ignored her instinct to rush to him to soothe away his pain. "I'll be in the kitchen if you need me, okay?"

He had never looked up as she closed the door.

She had spent the rest of the day crossing items off the To Do list. She had vacuumed the living room and cleaned the windows. She had fixed the broken pipe beneath the kitchen sink and mopped the floor again. She had stuffed Jason's dirty clothes from the hospital into a bag she would take to the laundry. She had scoured the apartment's bathroom tiles from top to bottom. When two hours had passed, she again looked in on her son. He still sat on the bed, his sandwich and milk untouched. She picked up the tray.

"I'll leave this in the fridge," she said, but he looked only at his monkey. "Sweetie, do you have to go to the bathroom? Come on, I'll go with you." He refused to budge.

For the rest of the afternoon, she had displaced her concerns with the balance of the list. She had phoned work, explaining to the receptionist an emergency had come up and she would have to take the rest of the day off. When Dawn was told it would be better to talk directly to Mister Saunders, she couldn't face it.

"I'm sure he's busy. I'll phone back later." She had hung up before the receptionist could object.

The phone call had made her remember tomorrow's exam. She had sat on the couch, listening for Jason while studying the training manual. She had grown confident she knew the technology backwards. Believing she would ace the test, she had convinced herself it would be enough to make Saunders overlook her absence. The thoughts of her boss made her think again of Jason.

'Christ, what am I going to do with him? I can't leave him in the apartment alone.' Then she remembered Joyce and how, throughout the months of her son's illness, her friend had offered to lend a hand. 'I'll phone her after work. She can watch him while I take the exam.'

But the thoughts of Jason also made her realize that she would have to tell Saunders she was again a fulltime mother. She worried how she would balance a life of caring for her son with her boss's demanding schedule. But her attitude swung again when she remembered the increased salary that went with the promotion, and decided to argue for enough money to hire a special needs assistant to care for her son while he recovered. She even thought of how she could home school Jason until he was ready to return to a classroom.

As the day turned toward evening, Dawn had sliced up a hotdog into a pot of Boston baked beans, a meal that had always been a family favorite. When it was heated, she took it together with thick slices of brown bread and butter into her son.

"You never got this in the hospital. Doesn't it smell good, Jason?" she had asked, again placing the tray on his desk.

Jason lay sprawled on the bed with his monkey. He would not look at her.

"Come on sweetie. You have to be hungry," she had coaxed. "Won't you eat?" But he had replied only with silence.

Back in the kitchen, Dawn had pecked at her dinner. She worked hard to quiet the critical voices in her head and decided to focus on the positive. She resolved that somehow, she would find a way to help her son where others had failed. She would lead him back from whatever dark place he had gone and then he would talk again. As she finished dinner and washed the plate and pot, she had smiled at the joy they would experience on the day Jason uttered his first word.

Still sitting at the table, she again looked at the clock. A half-hour had passed. She crossed the last item off the list then reached across the table, grabbing her handbag. As she emptied it, she pulled out the paper bag containing the sedatives. She tore it open, finding a plastic bottle. She shook it, peering in at a pile of white pills. Reading the instructions on the bottle, she saw that Jason was to be given two a day when required. She picked up the bag again, finding a thin piece of paper at the bottom. Unfolding it, she read about the possible side effects.

"Nausea, sleepiness, shaking, loss of appetite," she intoned, continuing down the list, "infection, sweating, and — what the hell? Slowed growth and weight loss? Bullshit!"

She stuffed the bottle back into the bag, stormed to the garbage can and threw it in. Sitting again, her exhausted gaze slid to the empty chair at the head of the table.

"Where are you, Michael?" she whispered. "God, he needs you. We both do."

She managed to get up. Turning out the light, she again went to check on Jason. She tiptoed into his room, hoping he was asleep. In the shadows she saw toys piled high on his shelves, the backpack tossed in the corner. She could make out the large letters JASON'S ROOM she had cut from construction paper and pinned to his wall when they had first moved in.

She heard him whimper. Suspecting he was on the edge of a nightmare, she stepped to his bed. He lay asleep, his blankets tossed aside. She rearranged them, covering her son as if he was the most precious glass ornament in the world. Within the warmth of his own bed, the whimpering stopped. She waited until he turned on his side and his breathing quieted.

Noticing his monkey lying on the floor, she bent to retrieve it. She recalled the day Michael had brought it home and her son's whoops of laughter at seeing its lopsided grin. She remembered how, when they had anchored near the island before the storm, her men had used it as part of the surprise they had planned for her. With a finger she traced its eyes and mouth, her hand falling to its long tail. Stroking it, she found she could not shut out the memory that followed.

The swinging tail tickled her nose but she was too comfortable to see what was intruding on her nap. Dawn reclined on the sunchair Michael had fixed to the foredeck of the *Margie M* after he had anchored the half-decker near the yellow buoy. Wishing she had not had that final glass of Guinness at the pub the previous evening, she had fallen asleep as the boat rocked within gentle swells. She had slept as the sea buoy's bell clanged and even as her men tied Jason's monkey to a fishing line, fixing the animal to swing close above her head. They had run the light line across the boat's rigging then in through an open window. Her men stood in the wheelhouse trying not to give the game away. Jason grasped the fishing line as Michael peered out at his sleeping wife.

"You ready, monkey?"

Jason giggled then gave the fishing line a tug.

Above his mother's head, the monkey's tail dropped another inch and swung faster. As it ran across her face her eyes opened. Shielding them from the strong sunlight she looked up, seeing the monkey. She saw the note attached to its tail, reading the words penned in her husband's strong hand. TUG ME. She chuckled, reaching up.

"Get ready," Michael whispered.

The boy found the huge bunch of flowers his father had hidden earlier in the locker beneath the instrument panel. Jason waited, a hand over his mouth, trying to stop his laughter. Looking out the window, he watched his mother pull the monkey's tail. The fishing line went taut and the bell, screwed to the wall and tied to the fishing line, tinkled like an old-fashioned door chime. Hanging on to the bouquet Jason bolted through the door, out on to deck. He threw himself on her.

"Happy Mother's Day!" he shouted as Dawn took him in her arms.

"Look at these," she said, seeing the bright freesias and gladiolas. "But it's not Mother's Day."

"Oh yes, it is. Dad says every day is Mother's Day."

She laughed at her son's serious face. "And what's in it for you?"

"Swimming!" he shouted as Michael walked on deck already wearing swimming trunks. "Please, Dad. You promised."

"I said 'might'," Michael laughed. Dawn handed him the flowers and he helped her up from the sunchair.

"'Might' is the same thing as 'yes', isn't it?" Jason begged. "Please?"

"Go on then," Michael grinned. "Get into your kit."

The boy squealed, running into the wheelhouse. They could hear him hop down the steps to find his wetsuit hanging below in the cabin. The deck was quiet except for the hollow slap of waves against the hull and the muffled tolling of the buoy bell. Dawn scanned an open sky above them filled with a blazing sun but an overcast of stratus and torn cumulus scudded low across the western horizon. Mist still obscured Solas Mór in thick fog.

"Are you sure you'll have time to go swimming?" she asked as Michael wrapped an arm around her.

"The Met Office says it's supposed to be fine until sundown. It's only some weather and if it threatens, we'll pull out quick. We won't be long. I promised the lad."

"You're always promising things."

"Like what?"

"Like everything. Last night you promised we'd be happy."

"And aren't we?"

She heard his worry, thinking he could be as naïve as a child. She smiled in that way she knew always hit him hard, a post-coital look of pleasure and promise of more to come that always stirred him. She remembered yesterday and the pleasure they took with each other in his old bed but pushed the thought away until a time when they could be alone again. As if reading her thoughts, he pulled his wife tight to him and kissed her.

"I don't think we'll get to the island today," he said. "See? I don't always keep my promises."

"Would it be that bad?"

"No, but it wouldn't be very pleasant. The lagoon will be rough and the sea fog wouldn't make for good walking. I want it to be special for Jason's first time."

She looked again for their island but the fog had dropped like a curtain, even thicker.

"Where is it?"

"Out there," he said, pointing. "You can't see it now because of the fog. We'll come back another time."

"I'd like to. I want Jason to see it and I want to see it again. Not that we can if you sell the boat."

She saw his surprise at her sudden change of tack. He studied her face and she knew he was trying to read her. Even after years of marriage, she was never certain if they always spoke the same language despite the strong bond they had built.

"Can you be honest with me about something?" she asked, squinting up at him.

"I'm always honest with you."

"No, you're not. You have secrets. Everyone does."

"And just what secrets would a fella like me have?"

"You miss it."

"Miss what?"

"Ireland, that's what. You miss your home."

She could see he was afraid he might hurt her, knowing what he would say next would not be the truth.

"I don't think about it," he said, and she thought of trapping him into a confession. He was easy and fun to trap but now wasn't the time. The worry in his eyes made her reach out, touching his cheek.

"You might not think about it but I think about it all the time. Michael, you're a good man but it's not going to work, not if you won't tell me the truth. Can't you?"

When he looked away, she decided to tell the truth for both of them.

"You can be such a Bozo," she said and, when he laughed, she pressed a finger to his lips. "This is serious. I don't want you to sell the boat."

"It makes no sense keeping it."

"It would make sense if we lived here, wouldn't it?"

"Sure, it would. But we don't."

"But we could."

"No, we can't," he said smiling, and she knew he was using their old game to distract her.

"Michael, I'm serious. Yes, we can. I want us to come back."

"Back?" he said, not understanding. "Back where?"

"Back here. To Ireland. Back to Kilcastle."

"You mean move here? Permanently?"

"Don't you see, you goof?" she said. "It doesn't matter where we live. Anywhere you are, we are. It's time to bring you home."

His stunned face broke into an enormous smile. He held her so tight she thought she might break. In his arms, she looked up at him.

"Don't ever let go, okay?" she asked.

"You're never going to get rid of me," he said. "Not ever."

CHAPTER TEN

A s the sun rose over the Boston apartment, Dawn startled into consciousness. Lying in bed, she thought she had heard Jason cry-out. Throwing off her tangled blankets, she rushed to his bedroom. It was empty. She hurried to the bathroom, thinking he was there, but a clatter of dishes drew her to the kitchen. She crept down the hall, hesitating at the door.

A chair had been dragged up to the kitchen counter top, a cabinet door above the sink opened wide. Her gaze was drawn to the table. Jason stretched across its surface, rearranging the place settings she had laid the night before. She had set the table for two but, for reasons that became all too apparent, he was unhappy with the arrangement. Another cereal bowl and plate lay at the head of the table. As she watched, he padded barefoot to a drawer. Oblivious to her presence he opened it, extracting a knife, fork and spoon. Anxious not to startle him, she cleared her throat.

"Good morning, Jase. Did you sleep well? You must be hungry."

He froze. Ignoring her, he stepped again to the head of the table, first laying the cutlery then readjusted the dishes to perfect symmetry. Thinking to distract him Dawn walked to the stove. Sliding open the bottom drawer, she withdrew a frying pan.

"How about pancakes?" she called with forced brightness. "You love pancakes."

Her smile cooled as he stalked past her, unseeing, as if she were a ghost. His eyes rose to a cabinet high above the counter. She held her breath as he slid the chair beneath it. Climbing on, his naked feet slipped on the seat before

115

he regained his balance. Stretching, he opened the cupboard and peered inside.

"What are you looking for, Jase? Can I help?"

Following his gaze, she realized he had found the target of his search.

The coffee mug rested on the top shelf, hidden behind some others where she could ignore it but safe because she knew she would never part with it. Jason had spotted it in a specialty store on a shopping trip which seemed a lifetime ago. She recalled his excitement when he had found it, burbling how Dad would love the blue mug with its bold white lettering. As she watched him push aside a line of other mugs, his gift's words peeked out like a forgotten love letter: WORLD'S BEST DAD.

As he strained to reach the only mug that mattered to him, she commanded herself to keep still. He stretched higher, wrapping his index finger around the handle. She was certain his tenuous grip would never allow him to lift it.

"Sweetie, let me get that."

Suspecting it was wrong, she strode to his side anyway. Reaching over him, she brushed his shoulder. He shrugged her off with brusque impatience. Placing her hand over his, she tried for a better purchase.

"Honey, let it go. I'll get it."

Jason tightened his finger and yanked. As he pulled, the mug slipped from his grasp. Dawn stretched to catch it, freezing in horror as it fell between them. World's Best Dad exploded on the floor, fragments scattering in a myriad of blue and white memories. When she looked up, she was caught in the glare of her son's accusing gaze.

"It's okay, Jason. We'll get another one." But even as she said it, she realized it would never be okay.

His scream pierced the room, terrifying in its intensity. Leaping from the chair, he howled like a wounded animal. He ran to the table, arms swinging, sweeping plates and cups to the floor where they shattered, strewing the room with wreckage. Horrified, she watched as he ran barefoot through the sharp flotsam. He screamed again as he dashed to his bedroom, the slam of his door waking her from stunned paralysis.

Running to his room she threw open the door. She stooped as his monkey zipped past her nose, striking the wall with a hollow thud. Helpless, she watched her son act out his fury. He pulled down the wooden shelves, a mountain of toys cascading to the floor. She reached to stop him as he ripped the bright paper lettering from the wall but he fought back with swinging fists. Tasting blood on her lip, her mind twisted for ways to protect him.

She raced back to the kitchen, the racket of his rampage in her ears. Emptying the contents of the garbage can on the floor, she pawed through yesterday's wet coffee grounds. She spotted the white prescription bag at the bottom of the heap. As she picked up the bag the bottle fell out, bouncing off the tile floor. She grabbed it, twisting off the cap, spilling two sedatives into her shaking hand.

Rushing back to his bedroom, she ducked as a baseball whistled over her head, smashing a lamp on the nightstand. She turned as he charged her, howling with rage. She threw herself on him, gripping him hard around the waist. He bent his head, sinking his teeth into her arm, biting so hard his jaw trembled. She gasped in pain but hung on. Swinging him on to the bed, she pinned him under the full weight of her body. He squirmed, bucking, but she gripped his arms with her knees. Taking his head in her hands she strained to open his clenched jaw. When his sobs loosened it, she forced open his mouth. She thrust in the pills, holding his jaw shut until she heard him swallow. Then, for reasons she did not understand, he was in her arms, holding tight like he had when he was Jason and not a boy she did not understand. She could feel his body shake as he sobbed, and she was crying too.

"Oh Jason, oh God, Jason. I'm sorry, I'm so sorry."

She held on until the medication took hold and he slept. She held him even longer after that because in his sleep he would not let her go.

Much later Dawn woke, slipping from his arms. Jason lay on the bed, legs sprawled wide as he slept. In the late morning shadows, she limped to the bathroom and, turning on the light, rummaged for the first aid kit. She examined her forearm, gazing at it as if it was someone else's arm because she could not accept that her son would bite her. She washed the wound and bandaged it then filled the sink with hot water. She bathed her face until the dried blood was freed and picked it from her lip. Looking in the mirror, she inspected the swollen mouth and bruised cheek where Jason had hit her. As she studied the red-rimmed eyes she realized she hated the woman who stared back.

"Don't say you're sorry. I'll never forgive you. Neither will he," she hissed at the reflection. Then, her mouth filled with bile and she dropped to the toilet, vomiting until there was nothing left in her belly. As she rose on unsteady legs, the telephone rang. Angry at the intrusion, fearing it would wake Jason, she wiped the stink from her face and stumbled to the hall table. The voice recorder kicked in just as she reached to cut off the call.

"Dawn? Dawn, are you there?" her mother-in-law's voice asked. "Did you get my message? I've not heard a word from you."

She reached for the phone but pulled back, hesitating. "No, Margaret, not now. What would I say?"

"Dawn, please pick up," Margaret pleaded, and she could visualize her mother-in-law's disappointment furrowing the kind face. "You must be busy. I'll call back later."

Dawn turned from the table, stepping toward the kitchen then changed her mind. She swung back, lunging for the phone.

"Margaret? Margaret, are you still there?"

"Dawn is that you? What's wrong, chicken. Is it Jason?"

"Nothing, he's fine," she said but the truth tumbled out before she could stop it. "Oh, Margaret, oh God what have I done."

"Tell me what's wrong. I'm here, Gersha. I'm listening."

Gripping the phone like a lifeline, she told Margaret everything. She admitted the mistakes she had made and the fear she had for Jason, and how every action she had taken seemed to be the wrong one. Running out of words, she sat on the chair next to the telephone, her chest heaving.

"Dawn, are you still there?"

"Yes," she whispered, gripping the phone so tight it shook. "Margaret, I don't know what to do."

"Yes, you do."

"What?"

"Come home."

"Home?"

"Yes. Home to Kilcastle. You can't do this on your own. We can take care of Jason together."

"It won't work," Dawn quivered, thinking of her son's unpredictable behavior. "Jason can be...difficult."

"Nonsense. He's my grandson. If I can't help him, who can?"

Dawn's lips tightened. "Margaret, I don't know what to say."

"Say you're coming home. Not next month. Not next week. Bring him home now, Gersha. Please."

The offer drifted in front of Dawn like a lifeline. All she had to do was grab it. She thought of Margaret's kindness and the town she and Jason loved, and what her husband would say if he were here to advise her. She swallowed hard.

"You're right. I'll bring him back. I'll start packing right now."

After the call, Dawn sat at the kitchen table surrounded by the wreckage of her son's anger which still lay scattered across the floor. With the decision made her mind focused on all she must do to prepare and, with it, the thought that she should take Jason back to see Morrison for a check-up prior to the trip. Then she thought of the questions he would ask and what she would say because she wouldn't lie.

"He did what?" Morrison would protest when she told him about that morning's trauma. "You reacted how?" He would shake his head in that way of his and look her in the eye. "I'm sorry, Dawn. Taking him home was risky enough. But now you want to take him to Ireland?"

No, she decided. She would not take Jason back to see Morrison.

As she took out the broom to clear the kitchen floor, she realized that while she might avoid Morrison there was another person she could not escape seeing. She would need to ask Saunders for time off.

"Three weeks should be enough," she muttered, pushing broken plates into a pile. "He won't like it but he'll have to live with it. But what if — what if he doesn't?" She pushed the broom faster. "You'll have to convince him, that's what. You'll promise him you'll work harder than anyone in the company when we get back. He'll understand it's for Jason, not for you."

She stopped sweeping. Seeing Saunders's angry reaction in her mind, she lifted the broom. Standing it upright, she imagined it was her boss as she rehearsed her speech. "Bill, it's only three weeks. When I'm back I'll bring in a million bucks next quarter. What do you say?" She stretched her hand out for an imaginary handshake. "He'll buy that, won't he?" she asked the broom. "It'll be easy, don't you think?"

But her lips tightened because she had learned that nothing was easy.

Finished with the kitchen and with Jason still asleep, she gave herself an hour to complete the rest of her preparations. She wrote a note to the landlord, promising she would send the overdue rent as soon as possible, pleading with him not to turf them out while she was away. She used the Internet on her cellphone to book the e-tickets, paying for the flight with the credit card she used only for emergencies, knowing it would be maxed-out when the expense cleared. Then she crept into her bedroom and packed for the trip. As she was shutting the closet door, she spotted Michael's green wooden box.

"You're coming too," she whispered. "Michael won't be there but you're coming because you always do."

She lugged the box from its hiding place then pulled down Jason's small suitcase from the shelf in the hall closet. Lifting it, she let herself into his room. As she sat on the bed his eyes opened, the puzzled gaze filled with the power of the medication.

"Jason," she whispered, "how would you like to go visit Nana? Nana misses you so much. Wouldn't it be nice to see her?"

His expression did not change and she hoped he would understand when they reached the airport. She straightened out his room, carrying anything damaged down to the basement skip, then turned to pack his clothes. Finished, she booked a cab to take them to Logan, requesting one stop first in the city.

An hour later, as the cab pulled up in front of the World Connect office, Dawn remembered.

"Oh, shit."

She had forgotten the supervisor's exam scheduled for that morning. Helping Jason from the car, she peered up at the towering office block. She realized that convincing Saunders to give her time off was now complicated by her own idiotic neglect.

"Come on, Jase," she said, gripping his hand tight. "Let's get this over."

When Dawn led Jason upstairs and into the busy office, she tried to make a beeline for Saunders's glass cage. She had no desire to run into anyone else and the awkward questions she was too tired to answer. But slowed by her drowsy son, she saw Joyce peering at her from behind her cubicle.

"Dawn?" Joyce called, removing her headset. "Hey, wait a minute."

Dawn stopped as her friend hurried toward them.

"What happened to you?" Joyce whispered, slowing to study Dawn's bruised face.

"I ran into a door," she lied and, raising an eyebrow, hoped Joyce would understand and not ask any more questions.

"But, honey," Joyce yelped, not getting it, "you need to have that looked at."

"Honestly, it's nothing. I'm fine."

"Don't tell me that because it looks anything but fine." Then Joyce's gaze fell on Jason. Smiling, she knelt eye-to-eye with him. "Well, look who's here. You must be Jason. It's so good to finally meet you." She glanced up at Dawn. "They let you bring him home? Why didn't you call me?"

"It's a long story."

"I'll bet," she said then opened both arms wide. "Jason, give your aunt Joyce a big old hug." When he didn't react, she stood, frowning. "Okay, Dawn. Spill it. What's going on?"

"Can we discuss it later? I need to talk to Saunders."

"Saunders?" Joyce hesitated. "Dawn, I don't think you want to do that."

"Why not? Joyce, what's going on?"

Dawn scanned the busy office. She spotted Steve standing in her cubicle, rummaging through the drawers of her work station. An open cardboard box sat on the floor beside him.

"What the hell is he doing?"

"Dawn, don't," Joyce warned.

"Jason, come on." Grasping his hand, Dawn marched across the office floor. As she approached the cubicle, she saw Steve throw a hairbrush into the box. "Hey, you! Get your hands off my stuff."

"So, you decided to show up?" Steve sniffed, turning to her. "A little late, aren't you?"

"You wait until I talk to Saunders. Stealing personal property could get you fired."

"By all means, go talk to him," he cracked, leaning against the wall. "He's the one who told me to do it."

"What do you mean by that?"

"Ask anyone. Sweetie, this morning you made front-page headlines."

Dawn glanced around the office. A few heads popped up catching her eye, swinging away as if too embarrassed to connect. A young sales rep hurried past, his eyes on the floor. Dawn pivoted back to Joyce.

"Joyce, what's going on?"

Her friend shook her head in sympathy.

"Dawn?"

She spun around. Saunders stood at his office door. He cocked his head at her like a master beckoning for his dog then strode back inside.

"Come on Jason," she said. Stepping to the office, she hung back as Saunders sat down behind his desk.

"Come on in," Saunders stated, waving a hand. Then he noticed her bruised face. "What happened to you?"

"I slipped."

"Really?" he replied, his eyes falling on Jason. "So, this must be your son. What a fine-looking young man."

"I'm glad you think so. But I don't think Jason is what you want to talk about."

"Maybe you better sit down. Jason, do you want something? How about a Coke?"

"He doesn't want anything, do you sweetie?" She looked down at her son. His gaze was fixed on the carpet, his stare still filled with the effects of the sedative.

Saunders stood, walking to his office window. Hands in his pockets, he gazed out on a sea of employees. Dawn glanced at her watch.

"Bill, I've got a cab waiting outside. Can we make this quick?"

"A cab?" he asked, turning to her.

"Yes, a cab, and well, see, there are some things we have to do, Jason and me, and I was wondering if —"

"You don't have to explain."

"Of course, I do. If you'll just listen to me for a second…"

"Dawn, really, it's not necessary. Look, I've got something to say but —"

"But what?" Her heart missed a beat. "Bill, you're not firing me, are you?"

He raised his head. "Yes."

"But you promised to promote me!"

"Only if you aced the exam, remember? Steve passed it this morning."

"I don't believe this. You promoted Steve?"

"What choice did you give me? You weren't here!"

Dawn looked at the floor. "Bill, I'm sorry. I really am. Jason came home yesterday. It was unexpected. That's why I wasn't in. Then early this morning he got…sick… and I forgot about the exam. It wasn't intentional. I swear to God it wasn't. Bill, I'm so, so sorry."

"I understand."

"No, you don't."

"Yes, I do. If I had a kid who was sick, I'd probably forget too," he replied, sitting again in his chair.

"But you don't have a kid, do you?" She placed both hands on his desk, leaning across it. "Bill, I need this job. You know I'm good at it. Give me another chance. Please don't fire me."

Saunders looked across at Jason, noting the boy's vacant gaze. "Dawn, what are you even doing here? He doesn't look well."

"You know he was in the hospital."

"But they sent him home?"

She nodded. "It was time."

"I'm glad. Every kid needs to be with his mother." He considered her son then looked her in the eye. "Dawn, can I ask how you're going to take care of him if you're working ten hours a day?"

"I'll figure it out. You know I will."

"Ah, I don't know," he sighed, leaning back in his chair. "You told me you needed more time to be with him. That was when he was in the hospital. With him home, you'll need even more time. Dawn, you can't do it all. No one can. You'll get another job. Something part-time and not as demanding. You'll have plenty of time to take care of Jason." He reached down, opening a drawer. Withdrawing an envelope, he held it out to her. "HR transferred that an hour ago. It should hit your bank account tomorrow. I told them to add a couple of bucks. You know, just as a thank you."

"You added it because you feel like an ass for firing me," she snapped. "Drop dead, Bill. Come on Jason. Let's get out of here."

She snatched the envelop from her former employer then strode out the door. Crossing the open plan office, she passed colleagues who wouldn't look at her. Leading her son to the cubicle, Dawn unpinned the family photo of Jason and Michael from the wall and shoved it in her coat pocket. She turned, spotting Steve leaning against his cubicle.

"Hey moron," she called, pointing down to the cardboard box at her feet. "You can keep it. I'm sure you'll get a thrill out of it."

"I'd rather drink acid," he smirked.

"Jason, cover your ears," she instructed then glared at her adversary. "Steve, you're the only guy I know who has two assholes."

"Make that twice and you get four," she heard, and found Joyce standing beside her. "The man is a menace to the human race," Joyce added, taking Dawn's arm. "Come on before I do something that will get us arrested."

Swinging from Steve, Joyce led Dawn and Jason to the front door. They stood for a moment, tears in their eyes. "Dawn I'm so sorry. I told Saunders he was a jerk but there wasn't anything I could do."

"I know. It isn't your fault."

Joyce looked down at Jason. "What are you going to do now? Dawn if I can help…"

"We're going to Ireland. We're going to stay with Michael's mother. Jason likes it there. We'll be okay. I know what to do now. At least I think I do."

"I know you do. If anyone can help Jason, it's you. Oh, come here." They clung to each other like old shipmates casting off for different ports. "Keep in touch, okay?"

"You know it."

But as Dawn walked out the door with her son Joyce sensed she would never see her friend again.

PART III

IRELAND

CHAPTER ELEVEN

"Did you lose this?"

Dawn did not hear the flight attendant because her gaze was fixed on Jason. She had belted him tight into the seat beside her due to the turbulence that had shaken them since leaving Heathrow. As she examined his sleeping face, she worried about the perspiration beaded on his pallid forehead, certain it was a side-effect of the sedatives. The plane lurched again, bumping his head against the window. She grasped his shoulder to steady him and, as she did, her mind filled with a thousand voices screaming her failures.

They screamed she had failed at the therapies that should have helped him and also because she had taken him from Morrison's care, too stupid to realize the harm she might cause him. They chided her for losing a job she depended on, the bills she owed, and an almost empty bank account. They scolded her for the decision to fly him to Ireland and she wondered, not for the first time, what business she had taking her son on a journey that caused him more distress. Trapped in a tin can flying at forty-thousand feet, her foot had tapped the floor in time to the voices that had pummeled her all the way across the Atlantic.

"Excuse me. I'm sorry to bother you. But did you lose this?"

Dawn looked up. The young flight attendant stood beside her in the aisle, the same one who had helped them board in London. She shook a bottle of pills. "I found these on the floor. Are they yours?"

Dawn peered at the bottle and realized they must have fallen from her bag. She had relied on the medication to calm Jason's outbursts over the course of their travels but felt terrible whenever she had to reach for the prescription. The nonstop flight from Logan had been overbooked and they were forced to fly to London rather than direct to Dublin as was their custom. Having re-read the sedatives' instructions, she had given Jason a pill when they boarded in Boston, which she thought would be enough for the entire journey. But having arrived over an hour late at Heathrow, he had grown anxious in the crowded terminal. When he had erupted in a tantrum, she had been forced to give him another dose.

Having missed the Dublin connection due to their late arrival, Dawn had rescheduled the last leg of their journey direct to Cork City Airport. She had given him another pill prior to boarding, scared to do so but scared not to. Helped by the flight attendant, she had lugged him onboard. His dead weight had frightened her so much so that she had become terrified that the drug was destroying him.

The flight attendant again shook the bottle. "I found these," she repeated. "Are they yours or not?"

"Those are my son's."

"Don't you want them?"

At the question, Dawn thought how Morrison would insist she keep them as security against Jason's next outburst. Instead, she found herself making a decision, one she feared she might later regret.

"No. He's finished with them."

"If you don't want them, I'll have to throw them away."

"As I said, he's finished with them."

The flight attendant glanced at Jason's sweating face. "I'm sorry he's not well. We'll be landing in a few minutes. Can I get you anything?"

"Would you have a cloth? I want to cool him down."

The flight attendant walked back up the aisle, balancing like a dancer against the turbulence. When she returned, Dawn bathed her son's face.

"You'll love being back in Kilcastle," she whispered as she swept away the perspiration. "Nana will be there. You'll see all your friends again. What do you think of that, sweetie? You'll have so much fun." Feeling his hot cheeks beneath the cloth, she feared her promises to him were lies.

After they landed and as Dawn carried him through the quiet arrival's area he woke, startled eyes filled with fear.

"Hey buster," she chirped as they walked out the front door of the small Cork airport. "Did you decide to wake up? Now all we have to do is find the bus."

She searched up and down the frontage road but couldn't see one. Approaching a taxi rank, she asked a driver. He informed her the bus to Kilcastle departed from the Cork City bus station, a twenty-minute drive away.

"If you take us to the station how much will it cost?" she asked. When he told her, her lips pursed as she remembered the condition of her wallet. Realizing she had no choice, they climbed in as the driver loaded their luggage. When he left them off at the bus station Jason came fully awake, his temper as dark as thunder.

"It's not far now," Dawn coaxed, trying to quell his whimpering. "See the buses? One of those will take us to Nana. You want to see Nana, don't you?"

He stared at a line of red and white Bus Éireann vehicles. Slapping at the air with hot fists, his whining caught the attention of milling passengers.

"Stop it, Jason. Please stop. If we miss the bus, you'll make Nana really sad. You don't want to do that, do you?"

The words were enough to get him up the vehicle's stairs and into a seat. He spent the rest of the journey gazing out the window. Dawn sat next to him as if sitting on the point of a needle, waiting for his sullenness to explode into rage. The voices in her jetlagged mind re-surfaced, chiding her for having thrown away the pills; overwhelming her with so many thoughts that she did not notice the mist break into a bright morning. They drove past the rolling green hills of West Cork, the sunlit rivers coursing between moss-covered rocks as they traveled southwest on narrow rural roads. When they reached the harbor town of Bantry, only half-way to Kilcastle, the bus broke down. As Dawn and Jason stood on the street watching the driver pull their luggage from the storage compartment, she wondered what else could go wrong.

"When's the next bus to Kilcastle?"

"Not until tomorrow morning," the driver answered in a soft West Cork accent.

"Tomorrow?" She looked down at Jason. "Isn't there anything sooner?"

"Afraid not, missus. Sure, you could take a private bus. Or there's the taxi, of course, but that would cost a fortune." The lean Corkman studied her anxious face. "Yer sure it's Kilcastle you want?"

"If I'm on a Kilcastle bus, where else would we be going? My son isn't well. Come on, there has to be a way of getting there today."

The driver scratched a thin cheek, thinking. He looked at his watch, then pointed across the busy town square. "The ferry. Leaves in ten minutes. It'll take you right there."

She turned, seeing trawler booms thrusting up from behind a harbor wall. Her foot tapped as she remembered the last time they had taken a boat trip.

"Are you sure there's nothing else? My son is afraid of boats."

"Now, how would that be? Every lad I know loves boats," the driver chuckled, kneeling by Jason. "What'cha say, young fella. Want to go for a boat ride?" Rather than lash out as Dawn had feared, her son's eyes opened wide. The driver laughed. "He doesn't seem afraid. You grab the lad and I'll carry the luggage. Come on and I'll show ye the way."

They followed the driver to the pier and, after he carried the luggage on to the ferry, she tried to tip him but he refused the few coins.

"Buy the lad a lemonade," he said in a familiar rhythm which sang in her ears. "And a *céad míle fáilte* too, while I'm thinking of it."

After he left, she paid the ferryman with almost the last of her cash. Remembering that Margaret would be unaware of their new travel plans, she shared her concern with the ruddy-faced skipper.

"You're Margaret McCarthy's daughter-in-law?" he asked when she explained. "I know the McCarthy's well. Used to fish with Michael's father years ago, God bless 'em. I'll phone and let her know you're coming. Now get up the ramp with ya. We'll be pulling out in a few minutes."

As she led Jason up the steep gangway to the ferry's deck, she was terrified at how he might react and the memories it would stir in him. But seeing the box-like structure of the wheelhouse, he bolted ahead. He ran between the few cars being ferried to Kilcastle and to the far side of the boat. She hurried after him, finding him clinging to the railing, gazing west as if willing the ferry's engines to life.

"It's good to be back, isn't it, Jason?" she asked, stepping to the railing beside him.

Seeing the excitement in his face, she suspected he at last looked forward to seeing the Nana he loved so much. She pushed her hopes upriver, forcing herself to believe the journey would mend a variety of wounds and that they would enjoy their time together. But when she reached for his hand, he jerked it away. As the boat's engines started, he sidled down the railing, wanting nothing to do with her.

When the ferry slid into the main body of Bantry Bay, the sunlit sky filled with cloud. Dawn stood in the misting rain, watching Jason search the steel-grey water. He peered into the fog and she thought he was trying to find the rocky shoreline where, in another life, he had played with his father. She rubbed her hands together, looking toward the wheelhouse. An open steel door led into a sparse cabin. She could see passengers sitting on benches, sheltering inside from the wet of the sea.

"Jason, let's get in out of the this. Don't you want to get warm?"

He ignored her, still searching the sea-mist.

'At least there's not a storm,' Dawn worried as she watched her son. 'I don't know how he'd react if there was a storm.'

She stepped further down the railing, standing in the rain as close as her son would allow. Feeling the vibration of the engine through her feet, she tried not to think about the steel decks of other boats she had journeyed on, or the coves they were sailing past where her husband had taught her to drive the rib, or the beaches where they had picnicked when the family was whole. As they steamed west, the fog cleared a little and she could make out the bulk of Bere Island. She saw the Martello Tower built on its peak, squatting like a fat king in a game of checkers. She remembered how Michael had once told her the British had built it to signal an impending invasion by the Empire's enemies.

She also remembered how he had pointed it out as a final waypoint on the journey back to Kilcastle. She realized they were almost home.

The fog cleared suddenly and sunlight struck the water. She gripped the railing as the ferry listed in a turn. The red buoy came into view as they slid past the point. Beyond, she could make out the harbor and the boats moored there. The town of Kilcastle rose behind it, the tall houses and shops nestled side-by-side, a view which always reminded her of a toy village in a Christmas shop window display.

She glanced sideways, seeing Jason's small hands still gripping the railing. As the ferry slowed, pushing into the busy fishing port, he studied the dories and punts tied to their moorings, left to swing on the tide. She tried to interpret his expectations as his gaze swung to the pier. There, huge trawlers were lined up like warriors, all tied up stern first, tall bows curtsying above oil-stained harbor water. She realized he was watching a trawler offloading its catch. Fishermen operating a crane swung blue and white fish boxes from the stern on to the concrete pier. There, forklifts lifted them on to trucks which, she remembered, hauled them off to market. Beyond the line of trawlers was the town which this close in was mostly hidden by the busy dock area. She could see the church steeple rise at one end and, perched on a hill at the other, the windows of Margaret's house which flashed gold in the sunlight.

Gulls swooped overhead screaming for their supper, fighting for scraps. She looked up as they cartwheeled and noted the dark rainclouds marching in again. She inhaled the thick smell of seaweed that rotted at the shallow end of the harbor. Its richness stirred memories and she wondered how much of his time here her son remembered. Part of her hoped he did but she also worried what those thoughts might trigger in him.

As the ferry slipped toward shore, ferry passengers climbed into their cars while those on foot lined the deck for arrival. The ferry turned again and the RNLI boathouse came into view, the blue and orange lifeboat tied fast to its station. For a moment the memories tried to overwhelm her. She turned anxious eyes on Jason, worried what would happen when he saw the lifeboat, but his gaze was locked on a spot further up the pier. She swung her head around, drawn to the familiar voice that called to them.

"Dawn! Jason!"

Margaret's slight figure stood at pier-side, her silver hair tucked beneath the bright woolen cap she wore in inclement weather. As she raised two arms in greeting the ferry's engines reversed, the deck shuddering as the boat lost way. The winch rumbled as the bow ramp fell, grinding against the concrete embankment in arrival. Dawn stepped toward her son, his eyes still hunting up the pier.

"Are you ready, Jase? Let's go see Nana."

He swung from her, scampering away down the ramp. She hurried after him, assuming he would go to his grandmother. But Jason did not stop. He twisted past his Nana's outstretched arms, running on.

Dawn did not have time to think. Sidestepping her mother-in-law's surprised look, she pursued her son up the pier, losing sight of him in a sudden downpour. Wiping her eyes, she spotted him again as he came level with a reversing forklift. She yelled a warning and the driver braked hard. Jason dodged around the vehicle and kept running. She followed again as he bolted past fishing boats and trawlers, their crews working on the pier. He bowled through a knot of fishermen lifting fish boxes and past Jackie who called out with a surprised greeting. She raced by him, running harder.

As she came around the stern of a trawler, she spotted the Irish flag drooping from its flagpole. Slowing, she saw Jason standing beneath it, gazing up at the drenched Tri-color. He grasped the metal pole with both hands then turned to the pier. She looked too, seeing the tie-up where the *Margie M* had departed on that morning a year ago. It was deserted now, empty except for rain-spattered water. She thought back to the excitement she had seen in Jason's face during their ferry crossing to Kilcastle. She had thought he was looking forward to seeing his grandmother. She had been wrong.

"Dawn?"

Her mother-in-law stood near, her eyes filled with bewilderment. Dawn heard a sob. Turning back, she saw Jason hunched over, crying.

"I'm so sorry, Jason," she murmured, and wanted to crush the words as she said them because they had no power to change anything. When he ran toward her, she opened her arms to comfort him. But he dodged past, flying instead to his grandmother.

"I don't understand," Margaret said, holding her grandson.

"He thought Michael's boat would be here," Dawn answered. "He thought his dad had come home." She wiped her eyes, unable to look at them. "I'll get the bags."

Alone, she walked back down the pier in the pouring rain.

CHAPTER TWELVE

According to town records, the two-story cottage had been constructed in 1903 by an English businessman who had a penchant for seaside vistas. Tomás, Margaret's husband, had bought it when they had first married because he said its broad beam reminded him of a compact trawler and was as solidly built. Margaret had liked it too and, being a stubborn blow-in from County Mayo, became determined to make a home of it.

It was not a large house compared to Ireland's modern standards but the kitchen was bright and airy, with pretty views of the back garden and robins foraging for insects in the winter grass. It had two small reception rooms downstairs which included the living room and a dining room plus the larger spare room she had transformed into an art studio after the death of her son. Then there were the two upstairs bedrooms and the family bathroom tucked beneath the eves, as well as the attic they had planned to convert after Michael was born to give them room for a larger family. Unfortunately, they were never blessed with more children.

Margaret had always liked that their home was warm and cozy and only a few minutes' walk from the town center. Tomás had appreciated the view of his half-decker from the wide living room window where he could keep an eye on the *Margie M* whenever a storm blew up. When he was alive, her husband had been the envy of his fisherman friends. They begrudged him the pleasure of knowing his wife was only up the hill and Margaret had lost count of the times he had pushed through the back door to lead her, giggling, to their bedroom.

When Michael was only an infant Margaret would stand with her son in the back garden, on the hill above the harbor. Always anxious, she watched for the return of the blue and white trawler home from its fishing trips. Seeing it steam back into port she would hoist the child on to her hip, rushing to the kitchen to warm her husband's dinner of boiled ham, potatoes and mashed carrots covered with the thick white sauce he liked but which she detested.

She was comfortable in the house, with a special fondness for the kitchen due to the warmth of the cast iron Aga cooker and its coal fire she lit every morning. After more than thirty years, the kitchen held many memories for her of Tomás and Michael. When she lost them both she clung to her remembrances though not so tight as to strangle the life from her, and learned to live with the dark tragedies. Except for the lingering days of grief that still tried to shipwreck her, she attempted to fill her life with light. But on the evening of her daughter-in-law's homecoming from America, and the grandson she had brought with her, Margaret anticipated a day that might bring only sorrow.

"Come on, Jason, you have to eat," Margaret begged, and once again pushed the untouched dinner plate closer to her grandson.

Jason sat at the kitchen table refusing to look at the chicken dinner with its stuffing and rich brown gravy that had always been his favorite. When she had led her grandson into the house, his cheeks still wet with tears, she had noticed how thin he looked. He had been unwilling to let her tease him into a smile as she always did to soothe him. When she had asked for a hug, he would not repeat the embrace he had given her earlier on the pier. Most of all, Margaret was worried because he had not uttered a single word since their arrival.

She glanced at Dawn who stood near the warm cooker, catching the look of exhaustion in her daughter-in-law's face. The frazzled, wet hair and facial bruise made her look ten years older than her age. Margaret's instinct warned her not to ask what had caused the injury. She pushed back the question and looked again to her grandson.

"Please, Jason, you have to eat something."

"He's not hungry," Dawn said, not taking her eyes from the cooker.

"Of course, he's hungry. He's always hungry," Margaret replied, bending to him. "Jason, I made an apple tart just for you. How about that?" But he only swung his head away. "Oh Jason, forget about it. Give your old Nana a hug."

Instead of holding up his arms as he always did, he scowled at her. Pushing back from the table, he ran past the adults, dashing into the living room. Through the open kitchen door Margaret watched him stand at the front window, gazing out across the harbor. Even from where she stood, she could read the sadness in his face. She yearned for his cheeky smile and the voice that had always filled her home with laughter.

"I'll get him," she said, starting from the kitchen.

"Margaret, just leave him alone," Dawn snapped. She weaved to the table, sitting, her head falling on to her hands. "I didn't mean that. Margaret, I'm sorry. I'm just tired."

"Dawn, he has to eat. Is he always like this?"

"Yes."

"It's terrible," Margaret said, carrying the untouched dinner to the sink. "After all this time, wouldn't you think the doctors would have done something? Jason should be talking by now. Dawn, you need to try something else."

"Don't you think I have?" she countered, and counted off the list on stiff fingers. "Cognitive behavioral therapy, exposure therapy, self-modeling, stimulus fading, desensitization, art therapy, spacing, shaping. There isn't anything else. It's driving me nuts. I don't know what else to do." Dawn rubbed her temples in tight circles.

"If you have a headache, you should start by going to bed."

"I can't. I have to get Jason changed."

"Let me get him ready for bed. Go upstairs and unpack. Then I'll get some tablets for your headache." She peered at the dark bruise on her daughter-in-law's cheek. "Chicken, what happened to your face?"

"It was an accident." Dawn dropped her head, hiding the injury beneath a cascade of wet hair.

Margaret scolded herself for not leaving it alone. She hesitated, then murmured, "I put you in Michael's old room. I hope you don't mind." She glanced at her son's battered green travel box. It sat near the back door with the other luggage. "You brought home his Uilleann. He would have liked that."

Dawn flinched, eyes filling with tears. Then she was out of the chair, sobbing in her mother-in-law's arms. "I didn't know where else to go. We don't *have* anywhere else to go."

"You did the right thing," Margaret said, cradling the young face in both hands. "You came home."

"Home?"

"This is your home, too, isn't it? Now go on up to bed and stop your worrying."

Dawn dried her eyes and, lifting the green box, left the room. Margaret gazed in at her grandson who still stood at the picture window, his sullen eyes fixed on the harbor. She sighed, wondering how in God's good name she would ever get him ready for bed.

Dawn stood outside the bedroom's open door feeling the cold hand of loneliness on her neck. She hesitated for a moment, wanting to be anywhere else but here, longing to hide from this nightmare beneath thick blankets as she sometimes did as a child. Unlike her childhood nightmares, however, this one wouldn't stop.

She forced herself to enter, reaching for the light switch. Her gaze took in his room. Unchanged since their last visit, it was as if Michael was waiting for her as he always had before. Her eyes shifted to a wall and the photos that hung there, frozen snapshots of his youth. Her gaze lingered on the image of her husband as a boy of Jason's age. He stood on a beach, his curling hair blown by an unseen wind. Holding a fishing rod, he smiled into camera. Another showed him with his father on the stern of the trawler, the sun in their eyes. They both wore foul-weather gear, arms folded high across their chests, a young Michael trying to look as tough as any Kilcastle fisherman. Another photograph was taken in his late teens in the pub. He held tight to his Uilleann as a young Jackie lurked over his shoulder, their faces split by laughter.

Her eyes moved up to more recent photos taken two summers ago: group shots of Michael and Margaret and Jason; of her and Michael; of her and Michael and Jason — all taken on the Allihies beach where they had gone to picnic. She remembered how her men had laughed when Margaret had ordered them to stop acting like clowns and the happiness of that day.

Her gaze shifted to the wooden bureau. It squatted beneath a window which looked out over the harbor. She remembered that if she opened the bureau's top drawer, she would find the spare T-Shirts, socks and shorts which Michael wore during their visits. She placed her hand flat on the worn oak surface, recalling how only a year ago his hand had rested there, too. She took a shaking breath, struggling to feel his presence.

She reached down, grasping the handle of the green box which she had carried up, lifting it on to the bureau. Caressing its surface, she remembered what was inside and would never be played again. Her gaze shifted to the huge overstuffed chair crammed into the corner. It was a hideous piece of furniture Michael had found at some flea market during a visit years ago, one which Dawn and Margaret had begged him to get rid of.

"Okay, I'll tell you what," she remembered him saying, a smile cracking his face. "If you two haul this monster back downstairs, I'll toss it. What do ya say?" But the thing weighed a ton and the women knew they were stuck with it no matter how ugly it was.

Dawn bent to it, fingers touching the discolored fabric where his head had always rested. She couldn't help but remember how just over a year ago he had sat there, his eyes filled with a look of love and lust as they made plans for the next day. She remembered how, after returning from the pub in the early evening, she had showered while Michael waited for her in the bedroom. When she walked in, she found him lounging in the chair, hands clasped behind his head. She could feel him watching her as she stood at the mirror.

"Michael, I want to ask you something," she said, brushing her thick wet hair.

141

When she glanced at him in the mirror, she realized he wasn't listening. She could see his reflection studying the curves beneath the thin robe she wore, his eyes shifting to her back where the exposed skin was covered in water droplets. Warm desire flushed through her which she did her best to ignore.

"Are you listening to me?" she asked.

"Course I'm listening to you. Don't I always listen to you?"

"Not always. Not when your head is on something else." She grinned at him. "Seriously. What did you mean in the pub about selling your father's boat? That's what you said to Jackie."

"What pub?"

When she swung to him, his eyes fastened on her breasts.

"I'm up here, remember?" she said, pointing to her head. "Now what about it? What about the boat?"

"What boat?"

"Don't go all Irish on me. You know what boat." She turned back, pulling the brush through her hair, a tease which she had learned through experience always drove him mad. In the mirror she saw him cross his legs.

"So, go on. Why are you selling your father's boat?"

"I don't give a damn about the boat."

"Like hell you don't."

"Can't we talk about it later?" She could hear the strain in his voice as he patted the arm of the chair. "Come on over here, why don't ya?"

"Forget it, Michael. We need to talk about it."

He grabbed the tie of her robe. With a playful tug, she let him pull her on to his lap. She snickered as he buried his face beneath her chin, tickling her neck with his beard's day-long growth.

"Stop it, Michael, stop! They'll hear."

"The walls are concrete and a foot thick. What's to hear, anyway?"

"Shut up and listen," she said, taking his hand. "Tell me the truth, Michael. Are you happy?"

"I'm bloody miserable," he replied. He sat straight up and, as he did, lifted her, her weight nothing to him. "Ah sweetheart, you know I'm the happiest, luckiest man alive. I've told you that."

"You're a plozie, that's what you are," she said, and he laughed because he had taught her the Irish slang word only that morning. "That's how you pronounce it, isn't it? *Plozie?*"

"Yeah, that's how you pronounce it. But I'm no plozie."

She nestled in close. "I know you're not. But you're selling the boat."

"Feck the boat. We don't need a boat to be happy."

"But what if we did live here? You'd keep it, right?"

"We've discussed this a thousand times. America's our home."

"America is *my* home."

"It's our home. We're happy there. Let's just enjoy tomorrow, okay?"

She decided to let it go, at least for now. "So, what do you want to do?"

"We're taking out the *Margie M*, isn't that what I promised at the pub?"

"Jason would like that. We could take him back to Bantry."

"Bantry? What's special about that?" He grinned, his face full of surprise. "Let's take him to the island. You've been on to me long enough to take you back."

"Solas Mór? I never said anything about Solas Mór. Really? You're sure?" She pushed away so she could see him. "God, Jason will love it. Can we take him to the lagoon? What about the dolphins? Maybe he can swim with them, too. That would be so —"

He put a finger to her lips. "My God woman. Now whist, will ya? You're interrupting me."

"What? How?"

"I've things on my mind."

"Oh, really? Like what?"

"I'm plotting our course to the island," he said, his hand moving to her cheek. "First out the harbor's mouth and across the waters of the bay," he whispered, his hand falling lower. "Then west past Bere Island where it can always get a little choppy." His fingers were busy beneath the delicate robe and she could feel them inching toward her breasts. "Pushing west, always west, where the island thrusts from the sea like a golden treasure." She felt a tug and the robe fell open. His palm was on her nipple and she sucked in. She kissed him hard then stopped, pulling away.

"What about Jason?"

"He's with my mother. Besides, we only need a few minutes."

"A few minutes?" she whispered, touching him. "Michael, we're going to need much longer than that."

Jason's scream shattered the memory. Dawn bolted from the bedroom, rushing down the stairs, finding Margaret holding her grandson's shoes. He stood barefoot on the couch, quivering with rage. Seeing his mother, the boy screamed again, the howl threatening to shake the house from its foundation.

"I only took off his shoes and socks," Margaret cried.

"Jason. Jason, look at me! It's time to go to bed." When he kept screaming Dawn bent to him, arms opening wide. "Come on. I'll give you a piggy-back upstairs. You always like piggy-backs."

Jason studied her then his clenched fist slammed into the bruise on her cheek. As she recoiled, Margaret rushed to help.

"Don't. He'll just get worse," Dawn warned, then turned back to her son. "That's it, mister. Come on!"

Ignoring the pain that blistered in her head, she grabbed him around the waist as he fought, twisting and screaming.

"What can I do?"

"Nothing. Just stay here."

Margaret watched Dawn carry the struggling child up the stairs. She heard Michael's bedroom door slam shut, Jason's muffled screams punctuated by sobbing. She drew a shaking breath, feeling her heart pound. Part of her wanted to deny what she had just seen; that her grandson could ever strike his own mother. Not like that. Not with such hatred. She now had no doubt what had caused the injury to her daughter-in-law's face. She found herself fearing for their safety, wondering whether the decision to bring the boy back home was a wise one. Annoyed at the thought, a hand to her mouth, she realized she could never turn her back on her son's family.

She found herself at the kitchen table, a mug of tea at her elbow. She rose, stepping back into the living room, to the bottom of the stairs. She listened, feeling like an intruder to their pain. Jason had stopped crying, the house shrouded in silence. She considered going upstairs but did not know how she could help. Instead, she moved back into the kitchen. She decided to sit at the table for a half-hour, nursing her tea. She thought of Jason and Dawn and what they were going through and, though she believed she understood grief and how to manage it, she was not certain how to pass such knowledge on to her daughter-in-law.

'Dawn is facing a different kettle of fish,' Margaret thought as she got up and used a poker to stir the cooker's dying coals. 'When Tomás was lost, Michael was a teenager and old enough to give a hand. Mind, he had his own problems when his father was drowned.' And she recalled how her son was always getting into innocent trouble and because of him she didn't have time to think of much else. She found herself smiling at the memory. 'Which is what Michael probably had in mind all along. It was his way of keeping me busy rather than thinking on Tomás.'

The memory of her son led Margaret to think more of him; of how, when they had learned of his father's missing trawler, he had continued to search for his Da' even though everyone thought it was hopeless; of how, after three weeks, Michael had found the abandoned *Margie M* wedged between the sharp rocks on Dursey Island and, despite being told of the danger, had pulled it off the island's restless shoreline before the next storm could shatter its wooden hull.

She recalled how he had spent the next few years tearing around the town, playing his Uilleann, getting drunk and chasing the girls, though he always gave her an embarrassed apology when she found out. She remembered how, without ever being asked, he had repaired the boat and worked his backside off at the fishing to keep food on the table and coal in the bunker.

She was proud of him, she knew, in the way of all mothers. But there was something more to him she always had trouble defining; something to do with his softness and the pain he had also suffered when his father had died, and the beauty that sang from his Uilleann whenever he played. In this day and age some might call him spiritual but she was of a different generation and the word held little meaning to her.

She glanced up at the wall clock. A half-hour had turned into much more and it was past midnight. She placed the empty mug in the sink and turned out the lights, then tip-toed up the stairs. For ten breaths, she stood outside Michael's room wanting so much to go in but afraid she would be unwelcome. Finally, she tapped on the door and opened it a crack. The room was bathed in soft light. Dawn sat on the bed, her eyes rimmed with exhaustion. Jason slept on the far side next to the wall, clutching his stuffed monkey. Margaret could hear him whimper, watching his arms lash out as if fending off unseen attackers.

"Dawn?"

When her daughter-in-law raised her head, Margaret saw the depth of the woman's suffering.

"Nightmares. He has them most nights. He'll settle down soon."

Margaret couldn't think of an appropriate reply. "Do you need anything?" she whispered.

"How about a miracle?"

"I'll pray for it," Margaret promised, and tried to smile back. "If you need me —"

"We'll be fine. Go on to bed."

When Margaret went to her room, she sank to the floor on stiff knees. She knew that praying for miracles required a special effort.

"Lord, you're good at miracles and so are your saints," she said as if talking to a close friend. "I have a special favor to ask. It's not for me. But if You have time and aren't too busy —"

Then she bowed her head, praying twelve full rosaries, one for each month since the sinking, then seven more after that. She prayed to all the Angels and Saints and, in particular, the Miraculous Saint of the Lost. She prayed with such fervor that she did not notice how the rain had stopped or the sky beyond her bedroom window brighten into a new day.

CHAPTER THIRTEEN

The next morning Dawn found her mother-in-law busy at the kitchen sink washing her best set of Delft, the one reserved for Christmas and other special occasions. As the older woman worked, she hummed a pretty song which Dawn did not recognize and, due to the pounding in her head, didn't want to hear.

"Good morning," Margaret said when she looked up. "Gersha, how did you sleep?"

"Pretty well," she lied, trying to hide her exhaustion.

"Chicken, can I see your face? Please let me look."

"It's fine," she grunted, turning away. "It's no big deal."

"Then at least let me get you a cup of tea."

"No, I'll do it."

Dawn stepped to the kitchen table, pouring a cup of tea, remembering to add milk because that's what they did in Ireland. She glanced at the lit Aga cooker. Together with the morning sunlight that flooded through the open window and the hot fire, the room felt too warm. Her head spun and she reached out, steadying herself against the table.

"Is the headache back?" Margaret asked.

"It's only jetlag."

The older woman crossed her arms over a bright apron. "What time did you finally get to sleep?"

"About three, I think." Wanting to change the subject, Dawn turned her gaze to the stack of delicate blue and white teacups drying on the sideboard. "Are you having a party?"

"Oh, just some friends stopping by later."

"Then let me help," Dawn said, taking a step toward the counter.

"Please don't. Jason's still asleep, isn't he? Why not go back to bed?"

"I wouldn't sleep now. It wouldn't be any use."

"Then how about a warm bath? It always works for me."

The mention of water stirred longing in Dawn's cramped legs. "I sure could use a walk."

"Then you go on. I'll watch Jason."

"Are you sure?" she answered, remembering how her mother-in-law had struggled with her grandson the previous night.

"I know what you're thinking but you've no cause to worry," Margaret replied, resting a hand on her daughter-in-law's arm. "I have to learn to help, too, don't I? Now go take your walk."

Letting herself out the back door, Dawn stepped into bright morning sunshine. Dew glinted silver on cobwebs hanging like crocheted scarves across the garden shed windows. Beyond the shed, she could see a trawler coasting across the harbor, its dark hull reflected in the glassy water. The boat was mobbed by a flock of seagulls hoping for an early breakfast. As they circled over the trawler, their screams echoed like children's laughter off the hills above the town.

She yawned, stretching up to a sunlit sky that floated as blue as the sea. As she did, she wished she could escape by diving into its vastness. Instead, she turned, walking out the north gate which led to the home's front garden. She took the cement steps two at a time down to Kilcastle's main street then turned away from the town center and anyone she might know. She walked by the closed Chinese restaurant with its jaunty red lanterns then a shop's window display where her family had purchased jackets and hats in days gone by.

As she approached the end of town, she turned at a fork in the road which led to the tip of the peninsula and the village of Allihies with its played-out copper mine. She recalled that further west was only the open sea and the distant island they had visited a year ago. She broke into a jog, trying to out-distance the memory. Turning again, she headed down the narrow road which descended toward the ocean and the cove hidden by the surrounding hills.

'It isn't much of a road,' she thought as she stepped between broken potholes where tall weeds had found a foothold. She remembered Michael telling her that years before the town had spent a fortune resurfacing it, but the hill was now intent on reclaiming what it had always owned. Few dared to drive their cars along it.

In the bright sunlight, trying to think of nothing, she did not notice the life which flourished around her. She passed sheep perched on craggy rocks studying her with odd slit irises, then clumps of yellow Saint John's-wort. Tall Soldiers were coming into bloom, reaching out with rows of orange blossoms. Delicate white-petaled watercress floated in a stream, pooling in rocky hollows. Pink-flowering heathers, alive with honey bees, painted the flanks of the road while spiders' webs tugged at the yellow flowers of blooming gorse.

As she walked, Dawn remembered how she and Michael had trekked this same way when they had first married and how he had told her the wild track was called a *boreen*, not a road.

"A *boreen*?" Dawn had asked, disbelieving. "It sounds like a drum."

"You're thinking of a *bodhran*," Michael had teased. "You haven't a clue about *focal Gaeilge*, have ya?"

"Don't tell me to fuck off."

He had laughed. "Not 'fuck'. *Focal*. It means 'word'. *Boreen* means a small road."

She had taken a mental note to remember it was a *boreen*, not a road and, as they walked, he had sprung the word *craíc* on her. He laughed at his wife's puzzled look when she at last understood it was not a gang's money-spinning nose-candy but only a bit of fun.

"Like, 'I'm going down to the pub for a bit of *craíc*'. Or 'the *craíc* is ninety', meaning it's a hell of a lot of fun."

"What's ninety got to do with it?" she asked, confused. "Just don't use *craíc* in Boston, Michael, or you'll get arrested."

He had laughed again then threw her other words in Gaelic and corrupted Irish slang like *gobsmack* and *rubber; múinteoir, gersha, garda síochana,* and *gobshite; pants, biscuit* and *fanny* and a hundred others. She discovered that while some sounded the same in American English, they had very different meanings in Ireland. When she tried them, the words had twisted on her tongue like thick fudge and she had laughed, enjoying them. But when he surprised her with the local meaning of *knob,* she'd had enough and chased him down the falling slope of the *boreen,* laughing like teenagers all the way to the sea.

Accompanied by the memory she made the final turn and, seeing the isolated cove, realized that last year at this very spot he had taught her the meaning of *plozie.*

When the shrill cry of a gull broke her thoughts, she found herself gazing out on the stone covered beach. She heard the sea breaking and the song of shingle tumbling within lapping waves. The beach was deserted, sheltered from sight by a forgotten cement pier. She yearned to immerse herself in the water, longing for the safety of the pool in Boston. Then, recalling that her husband had swum here as a child, she decided to do so now. No one saw her strip off the light jacket, blouse and track suite bottom she wore. In a bra and panties, she scampered across warm pebbles to the sea.

She suspected the water would be cold but the sea hit her like a fist of ice and she swam out with hard desperate strokes. When her ears filled once more with the memory of Michael's laughter, she stopped. Treading in the swells, she realized that even after a year, swimming in an Irish ocean was too much. She knew what was coming and her stomach tightened, preparing for the onslaught.

"God no," she shuddered. "I'm here. I'm safe. See? Just look!"

She swung around, eyeing the safety of the cove and the low rocks that protected it. It made no difference. She closed her eyes tight but the flashback came anyway.

She struggled within the grasp of the squall's heaving seas.

"Jason!" she screamed, searching through towering whitewater for her son. Above the storm, she heard his call and her eyes swept to the buoy. She saw him clinging to it, rocking in the heavy storm, fire reflecting off his contorted face.

She tried to yell his name again but the boiling waves swept over her, throwing her under the surface. For a long moment she was held there, arms thrashing against the strong currents. She could feel panic building in her constricted lungs, knowing that if she died so would her son. Desperate, she clawed up through the water. Arms quivering with exhaustion, she stretched toward a surface that seemed always out of reach.

Dawn's eyes snapped open. Breathing hard, still dog-paddling, she swung around to find her bearings. She had swum out further than she had intended. She turned again, facing the cove's outlet which flowed into Bantry Bay.

"If it was a year ago, I could see Michael's boat pass the mouth of the cove. I could swim out to him. I could warn him to turn back," she panted, then pounded both fists against the water. "But it's not a year ago, is it? He's not here. You can't help him."

She inhaled, glancing once more at Bantry Bay and the ghosts that sailed there. Then she turned her back on them and began the long swim to shore.

When she saw the tall triangular fin rise in front of her, she panicked, back-peddling. But she recalled what Michael had taught her. Few sharks visited these waters and those that did were harmless. When the fin turned toward her, however, she kicked hard, not caring what Michael had said. But then she remembered a similar fin slicing through an island's lagoon, and the white-faced dolphin that had swum with her when she was pregnant and happy.

The breeze went slack; the gulls' cries silenced and her fear was replaced by a sense of mystery. She put her ears beneath the surface but heard only the surging sea. Then she caught the sound of sporadic clicking and also something else. A song filled the ocean and she remembered the sensation of tickling that swept over her and her son when he was still in her belly. Forgetting her fear, she took a deep breath and dived.

Salt stung her eyes and she could not see clearly. But she could make out the sun as it streamed into the water and with it the glittering curtain of sealight that fell all the way to the bottom. The ocean was silent again, the song gone, and she turned a full circle disappointed not to find its source. But as she twisted toward the surface the dolphin floated up, tail standing before her like a sentinel.

She swam closer, noting the white spot painted on its face. Eye-to-eye with it, she was awed by its size but surprised because she felt no fear. It seemed to study her with an intensity that matched her own and, as she looked deeper into its eyes, she was drawn by the compassion and intelligence she found there. She peered even deeper. Light flashed. She could swear she saw a glimmer of firelight sparking beneath the dark iris. She pulled back, startled. Looking again, she saw only darkness.

The dolphin sang again, the ocean filling with its song. She could feel the vibration against her body and for a moment thought that it had reached inside her, as if connecting to her soul. It seemed that for once the world had stopped spinning and she could focus on this one, single, beautiful moment. She forgot everything else, captivated by its haunting voice. Suspended within a shimmering sea, she realized that for the first time in a year her heart had stopped racing. Her head wasn't swimming with horror. Instead, she felt only peace. She wanted to listen to the dolphin sing forever. But the mammal could hold its breath far longer than she could and she was forced to turn away.

She broke surface, searching the water, but the sea was quiet and felt much colder. She floated, recollecting the wonder of the moment and the tranquility she had experienced. It was as if the dolphin had reached into her mind and then beyond it, touching her very soul. Confused by the depth of the connection, she again searched the cove. All she found were lapping waves.

Fog was gathering thick over the bay and she realized it was time to return to her son. In the thinning light she swam back to shore, her steady strokes reflecting the peace of the encounter.

CHAPTER FOURTEEN

As she opened the back door, Dawn could feel her wet underwear cling to her blouse and track suite bottom. Deciding to change before Margaret could ask questions, she strode across the empty kitchen, grabbing a towel from the hot press where her mother-in-law stored them.

"Margaret? Jason?" she called, but her mind still boiled with questions about the dolphin. She crossed to the window and, gazing out on a foggy day, tried to hold on to the fragile tranquility the encounter had given to her. Her skin still tingled with the mystery of its song.

'I can't tell anyone,' she thought, toweling the sea from her hair. 'Margaret would never believe me. She'd think I was crazy.' The thought made her wonder if she really was crazy. Only a crazy person would sense such a deep connection with a wild animal. Only a kook could see, deep in a dolphin's eye, a wondrous glimmer of firelight.

'Maybe it was a dream, just like the flashbacks. Or maybe I really am nuts.' The moment of peace evaporated, her stomach churning with old anxiety.

"Margaret?" she called again.

Her eyes settled on the kitchen table strewn with a curious assortment of items. Branches of yew tree littered its surface together with unopened spools of purple ribbon and balls of wire. She heard laughter from beyond the kitchen door and remembered the friends Margaret was having over. Resentment rose at the intrusion because she had wanted to spend time with Jason and wondered if they could sneak upstairs together without being seen. But opening the door, she realized her plan was impossible.

The living room was packed with women, some of whom she had met but mostly whom she hadn't. A line of trestle tables had been erected in the middle of the floor; the furniture pushed against the walls to make room. The tables were piled high with more yew branches as well as wire, ribbon, scissors and garden cutters. Women stood in groups drinking tea from the Delft cups, their loud chatter filled with laughter and gossip. She peered through the crowd for Margaret and Jason but there were too many people.

"Ladies? Ladies!"

A large man stood at a table trying to attract their attention. Dawn recognized the religious garb and white dog collar as belonging to Father Danny, the local parish priest who had presided at her wedding. She recalled how, following Michael's proposal, she had cancelled her trip back to the States. Instead, a month later, they had been married in the town's church surrounded by her husband's family and friends. The sight of the priest brought it all back but the happy memories were now tinged with darkness. She had no desire to meet Father Danny again, at least not right now and probably not forever.

She found herself wishing that Margaret had warned her about the extent of the gathering. If she had known, she would have disappeared with Jason to the other side of the peninsula; maybe even the other end of Ireland. She did not want to talk to any of these people. But no one had yet noticed her and she wondered if she could escape back to the kitchen, or find Jason and take him upstairs. But that would mean running the gauntlet of the crowd. They would comment on her tangled hair, wet clothing and a face of bruises which could not be easily explained-away. Instead, she made herself as small as possible and stood unmoving at the kitchen door, searching the crowd for her son.

"Ladies!" the priest called again, and the chatter died. Father Danny's smile warmed the heavy jowls of his middle-aged face and behind thick glasses his eyes glimmered with kindness. "Thank you for being here this morning," he continued in his sing-song County Kerry inflection. "What you do today, what you do each and every year, demonstrates your faith in the love you have for those we have lost. It renews our belief that though we can no longer see them, our remembering keeps our loved ones alive in our hearts forever."

The ladies clapped as Carol stepped to the top of the table.

"Aren't we fortunate to have a priest as lovely as Father Danny," she said with sweet condensation, and Dawn remembered how much Carol's voice had always grated. "Okay everyone," Carol continued, and the sweetness was gone because she barked like a general. "We have our work cut out for us. Ninety-four wreaths and only a few days to go. So, let's get cracking, shall we?"

Someone turned on a CD player and loud Irish country music collided with the women's chattering. When the group broke like a rugby scrum, heading for the tables, Dawn realized there would be no escape. From across the room Margaret caught her eye, hurrying toward her just as Dawn spotted Jason. He stood at the edge of the crowd looking lost and wary. Carol's little girl, Lydia, a blonde-haired rascal of Jason's age, was trying to engage with him as she always did on every visit. Seeing his rigid posture, Dawn knew her son was having none of it. Forgetting her own anxiety, she pushed toward him just as Margaret walked up.

"Carol asked if we could make the wreaths here because there's a christening in the church," Margaret explained. "I couldn't say no."

"I wish you had," Dawn growled as Lydia ran up.

"Why won't Jason play with me?" the little girl asked with shrill disappointment because the pair had always played together during their visits. Dawn had always liked Lydia and did not want to see her upset.

"I don't think he wants to play right now," she explained, stooping to her. "He's tired from the long plane ride." She managed a thin smile for her mother-in-law. "I'll be right back."

Dawn turned away, walking to her son.

"Jason why don't we go upstairs?" she urged, bending to him.

He would not look at her. In his scowling face, the forewarnings of rage were balanced on the thin ledge of his silence. He would not take her hand when she offered it to him. Hoping he would follow anyway, she turned toward the stairs. But Carol had seen her and, crossing through the crowd, blocked their escape.

"Dawn, it's so good seeing you again," she gushed. Then her penetrating eyes assessed the bruised face, tangled hair and damp clothing. "What happened to you?"

"Can I talk to you later, Carol? I was just going up to change."

Dawn stepped toward the stairs but Carol caught her elbow.

"Of course, you can, but give me a minute, will you?" she said, leading Dawn toward a table. "We need your help."

"Help? What help?" Dawn asked, eyes still on Jason.

"Don't tell me Margaret forgot to tell you? Why, it's almost Remembrance Day! There's so much to do and the town has this horrible flu and so many are ill. Even Joan was sick but she's almost better now. See, there she is."

Dawn saw Joan at a table engaged in work with other women and remembered meeting the librarian in the pub a lifetime ago.

"Joan! Look who's here?" Carol called, and Joan looked up. The woman smiled, sneezed like a horse, then bent back to work.

Dawn watched as Joan and the women crafted large circular wreaths from the greenery on the table. But with her thoughts on more important issues, she turned back to Carol. She wished the woman who still held her elbow would stop prattling on so she could return to her son. She looked over the crowd, seeing Margaret trying to distract him, wanting to disengage herself before Jason erupted.

"Carol, thanks but I have to —"

"You remember Father Danny, of course," Carol went on, pointing out the priest who sat in a chair a safe distance from the maelstrom. "He has a wonderful heart but the poor man is never organized." She waved to the priest. "Father Danny, see who's come home!"

"Hey Father," Dawn called, but she turned away before he could answer. "Look, Carol, I really need to change."

Carol picked up a finished wreath, holding it out for inspection. "They're easy to make but take a bit of time, you see. Just bend the yew this way to make a circle. Then wrap the wire around it to hold it in place and add the ribbon. Do you follow? Don't you think they're perfect?"

"Carol, really, Jason is —"

"But we have so many to make!" Carol continued, and placed a hand on Dawn's back as if shepherding a wayward girl. "Now go change then get back here. That's an order!"

Dawn took a breath. Feeling a headache start to pound, she pushed down her dislike.

"Maybe later, okay, Carol? Jason is pretty tired from the flight." She took a step away but Carol again took her elbow.

"Did you say 'Jason'? Where is he?" she commanded, searching the crowd. "The poor, poor Gossan. I talked to Margaret. Everyone in town knows how he still suffers."

Dawn's skin went cold. She made a mental note to tell Margaret to keep her mouth shut. She reached down, removing the woman's hand from her elbow.

"Carol, let's make one thing clear. Jason is fine," Dawn said, her face flushing. "He's seeing a specialist. A doctor who knows what he's doing —"

"Oh, there he is!" Carol barked, and Dawn saw the woman's eyes fix on her son. Jason stood near his grandma, arms rigid at his side, eyes filled with silent anger. Dawn realized that for anyone familiar with the old Jason this new child looked decidedly strange. "I know it's none of my business," Carol ran on, "but Dawn, I know this amazing counselor. He was a wonderful help to Lydia when her Da' died. I'll make a call."

"That's absolutely not necessary."

"It's no trouble," Carol insisted, once more taking her elbow. She stepped so close Dawn could smell the woman's sour breath. "After Paul got drowned — did you ever get to meet my husband, Paul? — our counselor told me, 'You have to get Lydia out there. You have to get her to confront that grief.' And that's exactly what I did. Now look at her."

Dawn was forced to look. Lydia's small figure stood at a table, busy helping the women make wreaths. Unlike Jason, she chatted happily. Dawn found herself wishing Carol would drop dead.

"Take my word for it," Carol continued. "You have to get Jason out there right now."

"Really?" Dawn replied. She was aware of a dryness in her mouth, her head pounding to the music and the women's chattering. "Carol, I think you'd better excuse me," Dawn tried, but the woman held on with fingers as sharp as dogs' teeth.

"Mr. Jaffrey, that's our counselor, he told me —" and with the other hand, she tapped Dawn's arm to emphasize each word. "Grieve," Carol said, tapping. "Accept," she tapped again. "Believe," she tapped once more. Dawn felt the pressure in her stomach rise as she remembered what she disliked most about Carol.

"Carol, would you please stop that?"

"*Believe*. That's the key, you know," Carol said, tapping again. "We must believe in what we cannot see, just as Father Danny said."

"Carol, I said don't do that."

"The sooner you *believe*..." and the woman's fingernail jabbed once more, "...the sooner you'll find your answer."

"Carol, would you fucking stop that? Stop it right now!" Dawn roared and swung around, facing the jabbering crowd. "Everyone shut up. Just shut the fuck up!"

The chatter died. Someone turned off the CD player as startled eyes turned toward her. Margaret stood unmoving next to Jason, stunned. Father Danny rose from his chair, his heavy face bewildered. They all watched Dawn swing back on Carol.

"What did you say to me, Carol? I have to believe? Believe in what, exactly?"

"Well," Carol stuttered, "in Michael."

"What about Michael?"

"Why, that Michael is always here for you, of course. Just like all our dearly departed."

"Here for me? And tell me Carol, precisely where would that be?" Dawn pointed across the room. "Here?" She pointed out the window. "There? Come on, Carol, tell me. I'd really like to know."

Carol's mouth worked and Dawn realized she did not have a ready answer.

158

"I tell you what, Carol. Here's what I believe. I believe Jason is sick and I'm too stupid to help him. I believe I don't have a job anymore and I'm a schmuck for losing it. I believe the world is completely fucked up. And you know what else I believe?"

Carol could only shake her head.

"They're not here and they're never coming back. Not anyone. Not your Paul or your husbands or sons or your grandsons. No one's coming back. Nobody! Not even Michael. Particularly not Michael. He's dead. Gone. Vanished. POOF!" She took a step closer. "How's that for something to believe in, Carol? Or is that too much for your picturesque view of life?"

A careworn-looking woman asked in a trembling voice, "Doesn't she know we've all lost someone?"

Dawn inhaled hard, feeling the silence in the room. Hot embarrassment rushed to her face as she realized she had gone too far. Her mouth opened, hoping to bleat-out some sort of apology — any sort of apology — to the women who looked back at her with hurt-filled eyes.

A scream pierced the room.

Jason glared at her, his anguished face filled with accusation. Dawn remembered what she had shouted: his father was dead and never coming back. It was the truth but her words could not have been crueler.

"Oh Christ, Jason. Oh God, I'm sorry," she murmured but he ignored the apology.

He pushed through the crowd, rushing past her outstretched arms and into the kitchen. She ran, following, leaving behind a crowd of people too stunned to speak. Only Carol chose to break the uncomfortable silence.

"Poor Dawn. That woman definitely needs professional help."

Margaret turned on her, eyes flashing. "Carol, will ye not ever whist! You've said more than enough, don't you think?"

CHAPTER FIFTEEN

Jason was not in the kitchen and when she rushed through the back door he was not in the garden. But looking down the hill to the harbor, Dawn spotted him dashing across the main street and on to the square. Losing him in coils of descending fog, she flew down the steep steps, a hand to the railing.

Running across the street, she spotted him flying by a row of shops that peeked through the murk like phantoms. As he disappeared around the corner, she realized he was heading back to the pier. She took a shortcut across the square, running into the open space where damaged fishing nets were spread out like giants' cobwebs. A pair of men were repairing them with long needles and thick line much as a tailor would mend a knitted jumper. She bolted past them, turning for the trawlers.

"Jason!" she yelled. When he did not answer, she called his name again and ran on.

Jackie stood on the pier, at the stern of his trawler lashed tight at the water's edge. He concentrated on a wrecked, bulging fishing net which his mate, working at the davit crane mounted to the boat's deck, hoisted through the fog.

"Lower now, lower!" Jackie roared as the heavy load swung toward him. He ducked as it lurched past, just missing his head. "Stop. I said stop, ya gobshite!"

The mate cut the power and the net dangled in mid-air, swinging back and forth.

"What'cha got, Jackie?"

He turned, seeing Johnny. The old fisherman, dressed in a beat-up nor'wester, stood on the wheelhouse of his weathered half-decker roped to the pier near Jackie's boat. The old man peered through the fog for a better view. "What'cha catch?" he called again.

"Nuthin'!" Jackie barked.

"Jaysus, Jackie, what did that?" George bawled. Just back from a trip, the young fisherman tied his punt to a cleat and clambered up on to the pier. Jackie reached out, snagging the damaged net to stop its swinging as George whistled in disbelief. "What'cha got in there?"

"It isn't a load of cod now, is it?" Jackie snapped.

"Not likely. It's gonna cost a few thousand to replace that net, I'd guess," George replied and, peering in closer, whistled again. "Ah fer feck sake. Look what'cha caught."

The body of a dolphin lay in the net, its dark form unmoving.

"It's only a dolphin, George, so don't get your knickers in a twist."

"Hey Johnny, come look at this!" George yelled, and the old fisherman climbed off his boat and ambled toward them. He took in the dead mammal with a knowing look.

"You catch anything besides this beast, Jackie?"

"Not a sausage, Johnny."

"That's a pity, lad, seeing how you just paid for that engine overhaul," he said, glancing up at Jackie's boat. "Heard it cost you a fortune. You should've sold the thing months ago. It's nothing but a money sponge."

"The overhaul was over a year ago," Jackie grunted. "I'm doing fine now."

"So you say," Johnny said and turned to George. "How about you? Any fish?" When George shook his head, they all studied the dead dolphin. "It's no wonder no one's catching any fish. Not with the likes of them about."

"Who said there's no fish?" a voice called, and a crowd of fishermen approached them through the fog.

"Would you look at that bastard!" said one with a cast in his eye, spitting a gob of phlegm at the dead mammal. "Let's hope there's not another one."

162

"Unlikely," Jackie replied.

"Ah, now, Jackie, 'course there's another one," Johnny lectured, shaking his head. "Where there's one dolphin there's always another one, if not more."

"Johnny's right," the one with the bad eye said. "Where'd ya catch it, Jackie?"

"Just off the point."

"That close?" observed another fisherman. "Jaysus, Mary and Joseph, we're fecked."

"Now you don't know that for sure," Jackie said with a red face. "Maybe it just got lost."

"Lost me arse," George complained. "You know damn well they're after the same fish we are. Those are *our* fish, Jackie. I'm not sharing my catch with a fecker like this."

Johnny's lined face dropped into a scowl. "Watch yer tongue, George. You know they got every right to the fish. They're only trying to make a livin', same as we are."

"Ah come on, Johnny," bad eye replied, studying the destroyed net. "You know damned well they do more than take a few fish. If the government is planning on culling the seals because they savage the fish stocks, why not dolphins? They're worse."

"Look at that net," another fisherman added. "I'll be fecked if the likes of them are going to ruin me."

"So, what are you gonna do about it?" George bawled, turning on Jackie. "It's you who caught the damned thing. How ya going to make sure there's not more of the *craters*?"

The eyes of the entire group swung on Jackie. He picked up a long knife resting on the pier, shaking it at the carcass. "If I see one it'll run into this," he snarled, cutting at the ropes. "Bad suss to any of 'em if I find them."

The ruined net with its cargo fell on to the pier like a dead man.

"I hope you're right, Jackie," George said, standing over the body. "They're like locusts. What fish they don't eat they'll chase away. We'll be left with nothing." He kicked at the carcass with his boot. "The last thing this town needs is a group of those things about."

"I told you not to worry," Jackie growled. "If I see one, I'll kill it. So will any of us."

"Leave me out of it," Johnny replied. "The creatures mean no harm."

Jackie opened his mouth, ready to let fly. Then he saw a boy pelting through the fog toward him. "Now, what's got into him?"

"Isn't that the McCarthy lad? Looks like he's had a fright."

"Yeah, that's Michael's kid," Jackie replied and waved his arms over his head. "Jason? Jason, hey lad, slow down!"

But the boy dodged around him. Jackie watched as the lad headed down the pier, disappearing like a ghost into the fog.

Jason ran on past the line of tied up trawlers until he came to the flagpole. He leaned against it, breathing hard from his run. He peered up at the wet Irish Tri-color hanging dead in the mist then turned to look back at the pier. Through the fog he could see the empty slot between two boats, water sloshing against their hulls, and realized what his mother had said was true. His father was never coming back. He swung, racing on down the pier as fast as he could, his vision blurred by tears.

Since the accident Jason did not talk but that did not mean he did not think. He thought about his father all the time. Until his mother's angry words at his grandma's house, he was convinced that what he had seen after the sinking was true. He was certain his father was alive. But his mother had shaken the foundation of his faith like a sail blown hard in an unexpected squall. The anchor of his hope had come unstuck and he had nothing to replace it with.

Still crying, he bolted on through the thinning fog, stopping only when the pier ended. He stood quivering in the wet, snot running down his face, longing to be home. But he remembered that home was a house built on a Boston beach where they no longer lived, the one his mother had forced him to abandon much as she had forced him to abandon his father in the sinking boat. He stopped crying when there were no more tears left in him, his gut heaving, sick to his stomach.

When he heard the splash, he forgot about feeling sick.

He peered out to sea but the source was lost in the fog. Harbor swells washed against the side of the pier with a sound like a hollow drum and he crept forward to peek over its edge. All he found was oily water and discarded plastic bags. He used his sleeve to wipe the snot off his face and again scanned the water but nothing was there.

He turned from the sea, deciding to go back to his grandma's house because there was nowhere else to go. But sudden sunlight shone through a gap in the mist, striking his face. He heard the splash again and, turning back toward the water, became determined to find out what was causing it.

Dawn ran faster when she saw Jackie pointing the way down the pier. She kept calling for Jason as she ran, her worry mounting because the fog could obscure the edge of the pier and its sharp drop to the water. The fear descended into her legs, forcing her to run even faster, calling his name until she reached the very end. Here, the mist diluted into thin sheets. Within it she at last found him. He stood at the edge where the pier grew slippery with spilled engine oil and she inched forward not wanting to frighten him.

"Jason?"

When he did not turn, she thought he was still angry with her. His eyes were locked on a spot thirty feet from the pier, on a patch of sunlit water that rose and fell on the tide.

"Jason?" she called again but this time she followed his gaze. She heard a low whistle and saw a dark shape swimming low in the sea. It rose until its beak broke clear of the small crests and then she saw the spotted face. Its depthless eyes were locked on her son.

She took in a sharp breath, wondering why the dolphin was here. She inched closer until she could see Jason's wide-open eyes, and sensed within him the same depth of wonder she had experienced earlier that day.

"Dawn! There you are!"

Margaret hurried toward her, breathing hard, her hair matted with dampness because she had forgotten her hat. "I was trying to find you. Where's Jason?" When Dawn pointed, the older woman saw how close he was to the edge. She crossed herself as she moved toward her grandson.

"Don't," Dawn warned.

Margaret stopped then saw the spotted dolphin, too. "Oh my," she said as Dawn chanced another step closer.

Full sunlight struck the sea. Around the dolphin the water sparkled like diamonds. The mammal vented, the droplets of its breath drifting across to cover Jason in a fine mist which glowed silver in the sunshine. He reached high as if hoping to catch the glittering breath.

Then her son swung toward her. He erupted in a loud giggle, his face as bright as a shiny new penny. When he smiled at her, she felt as if she had been caught in his warm embrace. Dawn's eyes flicked from her son to the dolphin and back again.

"Oh my God," she whispered.

When they returned to the house and after Margaret had made excuses and asked her friends to leave, Dawn noticed Jason's calmness and how he obeyed her whenever she asked him to do something. He ate all of his dinner and when she said it was bedtime, he went upstairs without complaint. He allowed her to bathe him and waited in their room while she took a shower. When she walked in, she found he had put on his pajamas and crawled into bed all by himself. She hovered at his side, waiting for the inevitable explosion, but nothing happened. He held tight to his monkey and appeared to be sound asleep.

"Jason? Jase?" she whispered.

But all he did was snuggle deeper into his pillow. She could hear his even breathing, and knew he really was asleep and not pretending. She thought back on the day. Though she could not be certain of what had caused this sudden change, she suspected she had witnessed the answer floating in the harbor. She studied her son's face and remembered the smile he had given to her on the pier, the first one in months.

After adjusting his blankets, she turned from him thinking to shut the open window. But with her fingers on the latch, she smelled the richness of the sea and was struck by the beauty of the nighttime harbor below the house.

Its glassy surface reflected the red and green running lights of the trawlers tied to the pier. She looked for the dolphin but found only empty water.

Leaving the window open, Dawn noticed a bottle of pain killers on the bureau where Margaret had left them together with a full cup of water. Remembering her earlier headache, she took two pills with a sip of water then set the bottle and cup back near the green box of her husband's Uilleann. In the silence, she could see the gentle rise and fall of her son's chest and left the room so he could sleep.

She went downstairs to find Margaret. She stopped on the final step because she had never seen her mother-in-law as she saw her now. Margaret was dressed in a bright blue leotard, grey hair pinned back, sitting on a mat placed in the middle of the floor. She was practicing Yoga, her body stretching with a suppleness that denied the woman's age. She did not stop when Dawn came into the living room but instead closed her eyes as her chest expanded in a deep breath. When she let out a long exhalation, her daughter-in-law thought it was as if she was releasing the ballast of a heavy load. Margaret opened her eyes and Dawn saw the question in her look.

"He's sleeping," Dawn replied and the older woman smiled as if hiding a secret. "What?" she asked, but Margaret's smile only deepened.

Dawn sat on the couch, her left foot drumming a staccato on the floor. She could not dismiss the possibility that floated in her mind, but worried her mother-in-law would think she was crazy if she came out with it. Studying the wooden floor, she decided on a more careful approach.

"Margaret," she asked at last, "do dolphins live around here?"

"Dolphins?" Margaret answered as she raised her arms in another posture. "I've seen them in the bay, not that I've ever seen one in the harbor. It's unusual."

"Is it? Have you ever seen them do anything strange?"

"Strange?' What would you mean by 'strange'?"

"You know. Different," Dawn tried, but her face flushed as she looked back to the floor.

She did not want to explain the glittering light she thought she had seen in the dolphin's eye that morning when she found it in the cove, or the feeling of connectedness that had engulfed her. She could not explain the illogical emotions that had swept through her when she saw Jason on the pier with his eyes locked on the dolphin, or her restless desire to acknowledge a connection between her boy and a wild mammal when such a connection made no sense. All she knew was she had witnessed what might be the first sign of her son's healing, even though such an idea was as fanciful as wanting to again believe in Santa Claus.

Instead of saying what she wanted to say, Dawn glanced at her mother-in-law and said, "He hasn't laughed in a year, you know."

"I'd call it more of a giggle," Margaret observed as she uncoiled from the Yoga pose. "You know, Michael always liked dolphins."

"I know. He told me."

"He thought there was something special about them. Maybe…"

"Maybe what?"

"Jason is so much like Michael. Maybe he feels the same way."

Dawn rubbed her temples, a headache pounding despite the pills.

"I left some tablets in your room," Margaret said. "Did you find them? You weren't feeling well when the ladies were here."

"Yes, I found them. Thank you." She leaned forward on the couch. "Margaret, I'm sorry about today. I shouldn't have said what I did when your friends were here."

"You were upset."

"I hope I didn't hurt anyone."

The older woman laughed. "Don't you worry. Give the ladies a day and they'll pass no remarks."

"But I shouldn't have said it."

Margaret stood up, walking to a side table in the corner of the room. Two framed photographs rested there and she picked up the larger one. Dawn saw the strong features of Tomás and how much he resembled Michael who, in turn, looked so much like Jason.

"When I lost Tomás I thought I was going to die," Margaret said, sitting beside Dawn and peering at her husband's likeness. "It's bad enough to lose them. It's worse not getting them back. Not even a grave to visit. You're going through it too and I so wish you didn't have to."

Dawn found she couldn't say anything to that.

"Know you're not the only one to walk through such darkness. So many in the town have lost loved ones to the sea and have gone through this same nightmare. After Tomás died I almost went mad. Did Michael tell you?"

"You? You couldn't have."

"Gersha, I'm not as strong as you think. You wouldn't believe the crazy things I did. Do you know I went to the far point of the peninsula one midnight and wouldn't come home? I got as close to the place where Tomás was drowned as I could. Michael found me. He told me I was howling like a wolf crying for its lost mate. Do you know I don't remember any of that night? Now, if that's not crazy I don't know what is." She laughed but Dawn could see her pain. "I felt so horribly lost. So abandoned. As if it was Tomás's fault and he'd done it all on purpose. Dawn, back then my life wasn't worth living."

"What did you do?"

"I had a secret weapon."

"What?"

"Michael. Thank God I had him. His being here was a miracle. He picked up the pieces."

"But now you've lost him, too."

"He was my son. But he was your husband. There's a difference and we both know it. God alone knows how much I miss him and how much it can still hurt, but at least I was blessed with so many years of his life. But you, Dawn. You, Michael and Jason were just starting. I know what you meant to him. You were his everything. And I fear he was your everything, too."

Dawn thought she heard an appeal in her mother-in-law's voice. "Margaret, I can't let him go. Don't ask me to."

"I'd never do that. I won't be party to it. But you're living through something even worse than not being able to let go, aren't you?" She placed a warm hand on Dawn's arm. "When I lost Tomás I had Michael to help me. You don't have that. You don't even have the joy of your own son."

"I don't know what to do," Dawn whispered, and tears stung her eyes.

"You need to help Jason, but —"

"I've tried. You know that."

"— but," Margaret continued, squeezing her arm, "if you're going to truly help him, first you must learn to help yourself." Dawn stiffened at the words and tried to pull away but Margaret held fast. "Don't you think I know how much pain you're in? Don't you think I understand how upset and confused you are because your world fell apart and you don't know how to rebuild it? Let me ask you something. How can you possibly help Jason if you can't help yourself? Dawn, look at me. You have to make a start. You have to heal yourself."

"I don't know how," she replied, and felt Margaret's gentle touch on her cheek.

"I remember thinking the same thing. That's when I finally realized something. Do you know what that was?"

Dawn shook her head.

"If I was going to live again, I had to find something inside me, something that wasn't broken. I had to start by believing I could find what I thought I had lost forever." She touched her heart. "Something in here."

"I don't understand."

"Start with the basics. Slow down. Listen to yourself. Open up again to the world around you. That's the mystery of it because only then can you come to believe you can heal. Why do you think an old woman like me does Yoga?" She laughed, looking closer. "Does that make sense?"

"No."

"Okay, then how about this. Start by learning to breathe." She closed her eyes, taking a long breath, her face relaxing. "If you breathe, you live. And when you do, so will Jason. Can you understand that?"

"I'll try," Dawn replied. But even as she said it, she thought she did not understand at all.

After Dawn had gone to bed Margaret found she could not sleep. Instead of going upstairs, she covered the leotard with an old cardigan and pair of jeans. She put on her coat and walked out into the rain-swept night then through the town and to her church.

She found the sacristan at the front door, keys in his hand, getting ready to lock up. She promised she would only be a moment. Entering, she dipped her fingers in the holy water to bless herself then walked through the interior door and into the vaulting body of the church. She made her way through the shadows to the tall statue.

The wooden match lit in a sudden glow of light. The woman of strong but simple faith noted how small its flame was but how much depended on it. With the match she lit a candle and its diminutive light swept away part of the darkness. It flickered on the worry lines of her face and her caring eyes, and also upon the ancient wooden statue which had been carved over a century ago. She knelt before it, her gaze fastened on its compassionate eyes.

"Oh, holy Saint, gentlest of Saints, you are the patron of the lost," she intoned but this time did not finish the prayer. Instead, her troubled voice echoed up into the vastness of the church. "Blessed Saint, you are the saint of miracles. I need your help again. Please know it's not for me but for my family."

Margaret bowed her head, praying for her intention, then crossed herself again. She left the church, saying goodnight to the sacristan as she passed. Outside, standing in the rain, she wondered if the saint had heard her. She prayed that he did because she did not know what else to do.

"Please, dear Saint. Let the miracle come soon. Let it come with the dawn."

PART IV

DOLPHIN

CHAPTER SIXTEEN

The white-faced dolphin surfaced, venting into the pre-dawn light. Unseen, it navigated past the ferry transporting early-morning passengers to Bere Island and then, beyond that, the red buoy at the harbor's mouth. Wary, it crept half-submerged past the line of trawlers whose owners sometimes used methods to kill its kind. When the mammal reached the pier's end near the hill, it rotated its pectoral fins while swinging the muscular flukes, checking its momentum as it came vertical. With only its blowhole above the water, it lay unmoving in the shadows between two half-deckers, as lifeless as flotsam.

The being who had once been Michael but who was now changed beyond all recognition rested in the swells, thinking of nothing except the woman and the boy. When his longing shook him, he trilled, calling for the brother who was now part of him. The answer came from deep within, as it always did:

'Be not afraid', his brother spoke with thoughts that needed no words. 'I am with you.'

He let his sleek body settle to the bottom and in the darkness considered the improbable renewal he had experienced and, with it, the gift he had received.

Following the accident, in the early days of his transformation, he had floated cocooned within the quiet lagoon. There, he had been protected by those who had come to his aid and time did not matter. The days were counted in the sweep of rising and falling tides and the cycles of the moon. As he healed, he had dreamed. He dreamed first of the pod as it swam through bright waters hunting shoals of mackerel, or playing among the combers that beat against the coastline. He had dreamed, too, of another pod that trod the dry land but the image was distorted and not fully realized.

As he healed within pulsing filaments of light, he had dived deeper, dreaming he was a young boy again. Once more upright on two childish legs, he had discovered a furry caterpillar crawling beneath a farmer's fence. Cupping it in two small hands, he had raced home to the house overlooking the harbor where his mother had scolded him for disturbing what was natural. But his father had only smiled and, leading him to the garden shed, found a glass jar. They filled it with grass clippings and small twigs and he was taught to care for the caterpillar so he might witness a miracle. One day the boy discovered that the caterpillar was gone. In its place, a shell like a small fortress hung from a twig.

"Where has the caterpillar gone?" the boy wondered.

His father had sat him on a knee, explaining it had not gone anywhere but slept within the chrysalis. He explained the caterpillar no longer wanted to creep along the ground on tiny legs, and soon a miracle would transform it beyond all recognition. The boy begged to see the miracle but his father explained he would have to wait, and with rough fisherman's hands placed the jar in the window to warm in the sun. Every morning the boy ran to the shed to see if the miracle had occurred but his father told him he must be patient. One day, a miracle did take place. The jar was filled with a creature spreading gossamer wings in the sunlight.

"What happened to the caterpillar?"

"The caterpillar is still there but it made room for the butterfly and is no longer imprisoned on small legs," the boy's father had explained. "The two share a single body and together they will fly far and wide to explore all the world."

The boy took the jar back to the field where he opened it, and the butterfly flew high above him. As it fluttered over the tall grass, he imagined all the places it would visit that he could not and wished he could grow wings to follow it and share its body like the caterpillar. But mostly, the boy thought how wonderful it was when two creatures became one to live a life together.

In the lagoon, still sleeping as he dreamed of the butterfly, he shed the glowing exterior casing which bound him. In his sleep, he stretched the pectoral fins and flukes and the air in his lungs escaped through a cavity at the back of his head. As he exhaled, he dreamed he left his body and, like the butterfly, soared away from the lagoon and the island with its jutting peak and across a large body of water. He imagined himself speeding above a distant coastline, then a great city. He stopped only when he heard desperate cries calling to him.

The first came from a boy who lay in a hospital bed, asleep. The second from a woman whose cry caused his skin to crawl. In their voices he sensed the injuries they had suffered and, gliding to them, breathed out with his song to reach them. But in his dream, he found he could not touch them. He grew frightened because he knew they were important to him and yet he did not recognize them. They floated at the edge of his memory like photographs bent by age, their identities just beyond reach.

The fear of loss startled him awake. He found himself in the lagoon, fully conscious for the first time. He shivered, agonizing over the identities of the woman and the boy. His fear turned to terror as he realized he could not remember who he was or what had happened, or how he had come to be on the island. He turned to see fins sprouting from his sides, strong flukes sweeping the water, and thrashed with appendages he could not control.

'Be still,' a distant thought whispered to him. 'Wait so you may understand.'

He swung, searching for the voice but found only empty water. When he tried to yell, mad squealing escaped from behind a thin tongue.

'Have faith,' the wordless voice sang. 'Believe and you will master what you do not know.'

It was then he realized the voice spoke from within him. "I've lost my mind," he cried in a song unrecognizable to him. "Either that or I am dead."

He heard laughter in his head.

'How could you be dead when you see and hear and your heart beats? Remember how once, when you trod the ground on two legs, you were taught about the butterfly and the caterpillar? Isn't that what we dreamed?'

He thought back. "The caterpillar made room for the butterfly so they could share the same life together. It was a miracle."

'And so it is with you. I am the caterpillar. You are the butterfly. We have woken from our chrysalis and, because I have made room for you, we are now brothers on the same voyage.'

His great body shook as he sought to make sense of the words. Then his fins stirred as he remembered the woman in his dream.

"Then who is the woman? How can I believe anything if I can't remember what is important to me?"

'It will come but only with the tides,' his brother comforted. *'Sleep now. Sleep so you might gain the strength to learn.'*

When he at last slept, the pod of dolphins swam into the lagoon, venting in the sunlight. They swam close, caressing his sleeping flanks. "We will show the new swimmer how to play among the curling waves because he was a land-walker and does not know," sang one. "We will help him learn to fish the mackerel by herding them into a tight ball," sang another. "We will teach him about the gift and the blessings it bestows," sang a third.

'No. It is I who will teach him of the gift because I am his brother and am now one with him,' the voice whispered. *'When you are chosen to cocoon with a swimmer then it is you who can teach the gift.'*

Just as his unseen brother had counselled, it took many tides for the being who had once been human to become accustomed to his new form. Like an infant, in the shallows of the lagoon and guided by the pod whom he learned to love as kin, he came to master his strong flukes and pectoral fins. He learned to leap through the lagoon's sunlit water, and chase mackerel, and talk with song and squeals to those around him. Throughout his convalescence he remembered his dream of the woman and boy and longed to find them though he could not explain why. At every sunset when the pod swam back through the rocky entrance to the sea beyond, they would never take him though he begged them to do so.

'They do not take you because you are not yet ready,' his brother counselled.

"You know I am ready," he whistled through the bright water. "I have learned to swim. I can chase fish and catch them. Why do you hold me prisoner if I can do these things?"

'You are not imprisoned. No one stops you. One day you will know freedom more powerful than even the strongest flukes and fins. You will learn of the gift that is yours and then you will be free.'

"Gift? What gift? Tell me."

His brother laughed. *'You still have not learned patience. When the time comes you will know.'*

As he fell asleep, he thought again of the woman and the boy and wished the time would come when he might find them. He wondered about the gift his brother talked of and what it might do. He was forced to be patient for many more tides. Then, during a fitful sleep, he again heard the woman's desperate cry. This time it did not come from a dream. The call was as solid as his flanks and came from the east.

"I hear her. She calls for me. I know I am ready. It is time that I find her."

'I cannot stop you. Let us swim, swimmer, to the land from whence you came.'

Escorted by the pod, he headed out of the lagoon toward the mainland and then, alone but for his brother, swam on into a familiar cove. Within it, he found the woman crying. When they hung together underwater and she peered into his eyes, his heart stirred. Then the storm in his mind cleared as if swept away by a sparking breeze and he remembered.

He remembered the name he had been given at birth, and walking on two legs to a home on a hill. He remembered a cottage built near a city beach and the woman and boy he lived with, and a loving life that had been stripped from him. He remembered the squall and the storm-surge of whitewater; the murderous tongues of fire and the hollow song of a tolling bell. He remembered being trapped in a sinking vessel and the knowledge he would die. But he also remembered how a pod of dolphins had swept out of the darkness toward him, and the explosion of light that had transformed the sea's darkness into sunlit brilliance. He remembered, too, the spotted dolphin that had found him and how it had gazed at him with depthless eyes. The knowledge shook him because he now understood.

Suspended in the waters of the cove, he looked back at his great flukes and fins. He realized that he had been saved from death by being transformed beyond all recognition. Like the butterfly and the caterpillar, his brother had made room for him so that, together, they could share the body of a dolphin.

When the woman whom he now remembered to be his wife was forced to the cove's surface to breathe, he shook with the recollection of their love and longed to be with her again.

'I have seen other Swimmers try to walk the earth, to find what they have lost,' his brother whispered. *'I warn you, swimmer. It is a difficult voyage.'*

"My name is Michael, not swimmer, and I must be with her. If you are my brother, you will help me."

After a long silence, his brother sang, *'Then I will show you so you will be free.'*

As the dolphin hid between the trawlers the sun burst over the horizon, burnishing the ocean in gold. Rousing from his memories, he willed his great flukes to sweep the sea and, moving from the shadows, edged closer to the land of his old life. Making his way to the dock where he had been taught to swim as a child he surfaced, eyes above the water. Looking up at the quiet house perched on the hill, he saw an open window.

"It's too high."

'Nothing is too high,' his brother sang. *'Look within and see the gift you are given.'*

In his mind the darkness parted, and he beheld his brother floating in his consciousness. Within its depthless eye the sun rose in glory and within the brightness hung a chrysalis. As he watched, the shell split and a multitude of butterflies stretched their glowing wings.

'Catch them tight. Hold them and the gift is yours.'

As he reached out with his mind, the butterflies transformed into bright stars, the stars multiplying into clusters of glowing galaxies. They poured into his being like a sunlit waterfall. He vented into a clear sky, his glittering breath stretching toward the window.

'Go now. Rise upon the gift. But be patient or you will frighten them. I will wait for you here.'

Again, he vented. The droplets swirled like a galaxy, coalescing into a curtain of sealight which danced high above the water. Like a butterfly he ascended within it, up along the hill then through the open window.

Emerging from the womb of light, cloaked in a fog of ocean mist, he stood once again on two legs as humans do. In a familiar bed he found the woman and boy, asleep.

Dawn tossed, moaning, again clutched by nightmares. The sky was black with driving rain and she swam within mountainous seas. Thunder crashed and lightning lit the whitecaps. She flailed within the chaos; her face lit by fire as she screamed her son's name.

Within the glowing fog that encased him, the being who was Michael took a cautious step toward her. He heard her frantic breathing and the cry for their son. As he sang her name, the water within the cup she had left on the bureau vibrated as if a pebble had been dropped dead-center. He saw the green box next to it and, longing to hold the instrument again, reached for it.

The movement of his hand dissipated the fog that surrounded him as if by an unseen breath. He crept toward the bed, looking down on his wife. He reached out, water streaming from calloused fingers. Like tears, they fell on to her face and she startled in her sleep. He pulled back, remembering his brother's warning. Patiently this time, he reached again. He stroked her head with fingertips of dew, her hair glittering in the light. Her moaning quieted, then stopped. In her sleep, she turned to him, nestling her cheek into his palm.

When her breathing slowed, he turned to the boy but the child lay untroubled. As morning whispered into the room, the fog again encased him.

He dispersed back into the sealight, the shimmering coils withdrawing out the window then down to his brother who waited in the harbor below.

When Dawn woke, she rolled over, stretching in the morning sunlight. She smiled, not understanding the source of her contentment. She tasted saltwater on her lips. Curious, she looked around the room but could not find its source.

When she heard her son cry from downstairs, her contentment vanished. She pulled on her jeans, running from the room to find him. For that reason, she did not have time to look out the window or see the dolphin who waited patiently in the harbor below the house.

CHAPTER SEVENTEEN

"No, Jason. I already told you. You can't go outside."

Margaret hovered over her whining grandson as he pulled at a handle with both hands, straining to open the locked back door.

"Wait for your Mam. You don't want to get me in trouble, do you?" she pleaded, wishing Dawn was here to help. Margaret had woken early and, coming down to make up the fire, had found her grandson in the kitchen already dressed. As he continued to whine, she turned to the table where she had placed a bowl of hot oatmeal, hoping to distract him.

"Please, chicken. Come sit down and eat."

Glancing at his breakfast Jason swung back to the door, his whine mounting to a roar.

"Please stop," she appealed, hands covering her ears. "You'll wake your Mam."

"What's wrong?"

Margaret turned as her daughter-in-law strode into the kitchen.

"Thank God you're here. I don't know what he wants."

Dawn rubbed the sleep from her eyes, focusing on her son. He knelt against the door, screaming, hands stretched up to the handle.

"Hey, Jase. Jason, what's up?"

"Where's his monkey?" Margaret yelled over the din. "Maybe that's what he wants."

"No, that's not it." Thinking she knew what he wanted, she crouched next to him. "Hey kiddo, look at me. Do you want to see your friend again? Is that it?"

"He wants the dolphin?" Margaret asked. "But that's impossible. It won't be there."

"Jason, tell me what you want. Is it your friend?"

When his eyes opened wide, she reached over him, sliding back the bolt. Jason yanked the door open, running from the house. She ran after him.

"I'm coming too," Margaret said, and grabbed her coat.

Outside, Jason dashed past the wooden shed, disappearing down the back steps. Dawn followed, grabbing the railing, taking the stairs two at a time. At the bottom, she kept an eye on him as he cut away from the square. She chased after him, running along the sidewalk that led to the dock below the house. As she trotted on to its wooden planks, she found Jason scanning the sea, eyes round with expectation. She looked, too, but all she found was the quiet water of the harbor.

"Maybe the dolphin is having its breakfast," Dawn suggested. "Let's go eat and we'll come back later, okay?"

"Ah, the poor Gossan," Margaret called as she hurried up, seeing his disappointment. "I told you it wouldn't be here."

"I had to let him try," Dawn replied, then turned back to her son. "Come on, Jason. Let's go home." But then she saw how he stretched tall, his eyes fixing on the water. She heard a gentle whistle then a geyser of mist wafted into the morning light as the dolphin drifted toward them.

"Oh, my Lord," Margaret gasped as Jason skipped to the edge of the dock.

"Jason, be careful!" Dawn warned, stepping to his side. He giggled as the white-faced mammal inched closer. When it vented again, his giggles turned to laughter. But when it stopped twenty feet from the dock her son whined in frustration.

"He wants it to come closer."

"Closer? But it's a huge *crater*," Margaret fretted. "Isn't it close enough?"

Men's voices drifted toward them from up the pier. Dawn turned, seeing a group of fishermen hauling fish boxes off a trawler.

"I'll be right back," she said, striding toward them. "Watch Jason for a minute, will you? I have an idea."

On the pier Jackie worked with his mate, hand-balling a heavy box on to the cement. They placed it next to stacks of full fish boxes towering into the sunlight.

"Jaysus, you must have almost a ton there," George whistled. He walked over, sizing up the catch of mackerel. "Jackie, you were right. That must've been the only dolphin. Where'd ya find the fish?"

"As if I'd tell you, George," Jackie grinned as he lifted a mackerel by its gills. "You want some, go find 'em yourself." He turned to a group of fishermen who had gathered around his catch. "Didn't I tell ya it was the only *crater*? The dolphins are gone so there's fish for everyone. Now feck off with the lot of you and let me get back to work."

As the group broke up, Dawn hurried through the scrum. She slowed when she saw Jackie with the long fish dangling from his forefinger.

"Good morning, Jackie."

"Morning, Dawn," he replied, a smile on his broad face. "And a mighty good one at that. Now isn't this a fine fella?"

"It sure looks like it," she replied as he presented the fish. She pointed to a full fish box. "Jackie, how much do you want for one of those?"

"Now what would you want with an entire box of mackerel? You aren't wanting to sell 'em in the market, are ya? You aren't trying to give old Jackie a bit of competition with his own catch?"

"Of course not. I don't want to sell them."

"Ya can't be needing a whole box of fish," he hemmed, an eyebrow cocked high. "You sure you don't want just a few?"

"A full box," she insisted. "Please, Jackie."

"Ah, for Jaysus sake," he muttered and, tossing the mackerel back into the box, cocked a thumb at it. "Go on. Take that one."

"You're sure? Jackie, thank you so much. What do I owe you?"

"You mean money? As if I'd charge Michael's wife for a few fish. Take it."

"You mean for free?" she asked, surprised. But his lips tightened as he thought again.

"Well, Dawn, I tell you what and just so you don't feel bad about it," he continued, thick forearms crossing over a barrel chest. "How 'bout a few pints waiting for me at the pub tonight and we'll call it quits?"

"That's perfect," she replied, and they shook hands on the bargain.

"Good," he said, releasing her from his powerful grip. "We're agreed. Now go on with ya and let me get back to my work."

Dawn bent, lifting the box, staggering under its weight. "I'll manage," she said when he reached to help. She hoisted it high, and walking back down the pier felt pleased with her catch. When she made it to the dock, she dropped it at Margaret's feet.

"What do you want with all of those?" her mother-in-law asked. "They must have cost you a fortune. Who sold them to you, anyway?"

"Jackie, and he never charged a thing."

"For free? That's not like our Jackie," Margaret observed as Dawn pick up a foot-long mackerel. She held it high, its blue and silver stripes flashing in the sunlight.

"Jason? Hey Jase. Look!"

Her son still stood near the water and the dolphin still floated twenty feet away. Jason watched his mother wind up and throw. The mackerel hurtled over his head, striking the sea between the dolphin and the dock. The mammal swept toward the fish, taking it in its beak, coming a few feet closer at the same time.

"My God it worked!" Dawn cried. She hoisted another mackerel by the gills just as she had seen Jackie do, and stepped closer to her son.

"Okay, Jase. You try it." She held out the fish and he took it in fumbling hands. "Slippery, isn't it? Go on. Throw it to him."

Aiming at the dolphin, he slung it with all his strength. It spun end-over-end, glittering in the sunlight, but landed only a few feet from the dock.

"Don't worry," she said to her son's disappointment. "Watch."

Jason's eyes grew wide as the dolphin dived, disappearing from sight. "Wait for it… wait," Dawn counselled. Then the sea stirred beneath the floating fish, vanishing as the dolphin devoured it. The dorsal fin emerged from the sea, the dark shape floating inches from the dock's edge.

"That's awesome, Jason! See how close it is now?"

Carol was already in a foul mood. She had not slept well due to her worry about the wreath-making, and still smarted from yesterday's blasphemous language shouted by the American visitor. When Margaret had asked them to leave the house, resulting in hours of lost work, Carol had done her best to keep her temper, knowing it was up to God to judge the sinner. Yet when she'd woken that morning, and as she walked Lydia down the main street to school, she could not help but think how satisfying it would be to give the Yank a piece of her mind.

"Mam, slow down," Lydia protested, hanging from her mother's hand.

"Lydia, we're late for school," Carol barked between hurried strides. "You don't want Mrs. O'Driscoll to get angry, do you?" When her daughter slowed to a stop, Carol was forced to turn around. "Now, what is it?"

"What are they doing?" Lydia asked, looking toward the dock.

"Who?" she grunted, but Lydia was already running across the road. "Lydia! Come back here right now!"

Carol chased her daughter down the square, coming up short when she spotted her on the wooden dock with Dawn and Margaret. She clucked with impatience then hurried on, arms swinging.

On the dock, Lydia squinted through the bright morning mist. "Dawn, what's Jason doing?"

"Watch," she said, smiling down at the young girl. "Jason! Throw another one!"

When he heaved a fish into the water, Lydia's face lit up as the dolphin swam to its quarry, snagging it with conical teeth.

"I saw a dolphin in Kerry once," the girl burbled. "Will Jason swim with it like the people there do?"

"Fat chance," Dawn replied, and held out a fish. "Want to give it a try?"

"Lydia, don't touch it," Carol commanded. Her low heels clattered across the wooden dock as she hurried toward them.

"Carol, it's only a mackerel," Dawn said, hoisting the fish. "See?"

"It smells," Carol responded, stepping away. "My daughter is not going to school smelling like a fisherman. Come on, Lydia. We're late."

"But I want to stay here. See what Jason is doing?"

Carol saw the boy and, in the water close to him, the object of her daughter's interest.

"Is that a dolphin? What's that thing doing here?"

Margaret, who had been listening from close by, decided to step in. "I was telling Dawn that it's so unusual to have a dolphin in the harbor. It's so interesting."

"Interesting?" Carol barked. "Nonsense. Dolphins can be quite dangerous."

"Really?" Dawn smiled. "I hadn't heard that one."

"Well, it's true," Carol sniffed, and held out a hand. "Lydia, we're leaving."

"Maybe you can come back later," Dawn said to the disappointed girl, and turned to her son. "Jason, throw one more for Lydia before she goes."

Jason hurled the fish. This time the dolphin stretched high, water cascading from its graceful body. Opening its smiling beak, it caught the fish in mid-air.

"Jason, that's massive!" Lydia shouted, laughing.

Her son turned, his proud smile flashing. Dawn looked, taking it in. She realized she was seeing the old Jason again, if just for an instant, and wondered what she else could do to bring him closer.

The first fisherman to see the white-faced dolphin was old Johnny. He had pulled himself atop his wheelhouse to check the condition of the half-decker's life ring as part of the weekly safety inspection. Having made sure the ropes were clear, he stood tall to take in the view. Looking to the pier, he watched Jackie and the mate still offloading fish boxes. Then he turned toward the water while patting his boiler suit, looking for his pouch of tobacco and cigarette papers. As he squinted into the sunlit harbor, he made up his first rollie of the day. Lighting it behind cupped hands, he happened to glance down beyond the end of the pier. At first, he thought his old eyes were playing tricks. But when he rubbed the sockets and looked again, he realized what he was seeing was as solid as a winter's storm.

"Jackie? Hey Jack!" the old man yelled, throwing his butt into the water. On the pier, Jackie looked up from a fish box. "Lad, you were wrong," Johnny called, pointing. "There's more than one!"

Jackie looked but a line of parked trawler sterns obscured his view.

"Right back," he said to his mate. Jackie clambered on to his boat, then up to the roof of the wheelhouse. His trawler rode higher on the water than most of the fleet and he had an easy view all across the pier. He pulled at the visor of his old ballcap to cut the glare and peered as hard as he could.

"The old man's lost his marbles," Jackie muttered. "Nuthin's there at all." But as he scanned toward the dock below Margaret's house, his face went slack. "Feckin' shite. Damn that monster to hell."

He slid from the wheelhouse roof, leaping over the gunwale on to the pier, breaking into a run.

"Ya see it, Jackie?" old Johnny called as he ran by.

"I'll gut the bastard!" Jackie yelled, not breaking stride.

On the dock, Dawn lifted the heavy fish box with both hands.

"You're not going to keep feeding it, are you?" Carol carped. "It will hang around like a feral cat."

"Carol, I thought you were leaving," Dawn replied, winking at her mother-in-law. "Margaret, are you coming?"

"I most certainly am," she replied and, leaving Carol and Lydia behind, they headed toward Jason. Placing the fish box within easy reach, Dawn knelt by her son.

"Want to do it again?" she asked, holding up another fish.

She heard the dolphin vent and, looking over the side, saw it floating so close that if she had a mind to, she could reach out and touch it. "Okay, give it a throw."

He took the mackerel but instead of throwing it Jason leaned out over the water, the fish dangling from his fingers.

"Dawn, do you really think he should?" Margaret asked.

"Don't worry. I've got him," Dawn said, and took Jason around the waist. She was surprised when he did not protest at her touch but instead leaned out even further.

"You're crazy! He'll fall in!" Carol yelled.

Dawn turned, seeing the woman still prowling at the edge of the dock. She stuck out her tongue then looked back to Jason. "Just be careful, okay, Jase? Go real easy."

She heard venting again as the white-faced dolphin surfaced. She saw how it used its tail to push higher out of the water. Eye-to-eye with her son, their gaze seemed forged in steel. She remembered how, in an island's lagoon, she had swum with a similarly marked dolphin, and also thought about the one she had encountered in the cove yesterday, and was convinced they were all the same. Holding her son close, she could feel the even rise and fall of his chest and wondered if he was experiencing the same sense of peace she had discovered on both occasions.

The dolphin stretched higher and she held her breath as it plucked the fish from her boy's fingers. For a moment, Jason's hand lingered near the dolphin's head and Dawn realized he wanted to touch it. She shifted a palm flat against his belly, ready to pull him back.

"Go on, Jase. You can pet it."

But as he reached, the dock vibrated to the whack of heavy boots against the wood.

"Get out of here! Go on! Get the fuck out!" Dawn swung around as Jackie charged toward them, arms waving like a madman. "Go on! I said git!"

The dolphin ducked under the water as Jason stumbled on to the dock. He whined as the dolphin broke away, its dorsal fin slicing a clean line past the trawlers. As Jackie heaved closer, his eyes settled on the blue fish box.

"That's mine!" he bawled. He reached for it, thick anger in his cheeks.

"You gave it to me, remember, Jackie?" Dawn answered, standing in front of it. "You're not welshing on a deal."

"Welshing?" he asked, confused by the Americanism. "The neck of ya. Feeding that thing with my own fish! Now go on and feck off. Get off the dock, the lot of ya!"

"I didn't realize you'd elected yourself king around here, Jackie. Stop being an ass."

"I said get off!"

"Dawn," Margaret said. Turning, Dawn saw the warning in her mother-in-law's eyes.

"Come on, Jason," Dawn snapped. She reached for him but he slapped her hand away, racing toward the house. Giving Jackie a scowl, she lifted the fish box, marching after him. Margaret sighed and followed, leaving Carol to comfort the fisherman.

"What's got the Yank's knickers in a twist?" Jackie asked, scratching his balding head. "I only wanted to chase the *crater* away. I only did what was right."

"Of course, you did. Did you see the size of that thing? It's a menace." Carol swung to him with a look as tough as steel. "Jackie, you're an important fisherman in this town. People look up to you. It's your responsibility to do something about this."

It was a calculated order that played to his ego and, though he did not want to anger his dead friend's wife, found himself hitching up his trousers. "And so I will."

With a snort he turned inland, setting his eyes on the house on the hill.

Dawn paced the length of the living room. "Since when was it his dock? It's a public place, isn't it? We have every right to be there."

"But then so does Jackie," Margaret replied, trying to sound reasonable. She sat in an armchair near the window as her daughter-in-law cut a valley in the floor, a sight that competed with her grandson who writhed on his back, whining and very near a tantrum. "Jason how would you like some ice cream?"

Margaret tried, hoping to quell the storm, but all he did was slap at the air. She found herself wanting to give Jackie a piece of her mind which is when she heard the knock at the front door.

"Now, who could that be?" she asked, but suspected she knew exactly who it would be. Opening the door, she found Jackie spinning a grease-smeared baseball cap in hard working hands.

"Jackie," she said, nodding.

"Margaret."

Over his shoulder, she saw Carol standing with her daughter on the steps below the house. The woman's black look resembled an incoming gale. "Is that Carol? Is she coming in?"

"No," Jackie huffed. "Just me."

"Then wipe your feet."

As his bulk brushed past her, she reminded herself that Jackie had always been welcome in their home. She had the sudden image of a hefty, tousle-headed youngster pounding up the stairs to Michael's room for an hour of horseplay. But those were yesterday's memories and she steadied herself for the trouble that was brewing.

"So, what brings you here?" she invited, intending to nip any argument in the bud. But the room was full of Jason's whining, and Dawn had taken a stubborn position at the window with her back to them.

"I just want a word with —" he said, and nodded toward her daughter-in-law.

When Dawn heard the fisherman stalk up behind her, she spun to face him.

"Well then," Jackie hedged, seeing the anger in her eyes. His argument forgotten, he fumbled for words. "I, ah, ya know Dawn, it's just I never had a chance to really say it. Welcome home."

"You could have said that on the dock. Don't you think you've said enough?"

"I, no, that is…" he mumbled, looking at the floor. "I think there's been a misunderstanding."

"Oh, I understand all right. I understand you scared the shit out of my son."

"Dawn!" Margaret yelped.

"Well, he did. Didn't you, Jackie? Didn't you scare the shit out of him?"

"Maybe I did. And if I did, I'm sorry."

"Sorry? Look what you did!" Dawn demanded, and Jackie was forced to look at Jason who lay whining on the floor.

"I think we're getting off on the wrong foot. Margaret, you know how it is. If we don't fish, we don't eat."

"What's that got to do with anything?" Dawn demanded.

"Everything," he said, wondering how a fisherman's wife could be so ignorant. "Let me explain. We catch fish. Dolphins eat fish. We're both after the same thing. We don't like them and they don't like us. We don't want them anywhere around. So do me a favor and stop feeding the fecker."

"Are you telling me Jason can't give an innocent dolphin a fish?" she replied, leaning in. "Are you telling me what I'm allowed to do and not do with my own son?"

"Ahhh…" he hemmed, then looked her straight in the eye. "That's exactly what I'm saying. I got enough problems making a living without you stirring the shite."

"I think we should all take a deep breath," Margaret tried, but Dawn stepped so close she could count the hair in Jackie's nostrils.

"The fish belong to everybody," she snarled.

"Says who?" Jackie bawled, swiping the cap off his head.

"Says me!"

"Not my fish!" he yelled, slamming the cap to the floor.

"I don't give a damn whose fish they are!"

"Stop it. I said stop!" Margaret shouted, coming between them.

Dawn took a step back. She glanced at Jason. He had stopped whining and instead his eyes pleaded at her. "Case closed, Jackie. We'll have to agree to disagree. We're feeding it and that's final."

"It is *not* closed! Margaret, you know what I'm saying. The entire town depends on the fishing. Michael would understand, wouldn't he?"

"Yes," Margaret said reluctantly. "Michael would care about the town. Mind you, he would also say —"

"See?" Jackie crowed, rubbing his hands together. "Margaret agrees and so would Michael. Why can't you?"

Dawn wanted to kill Jackie. She wanted to rebuke Margaret for agreeing with him, however reluctantly. She realized she could continue this fight and perhaps alienate every fisherman in Kilcastle, as well as their families. She also realized that should she agree with the demand she would be betraying her son.

"Well, Dawn?" Jackie said. "What's it to be? Are you with us or against us?"

She swallowed hard. "With you," she muttered.

"I didn't hear that," he said, peering at her. "Are ya saying you won't be feeding the *crater* in the harbor again? Is that what you're promising?"

She jerked her head in a quick nod. Glancing at Jason, she saw his look of frozen disbelief.

"Good. Then we're agreed. The last thing I want is to fall out with Michael's wife." Jackie picked up his cap and held out a hand to cement the deal but was met with a cold glare. Withdrawing, he backed off. "I'd best be on my way, then, so. Dawn. Margaret," he finished, and skedaddled out the front door.

Dawn felt Jason's gaze on her neck. She turned, finding him staring at her with icy contempt.

"Jason," she said, taking a step toward him, "sweetheart, I'm sorry."

When she reached for him, he slapped at her outstretched hands. Then he bolted, screaming, into the kitchen.

"Oh, Dawn," Margaret whispered, "it's me who should be sorry."

"All he wants to do is feed a stupid dolphin."

CHAPTER EIGHTEEN

When Margaret found them in the kitchen, Jason was sagged against the back door, crying, while Dawn stood above him surrounded by an air of angry guilt.

"Jason, stop that!" she reprimanded. When he hammered on the door with swinging fists, she responded, "I said stop it! Didn't you hear me?" When he didn't, she sank to her knees beside him. "Why don't we go find Mister Monkey? He misses you," she tried, but Jason collapsed on the floor in a flood of screaming anger.

"We'll have to find something else," Margaret floundered.

"Really? Like what? Jason, I said stop!" But the child only cried harder.

Margaret cast around the kitchen looking for anything that might help. She rushed to a drawer, pulling out a wide plastic folder. Opening it, she removed a bundle of colorings Jason had drawn on previous visits and spilled a set of crayons on to the table.

"Jason, look what I found," she called, holding up a crayon. "Remember these?"

"Margaret, he won't color anymore," Dawn protested, remembering the failed treatments.

"Well, he always did before. Look, Jason," Margaret tried again, waving the crayon in front of him. "Why don't you draw a picture for Nana?"

Jason stopped crying long enough to look. A scowl like thunder crossed his face. He slapped the crayon from his grandmother's outstretched hand and started howling again.

"Jason that's enough!" Dawn ordered.

"Jason. Jason! Look at me!" He glanced up, startled. Margaret glared first at Jason, then Dawn. "Enough of this nonsense. You two. Come with me."

They followed Margaret down a narrow hallway at the side of the house, waiting while she opened a set of wide double-doors. Looking into the space beyond, Dawn was staggered by what she saw. It was a large room for such a small home. Sunlight flooded in through an expansive window that overlooked the harbor. She remembered how, during their visits, Michael sometimes led her here to fetch footballs or fishing rods for Jason to play with because it had always been a junk room. But the room had been cleared, leaving a bright, airy space filled with paintings.

"Who did these?" Dawn asked, her eyes surveying the walls.

"Me," Margaret replied.

Forgetting her son's anger, Dawn stepped into the room. "I didn't know you painted."

"I started after Tomás died but I worked at a friend's house. A few months ago, I brought them back here."

"You never told me."

The walls were hung with framed paintings, much like a small gallery. Dawn's attention turned to her son. Jason was drawn to a picture of a man that looked like an older version of his father. The subject's strong arms were crossed, the weathered face contrasting with the clean blue and white lines of the fishing boat he stood on.

"That's your grandpa, Jason. That's Tomás," Margaret said.

"That's the *Margie M*, isn't it?" Dawn whispered, recognizing the half-decker. She felt the old pain as the memory tried to take hold, but Jason had already walked on. His eyes were locked on a painting of a craggy boulder. The face of an old woman was painted into it, as if her form was rising from the very rock.

"Those are Irish legends," Margaret explained, pointing to a group of paintings. "That's the Hag of Beara, Jason. She's an old crone just like me, isn't she?" she smiled, and stepped to the next painting. An acrylic of three swans floated over a golden sea. "Those are the Children of Lir," she continued. "It's a wonderful story. You know that one, don't you, Jason?"

"Michael told him. At bedtime, he read Jason many of the Irish legends."

Her son moved on to an easel which stood in full sunshine near the window. It held a painting still in progress and he was transfixed by it.

"Look at that," Dawn said, stepping to his side. "Jason, isn't that amazing?"

"Oh, that old thing," Margaret scoffed. "It's not even finished. That's the Legend of Solas Mór."

"Solas Mór?" Dawn replied, looking at it with new interest. "I didn't know there was a legend about it," she whispered, and examined the picture which Margaret had outlined in pencil and had only started painting.

The fantastical island ascended from the sea, its peak towering above a fist of storm-clouds. Behind it, the sun rose in glory. On the rocks, a three-masted barque lay foundered, her hull broken in two. Desperate sailors, hands clasped in penance, knelt on the splintered deck, some falling into the savage whitewater and certain drowning. Dawn fixed on the round horror in the sailors' eyes. A shuddering flashback threatened and she swung to Jason to steady herself. She saw how he stared at the picture, irises as hard as pebbles, and she realized he was studying a group of dolphins Margaret had outlined but had not yet painted in. They leaped like ghosts through violent seas, speeding toward the doomed sailors. A large space near the dolphins was still blank canvas.

"What will you draw there?" Dawn asked, pointing to the section of white.

"I've been thinking about it for months but I'm still not sure," Margaret said, contemplating her work. "The legend has been around since the days of the ancient Greeks and it's always fascinated me. Who knows? I might never finish it."

Margaret glanced toward her grandson. Then she bent to a table littered with the tools of her trade: tubes of acrylics in a variety of bright colors, old saucers on which she mixed them, a jar holding pencils and paintbrushes, a full glass of clean water, and pads of sketch paper.

"Jason, your Nana is full-out of ideas," she said, reaching through the clutter. "Maybe you'd like to help me finish it."

She selected a tube of blue acrylic as well as one of white and squeezed a glob of each on to a clean saucer. She chose a paintbrush, dipped it into the glass of water and mixed the paints while also thinning them. Next, she picked up a sketchpad and stroked a bold line, covering the thick paper in color. Finally, she mixed vermillion and yellow to a startling autumnal orange and applied that to the paper, too.

"See how easy it is, Jason? See how you can make anything you want?" she said, and Jason saw how his grandmother had painted beautiful rainbows of color. She picked up a new paintbrush, squeezing the soft bristles to a point. "This is special and meant just for you," she said, offering him the brush and sketchpad. "If you have any ideas, why not paint them in here?"

"Go on Jason," Dawn joined in, realizing how smart her mother-in-law was. "Don't you want to help Nana?"

But Jason only looked at his grandmother's gifts with vacant eyes.

"Well, maybe later," Margaret sighed, placing the paintbrush on the table with the pad. "I'll leave them right here. Now," she said smiling, "why don't we all go have a nice cup of tea."

As they left the room, the painting of Solas Mór rose high in the sunlight waiting for someone to finish it.

That night they all slept without dreaming but woke un-refreshed. As the women gathered in the kitchen, boiling eggs and toasting bread for the first meal of the day, they said little to each other because they were unwilling to say what needed to be said: the hope for Jason that had come with the white-faced dolphin had been extinguished by an unwelcome promise and there was nothing to replace it with. When the women sat down to breakfast, Jason would not eat. Instead, he stood at the living room window looking out to sea. Even as he scanned the ocean, he knew the harbor would be empty of the dolphin. He wondered what it would be like to feed it again and perhaps stroke its sleek head and, as he did, imagined he could swim with it across the harbor and maybe beyond that, out into the open sea.

The thoughts of the wide ocean made him recall the night of the squall and how, despite his terror as he clung to the buoy, he had seen the dolphins leap over cresting waves. From that night, he had always thought of the dolphins and his father at the same time because of the grief and fragile hope he had endured, and also because he had come to believe they were responsible for his daddy's disappearance. Though he would always remember the event that made him believe his father was still alive — the impossible image that occurred following the false golden sunrise — he also thought that if he ever saw another dolphin, he would be frightened of it or angry. But when he had encountered the white-faced dolphin at the pier, then later at the dock, he had experienced neither. Instead, he thought it the most wonderful creature in the world and felt a closeness to it that puzzled him. He wished he could see it again to understand the dolphin better, but his mother's promise to his father's friend had denied that to him.

"Jason?"

He felt tears on his cheeks. Wiping his face he turned, seeing his grandmother at the kitchen door.

"I've poured you a cup of tea. Come and have your breakfast before it gets cold."

He frowned in reply. He was not hungry and resented her as well as his mother because of what had happened yesterday. Instead of obeying, he ran.

He scurried past the stairs because he did not want to go to his room and his mother had forbidden him from going outside. With nowhere else to go he snuck down the back hallway, finding his way again into the sunny room that was his grandmother's studio. He did not want to look at the paintings. Instead, he wished he could hide behind a couch like he sometimes did to surprise his father when he came home.

A deep armchair was pulled against a wall and he dragged it to face away from the door so he would not be seen. When he sat in it, drawing his legs beneath him, he tried not to think at all especially of the dolphin because everything made his stomach hurt. He closed his eyes tight and for that reason did not feel the warmth of the morning sunlight pool on to his lap, or see the floating motes of dust that sparkled like stars where the light touched them, or feel anything but his misery. He did not look out the window to again search the harbor, or watch the bright morning mist the sun had not yet burned off, or the calm water near the dock that was suddenly disturbed by the mammal which had hidden there since before sunrise, waiting for him.

In the shadows at the side of the dock, the dolphin broke surface. As he vented, his eyes roved to the house that perched high on the hill above him. Exhaling again, he gave substance to the thin mist that covered him. Dancing to his command, it rose like a glittering curtain as it had before. At the top of the hill, the mist gathered at an open window on the side of the house and through it he could see his son resting on the chair. Remembering the warning his brother had given about patience, Michael decided against visiting on two legs. This time he exhaled, reaching out with song to the boy who needed him.

In the studio, Jason heard something clatter to the wooden floor. Curious, he rose from the chair, bending to pick it up. It was a paintbrush, the one his grandma had offered to him, and he placed it back on the table. When he was sure it was safe, he ran back to the chair. As he settled, he again heard a clatter. The paintbrush had fallen once more.

When he picked it up this time, he studied it with great care. It looked just like any old paintbrush and seemed normal in every way. Suspicious, he again placed it on the table. Pacing back to the chair, in his head he counted off his steps. 'One,' he said to himself as he walked. 'Two, three.' He suddenly swung back, hoping to catch-out the wayward paintbrush. But it lay on the table exactly where he had put it.

As he turned once more to the chair, he thought he again heard something. He crept back to the table like a cat, peering over the edge. 'It can't move. It's only a brush,' he thought to himself. But as he watched, the paintbrush moved at first so imperceptibly he wasn't sure it was real. Then the brush rocked back and forth and, when it had gained enough momentum, rolled off the table, clattering again to the floor.

This time when he picked it up, he did so with careful fingers. He was not afraid of it, only puzzled. When light sparkled off the wooden handle, as bright as a lighthouse beam, he swung to the window to find its source. But he saw nothing except a dense mist hugging the outside of the glass, glowing gold with sunlight. As he watched, the mist began to fold in on itself like a spinning top and he thought he could smell the sea.

'Jason.'

He looked to the door to see who had called to him but it was closed, just as he had left it. He turned a complete circle but no one else was in the room. He frowned at the paintbrush, knowing he was being silly, and placed it again on the table.

'Jason?'

He sucked in hard, eyes opening wide.

'Isn't that a wonderful picture your Nana is drawing?' it sang in his head.

He glanced toward the unfinished painting of the island. It stood where it had always stood and, though he felt silly to be answering something he could not see, he nodded, saying in his head, 'It's wonderful but Nana, well, she hasn't —'

'Finished it? No. Now wouldn't it be lovely to help her?'

Jason rubbed his ears at the whispered words which he was certain were something else, as if someone was singing images into his head. But he found himself looking again at the unfinished painting of the island. Another melody of thought struck him which he suspected was not quite his own.

His hand moved to the table though he never told it to. He found himself selecting a tube of paint and then another and, squeezing them on to a saucer, mixed the acrylic with a few drops of water as he had watched his grandmother do. Then he grasped the sketchpad that lay on the table. As he picked up the paintbrush, the song whispered,

'Let's show Nana what's missing from her painting. Isn't that a grand idea, Jason? Wouldn't that be fun?'

As Margaret poured another cup of tea she glanced across the table, noting Dawn's brooding face. She wished she had told Jackie to drop dead

201

rather than be an accessory to an unwanted promise, but it was too late to change anything. Brushing up crumbs from the table, she could not stand the thick silence in the room. When she at last cleared her throat, her daughter-in-law looked up.

"Dawn, we're making wreaths in the church today. Maybe you'd like to join us."

"I don't think the women would want me. Not after what I said."

"Of course, they would. Please come." But Margaret gathered from her daughter-in-law's expression that any argument would be futile. She glanced at a boiled egg resting on the table, nesting in its egg cup. "I wish Jason would eat. He hasn't had any breakfast at all."

"I'll get him." Rising, Dawn strode to the door. "Jason?" she called. "Jason, come get your breakfast." Finding the living room empty, she swung back. "Where's Jason?"

"Has he gone upstairs?"

Dawn walked into the sunlit living room, standing at the foot of the stairs. "Jason, come down for breakfast," she called up.

When he did not answer, she found Margaret at her elbow.

"He has to be up there. He couldn't be anywhere else," Margaret said.

"I'll go get him."

Dawn trotted up to their bedroom but found it empty. She looked into the bathroom but he was not there and then into Margaret's room where Jason never ventured. But she looked anyway and, when she didn't find him, ran back downstairs.

"I'll look too," Margaret said. "He's hiding somewhere."

As Margaret looked through the house, Dawn unlocked the kitchen door to scan the back garden in case he had somehow got out. She looked into the old shed to make sure he was not hiding there, then down to the pier and dock below but saw nothing except the last of the mist burning off in the morning sun. When she ran back inside, she met Margaret standing in the middle of the kitchen.

"He has to be somewhere," Dawn said. "He couldn't just disappear."

"Did you look in the studio?"

"I thought you did."

After Margaret shook her head, they both hurried out.

When Dawn opened the door, the studio appeared to be empty. She was closing it when she noticed the armchair. It had been turned around so its back was facing the door. She walked closer, peering over the top. Jason sat beneath her. She saw how he had opened tubes of paint, mixing them in saucers to achieve his colors. He was finishing the bright painting of a dolphin in the sketchpad. Margaret joined her and looked, too.

"But he doesn't draw anymore," Dawn whispered.

"He certainly draws now."

When Jason looked up, Dawn could see his face glowing with pride but also mixed with fear and she realized he worried he had done something wrong. But his grandmother had also seen his look and studied the page with a keen eye.

"Jason, can I see that?" Margaret asked and, when he gave her the pad, she assessed it like an art critic. "It seems we have a professional in the making. Jason that's very, very good."

When Dawn studied it too, she realized what Margaret had said was true because the small painting of the white-faced dolphin was perfectly formed and it floated within the serenity of a sunlit sea.

"Jason, that's terrific!" she said and, when he smiled at the praise, the frustration of the day was gone. His face looked so fresh, so normal, and Dawn remembered the Children's Hospital and how Sam had growled with the voice of the dog he had drawn. She decided she had to try.

"Jason, can you look at me?" When he did, she asked, "Sweetie, can you tell me what the dolphin says? Can you do that? What does the dolphin say, Jason?"

But she realized her son was not yet ready because of his silence. Instead, he got up and walked to the window. As he stood in the sunlight his head rose quick like a hunting dog spotting its quarry. Following his gaze, Dawn looked too.

"It's back. It's like it's been waiting for us."

"So it seems," Margaret said, and the three looked down to the harbor where, at the dock, the dolphin drifted. Jason placed his hands on the glass as if wanting to call to it but the mammal suddenly submerged and was gone.

Margaret looked to her grandson and saw his disappointment. She glanced down at the sketchpad she still held and the painting of the dolphin he had drawn and a plan began to take shape.

"You know we have a great big coastline around here," she observed.

"What that's supposed to mean?" Dawn asked.

"Just up the bay. There's a small secluded inlet."

"You mean the cove? Michael and I used to go for walks there."

"Then you know how hard it is to get to."

"I don't understand," Dawn said, not sure where this was leading.

"It's just, well, not many people go there because the road is so bad. Certainly, no one is there most mornings or in the evening either, come to think of it. And if you happened to take a walk and accidentally ran into that dolphin while you were up there…"

Dawn finally understood what Margaret was driving at though she decided not to mention she had already run into the dolphin 'up there'.

"But what about Jackie? What if he saw us?" Dawn asked.

"As I recall, you promised you wouldn't feed it in the harbor," Margaret replied. "The cove isn't the harbor. Besides, Jackie can't be everywhere at once, can he?"

"No, he can't," Dawn said, and her voice arched. "And how, pray tell, might someone get to this secluded inlet if someone doesn't want to be seen?"

"You can walk there, of course. And there's the car if you can make it down the *boreen*. But the easiest way, the most — ah — unobtrusive way, is by boat. If you had one, of course."

"And who, I wonder, might have a boat?" Dawn asked, and looked her mother-in-law square in the eye. "You, perchance?"

Margaret's smile deepened. "Me, and no perchance about it."

CHAPTER NINETEEN

They found the punt in the boathouse at the very top of the harbor where Tomás had always stored it. As they stripped the wooden boat of its dusty tarpaulin, Margaret recalled the many times her husband had taken the family out in good weather to let Michael fish with his small rod. She remembered the time they had ventured to the mouth of the bay, where the water met the stiff chop of the real sea, and her son had hooked a sailfish. As he played it, the broad sail surfaced and Tomás remarked a fish like that was rare for these waters and that it had come in from the Gulf Stream miles to the west. While their son had fought the fish, Tomás had shouted orders and Margaret had given encouragement. But when it leaped, flashing blue and white as its long body slid up into the sunlight, it had broken Michael's light tackle and was gone.

She remembered what her son had said then as he leaned against the gunwale after the long fight. He had looked to the horizon and told her he was glad he had lost the fish because it was wild and free, and he hoped it would live forever. She was proud of him because he was only ten when he said it and, even then, seemed to understand the sanctity of life. She had made him a roast chicken dinner that night to celebrate the sailfish even though it was not Sunday.

As she placed the punt's tarpaulin on the floor against the wall, Margaret thought back on Michael and Tomás until she pulled the boathouse doors open. Then she asked Dawn for help and the two pushed the punt, which was cradled on a wooden trolley Tomás had built, down the cement ramp and into the tide. Margaret had remembered to bring the jerry can holding petrol and, after floating the boat, she filled the outboard engine and checked the oil level. Then she primed it and it started easily because Tomás had taught her, and since his death she had kept it well maintained.

"Take this in case you need to call me," she said over the belch of the idling engine, and held out a cell phone to her daughter-in-law.

Dawn remembered her own phone which was still hidden in her luggage. She had brought it from America but had not bought credit because it was too expensive to run in Ireland.

"But you might need it," Dawn objected as Margaret reached around, tucking it into her coat pocket.

"Take it. It will make me feel better if you do."

Dawn and Jason pulled on the life vests Margaret had brought and they both clambered into the punt. The boat rocked because of its narrow beam and Dawn grabbed the gunwale to steady herself.

"It's no different than the rib Michael taught you on," Margaret called from the dock. "It's longer and narrower is all. And it sits lower in the water than the rib so be careful how you go."

"That's easy for you to say," Dawn replied, but grinned to reassure her mother-in-law. She reached for the box of mackerel still half-full of fish that Margaret handed down, resting it in the bottom of the boat. As Jason climbed forward to sit on the cross-beam, she sat at the stern. When she gave the engine a bit of throttle the punt coasted into the harbor.

"I'll be at the church if you need me," Margaret called. "If anyone asks, you're going to the old castle up the bay."

"I'm more likely to end up in Africa," Dawn called back, and turned to check her pace across the water.

It was still morning as the punt motored into the main harbor and, as they moved past the pier and the line of fishing boats, Jason's face filled with excitement. But as they came a-beam Jackie's trawler, the wheelhouse door swung open and the fisherman stepped out on deck, stretching in the sunshine. When he leaned over the railing, gawking at the punt, Dawn swallowed hard and waved up at him.

"Jason, wave at Jackie," she said, and when he waved all Jackie did was wave back. Then Dawn gunned the throttle and they were past him, and she smiled to herself because Jason had understood she needed him and had helped.

They turned at the red buoy then into the bay where she set a westerly course. As they went, it seemed to Dawn that it could have been any other visit when she took Jason out while Michael waited for them on the pier. Just as always, Jason sat in the bow with a hand over the gunwale, playing with the waves while his mother steered. Like any other trip, Dawn called to him when she spotted a seabird. The gannet folded its wings against the long body, plunging into the water like an arrow as it hunted for fish. But she recognized there were differences, too, because Jason didn't chatter and laugh as he used to, and she was steering a punt not the rib, and they were transiting the deep waters of Bantry Bay and not the safety of an inlet or harbor. Most importantly, Michael would not be waiting for them when they returned.

'You take what you get and be glad for a day like today,' Dawn thought as she steered, watching the wind blow through her son's hair. Then she roused, looking toward the mainland for the cove.

"Jason, let me know when you see a marker. It's a big white stick. Nana told me to look for it."

Though he did not acknowledge her, his eyes hunted along the coastline. He pointed to a length of wood poking tall from the water where it had been driven into a snag. She slowed, turning. As they made their way in, she stayed in the center of the narrow inlet, afraid she would hole the wooden hull on a submerged rock. As they passed small islets, Jason shouted at a group of seals sunning themselves on the rocks. He laughed as one slid in, disturbed by his call. He turned to her, excited, as she aimed for the cove's center where she had swum with the dolphin. When they passed the final islet, she killed the engine.

Drifting on the light current, she looked to shore. The old concrete pier was empty as was the beach. She searched the *boreen* that led down to the cove, as well as the stand of yew trees behind the pier. Satisfied that they were alone, she pulled the fish box toward her as Jason scanned the water for the dolphin.

"It will come," Dawn said, and hoped all they had to do was wait.

Jackie worked on the pier beside his trawler, perspiring in the morning sun. As he stretched out the spare net for inspection — an old one he'd taken out of storage after the dead dolphin had ruined his good one — he kicked himself for his actions yesterday. He should not have scared the boy when he had chased away the other dolphin that had appeared near the dock nor angered the lad's mother. But as his hands rubbed a frayed section of the old net that needed mending, he remembered the promise he had extracted from the Yank and realized the bargain was worth the price.

"Feck it," he spat. "She should've known not to feed the fecker. Now she won't."

Anyway, when he saw them in the punt earlier that morning they had seemed in good form, so no hard feelings. He had been surprised when he spotted them but realized he shouldn't have been. The woman had always enjoyed playing around in Michael's rib so why not a punt?

The memory of his dead friend made his gut tighten. Before he had died, Michael had been a first-rate fisherman and good with money. Jackie had always gone to him for advice and thought how he could sure use it right now. But as he unknotted a tangle in the net stiff with salt, he remembered that Michael was not around and never would be again.

As he walked the net up the pier, he recalled how earlier that morning he had tussled with his money problems in the small house he lived in on the street above the town. He had thought about them as he made breakfast for his son, Peter, and throughout the drive as he took his son to school. They bothered him again when Peter got out of the car, turning back to remind his father that he wanted one of those expensive electronic games for his birthday which was only a few weeks away. When Jackie had suggested a bike instead, one he could get second-hand and on the cheap — not that he would tell Peter — the boy's disappointment overrode his financial burdens.

"Then the computer game it is," Jackie had found himself saying. 'If that's what you want then that's what you'll have." After the lad had given him a hug and run into school, Jackie had gripped the steering wheel tighter, worried about how he was going to pay for it.

Finished spreading the net across the pier, he thought hard as he walked back to the trawler, trying to reconcile the extra cost with the state of his bank account. Too many unplanned expenses had swept in, the latest being the destroyed net. But he remembered yesterday's catch he had managed with the spare net and the money he would make when it was sold, and how he could afford a few extra bob for his boy. He grinned in the sunshine, wishing Claire was around to see the look on Peter's face when he gave him the game on his birthday. At the thought of his lad's dead mother, he turned from the memory by tidying a hawser lying on the pier.

'It's only a trough of bad luck,' Jackie thought as he coiled the rope. 'Every boat rises on an incoming tide and tides always turn, don't they?'

But he knew this trough was a tough nut, and that his bad luck had started three years earlier with Claire's diagnosis for the breast cancer the doctors could not cure. A year later, he had buried her with his heart and used work as a salve and did his best for his son. He was aware that he was on a sort of human autopilot where days or nights or the day of the week mattered not at all. Since her death he had slept little and gained weight and, though he made sure Peter ate well, he no longer cared much about himself. Any time he had to make an important decision, he tried to calm himself long enough to think straight. But he seemed to fall from one bad choice to another, the worst being his decision to purchase the trawler.

Dropping the rope, he glanced up at his boat's shining superstructure knowing few would guess the sins that lay below the steel deck. He'd found her in Bantry, a class-looking fifty-five-footer with a host of modern gear going on the cheap. Smelling a bargain, he didn't even bother with the expense of an engineer's report. He had paid for it by selling the old tub he'd owned for years, together with most of his savings as well as Claire's life insurance. When he went back to hand over the cash, Jackie quashed the sudden worry he felt when the owner seemed too overjoyed to get the trawler off his hands. But he tucked away any misgivings and, steaming his new purchase down the bay to Kilcastle, believed Claire would have been proud of her husband's good judgment. But trouble started almost as soon as he tied up at the pier. First, it was the electrical system which shorted and had to be replaced. Then the hydraulics gave up and he spent a number of sleepless nights worrying until he got the trawler back in order.

With the boat running, he had fished her relentlessly and his bad luck seemed to change. The catches were good and the market prices high. But then the engine had started losing power and he suspected she needed a major overhaul which would cost a fortune. He was forced to bring her in to dry dock to have the work done and, though he had to borrow a fist-full of money, the engine now ran like a top. All that said, he had kicked himself hard about the boat's purchase ever since the day he'd bought her.

He thought how, back in the old days when his friend still lived in Kilcastle, Michael would have stopped him from such foolishness. He would have gone with Jackie to inspect the trawler using his proficient eye for detail and would have pointed out the pitfalls. Jackie would have let himself be swayed and Michael would have made him feel good about his change of mind with no loss of pride or self-belief at all.

Jackie frowned when he thought of what might have been and also the money he owed to the bank and almost everyone else. He thought of the ruined net he could not afford to replace and the dead dolphin, and the other one with the white face he had seen near the dock which would have ruined his livelihood had he not convinced his dead friend's wife to stop feeding it. He hoped no more would come into the area to spoil the fishing because Jackie needed every fish he could catch.

As his stomach played havoc with his breakfast, he looked up to see Padraig Downey, dressed in a swank business suit, ambling toward him across the pier. Having known the man since primary school, Jackie grumbled, remembering how Padraig had worked his socks off and, having left the town for university, had advanced in the world of finance.

Jackie waited, eyes narrowing on the man now thick around the middle. He seethed at Padraig's good luck: of how he had ended up with a cushy little number at one of the country's top banks while Jackie was forced to sweat for a living. He knew Padraig came back to town only to see his mother. But on this occasion, he suspected the banker's mam wasn't the only reason for the visit. Instead, it was due to another decision Jackie had been forced to make.

When his trawler's engine had neared meltdown and required an overhaul, he had approached the town's credit union for a loan. They had turned him down flat. Then he remembered Padraig and had run up to the bank's headquarters in Cork City. Sitting down with his old schoolmate, Jackie had perched on a high-backed chair as the banker examined the loan application.

"You want how much?" Padraig had grumbled, reading the bottom line.

"A hundred."

"*A hundred thousand euro?*"

"Maybe a bit less," Jackie had faltered. "Padraig, it's a complete overhaul, just as I wrote there. That's what it costs."

"But a hundred grand? Come on, lad. That's a bit rich."

"Keep reading. The fishing's good. Prices are rising. See the income line? You'll get it back," he had explained, pointing to the application and trying not to squirm.

"Jackie, those are projections," the banker had said, unmoved.

"Oh, come on, Padraig. We've known each other since we were in short pants. Remember all the football we played together?"

"That's true, that's true. But Jackie, this is business." The banker had leaned back, fingers drumming on his desk. "It's a lot of money. You sure you can make the repayments?"

"Isn't that what I just said?"

"What can you put up as collateral?"

"Collateral?" Jackie had replied, feeling sweat on his lip. "You know I got the house."

"But your house is mortgaged, isn't it? If something went wrong the mortgage company would have first call." The banker's eyes had focused on him like lasers. "What shape's the trawler in?"

"The trawler?" Jackie had asked, not sure where the banker was heading. "After the overhaul she'll be first-class."

"Then we'll use the trawler as collateral."

"My boat?"

"Your boat, Jackie," the banker had insisted, holding out a pen. "That's the deal. It's your call, my friend."

Jackie had to sign for the tough condition. For the first few months he had made the payments with no problem. But then he had hit more trouble as prices fell and catches soured. As his savings evaporated, he had found himself a-ground. Now, as the banker toddled across the pier toward him on this unexpected visit, Jackie swallowed hard and forced himself to extend a hand.

"Morning Padraig," he said as they shook. "Down to see the mother? How is she?"

"She's good," Padraig returned with a tight smile. He scanned Jackie's boat as if he had nothing on his mind at all. "So, Jackie, how's the trawler? Was that overhaul worth it?"

"Every penny. Running like she's brand new."

"That's good. And the fishing? How's that going?"

"On the up. Just took a couple ton to market."

"Tons?" the banker said, and Jackie saw the calculating look in the man's eyes. "And you got a good price?"

"Good enough," Jackie replied, feeling himself bristle. "Padraig, you didn't come down just to see your mam. If it was me you wanted to see I'd have driven up to Cork."

"Jackie, don't do that."

"Do what?"

"As if you'd drive up to see me. You told me when you asked for the loan that things were improving."

"And they are!"

"Are they? Then why haven't you made a payment in seven months?"

"Six," Jackie countered as he recalled how his financial condition had forced him to stop the bank payments. "Padraig, I was going to phone you about that."

"But you didn't. And you didn't answer the bank's warning letters. Jackie, you and I have known each other for over thirty years. When you needed the loan, I got it for you."

"It's not like the bank isn't charging any interest," Jackie grumbled. "You'll get your due. I'll have the money in for the catch this week and I'll write a check for a few pound."

"You don't understand, Jackie. The bank wants all of it."

"Six months? Where do you think I'm going to get six months all at once?"

"You're not listening. I said, *all of it*. We're calling in the loan."

"But that's a hundred grand! I don't have that kind of money."

"Yes, you do. Part of it anyway." When the banker's eyes swung again to the boat Jackie had to lean against her stern.

"You wouldn't do that. Padraig, we grew up together for feck sake. What's the bank going to do with an old trawler?"

"You never engaged with us. You never told the bank you were in trouble. You just stopped paying. What did you think was going to happen?"

"You're not taking my boat. It's mine. I can't make a living without it." He stepped close, eyes level with the banker's. "You try to take my boat and I'll fight you. I'll sue the bank for every penny it's got."

"And you'll lose."

"Then give me more time," he pleaded, wiping his lips. "The fish are back. I'm making quota again. It's just a matter of keeping at it. Padraig, don't do this."

The banker considered. "How much can you give us right now?"

"Two, maybe three months. But that's just a guess."

"You can't do the seven?"

"It's six, and no I can't. I got to live too, don't I?"

"Okay. Let me talk to the board but I'm not promising anything. Get the money in and keep it coming. Understood?"

The banker turned without even a handshake. Jackie kept his eye on the man as he strode back across the pier, past Jackie's mate who hurried toward the trawler.

"You! Gobshite!" Jackie roared, and the mate stopped in his tracks. "Get the damned boat ready. We're taking her out."

"You said we got two weeks off," his mate squealed. "I thought we already caught the month's quota."

"Feck the month's quota. Get her ready."

"What about the net? It's fucked," the mate said, kicking at the spare net stretched out on the pier.

"Enough of your excuses. Go on and get below!" As his mate scrambled below decks Jackie bent to the spare net, praying it would hold together long enough for another few trips. As he did, he remembered his son's birthday and hoped the good fishing would hold. Otherwise, Jackie realized, he'd have to break the promise he'd made to Peter for the present. He looked up, seeing the banker drive away in his expensive car.

"Feck the bastards," Jackie muttered, spitting on the concrete. "Feck 'em all."

In the cove, Dawn and Jason had floated in the punt for over an hour with no sign of the dolphin.

"It'll find us, kiddo," she ventured. But she worried it wouldn't and feared her son's new-found laugher would turn into a fading memory. She looked up at a sun that had climbed into a cloudless sky and again scanned the still water.

"Let's go further up the bay. We'll find it there," she said with false enthusiasm. But Jason's disappointed face was unchanged as she turned to the outboard motor and prepared to get under way.

She swung back when hearing her son's quick intake of breath. Looking out to the water, she had to shield her eyes against the glare. Then she caught the unmistakable sound of venting and saw the dorsal fin slice into the cove.

Jason scrambled to his feet, peering at the sea. She put a hand to the gunwale, steading herself against the boat's sudden rocking.

"Honey, sit down, okay?" she said, reaching for the fish box. "Here, give him this. You know what to do."

He sat and, taking the mackerel, stretched out over the water. The dolphin vented again, swimming toward the boat. But it stopped short of the dangling fish, floating just out of reach.

"What's wrong with it?" Dawn grumbled. Picking up another mackerel, she sniffed at it. "Christ, how can they eat these things?" she asked and her son grinned. She leaned over the gunwale and held out a fish, too.

"Come here, dolphin. Here's a nice juicy fish. Oh, come on and take the damned thing."

She watched the water stir as the dolphin edged closer but it stopped again.

"Quit playing with us," Dawn barked, waving the fish. "Look, here's a fish just for you. Now take it or we're leaving." She stood, stretching out even further. As the boat leaned, water sloshed over the gunwale. The ocean stirred again as the dolphin crept to the side of the boat. She could see its long beak and could swear she saw humor in its face. It bumped against the wooden hull but still did not take the fish.

"Oh, come on," she said, stretching out as far as she could. "Take it!"

The punt rocked again, her feet slipping on the wet wood. Arms flailing, she reached for a handhold but missed, falling headlong into the sea. She surfaced, sputtering. Jason laughed and, when she heard the dolphin squeal, could swear it was laughing at her, too.

"It's not funny," she said, but found herself giggling. "Help your mother up." Jason took her outstretched hand and helped to lever her back into the punt. When she was settled, the dolphin moved to the other end of the boat, taking the fish from her son. Jason looked back, his face shining.

"I guess he likes yours better than mine," she said. "Keep giving it fish so it won't swim off."

They spent a half-hour feeding the dolphin and, when Jason tired of being in the boat, she motored over to the pier and tied up. She stood in the warm sunlight, watching her son play with the dolphin. As it sped along the pier, Jason threw a fish high and the dolphin jumped to catch it. He threw another one still higher and the dolphin leaped just as high, water cascading from its back to reach it. She saw how her boy would fake throwing it one way then turn and throw it another, and how his actions forced the dolphin to change direction in mid-flight. He laughed brightly when his cleverness sometimes caused the dolphin to miss a fish, and he looked to his mother with pleasure. She thought how, just like any young friends, they mimicked and teased each other.

As the morning drifted by, she was swept up in the joy of watching her child. The dolphin leaped and Jason laughed as he ran along the pier, droplets glittering in the sunlight as the dolphin crashed back into the sea. Their fun was spoiled only once when the mast of a trawler appeared and glided past the cove's entrance, its hull concealed by the inlet's outer rocks. She thought it was Jackie's trawler and worried he might spot them but the cove was well hidden behind the hills and she thought they could not be seen.

In the early afternoon she heard the crush of tires against broken scree. Her mother-in-law's old green Morris Minor bounced down the *boreen*, its underbelly scraping against the ruined road. Margaret parked next to the water, waving as she got out, and stepped up on to the pier.

"The women are taking a break. I thought I'd visit before I have to go back to the church," Margaret said and, almost as an afterthought, added, "Did you see Jackie's boat?"

"I thought it was him," Dawn replied. "Let's forget about Jackie. As far as I'm concerned, he can take a leap."

"A true Irishman would say something less graceful."

"Like, he can piss-off?" Dawn replied. "Well, he can."

Margaret laughed, studying her grandson who stood on the pier. "How is he?"

"Watch," Dawn said, and turned to her son. "Jason, show Nana how good you are at throwing a fish."

Jason drew back, flinging a mackerel as far as he could. The dolphin leaped and Margaret watched the immense black and white body emerge from the cove, flutes swinging as water poured from its back. It caught the fish, crashing back into the sea.

"Oh, my Lord," Margaret said, hiding her fear at the dolphin's great size. "Jason that's wonderful."

"Jason, do it again!"

Spotting the dolphin floating in the swells, he picked up another fish. He wound up to throw but, pausing in mid-action, he instead knelt down on the pier. Dawn saw how his eyes met the mammal's. Her scalp tingled as the dolphin swam closer.

"What are they doing?" Margaret asked.

"Wait. Hold still."

Jason held out an arm, fingers splayed wide. Dawn caught her breath as the dolphin rose high next to the dock. As its beak touched Jason's hand, she realized it was their first physical contact. The white-faced dolphin rose higher to nuzzle even closer. Jason reached out with his other arm, taking the dolphin in an awkward embrace.

The dolphin released itself from the boy and submerged back into the sea, swimming up the narrow inlet to the safety of the bay. For a long time, Dawn stood watching the happiness in her son's face not ever wanting the moment to pass.

CHAPTER TWENTY

They had no trouble returning the punt to the boathouse nor were they questioned by anyone as to their destination. Dawn walked across the square with Jason skipping at her side, encouraging his joy by talking about the dolphin. After they climbed the hill to the house, she started making them a late lunch.

"Jase, go upstairs and take out a change of clothes. I have to shower but we'll eat first. How's that?"

He started out but at the door turned to her as if considering an issue of great importance. He ran back, coming into her arms. She held him tight, feeling the warmth of his breath against her cheek. When he skipped out of the room, she stood quite still thinking about the change in her son and this first embrace since the accident. As she took out a loaf of bread, her heart felt lighter than it had in months. Turning from the counter, her eyes settled on the kitchen table. A pile of cut yew lay there. Margaret must have forgotten it when she had returned to the church. Dawn picked up a branch, studying it. She recalled what Carol had showed her and how Joan and the other women had made the wreaths. She also remembered what she had said to them and the heartache her words had caused.

Dawn curled the piece of greenery into a circle and, picking up another branch, saw how with a little wire she could make a wreath. She suddenly wanted to talk to the women very much.

The Church of All Saints was built in 1907. It could hold a thousand worshippers and in the old days was packed tight on Sundays because back then the peninsula was well populated. But over the years families were forced to emigrate in search of work, as many Irish did throughout the country's history. In recent times half the pews stood empty. Yet, the church remained a focal point for the town's faithful and, as Margaret bent a branch into a circle, her eyes wandered to the soaring limestone columns which supported the nave's vaulted ceiling. She thought the architect had designed it that way, compelling worshippers to look to heaven as they prayed. On sunny days like today, the tall stained-glass windows illuminated the church in a glow of peace.

She glanced down the trestle tables which stood below the carved stone altar, seeing the women chatting as an Irish country tune tumbled from a CD player. They fashioned wreaths to remember lost loved ones but today there was no sadness because it was replaced by busy hands. The sadness would come later, on Remembrance Day. As Margaret worked, she thought of her late husband and son which made her think of Jason and the dolphin. There had been talk of the *crater* when she had arrived back after visiting her family at the cove, and Carol had started it.

"Did you see it?" Carol had asked the other women. "Did any of you spot it in the harbor?" But no one at the table had seen it and, at first, they did not believe her. "Ask Margaret," Carol had insisted. "Can you believe they were actually feeding it?"

"It's not in the harbor now," Margaret had replied without looking up. "Jackie chased it away."

The women chattered about its sudden appearance and worried how it might affect the town's income if it came back, and agreed that Jackie had done the right thing.

"Besides, it's dangerous," Carol had continued. "Lydia, tell them how big it was. Wasn't it a monster?"

But Lydia, who stood on the other side of the table helping an old woman bent with rheumatism, said nothing. Joan had rescued the situation by responding, "Oh for God's sake Carol. It's only a dolphin and it's gone now so why make a fuss over it?"

Margaret had suppressed a smile because she knew the truth to be far different. The conversation had turned to other things and, concentrating on her wreath, she wondered if her family had returned from their adventure.

As Margaret cut another length of ribbon, the front door opened at the far end of the church. When Dawn and Jason walked in, she noted how her daughter-in-law stood in the aisle looking like a lost soul. She glanced at Carol and, realizing the woman had not yet seen them, uttered a quick prayer that peace could be restored.

On the other side of the church, Dawn stood with her son surrounded by a sea of empty pews. She held a half-made wreath in one hand and, seeing the women, chided herself for talking to them like an ass.

"Okay, Jason. Here we go," she whispered, forcing her foot in the right direction.

They walked down the long center aisle and with each step she planned her words of apology. But then she caught Margaret peering at her with worried eyes and saw Carol noticing Margaret's look, and how the other women noticed Carol. When everyone looked up, whispering to each other, Dawn stopped dead in the aisle, her planned apology evaporating. She took a deep breath.

"Hello! I'm sorry to interrupt," she called but her words were too loud, echoing across the great vault of the church. The whispering stopped as the women stared. Clearing her throat Dawn wished the floor would open up. "It's just, well you see…look, I want to apologize," she tried again, but this time her voice was too soft.

"What's she on about?" the old woman working with Lydia asked, bending to girl. "Tell her to speak up!"

"She didn't say a thing," Carol trumpeted, having decided to ignore the intruder. "Joan, please hand me the scissors."

"Carol, shut your gob," Joan replied and, after sneezing, turned off the CD player. "Go on, Dawn. We're listening."

Dawn's cheeks turned crimson in the silence as she took another breath.

"I was saying I owe you all an apology. What I said when you were at Margaret's — the words I used — it wasn't right. I sort of, you know..." But their faces said they didn't know. "Look. I'm occasionally too direct, okay? That's what Michael always said. Sometimes I can be a real Bozo." The women reacted to the Boston term with puzzled looks. "Maybe that's not the right word. What I'm trying to say is, I wish I could take back what I said. I wish you could pretend it never happened. And I was hoping, maybe if you wanted me to, I could help. If you needed any more help, of course."

She held up the half-finished wreath. One of the branches came unstuck, falling to the floor. She saw the women shift as Carol frowned. Standing midway down a table, Margaret gazed back at her with pity.

"Or maybe not," Dawn said to no one. "Okay, Jason. Let's go home."

She grasped his shoulder, leading him toward the front door. A clatter of shoes hit the wooden floor behind her and a hand caught her elbow. Dawn turned, finding Joan and the old woman who had been standing next to Lydia.

"You want to help, Gersha? Is that what you said?" the old woman, whose name Dawn later learned was Mary, asked, and Joan took her broken wreath and examined it.

"If this is all you can do you better come with us," Joan sniffed, wiping her nose with a tissue. "My friend, it appears you're the one who needs the help."

"What about the others? Are you sure?" Dawn questioned, glancing to the women who still whispered at the tables.

"Most are as toothless as old flounders," Mary said, patting her arm. "Don't you take any heed of them. Now come along with us."

For the rest of the afternoon Dawn worked alongside them, sensing the women's forgiveness as they included her in their activities. Standing between Margaret and Joan, she relaxed as they showed her what to do. Joan tore Dawn's first poor attempt at a wreath to pieces, showing her how to shape one properly by fixing it with wire and finishing it off with a great bow of ribbon. Dawn was surprised by the careful attention the women paid to their task and how long it took to finish each wreath. As they worked, she listened to the women. They talked of the fine weather they hoped would last, and the progress of their children and grandchildren at school. They threw questions to her about her stay with Margaret and commented on how well Jason looked, and encouraged Dawn to join them in the infectious laughter which sometimes filled the church. When she placed her first finished wreath on the growing pile stacked at the side of the altar, she couldn't help but wonder at the number of them.

"How many wreaths did you say you're making?" she asked Joan. But Carol, who had ignored Dawn until now, answered.

"Ninety-four."

"Ninety-four of them?" Dawn asked, surprised. "Why so many?"

But Carol didn't bother answering so Joan explained the mystery. "We make a wreath for each person lost at sea over the past forty years."

"Have that many died?" Dawn asked, and did not know what else to say or if she should say anything.

"Joan, I thought you were going to cut some more yew," Carol barked, motioning to the small piles of greenery left on the tables. "I know you're still not feeling well so let me know if I need to recruit someone else."

"I'll get some if you tell me what to do," Dawn offered.

"I wouldn't want you exerting yourself," Carol sniffed. "If it comes to it, I'll do it myself."

When Carol turned away, Dawn saw Margaret's look of warning and schooled herself to remain silent. She looked for Jason, finding him sitting in the front pew. His eyes were fastened on Lydia who was still helping the old woman. He got up and, venturing to the table, stood in front of the girl who completely ignored him. Frustrated, he retreated back to stand beside his mother.

"Lydia won't talk to you because she's still upset," Margaret said as she worked. "You wouldn't play with her when she came to the house the other day. Remember, Jason?"

"Why don't you tell her you're sorry?" Dawn suggested. "If you do, she might make friends again. Go on. Give it a try."

Dawn watched as he shuffled back to his friend but Lydia still ignored him. At last, he held out a hand. The girl understood his silent apology and, when she took it, all was forgiven. The pair ran down the center aisle, hand-in-hand, hiding from each other in the pews.

"Wouldn't it be wonderful if we could all be like kids?" Joan grumbled, glancing at Carol. "Oh, if only holding hands could solve the world's troubles."

Dawn agreed though she said nothing.

At the far side of the nave the sacristy door opened. Father Danny walked out, stepping up to the lectern to organize some papers. Seeing him made her think again of what she had said to the women at Margaret's house and her cruel remarks about lost loved ones. She remembered that the priest had been there to hear every word and realized she had more work to do. When Father Danny walked back into the sacristy, Dawn glanced at her mother-in-law

"I'll be back in a minute," Dawn said, and stepped toward the sacristy door.

Father Danny walked through the clutter of the small room, trying to find his glasses. The sacristy acted as office, wardrobe and storage for the church. On one side his albs, chasubles, and stoles hung from a steel frame in a bright palette of colors. On the other, boxes of candles, missals, and old hymnals lay stacked on the floor. The priest used the disorganized silence to prepare for Mass or, on other occasions, to meditate with members of his flock over the troubles that sometimes visited them. At such times he worried his guidance would never be enough. But he took sustenance in occasionally seeing his counsel help bind the wounds they suffered, and prayed for the gifts of careful listening and the right words to help those in need. When he opened the door to the quiet knock and found the American waiting, the priest sensed he would require all the wisdom his gifts could muster.

"Dawn! Come in, come in!" Extending his hand, she grasped it tight.

"Could I have a word with you, Father? That is, if you're not busy?"

"Since when was I ever too busy for you? Let me get you a seat."

He moved piles of paper from two folding chairs and slid them side-by-side. But when he sat his visitor turned from him, pacing restlessly across the room.

"Father, about the other day at Margaret's house," Dawn said. "I'm sorry. I want to apologize."

"You were upset. That's understandable. Michael is a man to be missed."

But the priest realized he had stung her because the woman's face clouded with pain. He tapped the chair next to him and she sat. Finding his glasses in his breast pocket, he took his time polishing them as he chose his words.

"How well I remember your wedding," he said, balancing the glasses on his nose. "I don't think I have ever seen a couple more in love or so suited to each other. Is it any wonder you miss him?" When she did not answer he plucked some lint from his shirt, looking up at the sunlit window. "Dawn, you know what the Day of Remembrance is about, don't you?"

"Not the details. Michael mentioned it but he never really explained. I guess he used to attend when he lived here."

"That's right. Michael used to come to honor his father." The priest leaned back, seeking the words to explain. "Every year we hold a special Mass of remembrance for those lost at sea. After Mass we comfort the living by walking to the pier to bless the fishing fleet and pray for the safety of those who work on them. Later, we board the lifeboat and it takes us out beyond the bay. Out there, in the real ocean, anyone who has suffered the loss of a loved one throws their wreath into the sea. So, for everyone who has been lost, a wreath marks their passing as well as their lives and we pray it brings peace to those resting in the ocean's vastness."

She looked up, puzzled. "They throw in the wreaths we're making? I didn't know that."

"It's our way of remembering them. It's our way of learning to live without them."

"I don't think I can do that. I don't want to learn to live without Michael."

He shifted in the chair, knowing he must choose his words carefully. "I'm not asking you to forget him. That's why we remember them. But if you can't learn to let go, life is going to be harder for you than it has to be." He heard her foot tapping on the floor and prayed what he said next would give her comfort. "Dawn, remember this. Just because they're gone doesn't mean we won't be with them someday."

"Do you really believe that?" she asked. He suddenly realized the source of her anxiety and sensed just how careful he must be.

"It's the cornerstone of my faith," he said simply. "It's what the Church teaches. It's what Christ suffered for. My faith says that someday in Heaven I'll rejoin all those I've lost."

He worried he brought her no comfort because she rose, pacing back across the room.

"Maybe you'll think it's a sin, Father," she said, "but it sounds so airy-fairy. I remember the nuns teaching catechism at Catholic School. Heaven and Hell, Limbo and Purgatory. It's nuts. How can you believe in something you can't see?"

At her words, he remembered what she had said at Margaret's home.

"'Poof'. Isn't that the word you used?" the priest asked and couldn't help but chuckle.

"I said I was sorry. I shouldn't have said it," she replied, turning to him. "I'm damned forever, right?"

"Not at all. Dawn, you've put your finger on a point that has troubled religious scholars for two millennia and even longer than that. Let me tell you, if you're looking for proof of divine eternity you've come to the wrong man because I'm no authority."

"But you're a priest. You're supposed to know."

"Me? Know?" he laughed. "Dawn, all I know is how much I don't know. But I do know this. Finding faith is always hard work. Did you ever hear of a religious philosopher named Paul Tillich?" She shook her head at the name. "He wrote a very, very comprehensive text regarding the attributes of faith. Like many before him, he was attempting to prove faith should have some sort of basis in reality. Faith should have an *explanation*. But at the end of it all do you know what he advised?"

"No," she replied.

"This is what he discovered," he continued, chuckling again. "To believe you don't need to be a theological know-it-all. Instead, all you have to do is — are you ready for this?"

"What?"

"Jump."

"Jump?"

He smiled at her incredulity. "That's right. Make a leap of faith."

"A what?" Dawn asked, straining to understand. "But that's impossible. Are you telling me he never found any proof?"

"You mean in the hereafter? No. He didn't," he said, his smile filled with irony. "Dawn, no one has. And those who say they have are thought to be either crazy or liars." His forehead furrowed, thinking how he could help her understand. "You've heard of the miracle of Fatima, haven't you? Three children swore on a stack of Bibles that they saw a vision of Our Lady. Do you know what the initial reaction was to their claim?"

"I don't have any idea."

"People thought they were insane."

She frowned at that. "Insane? But the Church believed them, didn't they?"

"Eventually. But miracles will always be ridiculed. They seldom leave behind any evidence."

"So, no one can really prove it," Dawn said, finding his eyes again. "Father, do you believe what the children said about seeing Mary?" He nodded. "Even without proof?" He nodded again. "How?"

"Because I choose to take a leap of faith," he said, and placed a warm hand on her shoulder. "Dawn, did you know I've lost both of my parents as well as my younger sister? Of course, I can no longer touch them. And many believe I can no longer talk to them or listen to them or laugh with them or cry with them. And yet —" He rose from the chair, studying the quiet sanctuary and the light which danced through the stained-glass window. "I choose to believe differently."

"What do you believe?"

"I believe they're here," he replied, throwing his arms open wide. "Right here. I talk to them. I pray with them. I love them and they still love me. They give me strength and hope and I count on them to guide me through life's journey. I have no proof, of course, so I take a page from Tillich. I leap into my faith with my eyes wide shut and without any idea of where I'll end up." He walked back to her, placing his hand under her chin, lifting it. "Couldn't you do that too, Dawn McCarthy? Couldn't you jump into the unknown and trust enough to believe?"

"I don't know," she whispered, and he smiled at her words.

"Neither did I. But like me, maybe you could try."

She wiped away her tears and nodded. "How about if I try to try?"

"If trying to try is all you can do, it's good enough for me."

As she stepped to the door, he worried he had not done enough to help. "Dawn, at the Remembrance Mass, would you say a few words about Michael? I think everyone would appreciate it."

He saw gratitude in her wistful smile. "I think Michael would like that. Jason and I would like it, too. Thank you, Father Danny. Thank you for your kindness." Then she was out the door and he prayed he had said the right things.

When Dawn re-entered the main body of the church, she realized the women were taking a break because half of them were gone and the rest stood in a circle chatting and drinking tea. She looked for Jason and Margaret but at first couldn't find them. Then she saw them at the other end of the church. She walked down a side aisle to where they stood before a wooden statue hidden in an alcove. Margaret was lighting a candle.

"Who's that?" Dawn asked, looking up at the statue.

"It's the Saint of miracles," Margaret replied. "Do you want to light a candle?"

Dawn hesitated but Jason looked at her with the glow of firelight in his eyes. She picked a candle from a box and, lighting it from Margaret's, placed it in the holder. As she listened to her mother-in-law's words of prayer, she watched the candles burn side-by-side. In the steady flames she realized she did have faith if only in the love she held for her family.

CHAPTER TWENTY-ONE

That evening after a quick meal of rasher sandwiches and tea, Dawn and Jason again took the punt to the cove where they found the dolphin already waiting. Overhead, the clouds were lit in veils of pink, the sun's warmth reflecting off the water as her son played with his friend.

To Dawn, it seemed the evening's session was more purposeful because they dispensed with the need for fish as the two played games. Jason ran along the pier, the dolphin swimming close beside him and, when her son backtracked, the dolphin turned to follow. Or, as he spun like a top, the dolphin stood high out of the water, pirouetting in circles, and Jason shouted as the mammal acted the clown. Or, the dolphin leaped in multiple bursts as her son pursued him with skipping leaps. The dolphin brought an end to their play when it rose at the side of the pier and, as Jason reached out, nestled in close to him. Then it backed into the water and swam through the narrow inlet toward the open sea.

The distant call of a corncrake echoed between the hills. As Dawn watched the mammal's departure, her son's hand searched for hers. When she took it, he squeezed and she squeezed back. It was only a beginning, she thought, and understood they still had a long way to go before he might talk again. But she smiled, knowing a beginning was better than no beginning at all.

When they returned to the house no one was sleepy. Margaret made them a late snack as Dawn told her of their time with the dolphin and the progress Jason was making. Seeing her grandson's excitement and rather than taking him to bed, his grandmother retrieved the sketchpad and acrylics. As the women cleaned up, Jason sat at the kitchen table painting the dolphin leaping from the sea. When he finished, he was still not ready to go to bed. Dawn sat beside him, rolling her neck to loosen the stiff muscles.

"You two come with me," Margaret said, and led them into the living room. They waited as she went upstairs, coming down in a bright leotard.

"You can't be serious," Dawn laughed. "You're doing Yoga? At this hour?"

"That's right. And so are you two."

Margaret turned on some music and, standing in the middle of the floor, stretched and bent in time to the beat. "Breathe, one, two, three. Jason, come on! You too, Dawn. Get up here."

Jason gave a sideways look to his mother as they rose from the couch. They joined Margaret, moving to the older woman's instructions. "Now reach! one, two, three. And breathe! one, two, three. Now reach again!"

Dawn saw Jason breathing and reaching and, as he giggled, decided to spring a trap on him.

"Stop, Margaret, stop! It's too much!"

Collapsing to the floor in pretended exhaustion, Dawn watched her son fall for it as he ran to help her. She reached up, grabbing him, and as she tickled his sides he howled with laughter. She rolled him over, pinning him to the floor, recalling how Jason enjoyed the roughhousing he used to receive from his father.

"Okay, Monkey!" she said as he giggled. "You're going to get it!"

She tickled him again and, as he squirmed, realized she had not heard him laugh so hard in over a year. She stopped but his face was full of mischief as if saying 'Do it again, Mom. Please! Do it again!' He looked so healthy, so full of life, that she couldn't help but try once more.

"Jason, hey. Come on kiddo, look at me." When he looked, she asked, "Jason, what does the dolphin say? Can you do that? What does it say, Jason?" But all he did was turn away.

She thought hard and, deciding on a different tack, scrunched her face into a funny shape. "Does the dolphin say 'Cree-cree-cree'? Does it say that, Jason? Doesn't it say 'Cree-cree-cree'?"

He would not try. But because of his smile she suspected they journeyed down the right path. 'All I have to do is find the key that will open the door to him,' she thought, gazing at his glowing face. 'If I do, he'll talk again.' She pushed back his hair, planting a kiss on his

forehead. When he wrapped his arms around her, she was filled with renewed determination to find an answer.

That night Dawn did not have nightmares but dreamed instead that she swam through an open sea in search of treasure. She was not frightened by the ocean's depth but only at her aloneness and the conviction that her quest would never come to an end. Tiring, treading water, she saw a colony of seagulls fishing an empty sea. They swooped and dived, screaming at the fruitlessness of their hunt. She realized that like them she would have to continue her journey without the benefit of a chart to guide her.

It was then she heard the thundering song as a pod of dolphins stampeded toward her, the sea boiling from their play. Then she was within the herd and, covering her head, feared she would be crushed by their numbers. When she looked up the surging armada was gone and she thought she was alone again. But she heard a voice of laughter and found the white-faced dolphin tail-standing high beside her. Its eyes held a familiarity she had known before and, when it plunged beneath the surface, she felt it pushing her legs apart, lifting her from the sea.

She rode on its back, holding tight to the dorsal fin, skipping fast over gentle waves. She felt its strength beneath her, the warm heart beating against her thighs, and let go of her fear. The wind whipped through her hair and she laughed, thinking she was a creature of the sea and the ocean was her home, and all she needed was to find the treasure and her life would be complete.

They beat on for many miles and, as they approached a quiet shore, the dolphin released her. She floated in shallow waters and as the mammal gazed at her, she could see the beckoning in its eyes. When it dived, she followed but, swimming deep, feared she would drown. But she found she did not need breath because her lungs held all that she needed and instead she kicked hard to follow it even deeper. As they approached the sandy bottom, she saw something glitter and, moving closer, discovered it was a golden key. It rested on the sand behind a curtain of sealight. At first, she thought it was like any ordinary key. But then it pulsed and throbbed like a living thing and all she had to do was push through the shimmering light and the prize would be hers. But she discovered the curtain of light was as tough as old leather, blocking her efforts behind a glittering fortress. She pushed harder and the curtain bent further, and at last she broke through. When her fingers clasped the key, she saw how it was like any key except its teeth were not sharp, and it beat in her palm like a faithful heart.

In her dream, she thought, 'This is the key. The one that will open the door to my son. All I have to do is clutch it tight and he'll talk again.'

But as she closed her hand, blinding light filled the sea. When it receded and she opened her eyes, the key was gone. Instead, her palm was filled with golden sand. The sea's current swept it up and, though she clenched her hand tight, she could not stop the grains from drifting through her fingers. Frantic, she clawed at the sandy bottom where they had mingled with millions of other fine grains.

'It's gone. I'll never find it,' she thought.

'Oh, yes you will.'

Dawn bolted upright in bed. "Michael?"

She searched the bedroom but found only Jason sleeping beside her. Propping her head on the pillow, she dismissed the voice of her husband as wishful thinking. Yet, she couldn't dismiss the rest of the dream. She remembered the glittering key and realized there was something to it. The key was here, right here, somewhere around her. All she had to do was look and when she found it, hold on tight. When she turned back to her son, she remembered the plan to take him to the cove again that day. Getting up to look through the window, she saw the harbor covered in pelting rain.

"Don't worry," she said to Jason who, just awake, looked up with sleepy eyes. "It's supposed to clear this afternoon. We'll go then."

After they finished breakfast, Margaret suggested that her grandson paint with her while they waited for the rain to stop. Dawn told them she would use the time to run into town on an errand. She looked into the studio before she left and found both hard at work. Jason was painting another picture of the dolphin while Margaret was making sketches for her unfinished canvas of Solas Mór. Satisfied that they were happy, Dawn put on her coat and slipped out.

She had not stopped thinking about her dream all morning. As she thought it over, she remembered an article she'd read months earlier when Jason was still in the hospital. Wanting to research what little she remembered of it she decided to pay a visit to the town's library, hoping it might have the resources she needed.

Recalling its location on a narrow laneway between the main street and the pier, she walked through the town square to get to it. A weekday market was in progress, the line of stalls selling used tools, cheap fashion, and flowering shrubs in all shapes and sizes. Hawkers wearing slickers against the weather called to her, hoping for a purchase. She fended them off, hurrying past the Tea Kettle Coffee Shop which was crowded with people finding shelter. She caught sight of the old woman, Mary from the church, who sipped a cup of tea behind the front window. When she waved and Mary waved back, Dawn pulled her raincoat tighter and hurried on.

When she found the library she stood for a moment on the wet sidewalk, studying the long windows. Printed notices for mature student classes, cooking workshops, and photography competitions were taped to it as well as a notice about Remembrance Day. Though Margaret had mentioned the date she had forgotten how close it was. She found herself looking forward to it despite her original misgivings and recognized her thinking as a sea change, as if her old attitude had been swept up in a turning tide. Opening the front door, she stepped inside.

Dawn had never visited the library and it was even smaller than she had anticipated. As she removed her coat she wondered if it could offer any help at all. A half-dozen stacks contained a limited number of books. When she scanned the shelves she found only aging fiction, volumes on local history, a cooking section, another on spirituality and self-help, and a large children's area. She thought she didn't have a prayer. She heard a sneeze and saw Joan walk out from a back room.

"Bless you," Dawn said, stepping to the counter. "I thought you were over that flu."

"So did I but it's come back," Joan said, sneezing again. "Now, how can I help?"

"I was just wondering. You don't have anything on dolphin therapy, do you?"

"Dolphin therapy? I don't get many requests for a topic like that."

"I know it's pretty obscure. I read something about it in Boston and it got me curious. Would you have anything?"

"Are you kidding? Here? You'd have to go up to Dublin or Cork for such a specialized subject. Or I could order it for you if you've got a title."

"No, I don't. But if I did, how long would it take to get here?"

"Oh, maybe a couple of weeks."

"A couple of weeks?" she asked, and thought again. "Then could I use your Internet? Margaret doesn't own a computer and I'm sure I could find something if I had access."

"It's banjaxed. We're not getting a signal."

"Oh. When will it be fixed?"

"Maybe a couple of weeks," Joan replied again, and when Dawn laughed the librarian gave her a stony look. "Hey, you're on Beara, remember, one of the most isolated places in all of Ireland. It takes weeks to do almost anything down here."

When Dawn tried to hide her disappointment, Joan saw it. "You really want dolphin therapy? What are you planning to do, start a clinic?" The librarian rested both elbows on the counter, thinking. "What about something like it?"

"Like what?"

"Jaysus, I don't know. If I can't get you dolphin therapy what about another kind of therapy?"

"Such as?"

"Let me look. But if dog therapy is all I've got you're going to have to take it."

"Dog therapy? How could that be anything like dolphin therapy?"

"Hey, this isn't the Smithsonian Library you know," Joan retorted and, sneezing again, walked into the stacks.

She came back a few minutes later with a book on canine therapy which she'd found in the self-help section. "You're lucky I've got it. It came by way of a couple who owned a kennel nearby. I guess they were thinking of offering a service like it."

"What happened to them?" Dawn asked, thinking she might approach the kennel owners for advice.

"They closed up a few months ago when they emigrated to Australia. Anyway, why would the town ever need canine therapy? Sounds a bit cracked, if you ask me."

"I guess it does," Dawn hedged and, picking up the book, examined the cover shot of a boy with his arm around a coal-black Labrador. "If that's all you have, I'll take it."

"You don't have a library card, do you?" Joan asked, hustling back behind the counter.

"No, I'm afraid I don't."

"Let me set one up for you."

"Joan, how much does it cost?"

"Oh, it's nothing. Three euro, is all," Joan replied, and Dawn knew she was in trouble.

All she had to her name was a single one-euro coin as well as eighteen American dollar bills and twenty-seven U.S. cents in change, most of which she'd hidden in the bureau under Michael's old socks. Before she had left for

Ireland Dawn had withdrawn all the cash she could, a total of three hundred and fifty-nine dollars, much of which she'd exchanged for euro. But after buying some food at Heathrow Airport and spending money for the bus to Bantry, as well as the unanticipated expense of the ferry to Kilcastle, that was all she had left. She remembered Bill Saunders saying her final paycheck had been transferred and by her reckoning, and even if he added a little bit as promised, she would only have twelve-hundred dollars or so in her Boston checking account. But that would have to be used for credit card debt. Her savings account balance was at absolute zero and, as she considered Joan's request for three euro, wondered how in God's name they would survive except by Margaret's continuing good graces. While Joan readied the paperwork, Dawn rummaged through her bag as if hunting for the fee, eyebrows arching in panic.

"Oh God! I must have left my wallet at Margaret's," she fretted. "And Joan I just remembered. I haven't had a minute to get to the bank. You wouldn't take U.S. dollars, would you?" She held up three one-dollar bills she'd found in her bag.

Joan heard the worry in her voice and sensed something more serious than a forgotten wallet. Ignoring her visitor's embarrassment, she opened the book cover and, with a flourish, stamped the register with the return date.

"Are you sure?" Dawn asked, taking the book.

"If I can't trust Margaret's daughter-in-law to return a book, who can I trust? Take it."

"But what about the library card?"

"Just let me get back to my flu, will you please?"

"I'll bring the money for the card when I return the book. Thank you so much, Joan."

As she walked out the door, Joan thought about the woman and her boy who was still so very ill even if he looked beautifully healthy. She thought about the book the American had borrowed and the dolphin in the harbor and also that Dawn apparently had no money no matter what she might say. Joan added two plus two and, always good at arithmetic, came up with the right answer.

She drummed her fingers on the counter and, after sneezing once more, decided that after work she would make a phone call.

The rain never stopped and the family spent the day indoors. Margaret continued her work in the studio while Dawn read at the kitchen table, peeking through the open door to check on her son. Jason sat at the living room window, glum eyes looking out on a rainswept harbor. His silence motivated her to keep reading the library book and the lessons it contained.

Sweeping through the chapters, she learned that studies on canine therapy had proven that structured play between dogs and humans eased stress, increased physical activity, relieved depression and anxiety, calmed and motivated patients and helped to normalize difficult situations. She learned that treatments had benefited older people, hospice patients, autistic children and those suffering from behavioral problems. Because the book never mentioned acute traumatic mutism by name, she couldn't be sure of its relevance to someone like Jason. However, since the dolphin had appeared she had witnessed positive changes in her son's behavior and had become convinced the mammal was responsible. As she turned another page, scanning a list of therapeutic procedures, a sentence caught her eye:

"Autistic children frequently have impaired communications skills," she read out-loud. "Some won't talk at all. Canine therapy can positively affect non-verbal children by promoting speech."

While Jason was not autistic, he was decidedly non-verbal. The sentence got her wondering how she might adapt the book's advice to their unique situation. When Margaret's landline telephone rang not once but twice, she was so engrossed in her studies that she did not hear her mother-in-law whispering in the living room, or pay much attention when she poked her head into the kitchen.

"Dawn, I'm going out for an hour," Margaret said, already in her slicker. "Poor Jason needs something to do."

Dawn looked up, seeing her son at the door wearing a bored, distracted look. "Come sit with me, Jason. You can paint while I read. Deal?"

After Margaret left, Jason sat at the table painting in his sketchpad while his mother continued to study.

"Look at this, Jason," she said, opening a page to show him a photograph of a little girl with a golden retriever. But Jason's look was uninterested and Dawn realized the picture did not convey the real story of what the child was experiencing. As her son went back to his sketchpad she wondered if the book would prove useless. But she kept reading and Jason painted until Margaret came home, and it was bedtime. Dawn took him upstairs and, when he was asleep and after she had walked back into the kitchen, Margaret asked her if she'd like another cup of tea.

They sat at the table as they drank, listening to the patter of rain on the window. Margaret told Dawn that when she was in town, she had learned that a big high-pressure system was supposed to come up from the Sahara Desert in North Africa and would push out the rain.

"It would be great if it would improve by tomorrow. I want to get him back to the cove," Dawn said, but Margaret was skeptical.

"Never believe the weather reports. Best thing to do is, in the morning, stick your head out the window. That's the most reliable weather forecast you'll get in these parts."

Margaret sipped her tea, looking at nothing in particular, and Dawn realized there was more on her mother-in-law's mind than the weather.

"What's wrong?"

"Nothing. It's just…"

"What?"

"Remember Mary? The woman who was making wreaths with Lydia?"

"Of course, I do. I saw her today in town having a cup of tea."

"Well, she's in a bit of bother. She owns a shop on the main street. The Seashell, it's called. I'm sure you've been in."

Dawn remembered the tourist shop filled with plastic claptrap, with its dusty shelves and dirty front window display.

"I've only been in once, years ago with Michael. It's a nice place," Dawn lied.

"It's a mess of a place and Mary knows it," Margaret scoffed. "It wasn't always that way and she's finally decided to do something about it. She bought a load of new stock and hired a college student to work as a sales assistant over the summer season. But today, she learned the student had to cancel and now Mary's stuck because she can't find anyone else to help."

"You're kidding. I thought people would be lining up for a job."

"You'd think so but that's not the case. Most young people have left for Dublin or Cork for better opportunities, and everyone else is at the fishing or farming. I'm not sure what poor Mary will do. She needs help, that's all I can say."

Dawn looked into her tea thinking about the few bucks she had tucked into the bureau upstairs. "Is the job full time?"

"I think it's any hours a person wants to work."

"I was in sales in Boston," Dawn replied thoughtfully.

"That's right. That's what I told Mary."

"You told Mary?"

"I hoped you wouldn't mind. That's who phoned earlier," Margaret said, praying she wouldn't go to hell for lying. "Mary was so worried and that's why I went into town, to talk to her, and your name came up and, well, I said I'd ask you."

"What, to work for Mary?"

"Just for a few days. Just until she finds someone else."

Dawn thought about it. "I don't think I can work in Ireland. I don't have a work visa."

"Oh, I don't think you'll find a visa to be much of a problem. Not way down here in Beara," Margaret said, and winked. "You've heard the phrase 'under the table' haven't you?"

"What about Jason?"

"I'll watch him. Please Dawn. Mary needs the help."

As they finished their tea, it was agreed Dawn would talk to Mary in the morning if it was still raining.

Margaret went to bed feeling more than a little satisfied. As she knelt at her prayers, she realized she'd have to go to confession due to her duplicity. But a tiny white lie was much better than letting Dawn stay broke, a suspicion she'd learned from Joan during their earlier phone call. Margaret thought Father Danny would give her penance of only one decade of the rosary for such a small transgression. Blessing herself, she thought it worth the price.

CHAPTER TWENTY-TWO

In the morning the rain had not stopped. Jason sat at the kitchen table with a face as gloomy as a winter's storm because they could not go to the cove. As a distraction Margaret suggested she take him with her to Kenmare because she needed art supplies and, anyway, Dawn had to go to work. Jason swung to his mother open-mouthed at the announcement.

"It's not a real job, sweetie, and I don't know if I'll even get it," Dawn explained. "Don't worry. We'll go to the cove as soon as the weather clears up."

She helped Margaret wash the breakfast things then, in the rain, walked them to her mother-in-law's car parked on the road below the house. When her family was gone, she hurried down the main street and, arriving at the Seashell, stood on the rainswept sidewalk to take a closer look. A display window covered the entire length of the storefront but it was streaked with months of dirt and only a few dusty items were on show behind it. Dawn thought it could not possibly attract much attention. When she entered the shop through the creaking door, she found a large retail space deserted of shoppers and wondered at the emptiness of the shelves.

"Hello? Mary?" she called, but no one answered.

Wandering around, she inspected stacks of used books for sale heaped in a box near the door while cheap tin whistles, decks of playing cards featuring photos of tourist sites, and an assortment of tacky plastic souvenirs lay piled on a table. When she ran a forefinger across an empty shelf it came back coated with dust.

A door at the rear of the shop opened and the old woman shuffled out. Wearing a worn patterned dress and bent at the waist as if studying the dirty floor, the woman's grey hair covered her eyes like a dishcloth. Dawn remembered how welcoming she had been at the church and wondered if today was a bad day.

"Good morning, Mary," she said but the woman took no notice. "Mary?"

"Speak up!" the old woman barked, looking up. Limping behind a grimy counter, she lowered herself on to a plastic sun chair that had seen better days. "Bloody rain plays havoc with my rheumatism," she complained. Rubbing her legs, she took a good look at her visitor. "Margaret said you worked in sales. You ever work in a shop?"

"I worked in a call center."

"A what?" Mary snapped, a hand to an ear.

"A call center," Dawn replied, louder this time, but the woman didn't seem impressed. "I worked in a hardware store, too. I worked there in the summers and part-time during college."

"Hardware store? How's that like my place?" the woman grumbled, and Dawn found herself wishing she'd gone to Kenmare with Jason and her mother-in-law.

"It was a retail job. But you're right. It wasn't like your place," she said. "Mary, maybe I should come back tomorrow."

"Tomorrow? Now what good would that be? So, what do you think of my shop?"

"The Seashell is a fine place," Dawn hedged with a bright smile.

"That's a lie. It's a horrid place and I wish to God someone would take it off my hands so I could know some peace." She coughed into her sleeve then caught Dawn with a frown. "So?"

"So... so what?"

"So, what can you do to help?"

Pondering the question Dawn couldn't think of a quick answer. Glancing again around the store, she thought the only thing that could save the Seashell was a massive fire followed by complete demolition and an insurance claim.

"Not much, is that right?" Mary continued, shaking her head in self-pity. "It's a shame is all. My husband and I worked here for fifty years. Every summer, the tourists would throng into town in their buses, and we'd have a massive time selling out. Back then we were one of the most successful shops on the peninsula."

"What happened?"

"What do you think?" the old woman snorted. "Jack got himself drowned and I was left alone with the bloody thing. Now I don't give a toss. It's a pity because it being the start of summer, the buses will come again and tourists will throng like locusts but they'll walk right past the place because I'm not ready. Am I?"

The woman sighed again and started to shiver.

"Are you cold?"

"Of course, I'm cold. I'm not wearing my cardigan, am I?"

"Did you bring one with you?"

"Course I did. It's back there," she replied, pointing a thumb toward the rear of the store.

"Back where?"

"In the back room, Gersha. Aren't ya listening?" Mary snarled, and Dawn decided to go look for it before the old woman had a stroke.

As Mary watched the young American walk through the back door she smiled, hoping she wasn't putting it on too thick. Margaret would be livid if she messed things up. Cursing the uncomfortable plastic chair, she sat back to wait.

When Dawn turned on the light, she found Mary's cardigan hanging from a hook on the back of the door. Scanning the room, she realized it was used as a storeroom because it was filled with boxes. Half had already been opened and an assortment of new merchandise protruded from dusty wrappings. Curious, she stepped up to a tall box, bending back the cardboard to look. She pulled out a strong wooden walking stick, the type casual walkers use. Its lacquered finish sparkled in the dim light. She glanced at the label, reading it was handcrafted by a local artisan. The box was full of them.

She noticed a smaller box and, peering in, discovered an assortment of jewelry also made locally. Withdrawing a presentation carton, she opened it to find a pair of earrings. They were made from small seashells just like the name on the faded sign above the shop's front window. Delicate shells were suspended from fine silver chains attached to silver studs, and she thought them stunning. Taking the cardigan, she walked back into the front room clutching the earrings in her other hand.

"Did you know you had these?" Dawn asked, holding up the box.

"Why wouldn't I?" the old woman squinted. "I ordered them, didn't I? Where's my wrap?"

She helped Mary on with the cardigan and, studying the earrings, suspected how well items like these would sell to tourists.

"Mary, you asked me how I could help. I think I know."

"Oh, do you now? You Yanks think you have all the fancy ideas. But if you're sure by all means work away. I can't be paying much, mind you."

"That's okay," Dawn replied, and realized how much she looked forward to the challenge. "First things first. Tell me where you keep your cleaning supplies."

Dawn worked hard all morning, first by cleaning the front display window inside and out. That done, Mary showed her how to wind out the awning that extended over the front sidewalk to keep visitors dry and Dawn washed that even though it was raining. Looking again at the shop's exterior and still not satisfied, she borrowed a ladder from the hardware store down the street, climbing up to wash the blue and white Seashell store sign. With the outside of the shop finished she worked inside by removing the forlorn-looking items on the shelves and tables, then dusted everything. Next was the front counter and she cleaned that as well as the glass display case beneath it, then mopped the shop floor. When Mary announced it was one o'clock and she was closing for lunch, Dawn walked back to Margaret's house and made herself a sandwich. As she sat down to eat, she realized she had not thought about Jason's troubles all that morning. It felt good to be working again, if only part-time and probably for free, and she couldn't help but grin. She thought about her old job and wondered what Joyce was up to. When the image of Bill and that rat Steve came to mind, she found she was very glad to be in Ireland. After finishing lunch, she went back to work.

It seemed the old woman was not as afflicted by her rheumatism as she had been that morning because she helped drag out the boxes of new stock and together, they organized the store. Mary objected when seeing Dawn move the cheap souvenirs to the back shelves but she overcame the old woman's protests, convincing her that only newer items should be featured at front-of-shop to attract in the tourists.

"You're sure you know what you're doing, do ya?" the old woman grumbled, but only flapped a hand at her new employee. Mary sat again, grunting, to watch the young woman walk in and out of the back room, carrying armloads of new merchandise as she organized the rest of the store.

Posters, stationery, pens, key rings, mugs and crockery, maps, and books on Irish history and legends filled one side of the shop. On the other, Dawn laid out new woolen scarves and soft peaked hats in attractive piles. She dusted off the tin whistles and seeing a box containing small bodhrans — sensing the Irish drums would one day hang in distant living rooms — displayed them on mid-store shelving. After that, she filled the glass display cabinet with the earrings she'd found as well as silver necklaces, broaches and bracelets. When that was finished, she tackled the front window display.

Dawn stood at the window as Mary groused while handing up the merchandise and, as they worked and talked, she realized the old woman wasn't as hard of hearing as she'd let on. Mary asked how Jason was doing and had no trouble hearing Dawn's reply. She even heard Dawn whisper how worried she was for her son and how Margaret often walked to the church to pray for a miracle.

"Miracles are over-rated," Mary sniffed, and Dawn caught a glint of mischief in the old eyes. "Sometimes it just takes perseverance and hard work to win the day."

The old woman retreated back to her chair, lowering herself on to the plastic seat.

"I know a story about that. Want to hear it? Ah, but maybe not. You being a Yank you might not appreciate it." When Dawn protested that she'd very much appreciate hearing the story, Mary leaned back, bright eyes focused on the ceiling. Her voice lost its petulance, settling into the rhythm of a *Seanchaí*, an Irish storyteller.

"Once when I was just a girl, I knew a fellow named Oisin O'Herlihy. Oisin was an old man who owned a farm down close to Garnish near Allihies, and we all called him old Squint because he'd get so drunk, he'd fall off the ancient black Raleigh bike he rode because he couldn't see farther than the tip of his nose.

"Anyway," Mary continued, settling into the tale, "old Squint liked nothing better than to cycle into town seven days a week and sit at the counter of the pub with his mates. They'd drink pints of lager and recount stories of the old days. Because he was only a few months short of ninety, Squint told his mates that when he finally took his journey to the Pearly Gates, he hoped they'd give him a send-off of a fine wake.

"He told them he'd saved over a thousand pound — a fortune in those days — and the cash was stuffed in the ruins of his old mattress and, when his time came, he wanted them to use it to take care of all the details. It was enough for his funeral and the casket and a plot at the cemetery, with enough left over for a few crates of whiskey and a barrel of porter for the wake. All he wanted was a fine farewell and, even though he had a sister, he knew she was well set up in the city and, if they had any money remaining after arranging the wake and funeral, they could split any left between them. All he asked was they make sure he was dead proper before they started the proceedings. Following his speech his friends raised their glasses and promised to keep old Squint's wishes when his end finally came, and they drank on it.

"So, one day someone notices old Squint leaving the pub about midnight and he'd had more than he could stand. He was seen weaving and bucking down the main street on the old Raleigh and his cronies worried he might not make it back to his farm in one piece. Mind you, they also talked about the mountain of cash Squint had hidden in his mattress which brought them a bit of succor and, rather than go look for him which is what friends should have done, went back to their pints and plotted what they'd do with his treasure when he finally kicked the bucket."

Mary stopped because she had to take a breath.

"What happened next?" Dawn asked as she laid out a pile of new woolen jumpers in the front window.

"Turns out they were right to be concerned for Squint because the next day there was no sign of him. So, his friends embarked on one of the biggest manhunts ever to take place on Beara. They enlisted help from the town, and the crowds and Gardaí searched the entire peninsula all the way from Kilcastle down to Allihies and from there right up to Eyeries and Ardgroom and the Kerry border. After three full days, they still couldn't find the poor man and his mates had about given up."

"They never found him?" Dawn asked. "That's horrible."

"Ah, it wasn't so horrible as that," Mary said, and chuckled. "It turns out they found Squint on the morning of the third day not three miles from here. He'd ridden the bike off a curve and run down a hill into a stream. His bike was a shambles and the poor *crater* had almost drowned. Squint woke up in the chill water and felt a general weakness in his body which he could not attribute only to the drink, and crawled out of that stream but collapsed again. Even though he'd survived a drowning he still thought he was dead for sure because he realized he was at the bottom of a steep gorge, hidden by dense overgrowth. He was so weak he believed he'd never be able to climb the steepness and so hidden he knew no one would find him. But do you know what old Squint did?"

"No, what?" Dawn asked.

"He got stubborn. He crawled to his knees and, rather than pray for a miracle, he asked for the strength and perseverance he needed to help himself. He was an old man and felt horribly unwell and prayed for the courage to make it up that hill. When he was done praying, he got up from his knees and tried to stand but he was too weak to do so. Even though he thought he didn't have the strength to do it, he crawled up that hill on his stomach and made it to the top and on the verge of the road he finally collapsed. If he could have done it, he would have crawled all the way into town but he'd gone far enough because that's where they found him at last."

"They found him?" Dawn said. "Thank God."

249

"Didn't I say they'd found him?" Mary grumbled. "Now, where was I? Oh yes. So, the search party found him still breathing and rushed him to hospital in Bantry and the doctors stripped him clean and ran a whole series of tests, and it got back to his mates that it looked like Squint was doomed. So, they held a council at the pub over a few pints and it was decided they'd better get the wake prepared just like Squint wanted because it didn't look so good. And besides, even though Squint was not yet dead the idea of a thousand quid in their mitts sounded too good to be true. They didn't want to leave all that money in Squint's deserted farmhouse so they decided to find it to keep it safe, and that was their excuse and that's what they did."

"It sounds like they were good friends," Dawn said, perching on the glass countertop so she could hear better.

"Friends?" Mary said with a snort. "Friends me arse. All they wanted was the money. They went to Squint's farmhouse and turned it top to bottom looking for the stash. It wasn't in the mattress as Squint had said it was but they tore the old thing to pieces to make sure, and that's when Squint's sister showed up."

"Was she looking for the money, too?"

"Not the half of it," Mary replied, dismissing the idea. "She was a fine loving woman, a true Catholic, and she was there to protect Squint's property. She took one look around the house which the men had torn asunder and told them, 'You'd better get this all back in order or I'll tell the priest and he'll read your names out at the next Mass.' But the men explained why they were there and that Squint had made them promise to take care of the wake and they needed the money to do so, and if there was any left out of it they were instructed by Squint to split it equally so as to toast his good health. But they had a problem because they couldn't find his hard-earned reserves." Mary glanced at Dawn. "Of course, they never bothered telling her they'd also promised to make sure Squint was good and dead first. But anyway…

"Well, the sister listened and nodded and, even though she was Squint's only living relative and therefore legally entitled to the money when he was dead, decided Squint's promise had to be made good. She told them to buy what they had to buy and was certain she would find the money because she knew where Squint might hide such a fortune and, when she found it, would hand it over to them to make good on Squint's solemn word.

"So, the men, why they ran pell-mell back into town as fast as they could to carry out Squint's wishes. They went to the priest and bought the largest plot in the cemetery, the one near the end with a fine view of the sea. They went to the undertaker and purchased the best oak coffin the town had ever seen. They went into the pub and ordered cases of whiskey and a barrel of porter just as Squint had asked, and put their purchases on the tick in their names. They talked to the women of the town and asked them to prepare a big wake in Squint's honor to be held at his farmhouse the day his body finally showed up, to be followed by a hooley in the pub with enough to eat and drink for everyone, and they personally put up a down payment. They even took the bus into Killarney and bought a new mattress and had it delivered first class back to Squint's place to replace the one they'd torn to bits. They put all their purchases on credit, of course, knowing they'd be able to pay it all back when Squint's sister found the money, and they reckoned that even after all the expenditure they'd have over a hundred pound each held tight in their fists."

"What happened?" Dawn asked because the woman had gone quiet. "Don't tell me. The sister wasn't able to find the money."

Mary smirked. "Oh, she found it all right, exactly where she expected to. But in the meantime, do you know that after buying all that stuff and incurring all that debt, Squint's so-called friends got a shock because they heard from a Bantry-fella who knew Squint slightly, and he'd visited the hospital and talked to a nurse who was his second cousin, who in turn heard that Squint had turned the tide and was recovering. Squint's fiendish mates panicked because they'd begun to wonder what was taking so long for Squint's demise but they learned from someone else, and to their relief, that Squint really was on his way out and not far from the Pearly Gates. So, his mates took a bus up to the hospital to confirm the situation.

"They talked to the doctor and learned Squint needed a miracle to survive because all the tests pointed to heart failure and it was just a matter of time, and the men promised the doctor they'd say ten rosaries apiece that

Squint would get his miracle even though they had no intention of saying those rosaries at all. Then each of them asked permission to say goodbye just in case their cries for a miraculous recovery went unheard, and each one walked into Squint's room and saw the poor man with his ashen face and closed eyes and heard his shallow breathing, and knew what the doc said was true because Squint didn't stand a chance. They were already planning how they'd spend all that money and couldn't wait for the wake and the burial when they'd be free from Squint and could do what they wanted with the remainder of his cash.

"They also felt good because one of 'em had run into Squint's sister who said she'd found the money inside the tire of a retired tractor parked in Squint's ramshackle cowshed, just where she expected to find it, and she'd give it to them at the wake and they could pay off their debts with it and keep the rest just as Squint had promised.

"The men were delighted at the good news because they'd also thought of the bad. It had dawned on one of the mates that if Squint didn't die, they were on the hook for all the debts they'd incurred because they'd all signed for them personally, and fear struck their hearts. God alone knew they'd be run out of town on a rail if they couldn't pay up. But what with confirming that Squint was only moments from death and the sister having found the cash, they knew they could put their fears to rest.

"As you can tell," Mary said after taking a long breath, "Squint's pals weren't the brightest of lights. But anyway, it all turned out fine. So, let's get back to work, shall we?"

The old woman got up from her chair and limped toward the window display.

"You mean that's it? But what happened to the men and old Squint?" Dawn demanded.

"You really want to know?"

"Oh, come on, Mary. You can't leave it there. Tell me."

"Well, if you'd stop interrupting me, here's the big finish," Mary said, dropping back on to her chair. "Where was I? Oh yes. After their visit to hospital to see the last of Squint, the men ended up back at the pub where

they waited and waited to hear the news of his final passing which they were
confident would happen at any minute. They waited so long and with such
anticipation that they forgot to go to work, and they ran out of cash so they
had to put all their pints on the tick along with the whiskey and barrel of
porter they'd already purchased for Squint's wake, and they knew they each
owed a fortune. But they rubbed their hands at the thought of the money
when Squint died and kept ordering more pints of lager until they were
legless, and then the front door burst open — and do you know who it was?"

"Old Squint," Dawn guessed.

"You must have heard the story before," Mary laughed, and continued.
"When the lads saw Squint, one of them took him for a ghost and fell right off
his barstool. But old Squint was as alive as I am and, walking over to the
counter, pulled a huge wadge of cash from his pocket. 'Evening gents,' Squint
says. 'Just saw the sister and she gave me this. Pete, a pint of Guinness if you
will.' While the barkeep got the pint, his mates tried not to collapse from the
shock. They were as astounded by his sudden appearance as they were at his
order because Squint always drank lager even on the coldest days and never a
pint of black. Anyway, Squint took the Guinness and drained it in one
swallow and ordered another and said, 'Doc says I had too little iron in my
system and all I have to do is drink a few pints of porter and I'll be right as
rain for another twenty years.'

"'But what about the heart failure?' his mates croaked. 'We thought you
were dying of it,' and Squint just replies, 'Doc told me those tests aren't as
reliable as they're supposed to be and it was just a lack of iron all along that
was the trouble. But I prayed for strength and perseverance and God got me
through it. After I wrecked myself on the bike, I climbed up the hill even
though I didn't think I could do it, and now I've climbed out of that hospital
bed. After I did, I knew if I was to get better, I'd best start with a bit of
exercise so I walked from Bantry all the way to Kilcastle so I could share the
miracle of my survival with my good friends, and here I stand to tell the tale.'

"His mates were even more shocked. It was a good thirty mile from
Bantry to Kilcastle and even the heartiest of them would have trouble making
it, but Squint drank his next pint in another single swallow. As he ordered a

third, the men grew even more concerned because Squint looked healthier than he had when first entering the pub. Then Squint looked down at the thousand pound he'd laid on the counter.

"'Sister says you were looking for this?' Squint asked, taking up the wadge of money.

"'We thought you were dead,' his mates replied.

"'Seems I'm not,' Squint says and looks 'em straight in the eye. 'But I gotta thank you. I hear you bought me a cemetery plot and it's registered in my name. Seems you bought me a fine oak coffin and that's also in my name. Seems you bought me a couple crates of whiskey and a barrel of porter because Pete here has my name on 'em and I can call it down anytime I want,' and Squint looked at the barkeep who nodded and said, 'That's right, Squint. The lads bought it fair and square to be used whenever you want, and they put it on their own personal tick.' Squint smiled and looked back at his mates. 'Seems I even have a comfortable new mattress, and you've done me right by that too. I guess all you fellows have to do now is pay for it before someone chases you out of town or throws you in the Gard house for not making good on your debts.' Then he winked at the barkeep and, as he walked out of the pub, his friends realized they'd been duped by a professional.

"And that," Mary finished, "is the story of old Squint."

At last, she rose and hobbled toward Dawn. "You know what they say, Gersha," she said, placing a hand on Dawn's arm. "Miracles are two-a-penny. People keep wanting them, thinking they don't have to do anything in return. But those who persevere know they have to work for a miracle even when they're fortunate enough to be given it. Those people keep trying even if the task seems impossible. Those are the people God listens to. Remember," she said with a final squeeze, "God loves a try-er.

"A what?"

"TRY-er! Now if you're finished sitting on yer arse let's see what you've made of my front window."

Together, they walked outside and stood beneath the awning. Dawn was no professional window dresser but she suspected the window display looked better than it had in years. Woolens filled one side of it, draped across vintage wooden crates she had found in the back room, while jewelry sparkled in the light. Pottery was laid out in a grouping with a clutch of tin whistles arranged within them. She had finished it all off with pieces of taffeta which dressed the entire display in a sheen of green and gold.

"My, but isn't that wonderful," Mary said, her old cheeks glowing. "I guess Margaret was right. I guess you do know something about shops."

They went back inside and Mary saw that a large box of walking sticks had been pushed to one side. "What about those?" she asked.

"It's a surprise," Dawn said. "When are the tourist buses due in?"

"Day after tomorrow. In the late morning."

"Perfect. I'll tell you the day after tomorrow."

Mary hobbled behind the counter, pulling out an envelope and handing it to her. "Don't worry, it's not much. Open it later when yer home." Dawn put it in her handbag and was about to leave when Mary stopped her again. She held out a small gift box. "Open that at home, too. You just remember old Squint's story. You got to promise me."

"I promise I'll remember Squint and that God loves a try-er," Dawn said.

"Good. Now get home. I expect that son of yours is waiting."

When Dawn left Mary stood in thought, hoping the secret she shared with Margaret could be kept and that Dawn would never guess the identity of her true benefactor. Then the front door opened and two young American women dressed in hiking gear looked in.

"Oh wow, isn't this great? Look at these!" said a young woman with hair pushed beneath a soaking bandana. She walked to a display of woolens Dawn had created as her friend followed, both picking up warm jumpers. "Your front window display looks awesome and we just had to come in," the first woman gushed, holding out a sweater. "How much is this?" But there was something in Mary's face because the young tourist asked in confusion, "I'm sorry. You are open, aren't you?"

"Course I'm open," Mary grunted. "We've been open for fifty years and isn't it a miracle of perseverance? Now, let me help you."

CHAPTER TWENTY-THREE

When Dawn returned home, she found that Margaret and Jason were still not back. Sitting at the kitchen table, she examined the thick envelope Mary had given to her. When she tore it open a folded wad of notes slid out. Counting the tens and twenties, it came to a hundred and eighty euro — about two hundred dollars — for a single day's work in a dying business. She was certain it was a mistake.

Next, she turned to the small gift box. Opening it, she found a necklace different to any she had seen in the shop. The chain was made of gold and, when she picked it up, an elegantly-crafted dolphin spun within a thin circle of platinum silver. She thought she had never seen anything so beautiful. She did not know why Mary had given it to her but wondered if she'd talked to Margaret and worried the shopkeeper knew too much about their goings-on with the dolphin.

Then the back door opened and Margaret called, and they were home. Jason ran in holding a new sketchpad and a dozen small tubes of acrylics his grandma had bought for him. He held them up for his mother's inspection then skipped out of the kitchen, going to the studio to try them. Margaret bustled around the kitchen as Dawn explained about her day then showed her the money.

"Mary made a mistake," Dawn said, holding up the thick bundle. "It's too much and I'm taking it back."

"Don't you dare," Margaret replied as she dropped teabags into a pot. "If she counted wrong you can't tell her. All the woman has left is her pride."

"Then what about this?" she said, showing Margaret the necklace. "I can't accept this. It's too much."

"But it's lovely. It was a gift, Dawn, and a perfect one at that, don't you think? Giving it back would cause the old woman too much heartache."

Thinking she'd already caused enough heartache, Dawn agreed to leave things as they were. As Margaret sipped a cup of tea, she told her daughter-in-law that she'd heard on the radio how the weather would improve the next day because the big high was finally pushing in. As they talked, Dawn made supper for the family of eggs and sausages and, when it was time, went upstairs with her son. After they dressed for bed, she stood at the mirror to try on the necklace and admired the dolphin leaping through its circle of silver. She caught Jason smiling at her.

"It is pretty, isn't it?" she said, fingering the glittering dolphin. "But tomorrow we'll get to see a real one. What do you say to that?"

His grin answered her question.

For the next few days, the settled weather continued and Dawn took advantage of it. During the mornings she worked with Jason and the dolphin and during the afternoons she worked at the Seashell. On nights when the women gathered in the church Dawn helped make more wreaths for Remembrance Day. She kept her promise to Mary about the lesson of perseverance by continuing her studies of the canine therapy book. She also remembered what Mary had said of the tourist buses because on the day of their arrival Dawn rose early to visit the town's hardware store just as it opened. Using some of her new cash, she bought poster-sized pages of blank paper and an assortment of markers. She hurried to the Seashell and, letting herself in with the key Mary had given her, went to work. The owner was late arriving that morning, catching Dawn in the storeroom just as she was completing the posters.

"Now, what are you up to?"

"I didn't think you'd be interested," Dawn teased. "Stay right here."

She picked up the finished posters and scurried out front. The old woman groused as she waited but curiosity got the better of her and she followed. Mary found her assistant standing on a step ladder, taping posters to the inside of the display window. When they both walked outside to take a look the old woman wanted to faint.

"Fifty percent off the walking sticks?" she howled after reading the announcement printed in thick red marker. She frowned as the young woman hauled a full box of sticks out the door, standing them on the sidewalk. A smaller flyer was attached screaming the same offer. "Gersha, what are you thinking? I'll go out of business for sure."

"Just wait," Dawn said as she pulled the box into position. "I was the best sales person at my call company, you know."

"But you don't work there anymore. What happened? Did you get sacked for making your boss go broke?"

Dawn and Mary stood at the front door watching as the buses arrived at the square. The herd of tourists streamed off, milling like sheep as they took pictures of the trawlers and then the fisherman who frowned into the cameras pointed at their weathered faces. As the tourists stepped toward the main street and its line of shops, Mary studied them with the look of a quality control inspector.

"Ya gotta know those who spend and those who don't. The Germans, they spend the most, followed by the French. The English are so-so but will shell out on food and drink. The Spanish believe the Irish should give them money for visiting rather than the other way around. But the Americans, oh those Yanks! They hate parting with even a single dollar. You'd think they were all born in County Cavan they're so tight."

"Leave the Yanks to me," Dawn said, seeing a group meandering toward them. "Come on. Let's get ready."

Reentering the shop, Mary hobbled to a shelf, making final adjustments to a group of crockery.

"Jesus, Mary and Joseph!" she grunted, holding up a mug then looking at another. "The price tags are all gone."

"Don't worry. I took them off on purpose."

"You took off the prices? But why? We'll never remember what anything costs."

"Oh, yes we will," Dawn said, pointing to a fuzzy brown cardigan. "That sweater. Fifty-two-euro, fifty-cent. The woman's hat next to it? Twenty-two-euro, ninety-five-cent. The mug you're holding? Five ninety-five. And the walking sticks? Nineteen euro each. Want me to go on?"

"No," Mary replied, sitting behind the counter. "You have a memory like my poor dead husband. Just don't ask me to do it because I won't remember a thing."

Dawn heard a familiar twang outside the open front door as a woman called, "Harry? Would you look at this?" A middle-aged couple stood on the sidewalk examining the poster. The woman pulled a walking stick from the box, then steamed into the shop.

"Hi," Dawn said with her best smile. "Can I help you?"

"These walking sticks," the tall woman asked, pointing to the label. "Are they really made locally?"

"Sure, they are. They're made right here on the peninsula."

"You're certain? They're not cheap imports, are they?"

Dawn glanced at Mary, seeing the old woman's temper flare.

"No. They're Beara-made and that's a guarantee." Then Dawn made a point of examining the woman's raincoat. "That's a wonderful jacket you're wearing. Where did you get it?"

"I bought it at Macy's," the woman replied, pleased at the compliment. "It was on sale."

"Which Macy's? The one in New York?"

"Oh, God no. I never go to the one in New York. The Macy's in Boston, of course."

"I'm from Boston. I always shop at Macy's," Dawn said, and the woman turned just as her husband was sneaking out the door.

"Harry, get back here. This girl is from Boston, too!"

"Is that right?" Harry managed. "Where abouts?"

"I lived in Southie but worked at World Connect in the city."

"I know that company," Harry replied, and the three talked of Boston. Dawn learned that the woman's name was Fiddy and that her mother was in hospital recovering from a nasty arterial infection.

"Oh, that's terrible!" Dawn said. "I'm really sorry about your mom. You know, my aunt went through something of the same thing. When she got out of hospital her doctor recommended a lot of walking."

"Did he," Fiddy replied.

"Yes, and maybe a walking stick, you know, wouldn't it make a perfect gift for your mother? She'd have it forever, they're so well made, and we're having a very special sale right now."

"So I saw," the American said and, examining the handsome stick, asked, "Okay. How much?"

"As you can see, there's fifty percent off. That brings them down to twenty-three-euro, seventy-five-cent each," Dawn explained, seeing Mary almost fall off her chair at the inflated price. "But — and this is the great news — we're also having an exclusive offer running just for today."

"Another offer? What kind of offer?"

"Well, if you buy five, you get the fifth one absolutely free, which brings the price right down to nineteen euro each."

"Nineteen, is that what you said? Down from almost fifty?"

"Something like that," Dawn hedged.

"That's an amazing sale," the woman replied. She placed the point of the stick on the floor, testing her weight against it. "Okay, so what's the catch? You're not trying to off-load a mess of klunkers, are you?"

"Klunkers?"

"Klunkers. I want to know why they're so cheap."

Dawn took the woman's elbow and, leading her aside, nodded toward Mary.

"See the old woman behind the counter, the sad looking one? It's a pissa because she's owned the business for fifty years but lost her fisherman husband at sea. It's been terrible on her."

"The poor thing," Fiddy said with genuine sympathy, glancing at her husband who waited near the door. "I wish I'd lose mine."

"Mary was so grief-stricken she became confused and ordered too many walking sticks. And because there have been so few tourists this year, I suggested the sale or she'd be stuck with them. If we can sell a few she'll survive another year."

"Well, aren't you a wonder," the woman said, stepping toward the front door. "And you're certain the sticks are only nineteen euro if we buy five?"

"Fiddy, we don't need five walking sticks," Harry grunted.

"Oh, yes we do. Wait here. I'll be right back." Then she was out the door like a shot.

As they waited for Fiddy to return, Mary tossed Dawn a look of annoyance at her sales technique. Finally, the Boston woman reentered with what seemed to be the entire bus tour in tow.

"…and they're all made in Beara and I'm told they're constructed of oak or something because they're so solid and will last forever," the American rattled on. "But the best thing is, there's fifty percent off and get this: if we row in together and buy five, we get the fifth one free!"

Dawn heard the rising tide of delight as the crowd broke, attacking the displays like a well-seasoned army. While they shopped, she also informed the visitors that everything else in the store was thirty percent off and, what's more, if they bought four items the least expensive purchase had an additional twenty percent off. Of course, there were no price tags on any of the items but that didn't seem to bother the crowd. By the time the tourists left, the Seashell had sold out of all the walking sticks. Not only that, but the shop had been cleared of a quarter of its stock, all sold for full retail price or better. Mary looked to fall over because the till could hardly hold more cash, and when Fiddy and Harry finally left they carried three full bags including a clutch of walking sticks. At the door, the woman from Boston took Mary aside.

"You know your sales assistant?" she asked, nodding toward Dawn. "She's magic. Don't let anyone steal her from you."

As the front door closed Dawn looked at Mary and laughed.

"I forgot to tell you. There's one thing about Americans. They'll never pass up a sale."

"Particularly," Mary replied, "if a clever Yank is running it."

The high-pressure system remained settled over the southwest and there followed a period of fine weather with blue skies and no wind. When she was free, Dawn took long walks alone. She breathed in and breathed out and was surprised to discover what she saw, and asked herself why she had not noticed before. She saw the bell flowers of wild fuchsia peeking red-faced from the overgrowth and heard lambs in the high fields calling for their mothers. She smelled a raw sweetness as farmers harvested the first cut of summer grass and noticed the low-level acrobatics of swallows in flight. She tracked the play of a group of sea otters living along the coast and felt the sun warm her face.

She relished her time working in the shop and wore the dolphin necklace to show Mary how much she appreciated it, and sold goods to tourists who were happy to buy from her. During evenings at the church, she bent fresh yew into circles, and with Margaret and the women watched the pile of wreaths grow. She was afraid to admit it but she was content and Jason was content, too, though he still would not talk. But she buckled down and worked hard with him and, when taking the punt out through the harbor, saw that Jackie's trawler had not yet returned.

At night she no longer dreamed of the sinking.

She finished the therapy book and, figuring it was worth trying, early one morning she stood with her son on the pier in the hidden cove, the open book in her hand. She eyed the dolphin which floated in the water, and both the boy and the mammal seemed to sense something was up because they waited patiently.

"Okay, Jason," she said, looking up from the book. "Here's what I want you to do. First, I want you to kneel as close to the water as you can." As he knelt, she re-read the text, reminding herself that the first step was establishing a rapport between the canine used for the therapy ('Okay, the dolphin sure isn't a canine,' she thought, eyeing the mammal floating at pier-side) and the subject of the therapy, namely Jason.

"Jason, I want you to hold your arm out like this," she continued, raising her arm, "and then lower it." With her fingers splayed and hand held flat, she lowered it toward the pier. "See? You're asking it to sit, or in our case, telling our friend to dive underwater." Seeing her son's puzzled face, she held up the book. "That's what it says in here. Go on, try it." Jason frowned as he followed the command. But when she checked the dolphin still floated on the surface.

"Well, that didn't work," she muttered and, not quite sure what to do, flipped the page. "Okay, how about this. Rather than lower your arm, raise it. See? You're asking it to stand." She showed him a picture of a small child with his arm raised, a dog standing on its hind legs beside him. Jason glared at her as if she was crazy. Behind him, the dolphin clicked and sang and she could swear it was laughing.

"Oh, shut up," she said and, turning to another page, saw a new chapter which began: *The Next Step: Immersing the Subject within the Canine's Unique Environment.*

Below the heading, a photograph showed a boy working with a therapist in the confines of an outdoor treatment area. A large Labrador had its snout on the young patient's shoulder, the boy's face split with laughter. She studied the photo and its inviting environment and how relaxed the child looked to be in it. Peering over the edge of the pier, she remembered how safe she had felt swimming in the water with the dolphin. She glanced again at her son and snapped the book shut. Reaching into her pocket, she pulled out the cell phone Margaret had lent her.

"Hi, Margaret," she said, winking at Jason when her mother-in-law answered. "No, everything is fine here. I was just wondering, are you busy? I have a favor to ask."

It took Margaret only a few minutes to drive to the cove. After she parked the car, Dawn pulled the delivery from the back seat. Learning what her daughter-in-law planned, the older woman balked.

"I wish I hadn't kept these," Margaret fretted as Dawn sorted through the wetsuits and facemasks. "Can't you try something else?"

"I won't let anything happen, Margaret. I promise," Dawn replied, and waved to her son who waited on the pier. "Kiddo, come over here. Nana brought a surprise."

When he ran to her and saw what his grandmother had brought, his face split with delight. Fitting him into his suit, Dawn remembered how just over a year ago they had bought it at the town's marine chandlers. Michael had insisted they buy two for Jason, the second one two sizes too big because he had known his boy would grow. The first suit was at the bottom of the ocean because they had brought it with them on the tragic trip to the island. As for the second, Michael was right because even though Jason was a head taller than he had been when they had bought it, the wetsuit fit perfectly.

"Stand back and let me take a look," Dawn said as Jason spun around. "Well, don't you look like a professional?"

"You look like a seal," Margaret remarked, and as she walked to the pier with her grandson Dawn climbed into the backseat of the Morris. She struggled to change in the small cabin, thinking she'd never get the wetsuit on because the space was so tight. When she finished, she joined them on the pier and together they studied the dolphin swimming close by.

"Carol was right," Margaret worried. "The *crater* is huge."

"We'll be fine," Dawn promised, and turned to Jason. "If I tell you to get out of the water, you do it right now, do you hear me?" When he nodded, she said, "Okay, let me go first."

She studied the calm water looking for the dolphin but it had slipped beneath the sea. Placing the facemasks on the pier, she took a breath, jumping in feet first. She hit the water with little disturbance, feeling the happiness she experienced whenever she swam. Bobbing to the surface, she looked up at Jason and Margaret.

"Okay, Jason. Come on."

She saw the wicked smile on his face as he launched himself like a missile, hitting the sea in a cannonball of water that drenched her. When he surfaced, he screamed with laughter.

"You monkey!" she cried.

Then he was splashing water at her and she was splashing back, and for a moment they played as they used to as a family. But then she remembered the seriousness of the session. The sea glinted facet-like in the sun as she searched for the dolphin.

"Do you see it?" Dawn asked and, suddenly fearful, wondered what right she had to bring her son into the sea with such a gigantic creature. But she calmed herself by remembering the tranquility she had felt when swimming with it the last time. Jason saw it first and, pointing, she looked out to deeper water. Its dorsal fin sliced toward them and, because they were on the same level with it, it looked as tall as a fully-rigged schooner. When it was only a few feet away Jason whimpered and clung to her neck.

"Don't be afraid. You can touch it if you want. You've touched it lots of times, remember?" His grip loosened and when he looked over her shoulder, she knew it was behind them. She spun around to see for herself. The dolphin approached closer this time and she could feel its flanks caress her side. Jason reached out, his hand gliding over its beak then across its back and, when he growled in delight, she realized he was over his fear.

The dolphin turned, swimming toward them again. She reached for it as it came closer, and hanging on to its dorsal fin it pulled them through the water. Jason shrieked with laughter and she thought the dolphin heard his fun because it swam faster. Their passing left a small wake and she looked back, seeing how far they'd come from the pier. But the dolphin seemed to sense her fear because it circled and headed back to where her mother-in-law waited.

Margaret stood on the pier and, having worried as she watched her family being towed toward the mouth of the cove, allowed herself a relieved smile as they headed back in. Then she heard the crunch of tires and saw a car bouncing down the *boreen*. She looked back, seeing her family near the pier, but thought they could not be seen because of the low angle. Intending to keep it that way, she hurried toward the approaching car as it parked by her Morris. The door opened and a woman climbed out.

"Joan, whatever are you doing here?" Margaret called.

The woman looked miserable, with red eyes and wearing a cardigan much too warm for the good weather. "I promised Carol I'd get some more yew but I'm not up to it," Joan replied. "I thought I'd take a walk instead."

"A walk? Here?"

"And why not here? I always walk here," Joan said, and Margaret realized she had piqued the librarian's curiosity which is what she wanted to avoid.

"What I meant is, you still don't look well. You should be in bed. Why don't you let me take you home and I'll make you a cup of tea?"

"I'm quite all right, thank you very much," Joan grunted. "How about you? Why are you here?"

"Taking a walk, just like you," she replied and, glancing over her shoulder, was relieved Joan could not see anything going on in the water. But as it turned out everything was going on because hidden on the other side of the pier, her family still played with the dolphin.

When the mammal brought them again into shallower water Dawn let go of the dorsal fin and, clinging to the pier with Jason, watched it move back a few feet. She could swear she saw laughter in its eyes before it ducked below the surface.

"Where'd it go?" Dawn asked, and Jason hunted too but they couldn't see it. Then the water boiled around them and her son burst into giggles. She could see the huge shadow beneath them as the dolphin vented, blowing air bubbles. Jason laughed as the stream stroked his sides and tickled his chin. She grinned at his fun, then again thought of the therapy book and what it said about immersion in the animal's environment. She pulled herself up on the pier far enough to reach the facemasks where she had left them.

"Come on. Let's go play with it," she said, fitting Jason's mask as well as her own. When she took a deep breath, her son copied her. But before they could dive the bubbles started again and Jason shrieked with more laughter.

On the other side of the pier, Margaret was continuing her pitch to Joan. "Honestly, Joan, I think you must have a fever. I really think you should go home."

"And I think I should take a walk," Joan huffed, not understanding the woman's uncharacteristic meddling. As she marched toward the line of yew trees which protected the pier, she stopped.

"Did you hear something?"

"Hear? Hear what?"

"I heard someone."

"I didn't hear anything at all," Margaret countered, but Joan was already walking past her. When they got to the pier, Joan looked out on the quiet waters of the cove.

"I told you it was nothing," Margaret said.

"I could swear I heard someone laughing. Now if you don't mind, I'll get back to my walk."

As Joan turned again toward the yew trees, Margaret took a breath and followed.

Dawn and Jason swam beneath the surface through sun-streaked waters. They could not see the dolphin, even when revolving in a full circle to look for it. But when their backs were turned, the mammal rushed past them. Disappearing into the shadows, Dawn saw only its receding flukes. When it rushed past them again and they pushed to the surface for air, Jason howled with laughter.

"It's playing with us. Come on!"

At the line of yew, Joan heard a child's distinct laughter.

"That doesn't sound like nothing to me," Joan growled, and marched again to the pier. All Margaret could do was follow.

Below the water's surface, Jason spotted the dolphin first and swam after it. They were deeper now, swimming through a bright sea, and below them the pebbled ground turned to golden sand. The dolphin circled and, as it did, exhaled. From its blowhole a gigantic bubble of air emerged and grew. A perfect ring of silver floated in the water. As the dolphin danced through it, Jason kicked to follow. When her son swam through the glittering circle Dawn could not help but think of the necklace Mary had given to her.

The dolphin burst the ring with its beak and where there had been one glittering bubble now there were millions. She saw how her son was immersed in them and the laughing eyes behind his mask. The dolphin approached even nearer, now eye-to-eye with him. She saw how Jason placed his hands on either side of the dolphin's head, pulling himself close. She wondered if he felt what she had felt when looking into its eyes, and if he experienced the same sense of mystery, or saw the imaginary spark of firelight.

As Jason pulled himself in, looking deeper, his gut heaved. He moved even closer, hoping what he saw was real and not a dream. Behind the dark iris, light flickered. He thought he saw a butterfly opening gossamer wings, flashing like a firefly. Then there were thousands of them, dancing like faeries in a glowing pattern of light, sparking where they touched. The light grew more intense as a pattern took shape, settling into a form that looked so familiar. But Jason was out of air and out of time and, when his mother reached out and took his hand, he had to let go. As the boy kicked toward the surface, he could not take his eyes off the mammal receding into the shadows beneath him. Then they were on the surface and he was laughing and Dawn could not help but laugh, too, because he was so excited. She pulled him into her arms as he howled.

"Okay, kiddo. Let's get you out for a break." Turning to the pier, she found herself looking up at Joan.

"Oh! Joan! Hi!" she called.

Joan didn't say anything except stare down at her. Margaret, standing beside Joan, shrugged her shoulders in warning.

"Beautiful day, isn't it?" Dawn said, slipping off her facemask. "We're just having a little swim. Just me and Jason. Isn't that right, kiddo?"

The sea boiled behind her. The dolphin leaped, its great length sliding from the ocean. Water sluiced from its back as it swiveled, crashing back with a voice like thunder. Joan stood quite still, her eyes on the dorsal fin as it sliced toward the bay.

"Just you and Jason?" Joan asked, frowning. She stooped, picking up the therapy book then looked down at Dawn, her eyes full of annoyance.

"What about a cup of tea?" Margaret asked. "I have a flask in the car."

"I don't think so," Joan replied, laying the book back on the pier. She gave Margaret a dirty look and, marching to her car, started the engine and left.

After they got out of the water and dried off Margaret drove her Morris back to the house. Dawn put Jason in the punt, pushing the outboard motor to its limit. As she steered down the bay, her head raged at what a fool she had been and how she could ever think they could get away with it without being seen. As she turned into the harbor, sliding past the red buoy, Jason sat at the bow with his back to her, upset because he also understood the possible consequences of being seen with his friend.

That night he whined, not wanting to go to bed. Dawn hoped he was just overtired because she had not heard him like this in days. After she led him upstairs to their room, she and Margaret sat down at the kitchen table.

"I don't think we should take Jason back to the cove, at least not for a few days," Margaret said. Dawn studied the worry in her mother-in-law's face.

"Don't you trust Joan? Will she say anything about Jason's friend?"

"Of course, I trust Joan. It's just…well, it's a big secret. You know how important it is to the town. I'm not sure how she's going to react. I don't think we should take the chance for a bit."

"But Jackie could come back."

"Jackie will always come back."

Dawn put her head in her hands. "I don't know how Jason will react."

"Neither do I."

CHAPTER TWENTY-FOUR

For the next few days Dawn kept Jason away from the dolphin. She took two days off from the Seashell and, with Margaret, drove up to Kenmare to buy her son a new electronic games console, hoping to distract him. He wouldn't even open the box. They spent the rest of the day exploring the peninsula and places they had never visited before. Margaret took them to the copper mine museum in Allihies, then to the only cable car in Ireland which connects Dursey Island to the mainland. As they looked up at the small tram crawling along its cable, Margaret explained to Jason how, in the old days, the cable car had hauled almost everything, even cattle, across the dangerous channel to the island but Jason was not interested. When they returned to Kilcastle in the late afternoon, Dawn walked him to the local playground but he wouldn't so much as climb on a swing.

The next day, they packed a lunch and took a long walk along the Beara Way as they had when Michael was alive. Along the wild coast Dawn led Jason to a tidal pond, encouraging him to search beneath the rocks for small crabs and urchins but all he did was look out to sea. As the sun bent toward the horizon, he let her take his hand but held it only for a moment. She realized her son longed for what he could not have. Together, they watched the sun set and, as the high cirrus turned to crimson, she wished they were somewhere even more remote than Beara where secrets weren't necessary and Jason could swim with the dolphin. She watched as he left her, walking toward a beach where a soft swell lapped on to a pebbled shore. She did not follow him, thinking he needed room for his own thoughts. As she searched the sunlit horizon, wondering about the dolphin, her thoughts turned to Jackie and her stupid promise to him. She hoped the fisherman was having bad luck wherever he was.

Jackie stood tall at the wheel of his trawler, holding a cold mug of tea in one hand as he kept an eye on the deck below. His mate and the two crew members he had hired threw his catch into a saltwater tank already full of fish. Jackie whistled an Irish jig, believing his luck had changed on a turning tide, his good fortune rising with at least a couple ton of monkfish. He grinned, thinking how Padraig the banker would react when he handed him a few month's cash. He would also make good on Peter's birthday present and, while he was at it, take his son up to Dublin to buy more computer games at the stalls on Mary Street. He laughed as he imagined Peter's excitement. But sipping his tea, he also recalled that the fishing trip had not started out that way.

When the banker had left following the unexpected morning visit, and Jackie had ordered his mate to get ready to take the trawler out again, he had been half-bluffing. Jackie had already used up his month's quota for pelagic fish — mackerel, herring, cod and whiting — as well as the quota for flat demersal fish that hid on the bottom like sole, monkfish and plaice. No quota meant no fishing. However, the banker had meant business and if Jackie was to keep the trawler he needed cash, and to get the cash he needed fish. But to catch the fish he had to play a high-stakes game of cat and mouse with a faceless organization much bigger than him.

As the banker had climbed into his car and Jackie considered the fecker's threat, he had recalled the current value of every species of fish on the market. He realized that if he snuck out and worked quick, he might catch a good price. Deciding to take a walk to mull things over, he had wandered down the pier. He had found Johnny standing on the stern of his boat, squinting into the morning sun.

"Johnny," Jackie called as he jumped onboard.

"Jackie," Johnny called back, and they stood for a bit in silence.

"Fine weather," Jackie observed.

"It is. Real steady," the old man replied, and they stood there some more.

"Johnny, what's the score on monk?"

"Monkfish?" Johnny returned, his old eyes holding questions. "What'cha want with monk?"

"Just curious is all."

"Oh, are ya now?" The old man coughed, pondering as he made a rollup. "Well, I hear the *D'Eloise Dawn* put in last night with a load of 'em."

"Ah," Jackie grunted, looking out to sea. "Any idea where they caught 'em?"

"Now where do ya think? Continental shelf. Same as always."

"But where on the shelf?"

The old man squinted at Jackie's hard-headedness.

"What's wrong with ya, lad?" he said, raising an arm and pointing. "You aim your boat at two-seventy degrees, steam away and shoot your nets. Is that simple enough for you?"

Jackie thought hard. Monk was getting over five-thousand euro a ton, the best-priced fish of the lot right now. He'd have to steam a good six hours to get to the shelf, then add at least a half-day in finding them if he could find them at all. That meant a good three-thousand euro in diesel fuel alone. He'd need to hire two more hands to work with the mate. His crew would demand fifty percent share of any sale but he'd negotiate for far less. With hard bargaining, and if he could catch more than a few ton, he'd make a sizable profit. As he hitched up his trousers Jackie realized he could forget about using the legal fish marts dotted around the harbor to sell his catch. Not on this trip. But as he fidgeted with the buttons on his torn work shirt, he thought his plan was a reasonable one. If he fished beyond his quota and got away with it, it would give him the breathing room he needed. He leaned over and spat in the water.

"Johnny, what's the odds of lending me a net?"

"Every time you borrow a net it comes back banjaxed."

"That's not true."

"Sure, it is," the old man grunted. "Holed, every last one of 'em. That's a fact."

Jackie thought quick. The old man was right, of course. But he was planning on a get-in-quick and make-a-killing scheme and he wanted all the net he could muster. If the old man wouldn't lend him one, he could think of no one else he could turn to.

"Please, Johnny," he appealed. "I'd be grateful for the favor. I don't ask often."

"Like hell you don't." The old man sighed and gazed out at the harbor. "Ah take it, lad," he said, then gave him a sharp look. "Jackie, I know yer out of quota and on the tick to everyone in town. Even Liam at the fuel co-op and Donal over at the steel fabricators are saying ya owe 'em."

Jackie glared at the old man. "They'll get their money."

"You listen to me," Johnny said, hunkering down on the half-decker's gunwale. "When you fish beyond your quota it's never worth it 'cause someone's always going to catch you out."

"Go on with ya. I don't know what you're talking about."

"Course you don't."

Lighting his rollup, the old man decided to tack hard because the lad was as bull-headed as they come. Besides, he'd known Jackie's family for a lifetime. As he puffed, he looked up, considering the beefy fisherman and the trouble he might encounter.

"So, Jackie," the old man said, scratching his stubble, "if you did head out to the shelf, and if someone caught you, the Fisheries for instance, you'd say you're going on a long shakedown cruise, wouldn't ya? To check out that feckin' rebuilt engine again in that damned trawler of yours."

"You'd be right there," Jackie agreed, shifting his weight.

"And if someone asks why you're carrying so much net, you'd say you were checking the drums and hydraulics. Wouldn't ya?"

"That's exactly what I'd say," Jackie said, relieved the old man would play along. "Johnny, if anyone asks, I hope you'll tell 'em the same." He stretched out a hand and the old man shook it.

"The luck'll come back, Jackie. Just be careful how you go."

"That's a promise, Johnny."

Jumping back on to the pier, Jackie had walked back to his trawler with a spring in his step.

As his mate cursed, working to haul over the borrowed net, Jackie had made a phone call to the Russian called Skate, which everyone knew was not his real name. He had used the smuggler's services once before when times were tough and he was out of quota. Having made a deal with the crooked middleman, just before noon Jackie turned the key on his trawler's ignition. Engaging the transmission, he held his breath and prayed he'd be able to hold it for the next few days. As he steamed away from the pier he glanced at the pier-side sensor that would automatically inform Ireland's Sea-Fisheries Protection Authority of his departure. He had long learned that Big Brother would track the trawler across every nautical mile of his voyage. As he steered out of the harbor, he cursed the Authority because they regulated with an uneven hand. Instead of pulling over the Spanish, Dutch and French boats that were likely fishing over the limit, they concentrated on the local boats because they were easy pickings and couldn't escape the jurisdiction if fined.

And fined they were but the penalties were often much stiffer than a ton of cash. If a boat was caught over-quota, the result was most likely open and shut. The skipper-owner would be arrested by the Gardaí and the case scheduled for the District Court. If the skipper lost the case the trawler could be impounded, his license revoked, his fishing days numbered. Steaming down the bay, Jackie recognized that this was the risk he was taking.

But he remembered Johnny's advice and would follow it to the letter. He'd steam a few hours west on a shakedown cruise. He'd drop his nets in a hundred and fifty fathoms of water to test the drums and, while he was at it, find time to go bottom fishing. With the trawler's belly full, he'd creep back to Ireland but not to Kilcastle. Oh no, he thought, not Kilcastle, at least not at first. First, there was the smaller harbor to be navigated on the other side of the peninsula, one seldom visited in the wee hours. He'd meet the Russian there and in darkness they'd offload the catch. Jackie would make much less than market price, of course, but what the hell, he thought. If the catch was big enough, he wouldn't give a shite. As he throttled into the choppy waters of the Atlantic, he crossed himself, saying a quick prayer for a bit of luck.

When they hit the shelf, he ordered the mate and the two Polish crew members he had hired to shoot the nets. He'd decided on a twin-rigged configuration so there was plenty of it. As they got ready, Jackie looked out the wheelhouse window at a glass-smooth sea and thought it couldn't be a better day. When the nets with their wings, bridles and center weights hit the water a Minke whale broke surface off the bow, always a good omen. He became certain of his luck when they hauled in the nets. One was half-full while the other burst at the seams. When they offloaded, he discovered two-thirds of the catch was monk at five-thousand euro the ton with other bottom fish thrown in for good measure.

They worked hard for days and the crew complained about the lack of rest but Jackie worked them without mercy, promising additional shares to keep them at it. His crew also knew the price of monk and they busted their backs hauling nets and sorting fish to make more money. Jackie counted his blessings as the iced tanks below-decks began to fill and he felt sure his luck would hold. Then, on the third day, his mate hooked the cod-end line and started winching in, bringing up another load. When the net cleared the water Jackie saw the shark, a big blue, thrashing in it like Satan.

"You!" he yelled through the open window to his mate, frozen at the winch. "Dump it mid-decks!"

As the load swung over the gunwale Jackie went for his shotgun. He had owned the twelve-gauge for years but had only used it twice. On both occasions it had bought him out of a bushel-load of trouble. Unlocking the steel cabinet he grabbed the long gun, broke it, pulled two shells from a drawer, and chambered the rounds. He ran out the door and, jumping down to the deck, looked up at the hanging net. It twisted and shook as the shark fought.

"Drop it right there!" he yelled at the mate, pointing. The net parted and the deck streamed with a carpet of fish and a fourteen-foot blue thrashing for its life. It bucked, striking a sorting table. The steel buckled like cardboard. One of the Poles danced in, grabbing the shark's whipping tail.

"No, you gobshite," Jackie roared. "Get back!"

As the crew back-peddled, Jackie stepped closer. The predator could make kindling of his boat but he took his time, admiring the long pectoral fins and jaws filled with curving knives. He lifted the shotgun and pulled the trigger. The boom rattled the rigging but the shark's head was mincemeat. When the Poles lifted it, he realized they were going to throw it over the side.

"Shark's good eating," Jackie explained as his crew gathered 'round, staring at the carcass.

"It's shite," the mate said. "It'll be full of buckshot."

"Don't listen to him. We'll have steaks for lunch," Jackie said, and the Poles slid it to the side for later butchering.

They continued to fish for another few days, lifting one net after another until they had over five ton of monk in her belly, more than Jackie had ever caught on a single trip. He checked the barometer and, seeing its steady fall, glanced up at a darkening sky filled with torn stratus. His spine tingled cold as a feeling came over him that he'd stretched his luck far enough, so he ordered the crew to stow the nets then turned his trawler east.

As he advanced the throttle, holding a cup of tea in a calloused hand, he shook off his fear by belting out one of his favorite Irish rebel tunes and the wheelhouse shuddered with his song. He glanced to Heaven, raising his mug in gratitude for his good fortune, praying that his luck would hold for just a few more hours.

The trawler arrived at the meeting point early and Jackie sat off Ballycrovane harbor waiting for full darkness. Running lights doused, he hid his boat behind a point thrusting out from the mainland like a crooked finger. As he sipped another mug of tea, he remembered that the harbor had been used for centuries by local fisherman because it provided excellent shelter and a safe anchorage. But he also recalled that its narrow inlet and isolated location attracted users of a different breed and for other reasons. In the distant past, pirates secreted fast frigates from the English within its rugged confines. More recently, during the Irish revolution, gunrunners snuck past the nearby coastguard station to arm local militia intent on throwing out the British. In modern times, gossip had it that the harbor was familiar with drug smugglers intent on making an ill-gotten living. As Jackie looked out on the fractured rocks close by, he chuckled, draining his mug. For such a sleepy place, the harbor had attracted its fair share of criminals, infamous armies of invaders, famous saints on the run and innocents seeking sanctuary. Now it was his turn.

When the wheelhouse clock struck 2AM, and on a rising tide, Jackie advanced the throttle to slow ahead. Easing the trawler from its hiding place, he made way for the slot that led to the inlet and the harbor beyond. Peering through the window, he could make out the shadowed silhouettes of his men waiting on deck, surrounded by the boxes they'd filled with monkfish. As he turned into the inlet, he reviewed his plan to meet Skate's boat and sling the load across with the davit crane. Skate would weigh the catch and send across a bundle of cash. That was the deal. Then the smuggler would sail into the night, the load mingling with the confusion of the Dublin fish markets, and no one would be the wiser.

Jackie eased the trawler down the inlet, keeping an eye out for shoals on the starboard side. In the darkness, he made out the shadows of a half-dozen fishing boats where their owners had left them tied to the small pier. Spotting Skate's darkened trawler rocking in the estuary, Jackie throttled back and stepped out the door.

"You! Get up here!" he hissed to his mate who waited on the deck below. "Mind the throttle. Don't let her drift, hear me?"

As his mate scurried into the wheelhouse, Jackie jumped down and made his way to the crane controls. He waited as Skate put his trawler slow ahead until the hulls of the two boats touched. Someone threw a rope, tying the trawlers together. When a thin-looking figure walked out on deck of the other vessel, he recognized the man as Skate.

"You got 'em?" Skate called, his guttural accent traveling in the darkness.

"Keep yer voice down!" Jackie spit. "Yeah, I got 'em. You just better have the money."

Skate smirked, his crooked teeth flashing in the darkness. As he powered up the crane, Jackie could taste the cash. A huge box of fish lifted from the deck as the Poles worked to steady it. He swung it over the stern of Skate's boat and, as three of the smuggler's men grabbed it, Jackie lowered the box.

'That's one,' Jackie thought, grinning, 'and a whole lot more to go.'

They worked in darkness for over two hours. They had transferred most of the tonnage and only had a few more boxes to go. Jackie lifted another one and, as it hung ten feet above his deck, he heard a snap like ripping song. Then the heavy box pitched and Jackie realized a line was parting.

"Get out of there! Go on!" he yelled, and the Poles scattered.

Jackie worked the crane controls, hurrying to land the heavy load back on his own deck. Then the line parted completely and the box fell, striking the gunwale on its way down. It balanced on the edge then tipped, the box and its contents tumbling into the sea.

"Shite, ya fecker!" he roared.

As he grabbed a knife, Jackie heard laughter coming from Skate's boat. Rushing to the gunwale, he cut the ropes securing his trawler to the smuggler's and, turning, saw his mate at the wheelhouse door.

"Don't just stand there. Full astern!"

Jackie rushed to the side, peering aft into the darkness. The box floated upright, half-submerged. He had the idea of snagging the box with a long fishing gaff and rescuing what remained of his monk. But as he leaned over the gunwale the boat shuddered, wash boiling from the stern, and he realized that rather than reversing the mate had pushed the throttle full ahead.

"Gobshite!" Jackie barked and, leaning further over the side, scanned the water ahead. He saw a thick line, the one that had parted. It floated on the water forward the bow and his trawler was steaming right at it. Pushing past the Poles, he flew up the stairs and into the wheelhouse, seeing the mate at the wheel.

"What the fuck are you at?"

"You said full ahead," the mate yelped.

Jackie looked forward. The sea was empty, the thick line already under the hull. He shoved the mate out of the way and reached for the throttle. Before he could touch it, the trawler shuddered as the line fouled on the spinning prop. The vibration grew worse and he heard screeching from below decks. He closed the throttle and killed the engine but knew in his bones the damage was done.

"Jackie, I'm sorry. I really thought —" his mate whined.

"You stupid eejit!" Jackie roared, then stormed out to the bow. They floated without power and, gauging the distance to shore, he realized the incoming tide would carry them on to the rocks. He suspected the shaft was bent but he would worry about that later.

"You!" he yelled at one of the Poles. "Throw out the anchor!"

Jackie heard the clatter of chain and the splash as the anchor hit the water. He worried at the distance to the approaching shore but felt a tug as the anchor took hold and held them fast.

In the darkness an engine roared to life. He turned to see Skate's trawler make-way toward the inlet at full throttle, a wake of phosphorescence spewing from its stern. Jackie opened his mouth to yell but realized the pirate wouldn't hear him, much less give a damn. As the crook steamed out of the small harbor, he carried five tons of Jackie's monkfish and also the cash he was owed. He'd been screwed and there wasn't a thing he could do about it.

When he reentered the wheelhouse, he kicked out his mate and slammed shut the door. He stood at the wheel and thought about his son and dead wife and the disappointment they'd have in him. When he got hold of himself, he dried his eyes and clambered below decks to the engine room. He examined the shaft, seeing how it had bowed, busted, to sit tight against its housing. He'd have to disassemble it and thread it out the hull, and he'd need to buy a refurbished one which he could not afford except through some astounding miracle. He walked back on deck and, as the tide turned, ordered his crew to heave the remaining monkfish overboard. He leaned against the gunwale watching the shiny treasure drift away toward the open sea. As dawn brushed the horizon, he got on the radio.

Two hours later, in a freshening wind and light drizzle, Johnny's boat inched into the harbor. The old man threw a line and, a couple of hours after that, Jackie's trawler was towed through sweeping rain into Kilcastle. A crowd of fishermen gathered at the pier gawking at the busted boat. Jackie tried to find comfort in knowing that at least he'd not been caught for fishing over quota but realized he was playing games with himself.

Standing at the wheel of his wounded trawler he wondered if he wouldn't be better off in jail.

CHAPTER TWENTY-FIVE

A low-pressure system swept in on sheeting rain. The wind got up from the northwest, replacing the southern weather with an uncomfortable chill. When Jason refused to eat breakfast, instead slouching at the living room window, Dawn worried for him. But Margaret reassured her and insisted that she stick to her plan and go back to work.

In the rain the square was empty of tourists. Dawn hurried past The Lighthouse, the early-morning pub used by fishermen after every trip. Inside, Jackie hunched against the bar over a couple of pints and a half-one of Paddy's, beating himself up for his stupidity with hopeless thoughts of the future. He did not look up as Dawn strode by the window.

When she arrived at the Seashell, she found Mary sitting in her chair crippled by rheumatism. Dawn made her a hot cup of tea and, after draping a throw across her lap, swept the floor and tidied the merchandise. They waited but not a single customer entered throughout the entire morning. In the early afternoon they had one visitor. A tourist ventured inside, shaking off the rain like a wet dog, but he left without buying anything. An hour later, Mary hobbled to the front window. Gazing out on the rainswept street, she decided to close the shop because there was no point in staying open.

Dawn was home early on a day that felt of autumn and the family took dinner in the kitchen. She and Margaret filled the silence with idle talk while Jason picked at his cottage pie until he crept from the room. Dawn found him at the picture window hunting for the dolphin in harbor waters that looked as raw as hammered steel.

Thinking to dispel the gloom, in the early evening Margaret lured them back into the studio. She worked on the Solas Mór painting and, when Dawn glanced up, she noticed how her mother-in-law had taped Jason's dolphin drawings to the walls to showcase his efforts. Their colorful forms leaped from sun-dappled seas but her son wouldn't look. He lay sprawled across the big chair with his back to them, his sketchpad and paints untouched.

"Jason, I'm sorry. I really am," Dawn said, kneeling at his side. "We'll see your friend again, you'll see. We just have to be patient."

Working at her easel, Margaret tried to think of ways to change the subject. "Dawn, can you come look at this? You, too, Jason."

Jason rose from the chair, shuffling to his grandmother as Dawn followed.

"What do you think?" Margaret asked. "I was hoping to have it finished for Remembrance Day but I'm still not sure of it."

Dawn and Jason studied the painting which was now full of color. The island's olive peak thrust into swirling gold-lit storm clouds while sailors fell from the sinking barque as dolphins leaped toward them. A slate-blue sea boiled all around.

"What are you going to paint there?" Dawn asked, pointing to the foreground which was still blank.

"It needs something to catch the eye but I've still not decided."

"Jason," Dawn coaxed, holding out his sketchpad, "why don't you show Nana what to draw?" But all he did was turn his back.

Margaret glanced at the sulking pair. Putting down the paintbrush she grabbed her raincoat from where it hung behind the door. "Okay, you two. Come with me."

"Where are we going?" Dawn asked.

"Out. Quick smart, now, and I'll have no arguments."

Kilcastle Pub was packed with the buzz of local families trying to forget the rain with a drink and a chat. Margaret pushed past a group of fishermen, mouths flapping as they exaggerated recent catches, while farmers cursed the state of silage and their wives swapped gossip. Children ran laughing through the crowd and, as Dawn led in Jason, she was met by welcoming smiles even from those she barely knew. A woman asked her to stop and talk but Dawn begged off, unable to take her eyes from her son. He clung tight to her hand, hanging back as if seeking shelter from the crowd. She wanted shelter, too, realizing it was her first time in the pub since the accident. She squeezed his hand and they walked on.

She followed her mother-in-law past the crowd to the back, where town's people danced to the music of the traditional group gathered at the far wall. She remembered how Michael had played his Uilleann with the musicians only a year ago.

"Are you okay?" her mother-in-law asked and when Dawn nodded said, "Stay here. It's my twist."

As Margaret moved toward the bar, Dawn noticed Carol sitting at a table with Lydia. Seeing them, the young girl dashed up to take Jason's hand but he pulled away.

"Please, Jason," Lydia insisted. "Let's go play."

He looked up at his mother, hesitating.

"I'll be right here," Dawn said, forcing a smile. "Go find Nana. She'll need help carrying the drinks."

He shook his body like a border collie then took Lydia's hand and ran into the crowd. When he left Dawn stood alone, feeling like a stranger. Between dancing couples, she could see the table where last year her family had sat as Michael ate sausages and talked with Jackie. She remembered Jason running up wanting money for ice cream and how his father had lifted him with words of laughter.

"How's the dog therapy going?"

Dawn looked up to see Joan dancing past with another woman. The librarian's face was set with annoyance but she waltzed into the crowd before Dawn could think of a reply. She wondered if Joan had talked to anyone about the dolphin and worried that Jason might never swim with it again. She felt Carol's eyes on her. As the woman strode across the floor, Dawn stiffened.

"Just who I wanted to talk to," Carol brayed, hooking her arm. As the woman chattered on about Remembrance Day and the number of wreaths still to be made, the PA crackled.

"Now for an old favorite," the musician who looked like a fox announced. "We want more dancers out on the floor for *The Voyage*."

As the musicians started playing the classic tune made famous by Christy Moore, Carol's face seemed to dissolve, her voice drowned out by the familiar melody. Dawn looked across the room, remembering Michael as he was a year ago. She saw him stand tall and, lifting the green box, stride across the floor from the table where they had sat so close together. She saw him sit with the musicians, his strong hands on the Uilleann, and the way he looked at her. She heard his gruff voice sing the song meant just for them.

She remembered his voice as he sang the lyrics which describe loving families and the struggles they must endure. She recalled how he had grinned at her as he sang of the voyage they were on and reexperienced the joy she had felt as he sang it. She remembered how he had put down his pipes so he could dance with her and how she had looked up into his eyes, knowing she would never stop loving him no matter what storms they encountered or how far off course they might be blown. She recalled how Jason had run toward them, back from the shop with a face full of ice cream, and how Michael had hoisted him high. They had all danced together as he sang the final chorus and, as he held her, she had been touched by the words of *The Voyage* which reflected her own marriage because, as the song says, their love would keep them afloat no matter what troubled waters they might encounter.

Then she remembered how, when he finished his song, the room had filled with applause. As he smiled down at her, she recalled what he had said earlier to Jackie about selling his father's boat and had decided to spring one of her fabled traps. Michael had seen the teasing question in her eyes and frowned, suspicion.

"Don't look at me like that," he had said. "What are you planning to get me into now?"

She had replied only with a giggle.

"Dawn, are you listening?"

The image of Michael froze in her head. She focused, seeing Carol's glare. "Dawn, you need to pay attention," the woman snorted. "We all have to buckle down if we're going to get everything ready for Remembrance Day."

But Dawn could not buckle down because she was caught in the memory of her husband's question.

"Come on, out with it," he had growled. "Dawn, I know you're up to something. So, what is it?"

She had taken his hand, toying with his fingers, grinning. "Let's take the boat out tomorrow. We might not get another chance, not if you sell it. Anyway, you promised."

"I did?" he had asked, grinning. "No, I didn't."

"Yes, you did."

"No, I'm feckin' sure I didn't."

"Oh, yes you did!" Jason had chimed in.

"Oh, I did, did I?" Michael had chuckled, looking from one to the other.

"Can we, can we Dad? Please?"

Michael had laughed, pulling his family close. "What choice have I got between the pair of ya? If it's a boat trip you want, it's a boat trip you'll get."

Standing in the middle of the pub, Dawn looked down at her shaking hands that seemed to belong to someone else.

"… there's so little time and so much left to do," Carol continued. "We're almost out of yew but I asked Joan again and she promised to do it. Now listen carefully…"

Carol continued to yap but the words were lost in a rising storm. Dawn's mind spun, replaying her teasing request for an innocent boat trip. One which had snared her husband into an agreement. One which had led them to unthinkable consequences. The room reeled to the rhythm of her selfish words. *Let's take the boat out tomorrow. Let's take the boat out tomorrow. Let's take —*"

"Am I boring you? Dawn?" Carol stood there, arms crossed, frowning.

"I'm sorry, Carol. It's just …." Dawn murmured, and wanted to throw up. She swayed, stumbling backwards. She bumped into a pair of dancers, then turned, rushing across the floor, pursued by the memory of the trap that had killed her husband.

On the first morning of his family's absence the dolphin had waited patiently in the hidden cove for their arrival. When they did not come, he had searched for them. He had patrolled the bay looking for Dawn's punt and when he did not see it went into the harbor itself. There, he had waited in the shadows by the town's pier, noticing the empty berth where his friend's trawler often tied up. He had recalled the danger the fisherman might cause and was relieved that the boat was still at sea. He had moved from his hiding place, swimming to the dock below the house on the hill. Seeing that it was deserted, he had continued his search. He had swum back out of the harbor, then west down the bay and past the small island with its cable car. The wild part of him sang in longing and his pod had called back in reply. Their distant melody told him they had seen the land walkers who were his family on a beach he had visited many times before.

As the sun set, he had approached the rocky shore. Upon it he could see them standing in the evening light. In his joy, he had thought to stretch out with his gift as he had done before. He could sail to them on the sealight and sweep them into his arms. But he had held back, sensing that the surprise of his greeting would cause untold damage. As his family left the beach, he had worried he would never again know their love as he had when walking upon the land with them. That evening, with the weather again turning stormy, he had swum to the distant island to ride out the gale in the hidden lagoon. When the rising sun brought no comfort, he had sought counsel from his pod who floated with him.

"When I swim near them with flukes and fins, they do not fear me because they do not know who I am," he sang. "I can visit them with the gift or sing to them in their dreams. But if I make myself known as I am, they will run, afraid. They think I am dead. How do I bring them close, to know their love as I did before?"

"Do nothing," one had sung, "you must wait until they come to you."

"Go now, quickly, and reveal what you have become," another had whistled. "If you do not, they will never understand and you will lose them forever."

But the brother residing within him had said without words, '*Do not heed the pod. Instead, sing your song and feel its gift. Listen, and you will know when it is time to reach for the boy and woman. Until then we must wait.*'

Thinking of his brother's counsel, he had slipped back out of the lagoon, heading again toward the mainland. When he had arrived at the town's harbor he had reached out with his consciousness, sensing change. The trawler of his old friend was back. It nestled at its tie-up along the pier and even underwater the dolphin could feel the anger that surrounded it. He had remained submerged until after nightfall. But now, breaking surface, he crept toward the pier.

He sensed her without needing to see her. When he surfaced, he heard her weeping and rose upon her sorrow. The mist of his consciousness merged with the wind and he drifted over the pier and across the square to the gathering place they had frequented in another life. Below him, in the shadows of an entryway recess, he found her drenched by the falling rain. He watched as the older women he recognized as his mother lead his son on to the street to find her. As they consoled his wife, he longed to reach out to dry her tears; to show her the miracle of transformation he had been granted and bring her to him. But he again remembered his brother's warning and sensed it was not time, at least not yet. Instead, he drifted on the wind, following them to the house. He crept to the upstairs window and watched as the boy was put to bed. He stood guard until his son slept.

When the boy was sleeping, he willed the mist to carry his consciousness down the exterior wall of his old home. Huddled at the wide window, hidden within the wind, he could not help tapping his love against the rainswept glass.

"He's asleep," Margaret whispered as she crept back down the stairs. Her gaze roved to the window and the sound of the tapping rain. She glanced to the other side of the room. Dawn sat on the living room floor, hugging her legs like a child. "Dawn, I'm so sorry I brought you to the pub," Margaret continued. "I didn't think."

"No, it's just —" Then her daughter-in-law's voice trembled, her eyes swelling with more tears. "I miss him so much. I miss his smile and how he'd look at me. I miss when he'd laugh at me. I miss his touch. I miss sharing with him. Like when Jason was in hospital back in Boston. I needed to talk to him. I *had* to talk to him." She looked up. "Do you know I actually phoned him? Then I remembered," she said and her voice broke. "Michael isn't here anymore."

"I'm so sorry," Margaret murmured. She crouched on the floor, taking her daughter-in-law's hand. Dawn began to sob again, her head falling on to her mother-in-law's shoulder.

"I talked to Father Danny," Dawn said finally, "but I don't understand. He told me to jump, whatever that means."

"Jump?"

"But even if I could, how do you learn to live without someone you love so much? Michael wasn't just a part of my life. He was all of it."

Margaret reached out, cupping her face. "Oh chicken, don't you see what Father Danny means? Michael is here, right here all around you." The older woman's eyes drifted across the room. "He's in the air. He's in the light. He's sitting on that old couch he liked so much." She turned toward the window alive with pattering rain. "He's tapping on the glass, trying to get your attention. Can't you believe that?"

Dawn shook her head. "I don't think I believe in anything, anymore."

Margaret stood, walking to the window. She stared unseeing past the rain-spattered glass, through the roiling mist. She focused on the dim light of the harbor buoy as it swayed in uncertain seas.

"Dawn, if you can't find something to believe in for yourself, can't you at least find it for Jason? I told you before. It's you who must heal first if you're going to help him."

"I can't help him. Nothing works. I'm an idiot."

"Stop saying that. Of course, it's working. You know it is. Jason is getting better."

"You mean he *was* getting better."

Margaret realized Dawn was referring to the decision to stop visiting the dolphin. She marched toward the couch, scowling down at her daughter-in-law. "Then there's nothing left for it. If Jason can't get better here, you'll just have to take him back to Boston."

"Why would you say that? No one helped him there, either."

"Then what are you going to do? Give up? You're his mother. It's you who has to decide what to do. If you don't, he'll never talk again. Have you thought of that?"

"Of course, I have. I love him."

"Do you? I don't see that anymore."

"You think I don't love him? That's what you think?" Dawn snapped, rising to her feet. "You know what? Sometimes, you can be a real pissa. Everything I do is for Jason. It's been twenty-four-seven for as long as I can remember. All I want is for him to get better. Don't you believe that?"

"Do you?"

"Of course, I do. I have to believe it."

Margaret couldn't help but smile. "Good. It seems you believe in something after all."

Dawn took a step back. "You did that on purpose, didn't you? You wanted to make me angry."

"No, I wanted you to decide. You've heard Jackie's come home. So, what are you going to do? You need to know and I want to hear it."

Dawn walked to the window. She placed a hand flat against the glass, feeling the tapping rain. "Okay, so here it is. The dolphin is helping him. We both know that. So, tomorrow we take Jason swimming with the dolphin."

"Even if Jackie's back? You're certain?"

"Jackie can go fuck himself. That's what Michael would say, isn't it? Michael would want Jason to get better no matter what stood in the way." She swung back to her mother-in-law. "In the morning, he goes swimming with his friend. We do it again and again, for as long as it takes."

"Good," Margaret said. "We both know it's a risk. But Dawn, remember the Saint. Miracles happen all the time. It will happen for Jason, too."

"You promise?"

Margaret took the young woman's hand, squeezing it. "I promise."

Beyond the window, the mist shook as he heard them. He hid within the rain until they climbed the stairs. Then he drifted up into the night, watching as his wife nestled in bed close to their son. He stayed with them until the rain had passed and dawn lit the sky. With its coming, he withdrew back to the dock, his mind tussling with their words.

His mother had promised his wife a miracle. He intended to give it to her. All he needed to do was pull her to him without scaring her off. All he needed to do was make her believe. He sang his worry, not able to think how he would do it. It was his brother who gave him the answer.

'Your song is simple. The time for waiting is over. When we encounter them again, you must act.'

CHAPTER TWENTY-SIX

C arol thumped down the *boreen* toward the cove sputtering like a two-stroke engine. She side-stepped a pothole then tripped on a fallen branch waiting in ambush. Picking it up, she shook it.

"Why is it always up to me?" she bellowed at the stick. "Can no one keep to what they promised?"

An hour earlier, while rushing to get Lydia dressed, she had received a phone call from Joan. The woman who had seemed perfectly up to dancing last night had begged-off from her promise of collecting more yew due to a relapse of her flu.

"As if I don't have enough on my plate," Carol growled.

Slinging the branch aside and hitching up the basket she had brought to carry the greenery, she marched on, ticking off the items on today's mounting To Do list. At the top were the wreaths, still not finished despite the fact that Remembrance Day was fast approaching. Then the dwindling yew supply followed by Joan's broken promise. Then there was the scramble to get someone to take Lydia to the church while she addressed this unnecessary chore. But the final straw was the American.

"Oh, how I've tried," Carol muttered.

Though she had taken into account the loss of the woman's husband as well as her injured son, the Yank's attitude was impossible to accept. Carol had worked hard to forgive her for the unprovoked attack at Margaret's house and her denial of their faith. She had buried the woman's rudeness beneath thoughts of the Golden Rule and had spent time she didn't have praying for her soul. She had even tried to overlook the oh-so-American craziness of feeding a dolphin in the harbor which had stopped only because she had goaded Jackie into do something about it. But after last night in the pub?

"That's a right bitch, that one," Carol snarled. Recalling the encounter, she stumbled, sliding on loose gravel. Regaining her balance she thought how, despite her efforts to patch over their differences by including the American in what was left to be done for the Remembrance Day ceremony, Dawn had looked right past her. Carol had spent the night tossing in bed, settling only when she had reached a conclusion: the Yank was ignorant, a menace and not to be trusted.

"Never again," Carol bristled. "I tried. There won't be another chance."

As she rounded the *boreen's* final curve she made out the target of her morning chore: the line of yew trees swaying in the breeze. Pulling out a pair of clippers she picked up the pace, wanting to finish this entire episode. But as she descended toward the sea, what she saw stopped her dead. She looked again then scurried behind a clump of gorse, pushing down the branches for a better view.

"He's hungry, Jason. No one's here. Give him another one," Dawn prompted, kneeling on the pier with her son.

When an hour after sunrise they had arrived at the cove in Margaret's car, Dawn had worried the dolphin might not be there. But the mammal had been swimming at pier-side as if it had never left and Jason's face was once again as bright as a new penny. Her son reached out with another fish and the dolphin stood tall on its tail, brushing against the pier to take it.

"See? I told you it wasn't going anywhere," Dawn whispered as Jason wrapped his arms around the enormous body.

"Jason?" Margaret called as she stepped on to the pier. "It's nine-thirty. We have to say goodbye now."

"That's what we promised, isn't it?" Dawn said, seeing her son's disappointment. "I have to work then we're going with Nana to the church. But remember what we agreed? We're coming back this evening. Go on now and say goodbye."

The dolphin rose, hanging before them, its dark eyes hunting for hers. Her neck tingled at the familiar intelligence she saw in them and she wondered at its look. Its eyes seemed to pull her in, as if wanting to speak to her with a message of great import. Instead, it turned away and she watched as its dorsal fin sliced toward deeper water. Then, the sea exploded as the dolphin leaped. As Jason broke into laughter, she could not help but think that maybe Margaret was right. Maybe a miracle would take place and her son would talk again.

When Carol witnessed the dolphin jump from the water she almost fell over. She well-remembered the promise Jackie had extracted from the Yank. "And now she's broken it," Carol hissed. "The liar!"

Throwing the basket to the ground, she pushed through the overgrowth then scampered up a hidden sheep run. As she hurried back into town, she reminded herself of what she had decided last night. The American was never to be trusted. Marching across the busy town square to Jackie's trawler, she found the mate standing listlessly on deck.

"Where's Jackie?" Carol demanded.

"Inside," the mate said, pointing a slow thumb at the wheelhouse.

"Get him."

"But he's sleeping."

"Aren't you listening? Get him right now," Carol brayed, and the mate scampered off leaving her to fume on the pier. When Jackie emerged through the wheelhouse door, she marched up close to the stern.

"Jackie! We need to talk," she barked up at him as he rubbed the hangover from his eyes.

"Carol, not now. I got enough on my plate."

"Well, now you've got even more. You'll never guess what I saw at the cove."

Jackie clambered down on deck to hear better. As she finished her report, he tasted bile and spat over the side.

"Jaysus Christ," he said through thick lips. He spotted George further down the pier, climbing from his punt. "George, come over here!"

As George trotted over Jackie jumped down, joining Carol.

"Tell George what you told me," Jackie said.

As Carol repeated her story, fishermen from up and down the pier wandered over, listening. When she finished the crowd swung on Jackie.

"I thought you had this sorted," George scowled, and turned to another fisherman. "Hugh, what'cha catch yesterday?"

"Nuthin'," the fisherman said. "Didn't even pay for the diesel."

"What about you?" George asked another. They all agreed that their recent efforts had garnered few fish from the bay or along the coast. The hubbub of voices grew angrier. "She'll ruin the fishing," said one. "We got a baby on the way. What am I gonna tell the missus?" asked another. "Johnny was right. Where there's one dolphin there's always more," cried a third. In the hubbub, George raised his voice.

"Something's scaring off the fish and we all know what," he bellowed, and faced Jackie square-on. "You're the man who promised we'd be rid of 'em. So, what are ya going to do about it?" The crowd roared for a response.

"All right, all right!" Jackie shouted, his jaw setting as the voices quieted. "First things first. I'll get the truth straight from the horse's mouth. Carol, where's the Yank?" When Carol told him, Jackie swung toward the church. "Right. Follow me."

"That's not fair! You looked!"

Jason grinned and, as he ran back into the pews, Lydia started the game of hide and seek all over again. Dawn kept an eye on him as she worked at the trestle tables with the other women. She had been able to hold tight to the feeling of contentment all morning. From the moment they had left the cove to the time Mary had said they'd open the shop late because the ladies needed help with the wreaths until this perfect moment as she tied a ribbon around a circle of greenery, she found she could breathe easier. Standing next to her, the old shopkeep looked at her watch.

"The time's getting on. I'll go open up."

"Can't I do it?"

"You stay here," Mary smiled, and touched the dolphin necklace that hung from Dawn's neck. "You keep wearing that. You never know what it might bring."

As she hobbled down the center aisle Dawn wondered at the conspiracy in her voice. She realized Margaret must have shared their early morning exploits because Mary was a friend and could be trusted. She heard laughter and saw Jason scurry past Lydia's outstretched arm. Across the table Joan sneezed, looking up with a thin smile.

"Just look at him," Joan remarked. "Amazing what a dog therapy book can do."

"What therapy?" Dawn asked and Margaret, who stood next to Joan, heard the uneasiness.

"Joan, I don't know what you're on about. Dawn, you never mentioned a new therapy."

The librarian looked from one woman to the other. "You two must think I was born in a barn," she said, watching Jason skip down the aisle. She sneezed again then reached for more greenery, frowning at the small pile. "I wish Carol would get back."

"Carol?" Margaret replied. "Where has Carol gone?"

"Out getting more yew. She wanted me to do it this morning but I'm still not feeling well. Maybe I should have picked some up at the cove the other day," she said, meeting Margaret's eyes, "but after what I saw in the water, I had other things on my mind."

"Joan," Dawn asked, focusing on her work, "do you have any idea where Carol went?"

"How would I know? Somewhere outside the town is my guess. If she'd have asked me, which she didn't, I'd have told her the cove's the best place."

The front door opened with a bang. At its cracking echo every woman around the table startled. Jackie marched down the center aisle at full throttle, Carol in his wake.

"You!" he roared, pointing. "You promised! You told me you wouldn't but you did!"

His words hit Dawn like thunder.

"What's wrong, Jackie?" Margaret asked as he neared his quarry. "You look upset."

"As if you didn't know. You've been in on it all along." He swung around, both hands flat on the table. "You gave me your word."

Dawn glanced at him then at the floor. "Jackie, I don't know what you're talking about."

"Look at her. Just look!" he cried, leaning closer. "Oh, you know what I mean."

Dawn shrugged. "Even if I did, what's the problem?"

"Problem! You promised not to feed the fecker."

"Who said we were feeding it?"

He stood tall, turning to the women. "Do you hear the talk of her? She's lying!"

The ladies began to whisper. Someone raised their voice. "Jackie, you'd best explain why you're shouting in the house of God."

"Here's why. She's feeding that damned dolphin even though she promised not to!" He swung to Margaret, his face mottled red. "You tell 'em. You know what she promised."

"Jackie, that's not exactly what she said," Margaret replied.

"Oh, she didn't, did she? So, you'd lie too! Margaret, you told me Michael would always put the town first. That dolphin is going to destroy the fishing and you know it."

Carol, steaming to the head of the table, rapped hard on its wooden surface. "For God's sake Margaret. You were there. Did Dawn promise not to feed that monster or not?"

Margaret looked from Carol to Jackie like a mouse caught between two cats. She glanced at Joan. The librarian refused to meet her gaze.

"Well?" Carol demanded. "Tell us."

Every set of eyes around the table turned on her.

Margaret squared her small shoulders. "She promised she would not feed it in the harbor. But might I remind everyone that the cove is *not* the harbor."

298

She scowled, rounding on Jackie. "You of all people know I wouldn't do anything to hurt the town. So does everyone at this table."

"I thought you had more sense," Jackie rumbled. "Ask George. Ask any of 'em. The fishing's gone bad and there's only one person here who's responsible. And we all know who that is, don't we?"

Dawn looked down the table, sensing the shift in the women's opinion.

"I don't believe this," Dawn muttered. Swinging from Jackie, she stormed from the crowd, marching up the center aisle. "Jason! Come on. We're leaving."

His head popped up from behind a pew. At the same time, a clatter of footsteps followed as Jackie and Carol pursed her like a pair of snapping dogs.

"You're not from the town so you have no right!" Jackie barked. "It will destroy Kilcastle!"

"How can you be so ignorant?" Carol howled. "The *crater* is dangerous!"

"Michael was a friend but I won't stand for it, do you hear me?"

Dawn turned, swinging on them. "Back off! Back off both of you! It's only a dolphin, isn't it?" She peered down the aisle at the women. "Well, isn't it?"

No one would look at her.

She heard a whimper. Jason stood rigid near the front door with Lydia. Jackie thrust his face at Dawn. All she could see were his bloodshot eyes.

"You broke your promise and you've endangering our livelihood. But now you hear this, Yank. I'm going out to find that thing. And when I do — be it on your head."

"Try it, Jackie, and see what happens," she growled, then marched to Jason, taking his hand. "Come on. Let's go home." As they left, Dawn pushed the door shut with a bang.

"Good riddance to her, if you ask me," Carol snapped.

"What did you say?" Carol turned as Margaret advanced toward her. "Carol, you've always been a friend. But there are times when you can be such a —"

"Can be such a what? Go on. Finish it."

"God forgive me but I can't say it in church," Margaret blurted, then swung on Jackie. "If you touch that dolphin, you'll never be welcome in my house again." She steamed on, following her family out the door.

"Carol, don't mind 'em," Jackie growled as he stepped toward the door. "You did what you had to do. Now I'm going to do what I have to do."

As Jackie rushed to the pier, he cursed himself for the bent shaft of his disabled trawler. But experience had told him there were many ways to skin a cat in open water.

"You! Get off yer arse and give me a hand!" he yelled at his mate who lounged on deck. In the lee of the wheelhouse, they unlashed the trawler's rib from its tiedown and winched it over the side. As it touched the water Jackie noticed George in his punt. He floated by the pier, the engine idling.

"George, get over here!" When George motored over, Jackie told him what he had in mind. "Get anyone who has a boat. We need a big crew if we're going to find the *crater*."

"And when we find it?" George asked.

"What'cha think?" Jackie said with a grin.

As George throttled across the harbor Jackie climbed into the wheelhouse. He opened the locker, extracting the shotgun and two boxes of shells. Running back to the deck, he climbed over the side and into the rib. He ordered the mate aboard and, as he started the outboard, saw old Johnny standing on his half-decker. But after speeding across the small patch of water at near full-throttle, the fisherman shook his head at Jackie's request for help.

"First, ya can slow down," the old man warned then eyed the shotgun leaning against the rib's gunwale. "Second, don't ask again. Lending you some nets is one thing. Killing a dolphin is another. I'll have none of it."

"It's just a big bloody fish," Jackie said. "You know the trouble it's caused."

"Did you actually see it do anything? Well, did ya?" Johnny humped. "Dolphins are more than just a fish. Pity some don't know that."

Leaving the old man behind, Jackie ignored the speed limit, flying to the mouth of the harbor. There, he found a flotilla of ribs and punts waiting.

"I'll try the cove," Jackie yelled as he stood up in his rocking boat. "George, you have the fastest punt. Take two of the ribs around Bere Island then up toward Bantry. You others. Head down past the lighthouse. If you see it, put up a flare and call me on your phones." He held the shotgun high. "When ye find it, I'll do the rest."

"And so ya will, Jackie," George called as the others shouted in agreement. The meeting ended in wakes of spume as the boats roared toward their objectives.

"You drive and I'll keep a lookout," Jackie ordered his mate as they moved into the bay. He broke the shotgun, chambering two shells.

"We're gonna kill it for sure," the mate yelled above the outboard's din. Shouldering the long gun Jackie grinned, thinking for once his mate had it right.

They slowed, making a careful search of the crags along the shoreline. Not spotting their target, Jackie ordered a turn at the white marker. As they entered the cove, he heard a roar behind him. Two ribs and a few punts charged up the bay, still hunting.

"Steady now, take her in real easy."

The mate cut the engine and they drifted in. Jackie scanned the water between the snags and islets then looked below the deserted pier but saw nothing.

"Maybe it's gone," the mate said.

"Maybe it isn't. Now shut your gob."

Except for the small entrance the cove was as tight as a fish bowl. If it was here Jackie would find it and when he found it, he would kill it. "Make yourself comfortable. It might be a long wait," he told the mate. An eye on the water, he took a seat at the bow, the shotgun on his knee.

Hidden behind a rocky snag, the dolphin surfaced, holding his breath so its plume would not give him away. Eyes above the water, he saw the rib and the men in it. They floated near the cove's entrance, blocking his escape.

When sunlight struck black metal, he recognized the dangerous weapon the fisherman held. The human part of him remembered how he would carouse with his old friend and the jokes they would play on each other. His pectorals shook with laughter as he decided on the trick. Swinging his flukes he submerged, heading in fast toward the rib.

In the stern of the boat, the mate sat bolt upright. "What the feck was that?"

"What?" Jackie grumbled, rousing himself. He scanned the cove but nothing moved, not even a seabird. "Go on with ya. Ya heard nothing."

Under the mate's feet the fiberglass vibrated. He heard a hollow bump, as if a log had struck the boat's underbelly. "There. I told you I heard something."

"You've lost yer mind. I didn't hear a sausage."

"Jackie, come down here. I heard it. Honest."

Jackie eyed his mate then crawled the short distance aft. At the stern he bent, listening.

"Are you playing games with me? I don't hear shite."

"I heard it, Jackie. Honest I did."

They both heard a hollow bump. Jackie's head swiveled to the bow.

"See? Didn't I tell ya."

"What the feck is going on?" Jackie muttered, and scrambled back forward. He leaned over the bow's gunwale but saw nothing.

"Back here!" the mate said and Jackie heard it too. The sound came once more from the stern. The rib rocked and the mate clung tight to a lanyard. "God save us, it's a ghost for sure."

"Ah go on with ya, ya gobshite. It's no ghost," Jackie said, and bent over the gunwale for a better look. The bow halyard, floating in the sea, went taut. The boat lurched forward. Jackie got to his feet as the shaking rib accelerated, towed fast through the water.

"You! Hand me the shotgun!"

The mate got his hands on the stock and reached it forward. Jackie grabbed the barrel then shouldered it, pointing it over the swaying bow. A dorsal fin sliced through the sea in front of him.

"You fecker! Let go!" he roared, taking wild aim.

The halyard went slack and the rib slid to a stop. The water boiled to starboard as the dolphin leaped, rising from the ocean as enormous as a sea monster. Jackie swung, tracking the target. The dolphin twisted, falling hard on the gunwale. As the boat pitched Jackie lost his grip and the twin barrels of the shotgun swung down. He fumbled, regaining control. As he did his trigger finger squeezed tight, the shotgun firing both barrels. When the smoke cleared, he saw a hole the size of a football breaching the deck, seawater surging in like a river. He looked up, seeing the fin slicing toward the cove's entrance.

"Feck you bastard, feck ya anyway!" he roared, shaking a fist. He whirled to his mate. "Start her up and get us back."

"But Jackie, what about —" the mate replied, pointing to the spurting water flooding the rib.

"Just do it!"

Jason stood at the living room window clutching his monkey. He watched four boats speed past the harbor's mouth, angry white wakes spewing from their sterns.

"Don't worry. They won't find it," Dawn tried, but her son's lips only trembled.

"Dawn?" She turned to find Margaret. The woman's face was filled with unease. "Dawn, I'm sorry. I should have stopped him."

"How? Jackie's an idiot and besides, I'm the one who should have stopped him." Dawn looked back at her son. His hands were pressed flat against the window. She spun around, stepping toward the kitchen. "Margaret, mind Jason, will you?"

"Where are you going?"

"To find Jackie," she growled, and strode from the room.

As the back door slammed shut Margaret stepped to her grandson.

"She'll be back," she promised. Jason turned to her, tears glinting on his cheeks. Then his hands clenched hard and he bolted past her, down the narrow hallway toward the studio.

Margaret counted to thirty to give him time to calm down then followed him. She found Jason in the studio, lying flat across the big chair. His monkey lay on the floor and she stooped, placing the stuffed animal on the work table. She eyed the painting implements and clean glass of water and, hoping to distract him, picked up a brush.

"I'm still not sure what to draw," she hemmed, considering the unfinished painting of the island and its blank area of canvas. "Jason, have you thought of anything yet? Your Nana can't think what to do." But he only buried his face in the chair's cushions. "Then how about a cup of tea and some biscuits? I bought them 'specially for you." He whined, slapping the arm of the chair. "Okay, suit yourself. When you're ready, I'll be in the kitchen."

When his grandmother strode from the room, Jason whined again but there was no one to listen. He heard rain strike the window. Slipping from the chair he stepped across the room to look out on the harbor, discovering it was now covered in a fine mist. He searched the water near the dock but could not see the dolphin. Remembering the speeding punts, he worried that the men might find his friend and what they would do to it if they did.

As the dolphin escaped from the cove past the startled fisherman, he blasted himself for his folly. Beating down the bay, his dorsal fin cutting below the surface, he realized he should have taken action by reaching for his family that morning, as his brother had counselled. But he had hesitated, afraid of pushing them away by acting too fast, too soon. Yet his indecisiveness had proven a valuable lesson: he recognized that time was running out. His flukes doubled in speed, sweeping with new resolve.

At the dock below the house, he rose again on the mist, finding his son standing at the window. He tapped on the glass, his burbling song as tranquil as a mountain brook. He watched as the young lad stepped back, startled. But when he tapped again the boy opened the window, looking out at the opaque mist. The being who was Michael grinned at his son's puzzled look and when the lad ran across the room to throw himself back on the chair, he sailed in on a breeze of sealight. His keen senses turned to the monkey. It stood on a table, its long tail hanging above the floor. Michael reached out with his gift, focusing on it. The tail moved. Only a millimeter at first and not enough for the boy to notice. But he centered his gift, concentrating, and the tail swung again. Further this time. Then back and forth and back and forth, as fast as a retriever's welcome.

Hearing the swish of fabric Jason looked up, freezing at what he saw. He stood, trying to see what was causing the tail to swing but found nothing. Then he remembered how the paintbrush had moved and the song he had heard. He wondered if he would hear it again.

'*Hello, Jason.*'

He shook his head at the buzzing in his ears. Then the whisper turned to song and, as before, the notes took on meaning.

'*What shall we paint today? Wouldn't it be fun to draw again? Maybe we could help your Nana finish her painting.*'

Jason's eyes moved to the Solas Mór canvas and the blank unfinished section. He had no idea what he might draw. He wished he could ask for advice but that meant he would have to do what he had not done in over a year.

'*You want to talk to someone, isn't that what you're thinking, Jason? You could talk to your mother. She might know what to draw.*'

No, he wouldn't talk to his mother or even his grandmother. Without his dad it hurt too much to talk to anyone about anything, which is why he had decided a long time ago not to even try. He remembered what he had seen on the night of the accident and was still convinced his father was alive and all he had to do was find him. When he had first swum with the dolphin in the waters of the cove, he thought he had been given a clue with the dancing butterflies of light he had seen in its eye. He had wanted to look deeper to make sure, but there had been no time.

305

'Why don't you ask Mister Monkey what to draw? He's a pretty smart fella. Maybe he can tell you. Why don't you talk to him, Jason?'

Jason glanced at his monkey with its lopsided grin and, reaching to the table, picked up a tube of acrylic. As he mixed his paints, he thought how it wouldn't be such a bad idea to talk to Mister Monkey. Maybe he would know what to draw. And if he did talk to him, it would stay a secret because his monkey would not talk to anyone else.

CHAPTER TWENTY-SEVEN

Lydia waited at the back of the church for what seemed like forever. She squirmed against the pew's hard wooden seat, her head bursting with the hurtful words of her mother and the fisherman and the image of her friend's upset face.

"Why do some grownups think dolphins are hateful?" she sniffed to herself.

When she had watched Jason feed it at the dock it hadn't looked like a monster. It had looked wonderful. She had wanted to feed it too but had been stopped by her mother who had screamed that the *crater* was dangerous.

"It's not dangerous," Lydia whispered. Then she broke into a giggle, thinking of Jackie's bright red face and how angry he had been because the dolphin had returned. "But it's back, and Jason will love that." Then she scowled as she remembered the fisherman's threat to find it. If he did, she worried how Jason would react and wished she could be with him. She crossed her arms and huffed, remembering her mother's order to wait for her in the church. If she disobeyed the strict command there would be trouble.

"Lydia? What's bothering you, Gersha?"

A woman, an ancient friend of her mam's, stood at the end of the pew. She adjusted her horn-rimmed glasses and peered down in near-sighted concern.

"Oh, nothing, Mrs. Sullivan," Lydia shrugged.

"Well, you stay here and keep still like your mother said. She shouldn't be much longer."

As the old lady shuffled down the aisle toward the altar, Lydia looked back to the front door. No one was there. She waited until the woman hobbled up to the tables, joining the other ladies who chattered on like a gaggle of geese. No one would notice. Lydia slipped from the pew then crept up the aisle and out the front door.

Five minutes later, Carol stormed in lugging a full basket of yew.

"Here it is, finally," she barked to the ladies. "*Crater* or no *crater*, we have a schedule to keep." As she dropped the greenery on to the table she turned, scanning the church. "Where's Lydia?"

"She was here a minute ago," old woman Sullivan said as she pointed. "She was sitting in that pew."

"I know that. I'm the one who told her to wait there, didn't I?" Carol stood on tip-toe, hunting across the nave. "Lydia? Lydia! Come up here right now!"

Nearby, Joan sat on the altar steps. She had spent the time since Dawn had stormed out stewing over Carol and Jackie's hot-tempered remarks. Hearing the woman's yowl, she looked up with a smirk.

"Carol, don't tell me you've lost Lydia?"

"Of course, I haven't lost her. She was right there!"

"Well, she's not now. You don't think she's gone out looking for that dangerous *crater*, do you?"

"The monster? Oh my God!" Carol howled, grabbing her coat. "I'll be back as soon as I can."

As she rushed up the aisle Joan blew her nose. "I'll be in the library," she said to the ladies. "Let me know if Carol comes back. God forbid we should lose her, too."

Panting from her run up the hill, Lydia crept around to the side of the house and peered in through the rain-streaked studio window. Inside, she saw Jason standing at an easel, gazing up at a large canvas. She watched him frown and how he picked up his monkey that sat on a table. When he raised its fluffy ear to his mouth, she didn't think much of it. But then she saw his lips move.

"But Jason can't talk," she said to herself, looking closer. But her friend's lips opened and closed just like anyone did when they talked. When she knocked on the glass he looked up, caught-out.

"Jason, what'cha talking about?" she asked but he only glared back. "Fine. If you want to be thick about it that's up to you. Open up."

When he opened the window and helped her into the room she crossed her arms, scowling. "Jason, if you can talk to Mister Monkey, why can't you talk to me? Is it a secret?" When he wouldn't say anything, she followed him to the easel. He tapped the blank area of canvas with the end of a paintbrush. "That's your Nana's painting, isn't it? Don't touch it again or you're going to get in trouble." But he held up a sketchpad and she looked at what he had drawn. "Is that what you want to draw on your Nana's painting?" When he nodded, she peered even closer at his drawing. "I don't get it, Jason. What's it mean?" When he still wouldn't answer, she frowned. "You're being rude. I know you can talk. I saw you. If you don't say anything I'm leaving." As she swung toward the window, he stopped her with a hand to her shoulder. She turned back, seeing his look of indecision. Then his lips pressed against her ear, moving with whispered words.

"Are you sure? But Jason, that can't be right." He nodded back as fast as a top. "Okay, maybe," she said, looking again at his drawing, "but no one is going to believe you."

He took her hand, leading her to the table, motioning to the glass filled with dirty paint water.

"It's just water, Jason. You're crazy."

He pointed over her shoulder. Lydia turned around, seeing the glowing mist gathered at the window. Then the glass on the table began to vibrate, the water shivering. Dirty paint floated to the surface where it separated, oscillating, forming a silver circle that sparkled like starlight. Then the glass skittered across the table and over the edge, smashing on to the floor.

Lydia looked up, meeting Jason's eyes. "Or maybe they will believe you."

In the kitchen Margaret sipped at a cup of tea, worrying about her family. She glanced at the clock. Thinking she had given her grandson enough time, she rose from the table to fetch him. As she turned to the door Lydia marched in.

"Lydia? What are you doing here? Chicken, where's your mother?"

"I don't know. Maybe back at the church," the child said as she walked to the sink. "Margaret, could we have another glass of water?"

"A glass? But why?"

"The other one broke and Jason asked me to get a new one."

"Lydia," Margaret said carefully, sitting again, "Jason couldn't have said that. You know he can't talk."

"He can too," she replied, reaching up for a glass on the counter. "He said, 'Lydia, please go to the kitchen and get another glass of water.'"

As the girl filled it at the tap Margaret took a sip of tea, wondering how to respond to the child's wild imagination. "Gersha," she said finally, "it's not nice to stretch the truth. I know you want Jason to talk again. We all do."

"But I am telling the truth. Now if you'll excuse me, I have to go back to Jason."

Carrying the full glass she strode toward the door, then swung back around. "Margaret, I'm not lying. Jason can talk again and that's all there is to it." Then she marched out of the room.

Margaret sat quite still, reflecting on the child's adamant conjecture. Then the teacup slipped from her hand. It shattered on the floor as the back door flew open and Dawn strode in.

"It was a waste of time, Margaret. Jackie's still out looking for the —" She stopped. Noticing the broken cup, she spun to face her mother-in-law. "What happened? Where's Jason?"

"He talked," Margaret whispered, meeting Dawn's eyes. "He talked!"

Together, they ran from the room.

"Jason?"

He stood at the window, his back to her. Dawn reached out, pulling his chin around, searching his eyes. "I need to ask you something important. Lydia told Nana you talked to her. Did you, sweetie? Did you ask Lydia to get a glass of water?"

"He won't talk to you," Lydia asserted, crossing her small arms. "He'll only talk to me. And anyway, that's not everything he said."

"Then what did he say?" Margaret asked.

"Just like I told you," Lydia huffed. "First he wanted a new glass of water. Then he said the other thing."

"What other thing?" Dawn asked.

"Well, if you really want to know, Jason told me he wants to go swimming with his Daddy again. That's what he said, really."

Margaret hid her sadness behind a smile. "But Lydia, that's not possible. His Daddy isn't here."

"Oh, yes he is. That's what Jason says. That's why he wants to go swimming with the dolphin again. To make sure."

"But Lydia," Dawn replied, "the dolphin isn't here anymore. They chased it away."

"No, they didn't. Just ask Jason."

When her son turned back to the window, Dawn followed his gaze and saw it. The dolphin floated in the quiet shadows of the dock. Then she remembered what Doctor Morrison had said and how Jason might choose a single person to talk to as a test and, if he did, he was on the road to recovery. "Reinforce any progress with the object of his trust," she whispered to herself, recalling the doctor's words. She looked again to the harbor, studying the mammal with new eyes. "Jason chose Lydia as the test but he trusts the dolphin."

"What did you say?" Margaret asked.

"Jason, look at me," Dawn said, stepping close. "Do you want to swim with the dolphin again? Is that what you want?"

"But what about Jackie?" Margaret asked. "What if he sees it?"

"Margaret, if Lydia is right, if Jason is that close, maybe that's all he needs. One more push and..."

"... he'll talk again." Margaret stared out the window, thinking hard. "If we're going to do this, we need some help."

Dawn smiled. "And I know just where to get it."

She made her first stop at the Seashell. Inside, Dawn told the kids to wait near the door. She found Mary sitting in the chair at the counter, asking her for a quiet word in the back room. It took only a few minutes to explain the idea.

"Oh, it'll be grand to wind up Jackie," Mary laughed. "Have you asked Joan, too?"

"I didn't think she'd be on our side."

The old woman placed a warm hand on Dawn's arm. "Gersha, Joan has always been on your side. But that's our Joan. Always struggling to say how she feels."

When they left the shop, Dawn led the children through the light rain and across the square. As they walked past the line of trawlers, Jason whined. She looked out to the harbor. A rib edged toward the pier. Jackie and his mate were in it.

"Keep walking," Dawn told the kids. "Don't say anything."

"Why not?" Lydia asked. "Is it a secret?"

"That's right. Everyone keep their lips sealed."

As they came abreast of Jackie's trawler, Dawn saw the mate scramble up on to the pier, tying on the painter. Then Jackie climbed up. As she passed, she noted the fisherman's angry eyes.

"Come on, kids. Keep up," she whispered.

As they strode by him, Jackie eyed the Yank then spat on the concrete. Rather than bite her head off, which he was inclined to do, he swung on his mate.

"Get the rib up," he snapped. 'Now!"

After they winched the stricken craft back on to the trawler, he had a good look at the holed fiberglass. He'd have to buy special epoxy at the chandlers, two tins at seventy euro each, which he'd have to put on the tick like everything else. But he needed the rib and, having no other choice, sent his mate for the supplies. Then he carried the shotgun to the wheelhouse and cleaned it while cursing his useless attempts to kill his quarry. Finished, he scanned the harbor but there was no sign of the dolphin.

"You bastard. You're not making a fool of me again."

He broke the shotgun, pushing home two new shells. Then he laid it on the chart table within easy reach.

When the library book slapped down on to the counter's wooden surface Joan looked up to find Dawn, Lydia and Jason on the other side. Dawn tapped the book cover with a forefinger.

"I want to return this."

"You still owe me for the library card," Joan grumbled.

"It's in there. First page."

Joan opened the book, spotting the five euro note. She sneezed, blowing her nose again, and as she handed back the change winked at Jason. "I hope the book helped. I understand canine therapy can be tough. Particularly when you have to go swimming for it."

"It certainly is tough," Dawn agreed, leaning in. "Actually, we're not finished."

"You aren't?"

"No, we aren't."

"And why's that?"

"Like you said, it's tough work."

Joan studied the woman's face. "Maybe you should keep the book."

"I don't think so. I think we need something else."

"Do you, now?" Joan replied, and leaned in too. "And what, pray tell, might that be?"

"Actually, I'm looking for a book on friendship. I'm wondering if you have one?"

"I might. It depends on what kind of friendship you're looking for."

"The kind that helps, no questions asked. How about it?"

The librarian's thin face cracked in a smile as she leaned in closer. "You should have asked an age ago. Now what do you have in mind?"

After their chat, Joan closed the library and with Lydia hustled to the church. She found Mary already huddled around the tables with the other women.

"Where's Carol?" Joan growled.

"Still out hunting for her daughter, I suspect," Mary chortled, patting Lydia on the shoulder. "Before you came in, I was explaining to the ladies how young Jason needs our help. So does his mother. The two have been through enough. Isn't that right, ladies?"

The women's voices rose in agreement.

"But won't there be trouble?" an unconvinced woman asked. "Carol says the *crater* is dangerous."

"What about the fishing?" someone else rowed in. "Before he drowned, my husband always said dolphins made savage with the fish stocks."

"There's enough fish in the sea for everyone, including a few dolphins," Joan countered. "And as for the *crater* being dangerous, ask the expert. Go on, Lydia. Tell 'em."

"The dolphin isn't bad," Lydia chided. "Jason isn't afraid of it and he's only a little boy. You're all just being silly."

"There you have it," Joan said. "And if there's a bit of trouble, what about it? I always thought peace and quiet were highly overrated. So, what's it to be, ladies? Those in favor, raise their hands."

After every woman had voted to help, Joan explained the plan to keep Jackie out of the way. Then the front door opened and Carol stormed in.

"Okay here we go," Joan whispered. "Everyone get busy."

The women scurried to work on the wreaths as Joan nipped behind a pillar. She waited for Carol to stride past her then snuck into the sacristy.

"Has Lydia come back?" Carol demanded as she hurried toward the altar. "I've looked all over for her."

"Mam, I'm over here," Lydia called from her place at the table.

"Where were you? You just wait 'til we get home. You've been a bold, bold —"

The overhead lights in the church flickered. They flickered again then the nave was doused in darkness.

"Oh no!" a woman cried. "What do we do now?"

"We have so much work to do," someone else complained. "We don't have enough light."

Carol looked up at the ceiling, hands on her hips. "What else can go wrong? Lydia, you stay here and this time I mean it. I'll get help."

As Carol steamed through the shadows back to the front door, Joan emerged from the sanctuary.

"Guess who's been a naughty girl?" Joan gloated.

"Me?" Lydia asked.

"Nope. Me." The librarian opened her hand. In it lay the main fuse for the church electrical system.

Dawn sauntered across the square, stepping over sunlit puddles. The rain had cleared and gulls screamed as they fought for a late-morning meal. Approaching the trawler, she found Jackie on the stern using a palette knife to stroke white epoxy on to his busted rib.

"Hey Jackie," she called. "What are you up to?"

He looked up with fire in his eyes. "None of your business," he growled and got back to work.

She leaned against the stern. "You missed a spot."

"So says you."

"Turned into a nice day, didn't it?" she asked, looking to the sky. "You know, Jackie, I've been thinking."

He rapped the palette knife against the rib. "Can ya not see when a man's busy? Now, what the feck do you want?"

"Jackie, I want to apologize."

"Oh, do ya now?"

"I was wrong and I know it. I didn't understand. But hey, look at the bright side," she said cheerfully. "You've chased away the dolphin so the fishing is bound to get better, isn't it? It's vanished, so let's let bygones be bygones." When he looked ready to explode, she reached toward him, thrusting out a hand. "Well, what do you say?"

He glanced at her outstretched hand. "Feck off, that's what I say."

"Well, that's a shame. But suit yourself." She turned to go then swung back. "Oh, I almost forgot. Jackie?"

He looked up again, his face as red as a radish. "Are you still here? What do ya want now?"

"It's Father Danny."

"What about him."

"He wants you."

"What?" he said, stopping in mid-stroke. "What's he want?"

She shrugged. "I don't know. He's over at the church. I guess you should ask him."

"Can't you see I'm busy?"

"Okay. But I sure wouldn't want to disappoint the parish priest. Anyway, be seeing you."

He eyed her as she sauntered back down the pier. "Little vixen. Who the feck does she think she is?"

He sighed, thinking of the priest's request to see him and threw down the palette knife. Wiping his hands, he hopped off the trawler. As he stormed across the square toward the church, he thought how he'd find Father Danny, deal with whatever he wanted, then get back and finish the rib. He'd lose some time waiting for the epoxy to dry but feck it. When it was ready, he'd get back to the hunt. After all, the dolphin wasn't going anywhere and neither was he. Crossing the main street, he almost ran over Carol steaming up in the other direction.

"Oh Jackie! I'm so glad I found you. We have a major crisis."

"Who doesn't?" he growled. "Carol, can't it wait?"

"No, it can't. Now, come with me." Leading him down the street and into the darkened church, she pointed to the ceiling. "The lights aren't working. We can't see a thing."

"Is that a fact?" he grumbled. "Get the maintenance man. That's what he's there for."

Joan walked up, frowning in the shadows. "I heard he's away on holidays."

"That's right," Carol agreed. "He's gone for a fortnight. That's why we need you."

"Oh, for feck sake."

"Jackie, you're in a church," Carol warned. "Mind your tongue."

"Where's Father Danny?" he grumbled. "He wanted to see me anyway."

"In the loo," Mary said as she walked toward them. "Must be a tummy upset."

"Why don't I just pop in and get him?" Joan offered, turning toward the sacristy. "If he's finished, that is."

"No, no, leave him be," Jackie shot back. "Best not to disturb the man."

Carol looked to Joan. "When did you see Father Danny? I didn't think he was in today."

"Just now," Joan explained. "Turns out he's been in the gents for hours. The poor man was out of loo paper. I heard him calling from the toilet. I was on one side of the door and he was on the other side, of course, and he said —"

"Joan, I think I get the idea."

"Anyway, I got him the roll and explained about the power outage because he was wondering why it was so dark in the toilet, and to make a long story short," Joan stated, pointing toward the ceiling, "Father Danny said the problem's probably up there."

Jackie followed her finger toward the high ceiling. In the shadows near the choir loft balcony, he made out a fist-full of dangling wires. "Ah fer feck sake," he sighed, studying it. "Couldn't be more out of the way, could it?"

"Jackie," Carol demanded, "you have to fix it. You don't want to jeopardize the Day of Remembrance, do you? You know we can't work in the dark."

"It's not dark," he said, pointing to the sunlight streaming through the tall stained-glass windows. "You got plenty of light."

"Jackie, it's not enough and you know it," Carol barked.

He sighed again and turned toward the narrow stairs leading to the choir loft. The women heard his thick boots clump up the wooden risers, one reluctant step at a time.

317

"I'm not sure about this," Joan said, looking to the high ceiling. "I hope he'll be careful."

"Of course, he will. Why wouldn't he?" Carol asked.

"It's a long way up, isn't it? I just hope poor old Jackie doesn't fall and land right on his head."

"Oh my God. Do you think I should help him?"

"Oh, Carol, what a sweet thought," Mary said. "You go on. We'll be right here supporting you all the way. Isn't that right, ladies?"

At the tables, the women's voices rose in a chorus of encouragement.

"You stay here," Carol stated. "Help is on the way."

As she climbed the stairs, Joan grinned at Mary. "Step one complete. Now on to step two."

In the house Margaret helped Jason change into his wetsuit as Dawn struggled into her own. When they were ready, they climbed down the hill and, standing on the dock, looked for the dolphin.

"What happens if someone comes?" Margaret fretted.

"Just hope they don't." Dawn turned to her son. "Jason, are you ready? Let's go find your friend.

She helped him with his mask then fitted her own. Filling their lungs, they jumped into the sea. Peering through her facemask, Dawn made out the drifting shadows of a school of mullet but nothing larger. When they came up for air, she saw her son's disappointment.

"It's okay, Jase. Let's try again."

This time when they submerged, she heard the distinctive clicking. She followed it through the sunlit water to the far corner of the dock. The dolphin waited, floating in the shadows. As they surfaced for more air, Dawn saw her son's eyes glitter behind his facemask.

"See?" she grinned. "I told you it would be there. Come on!"

When they dived again, the dolphin emerged from the gloom. As it swept by them, Jason grinned wide. He turned, tracking it, as the mammal swung its great flukes, gliding deeper through curtained sealight. Her son kicked and, swimming to it, held out his arms. The dolphin nestled in close as

Jason grasped its beak, focusing on its laughing eyes. Hanging above them watching, Dawn's skin prickled as she remembered Margaret's prayers for a miracle and how her son might talk again. Then she thought of her dead husband and how much she wished he could be there to witness this.

'Please, Michael' she said to herself as she peered down through the water, 'he's been through so much. If there's going to be a miracle, let it be now. Right now.'

In the church Jackie reached over the railing of the choir loft toward the dangling electrical wires, swearing silently as he swiped at them with a rough hand.

"Another inch, Jackie. Come on, reach!"

"Carol," he griped, looking back at the woman. "Would ya shut it? I don't need your help."

He turned back to the wires. Adjusting his belly on the balcony handrail, he grabbed a wooden spindle for balance and leaned out farther. His hand slipped on the wood, his heavy body tilting. Below him, someone gasped. He peered down to the center aisle which seemed as far away as a canyon's floor and at the women who gawked up at him.

"It's all right ladies," he called with a plastered smile. "Don't get your knickers in a twist." Pulling himself back up on the railing, he counted to ten then looked back at Carol. "Grab me."

"I thought you didn't need my help."

"If I'm going to reach the feckin' thing, you got to grab me."

"Where?"

"I don't give a shite. Anywhere. Just do it, woman."

Carol grabbed him by the seat of his trousers and pulled. Jackie grimaced at the sudden tightness in his crotch.

"Is that okay?" she asked.

"Perfect," he grumbled, and turned back to his target.

As he reached out even farther his shirt inched up, his beer belly protruding into the void. He eyed the wires again, wishing to hell this was over and he could get back to his boat where he belonged.

319

Twenty feet below, Lydia gazed up at the spectacle. "What happens if Jackie falls?"

"Maybe it'll knock some sense into him," Joan replied.

They heard a loud rip and, peering up at Jackie's face, saw that it was as red as a navigation beacon.

"You okay up there?" Joan called.

"Just dandy," Jackie called down.

The women watched as the fisherman leveraged himself back into the loft, disappearing over the railing. After a clomping of boots, he emerged from the stairwell breathing hard. When he bent, stretching, they saw his jeans opened at the backside from stem to stern.

"You're going to have to get someone else," he gasped.

"You're not giving up?" Carol whined, following after him. "But Jackie, what are we going to do? You have to fix it."

He cursed under his breath, looking again up at the wiring. "Did anyone think to check the fuse box?"

"What fuse box?" Joan asked.

"Ah, fer feck sake," he muttered, and swung toward the sacristy.

"Jackie, maybe you should check later," Joan urged, following at his shoulder. "Father Danny might be in there. I'm sure he's busy."

"It's only a fuse box. I'm not asking for absolution."

As Jackie marched through the sacristy door the ladies and Lydia poured in behind him. Steaming straight for the box, the fisherman banged open the door. Searching, his eyes opened wide then closed as tight as a scallop shell. He grunted then swung around on the ladies.

"Where is it?"

"Where's what?" Mary asked. "What in heaven's name are you on about?"

"You know damned well what."

"Jackie, explain yourself," Carol insisted. "We've no time for a wild goose chase."

"This is no wild goose chase." His gaze shifted to Joan. "Father Danny was never in here, was he? So why did ya want to stop me?"

"He must still be in the loo," Joan retorted. "I'll get him."

"Don't you move. Give it here."

He thrust out a hand. Joan glanced at Mary, then shrugged. Reaching into a pocket, the librarian pulled out the fuse and dropped it into his palm. Jackie stalked back to the box. When he screwed it in tight, the lights in the sanctuary lit.

"Well, isn't it a miracle," Mary gasped, and the other women tittered in agreement.

"Miracle me arse," Jackie scowled.

"I don't understand," Carol said but Jackie would not take his eyes off Joan.

"Of course, you don't. They didn't want you to. They wanted us to think two plus two equals five. They wanted to steer us off course, which happens when someone is trying to hide something."

"Jackie, that's ridiculous." Carol barked. "What would anyone want to hide?"

"She knows," he grunted, thrusting his beer belly toward Joan. "So, what's the secret?"

"You know what it is," Joan hemmed. "I already gave it to you."

"Not the feckin' fuse. What else."

"Jackie, you can be as thick as a plank," she said, turning from him. "I don't know what you're on about."

He scanned the room, his glare settling on Lydia. She crossed her small arms, her lips working to hide a smile. "I bet you know what the secret is, don't you, Lydia?"

"You're never going to find it," Lydia said. "It's too smart for you."

"What is?"

"Why the dolphin, of course."

Jackie lowered himself to a knee. "Lydia, what about the dolphin?"

The young girl glared at him. "Like I said, you're never going to find it."

"Lydia," Joan warned, "don't."

"Well, he won't," Lydia continued. "Not even if it was in the harbor. Not even if it bit him on his big fat nose."

"The harbor?" Jackie's eyes went round as spotlights. "I'm gonna kill the fecker."

Jackie ran all the way to the pier, puffing like an overworked engine. Leaping on to the trawler and running past his mate he hurried to his cabin, hopped into an overall, then banged up the stairs to the wheelhouse. He picked up the shotgun and broke it, checking the brass ends of the fresh shells. As he secured the safety, he heard the roar of multiple outboard engines. Stepping to the window, he spotted four punts coasting to the pier. Taking the gun he ran down on deck, leaning over the gunwale as the punts arrived.

"That's far enough," Jackie yelled as George killed his boat's engine.

"What did'ya say, Jackie? We didn't find it if that's what you're asking," George shouted back, then spotted the rib upside down on the trawler's deck. "What the hell happened to your boat?"

"Never mind that. The fecker's here."

"Which fecker?"

"The dolphin, what do you think? It's in the harbor. George, you search between here and Dinish. I'll take the pier."

George restarted his engine, speeding away with the other boats as Jackie turned to his mate.

"You! Stay here. If you spot it come get me."

Jackie jumped off the boat, striding down the pier. He took his time, searching the dead water between tied up trawlers. When he got to Johnny's half-decker, he saw the old fisherman on deck cleaning a line of lobster pots.

"Johnny, you seen anything in the water?"

The old man stared hard at Jackie's shotgun. "Where the hell you going with that?"

"It's no one's business but mine. I asked if you saw anything?"

"I seen lots of things. Like what?"

"Like a dolphin."

The old man spat over the side. "I told you before what I think."

"Ah, go on with ya," Jackie retorted. "If you won't help, be it on your head."

322

He kept walking, keeping to his careful search along the pier. A couple of times he heard the ocean gurgle and raised the shotgun but only spotted trawlers emptying bilge water into the sea.

Margaret stood worrying on the dock, watching as the pair surfaced.

"Dawn, don't you think you've been long enough?" Margaret called. In the water her daughter-in-law only waved then turned back to her son.

"Wasn't that cool, Jase?" Dawn asked as they floated near the dock. "Tell me how cool that was. Go on, you can talk to me just like you talked to Lydia." When he didn't answer she pushed down her disappointment. Beside them the sea parted as the dolphin's dorsal fin rose from the water. The mammal breathed, air rushing in through its vent, then submerged.

"It's still here. Want to do it again?"

When Jason nodded the two ducked under the water.

From the dock Margaret watched as the pair dove, following the immense shadow that swam in front of them. She turned, putting a hand to her eyes against the glare, searching the harbor area. She could see some of the square but most of it lay hidden behind a line of shops. The bottom quarter of the pier was in view but the rest was concealed behind the sterns of parked trawlers. Though no one walked near she prayed that Dawn and Jason would finish soon.

In the water beneath Margaret's feet, Jason dived toward his mother. As he did, he thought of the song he had heard in the studio and recalled the silver ring in the vibrating glass of water. He thought about the disappearance of his father and how it all reminded him of what he had glimpsed in the dolphin's eye when he had first swum with it in the cove. He was sure Lydia thought he was crazy after hearing what he had whispered to her. Maybe she was right. Maybe no one would believe him. But no matter what anyone else thought he was determined to find out. He had already looked again for the sparking flash in the dolphin's eye when he had first clung to it during his first dive. But when he had peered in, he had seen only darkness. This time he would look deeper. As he swam to his mother's side, he again saw the dolphin suspended beneath him. Once more his mother held back as he kicked on alone.

As he approached the immense shadow the sea vibrated in whispered song. He grasped a fin, pulling himself up along the muscular body to the dolphin's beak. He hung on as sunlight played over its flanks and across the white patch on its face. Grabbing tight, he pulled himself closer. When his mask touched the skin, he knew he could go no nearer. The water around him stirred and, as light danced across his eyes, he peered even deeper.

He thought its eye was unlike any he had seen before because the darkness cleared like storm clouds running before a fierce wind. He stared into a vortex of sparkling color. At its bottom he saw a glittering butterfly break from its cocoon. Then there were thousands of them, sparking where their glowing wings touched, coalescing into something else, something much more familiar. He could feel warmth in his stomach and caught a comforting paternal smell he had longed for. The song grew louder. He wanted to laugh but the mask stopped him and instead he hugged tight to the dolphin. When his lungs were ready to burst, he pushed off, swimming up past his mother. As they broke surface together, he pulled off his mask, laughing so hard he gagged.

"Are you both all right?" Margaret called from the dock. Dawn looked up at her then turned back to her son.

"Jason? What happened?" she asked, holding him tight. When he would not stop laughing, she asked, "Hey, kiddo, look at me. Was it cool?"

He grinned at her in a way she had not seen since the accident: the mischievous, playful, healthy smile that had always been her son.

"Jason, what does the dolphin say? Can you do that? What does it say?" When he swung away from her, she worried that even now he was not ready.

"Try again," Margaret called.

Dawn pushed up her facemask, taking her son's head in both hands.

"Jason, remember when we were in the hospital and we drew the cat? Remember how I asked you what the cat says?" His smile broadened and he nodded. "Then please, sweetie. Tell me what the dolphin says. What does it say?"

His brow wrinkled as his lips compressed. For a long time, he studied her, his eyes filled with uncertainty. Then his mouth worked, opening wide.

"Cree-cree-cree!" he sang. "Cree-cree-cree!"

"Did you hear him, Margaret? Did you?" Dawn shouted. "Do it again, Jason!"

"Cree-cree-cree!"

"Holy mother of God!" Margaret cried.

On the dock, the older woman turned when she heard the roar of engines. In the near-distance a group of punts flew past. One of them slowed and veered toward her. A man stood up, peering at her, then turned to look beside the dock. Margaret heard the roar of the outboard engine and watched as the boat speeded toward the pier.

Jackie looked out to the harbor. George, standing tall in his punt, cut the engine, gliding in toward him.

"Over there!" George pointed. "The dock!"

Jackie shifted the shotgun, breaking into a run. He skirted the end of the pier then ran past the Lighthouse Bar, thumping down the path that led to the far end of the harbor. He saw Margaret standing on the dock at the same time she saw him. He heard her shout the Yank's name.

He spotted the woman floating in the water with her son. Then he saw the dorsal fin as it surfaced. The water boiled, the immense flukes thrashing as it turned toward the open harbor. Jackie bolted on to the dock, running past Margaret as he levered off the gun's safety. He took aim but checked. The Yank and her son floated between him and the dolphin.

"Get out of the way!" he roared at them. "Move!"

"No!" Margaret cried, and rushed him. Jackie sidestepped, striding past her as he raised the shotgun.

In the water, the dolphin saw the danger to his family. He reversed course, placing his enormous physical presence between the weapon and those he loved. He heard his brother's song call a warning then felt his gift exhale on a plume of light. He swung his body, facing the twin-barreled threat.

325

On the dock Jackie took aim at the *crater* that had stupidly swum back into range. He steadied himself, ignoring the boy who thrashed through the water toward the target and the Yank who screamed at him.

As he squeezed the trigger, Jackie smiled. He was so close he could not possibly miss.

PART V

ISLAND

THE LEGEND OF SOLAS MÓR
BY ANONYMOUS
(verse 9, 1 — 13)

Journey as you wish and choose as you will for salvation is at hand.
   The secret is nigh, the promises sharp,
      Keep swimming, Swimmer, swimming.

Believe with faith, with faith believe, in peace as your eternal ending,
   Despite your fear and longing past, be not afraid of dying.
      Keep swimming, Swimmer, swimming.

Hear young Swimmer the song we sing with promise of life's ardor,
   And join us in the steadfast walls of our forgotten harbor.
In the embrace of always-tomorrow the love you seek is given,
   On Solas Mór all storms will pass and all will be forgiven —
For here at last the bell will toll as you leap to an earthly Heaven.

The gift is here, within your grasp,
   So swim, brave Swimmer, keep swimming.

CHAPTER TWENTY-EIGHT

The squall howled with the shriek of a boar and Dawn was caught up in its madness. As she swam into the teeth of its power, all she could hear was the tolling of the bell and all she could feel was the panic of her search. When lightning lit the towering seas the yellow buoy appeared, swinging within wind-whipped swells. She stretched toward it but cresting waves tore at her. Caught in its claws she plummeted, twisting into the depths. Her lungs ached as her mouth opened. Water poured in.

Darkness

Doctor Morrison crouched over Rose. But when Dawn looked the girl was Jason and the warning the doctor uttered was lost in the gale of cold despair.

Light revolving, spinning

Carol stood on the dock, barking at the monstrous *crater* which floated near. The dolphin was huge with biting teeth and jumped, swallowing Lydia whole.

Deeper and deeper, water everywhere

Dawn kicked within the darkness, lungs on fire. Breaching the surface, she swam into an ocean of horror. The buoy was close; her son clung to it. As she reached for him, Jackie rose from the storm with a shotgun as big as a canon. He pulled the trigger and Jason fell, lifeless, into the sea. He drifted beneath her, his accusing voice echoing through the depths.

"You did it, Mommy. You did it, Mommy. You did it, Mommy."

She had killed her family.

Adrift

She found herself on an endless sea, the blue and white boat in flames. Clawing at a porthole, she beheld Michael's face grinning back from within the consuming blaze. He had been trapped by her own selfishness and nothing could change it, not even a miracle.

Sunrise

It streamed, blinding, through clouds rising toward Heaven. Hearing his song, she opened her eyes. His melody was gentle and warm and held her fast. She turned away, knowing she was no longer worthy. But he tugged at her, pulling her into his arms.

"Where's Jason?" she whispered.

"Soon. We'll be with him someday soon."

She looked into his eyes. His depthless blue eyes. Then she understood his meaning.

"Liar," she said.

CHAPTER TWENTY-NINE

"Jason?"

When Dawn had woken following the effects of the sedative the doctor had given to her, she had followed a nurse into her son's room. Now, she sat beside the hospital bed stroking his curling hair damp with sweat. "Jason, can you hear me, sweetie?"

He did not react. His arms lay lifeless at his sides. His open eyes stared unseeing at the ceiling. They did not focus or blink. They did not hold laughter or tears or even dreams. His eyes resembled those of a girl she had met in a Boston children's hospital. Rose had the same eyes. Rose was catatonic. Rose was beyond hope. She recalled Doctor Morrison's warning. Jason could suffer a similar fate if he was ever again exposed to extreme trauma.

"Like the one yesterday," Dawn shuddered. Tears fell on his blanket as she took his small hand in hers. "Oh God, Jase. What have I done?"

Though she willed herself not to, her mind filled with the images of yesterday's traumatic incident.

She was floating in the water with Jason, the dolphin close by. Then Margaret screamed. Dawn saw Jackie scramble on to the dock, lifting the shotgun as he yelled. She had reached for her son but he had slipped past her, plunging to protect his friend. Then the twin blasts, as loud as dynamite. The dolphin thrashed in the water. Jason screeched as if he had been shot. She had seen blood spattered on her boy's face, horrified that it was his. But she had turned to see that it was the dolphin's, its bleeding body sinking into the sea beneath her. When Jason's head slumped below the water she had finally reacted. She stretched for him, pulling him to the dock. She didn't know who had lifted him out. He had lain lifeless on the wood as they waited for the ambulance. When she heard its wail, Jason had opened his eyes. He had not closed them since.

Dawn blinked hard, forcing herself to remember where she was. She still sat at Jason's side, holding her son's hand as the doctor entered the room. The woman checked the monitor for heartrate and respiration then used a small penlight to sweep the boy's eyes. Dawn saw how the doctor tried again, looking for a response.

"There's nothing, is there?" Dawn whispered.

"I'd like to transfer him back to Boston as soon as feasible," the doctor said. "They have more resources and know his history. Is that all right with you? Mrs. McCarthy?"

Dawn blinked again. "What did you say?"

"This is a local hospital. We don't have the resources to treat him here. We could transfer him to Cork City but I'd prefer to move him back to Boston. Can you do that?"

Dawn couldn't think; she couldn't move.

"Let me know what you want to do." The doctor touched her shoulder then slipped from the room.

Dawn found herself looking at the bedside table. Margaret had thought to bring Jason's monkey and it sat unblinking next to a cup of water. She picked up the soft toy, studying its lopsided grin. She held it to her ear as if by habit.

"Mister Monkey wants to say hi. Can you say hi back to him? Jason?"

She looked into her son's eyes. His blank stare seemed filled with accusation for all she had done. She stifled a sob, fingering the necklace at her neck and the dolphin leaping through its ring of silver. She had long recognized that Jason blamed her for his father's loss but, until now, she had never tried to explain what had happened, fearing he would only hate her more if he knew the facts. However, she recognized that this might be her last opportunity. If she tried now, maybe he would hear her.

"Jason, on the trip last year. When we were on the boat with your Daddy. It's just… I felt so afraid and alone. I didn't know what else to do. Things happened too fast and don't you see? I didn't have any choice. But I got it wrong, so wrong, and all I ever wanted to do was love you and your Daddy and try to make things better. I'm sorry, Jason. So, so sorry."

Then she was crying, her head lying beside his still body. When she looked up his eyes were unchanged and she knew she had not reached him. She stood, then stumbled out the door.

When she entered the crowded waiting area, she couldn't look at the people who were gathered there. Joan, Mary, Father Danny and a group of church women stood together talking in hushed voices to Margaret. Carol sat with her daughter on seats pushed against a far wall, the woman's look full of defiant guilt. Seeing her friend's mother, Lydia rose, hurrying across the room.

"Dawn?"

Dawn looked down on the tiny girl whose eyes were brimming with tears.

"Jason won't talk to me again, will he? Not ever again."

Dawn couldn't take it, not even a child's honest question. She walked to a corner of the room. Facing the wall, she clasped shaking hands across her face as silent voices pummeled her. 'You fool. You knew this would happen,' the voices screamed at her. 'First it was your husband, now your son. You bitch. You stupid, fucking bitch.'

"Dawn?"

She looked up. Margaret stood at her shoulder.

"They want me to transfer him back to Boston," Dawn shivered.

Margaret stared at her. "I'm so sorry."

She glanced past her mother-in-law. Jackie was slouched in a chair, unshaven, looking as if he hadn't slept in a week.

"Margaret, what's he doing here?"

"He wants to talk to you. I told him you wouldn't."

"You told him right."

But Jackie had seen her. He stood, shuffling toward her through the crowd, twisting his baseball cap in sweating hands.

335

"Dawn, I'm sorry," he mumbled, looking up with red-rimmed eyes. "I didn't think the lad would come to any harm. I thought he was far enough away. I wasn't thinking straight."

"But it's too late, isn't it, Jackie? You didn't think at all. You never think."

Carol, who had strained to hear Jackie's apology, got up from her chair, striding to Dawn's side.

"Dawn, listen to Jackie. He's sorry, just as we all are," Carol said, tapping Dawn's arm. "We'll pray for Jason. We'll pray for him today and tomorrow and the next. We'll even pray for him at Remembrance Day. Isn't that right, everyone?" she asked, turning to the women. "We'll say a special prayer for the child's recovery."

"Carol?"

"Yes, Dawn?" Carol replied, turning to her.

"Do me a favor."

"Anything I can do to help."

"Keep your fucking mouth off my son. You've done enough!"

Dawn looked across the crowded room. The women stared back, their faces full of surprise at the outburst. Father Danny couldn't seem to take his eyes off the ceiling.

"I'm a lousy mother, okay?" Dawn yelled. "Isn't that what you're all thinking?" She swung back to Carol and Jackie, her eyes brimming with tears. "You two don't think you had anything to do with it, do you? You think it's all my fault. But don't you worry. I'll be leaving soon enough. Just leave Jason alone."

"Dawn, please. We'd never hurt the lad," Carol said, reaching toward her.

"Don't touch me, Carol. Not ever again."

Dawn stepped away. Her chin trembling, she bolted out the front door.

Jackie stared at the floor. "Margaret, I never meant to hurt the lad. Didn't you hear me say it?"

"Well, I did, Jackie," Carol sniffed. "What's wrong with that young one? No one accused Dawn of anything. And she dares to point a finger at us?"

Margaret raised her chin, facing them. "Jackie, you can be a silly, foolish, ignorant eejit. And as for you —"

"Go on, Margaret," Carol said. "This time, why don't you finish it?"

Margaret looked her square in the eye. "You're an insensitive, unthinking, self-absorbed Bozo! You can feck off, the pair of you. Isn't that what Dawn would say?"

She spun from them, following her daughter-in-law out into the rain. She caught sight of Dawn running down the hill toward the town. Margaret bowed her head, fearing that this time no amount of prayer would ever bring the young woman peace.

Dawn ran through the evening showers not thinking about a final destination nor caring. She ran down the hill into town and past the square, the closed shops and the deserted pier. She ran as the rain fell on her face and into her eyes, soaking her. But she ran on anyway, her desperate strides like those of a fugitive.

When she made it to the end of the town and turned at the crossroads she slid on the gravel, sprawling headlong into the muck. Stumbling to her feet, she sprinted down the broken *boreen* past sheep sheltering within the wild gorse who shivered at her passage. At the bottom of the hill, she could see the cove, waves cresting across it like ghosts. She fell again as she climbed on to the pier. Pulling herself up, she staggered to the end. She stopped because there was nowhere left to run. There, she fell to her knees, her sobs echoing across the water.

The sound of her grief mixed with the rattle of shingle as the tide washed the beach, breaking over the wounded mammal that rested there.

When the dolphin had been hit by the shotgun's twin blasts, he had sunk to the bottom streaming blood, the breath of his gift escaping from the shattered lungs. He had squealed to his brother but the reply was only silence.

As he had drifted to the bottom sands waiting for death, his consciousness had filled with fear for his family. His flukes had swung despite his injury. Battling to the surface, he had known the gun would be waiting. But the outgoing tide had carried him away from the dock to the harbor's deeper water and for a time he had floated within cresting seas, too injured to care if he was seen. In light rain he had struggled toward the bay, beaching for the night on a low sandbar as the blood of life seeped from him. As morning broke across the peninsula, he had made for the island and its hidden lagoon, seeking the company of his kind so he would not die alone.

But even as he had begun his voyage, he knew he would not have the strength to finish it. When he had seen the white marker, he had turned into the cove, sensing it would be his final anchorage. He let the incoming tide carry him in, grounding at last on the rough shingled beach. Here, he would be comfortable for the final waiting.

He remembered the simple boyhood prayer his mother had taught him. When he finished, he thought of his father and the butterfly and how he would soon fly to join them. As his consciousness ebbed, he thought one last time of his son and his wife and the great love he had for them. Then he closed his eyes and slept. As night fell again, he did not hear the woman call his name.

Dawn's hands swept the tears from her eyes as she looked across a sea of ghosting shadows. Her fingers found the necklace hanging between her breasts. She took the dolphin into her palm, seeing how its leaping form glittered in the rain. She ripped it from her neck, hurling the necklace as far as she could into the cove.

"Michael!" she howled. His name echoed back from the rain-drenched hills. She stood, glaring out into the darkness. "What do you want from me, Michael? I couldn't help Jason, okay? I can't fix this anymore. I need you to be here!" She turned a complete circle, searching. The wind came up, the night filling with the rustling voices of the yew trees. "Where are you? Where? If you were here like they say you are, you'd help him. This isn't my fault. It's yours! Do you hear me, Michael? Yours!"

She collapsed back on the pier, sobbing again. When she finished, she rolled on to her side. Looking out to sea, her whispered words came through her tears. "Oh, Michael. It isn't your fault. It's mine. All I ever did was fuck up. Why did I ever ask you to take us back to the island? I killed you, Michael. Oh God, I killed you both."

Distant thunder rolled in from the south. Lightning lit the cove in forks of silver and she ground both fists into her eyes to stop the flashback. But the year-old memory of her family's final trip on the *Margie M* bloomed like licking flames and there was no escaping it.

CHAPTER THIRTY

The fog over Solas Mór had dissipated in a freshening breeze. To the southwest, beyond the island, lightning backlit a bank of grey clouds scudding low across the horizon. Dawn leaned against the wheelhouse instrument panel, Jason kneeling on the steering seat beside her, watching Michael out on deck. He opened a side locker, stowing the sunchair she had reclined on earlier then untangled Jason's toy monkey from the fishing line where it still hung. As he singled up a rope he scanned the horizon, his brow furrowing with worry. When he noticed her peering out at him from the wheelhouse, he hid behind a wide smile. The sunlight washing the deck dimmed behind high stratus as he marched back through the door.

"Dad, I don't want to go home. I want to go to the island," Jason whined as Michael lifted him from the seat, handing him his monkey.

"Don't you worry," Michael replied. "We'll come back another time."

"We sure will," Dawn said. "Mister Monkey can come too. You can go swimming again."

Michael reached for the starter and the engine bellowed to life like an old sea lion. He peered out the forward window and Dawn followed his gaze. The angry squall line, green as cats' eyes, rolled in behind the scud, speeding toward the island. Within it lightning flashed like a row of gorse fires.

"Be right back," Michael said. "I have to pull in the anchor."

She sensed his anxiety as he hustled to the bow which had begun to pitch in the swell. As he bent to the anchor winch a fist-full of rain drummed against the wheelhouse window. She watched him get to his knees, examining

341

the winch motor. Then he stood, grabbing the thick hawser that was tied to the anchor which rested on the sea floor, pulling until the veins in his arms bulged.

"What's Daddy doing?"

"I don't know, sweetie," she said, and looked again to the horizon. The scud had moved over the island, the squall line behind it sweeping fast toward them. Within it, lightning forked. This time she heard a low rumble of thunder. She saw Michael let go of the hawser and start back. She could read his frustration in the thick lines of his forehead as he walked into the wheelhouse.

"What's wrong?"

"The anchor's snagged on the bottom. Don't worry, it's nothing that can't be fixed." He opened the door behind her, descending the few steps into the belly of the boat.

"Daddy, can you really fix it?" Jason called. They heard him rummaging below decks, then the clomp of boots as he came back up.

"Course I can fix it, Jason. It just needs a little persuasion." Michael grinned, swinging a short hatchet in his hand. He placed it on the steering seat then pulled on a yellow slicker. "I'll be two shakes. We'll be home by teatime as promised." He picked up the tool, ruffled his son's hair, then bounded out the door.

They watched him work his way to the bow. As the wind picked up, the deck pitched harder in the swells and he had to balance to its rhythm. The wheelhouse lit in sudden brightness as thunder ripped. There was no time between the lightning and the thunder's roar and Dawn realized the squall was on top of them. With the half-decker rolling in the confused seas, Jason clung to her and she reached for a handhold. Watching Michael lift the hatchet, she hoped the hawser would part easily so they could get back home where they belonged. But she saw how he had to lift it again.

"I hope Daddy hurries," Jason said.

"So do I, sweetie. He won't be long."

A sheet of rain slammed like gunfire against the window.

As they pitched, the heavy seas battered every plank, nut and bolt in the *Margie M.* Beneath the stern decking, buried below the water-line, the storm shook the old engine. It idled, coughing and vibrating, and so did its components. The engine's manifold was already hot enough to evaporate water. Above it, the steel fuel line ran from the diesel tank bolted to the hull and into the innards of the engine. Years ago, Tomás had covered the steel tube with protective foam but it had fallen away, leaving the narrow pipe exposed. Michael had not noticed it because the fuel line was buried behind the cylinders. Unseen, for years the naked metal had chaffed on a rusting spar. Every time the half-decker shifted the spar had peeled away a bit of pipe, one sliver at a time. When the squall again buffeted the boat, the fuel line holed. A thin stream of diesel fuel spilled on to the hot manifold and began to smoke.

Twenty feet forward of the engine, Dawn and Jason watched as Michael once more swung the hatchet. The hawser parted, slipping through its hawsepipe and into the sea. He leaned over the gunwale to make certain it wouldn't foul the prop then climbed back across the pitching deck. When he entered, he slammed shut the wheelhouse door, tossing the hatchet on the floor.

"All set," he said. "Let's go home."

His quick smile quelled her panic. She hugged Jason tight as Michael placed his hand on the throttle and advanced it. Below-deck, in answer to Michael's command, the thin stream of fuel began to flow faster. It hissed on to the white-hot manifold, then ignited. Balls of fire crept up the wooden hull to the fuel tank.

The tank ruptured, exploding.

In the wheelhouse the windows shattered. Dawn and Jason were thrown hard against the front panel then to their knees. The cabin below-decks filled with smoke. Its black stench rolled like soup through the open cabin door. Michael looked aft out the splintered window at the smoke and flames billowing from the stern. He reached down, hauling his family to their feet.

"Stay here!"

He pushed past them and rushed down the steps into the smoking cabin. Clutching Jason tight, Dawn looked through the broken aft window, seeing flames engulf the stern.

"Hurry!" she yelled, and heard Michael's coughing before she saw him. She looked in through the smoke. Carrying a heavy fire extinguisher, he struggled up the tilting steps.

The wheelhouse grew darker and she leaned against the sudden change in the deck's pitch as the trawler tilted. She turned, looking out the shattered starboard window. A solid wall of water, taller than a three-story building, bore down on them. She stared at the top of the wave, spume driven like a white avalanche as it curled, descending.

"Jason, get down!"

She dove, grabbing her son by the knees, forcing him to the deck as the rogue wave hit. Water poured through the shattered windows and into the wheelhouse, heaving them against the walls. As Jason sobbed, she looked down into the smoking cabin. Michael was on his belly, the extinguisher still in his arms. He staggered to his feet, struggling toward the steps. Then she heard the hollow clang of a bell.

She stood, clinging to the wheel, looking to port. The yellow buoy, hard as an island, appeared through surging whitewater, close on. The half-decker pitched again as a following wave hit the side. She reached for Jason as the boat slid sideways, the church-steeple structure of the buoy tipping over the gunwale. The boat shook as it collided, rupturing the hull planking below the waterline. Behind her, she saw Michael's surprised face as the cabin door slammed shut. She grabbed the door handle, pulling.

"Come on, you pissa. Open!" The door wouldn't budge and she realized it was jammed. She turned to Jason, seeing his terror. "Stay here!"

She stepped out on to the pitching deck and looked to the stern. Flame shot skyward. The trawler's rib was on fire, the boat's burning rubber obscuring the stern in smoke. Grabbing the steel railing, she inched aft across the narrow decking running between the wheelhouse and the gunwale. She glanced down: the ocean boiled a few feet below. She found the porthole and, squatting, peered in through the small window. Through the smoke, she could make out Michael. He was pounding at the cabin door with the fire extinguisher. Water covered the cabin, the sea spouting through the splintered flooring. She beat on the window. He turned and, seeing her, slogged through the water toward her.

"We have to get him out, Mom!"

She swung around. Jason stood next to her, balanced on a slick foothold. Dawn grabbed him, pulling him to her.

"What are you doing here?" she yelled. "Where's your life vest?"

"Up there," he called, and pointed to the bow.

She remembered taking it off him, leaving it on deck. By now it would have been blown halfway to Wales. She pulled him close as she heard a sharp rap. Behind the porthole, Michael waved at them to get back. She shielded Jason as he rammed the window with the butt-end of the extinguisher. Glass and smoke exploded outward. She reached in, clearing the jagged shards. She did not notice cutting her wrist nor the bleeding. Michael hacked, coughing up the smoke in his lungs as he breathed in the fresh air. He thrust his hand through the porthole and Jason grabbed it.

"I can't get the door open," Dawn yelled, taking their hands in hers.

"I noticed," he shouted, trying to smile. "What's it like aft?"

Dawn looked again. Flame and dense smoke billowed, fanned by high winds. "Bad."

"Can you float the rib?"

"It's burned to fuck."

He nodded then looked down at the water surging around his knees. "What the hell did we hit?"

"The buoy. Can't you stop the water from coming in?"

"The pumps won't work without the engine and that's burned to hell."

She stared hard at him. "What are we going to do?"

"You got to put the fire out."

"With what?"

He hoisted up the extinguisher, trying to force it through the porthole but the metal cylinder was too wide. He dropped it and, looking back at the flooding cabin, grinned out at her.

"Maybe it's a good idea if you got me out of here," he yelled, and Dawn could hear fear in his voice as she struggled to grin back.

"Maybe it is. Stay here."

"Baby, I'm not going anywhere."

He squeezed her hand then let go. Reaching over her, he grabbed Jason by the shirt, pulling him flat against the boat's superstructure. Dawn edged past her son then inched back to the ruined wheelhouse. At the door she slipped on the broken decking and fell in. The monkey floated face down in water sloshing across the floor. She bent, hunting through the seawater until her fingers found the hatchet. She stood, fighting for balance, turning to the jammed cabin door. Swinging hard, she could make only shallow cuts in the thick wood. Inserting the hatchet's cutting edge between the door and the frame, she pushed on it with her entire weight. The tool slipped, spinning back into the water.

She looked out the shattered forward window. Huge seas surged over the gunwale as the *Margie M* settled by the bow. Water sluiced in to the wheelhouse, deeper now. She dropped to her knees, searching for the hatchet but this time couldn't find it. Then she stood, tumbling back out into the teeth of the squall.

High gusts swept the deck, throwing her against the superstructure. The squall roared like an animal as hail hit her in the face. Turning again for the porthole, she saw whitewater cascading over the aft gunwales on both sides of the boat. When she inched back, she found Jason still grasping his father's hand. She grabbed on to them tight.

"Michael, I can't open it. You have to tell me what to do. What do I do?"

Another series of waves hit the boat hard. The *Margie M* swung, listing, the deck tilting toward the sea. Dawn slipped on the narrow foothold as Jason screamed. She looked down, seeing their legs dangling over the gunwale, her feet deep in surging whitewater. Michael grabbed both of them. She felt his grip tighten as he pulled them back into the lee of the superstructure. Clinging to Jason, she leaned back against her husband's arm, fear hitting her in waves.

"Dawn, look at me!" She glanced up wild-eyed. Michael seized her shoulder, shaking it. "I said, look!"

She looked. He was up to his belly in water but his solid gaze steadied her.

"Okay," she said. "I'm looking."

He wiped water from his eyes, his face hard.

"I want you to do something for me."

"What?"

"I want you to fix this."

"Don't you get it, Michael? I can't fix it!"

"Oh, yes you can. You know you can."

His voice made her focus on his eyes. Within them she saw his true intent.

"No, Michael. Forget it."

Jason stared at them then grabbed his mother's arm. "You got to get him out, Mom. You got to. Promise, you got to promise!"

Michael again grasped her shoulder, his grip tightening. "Dawn, for feck sake there's no time!"

"No, Michael. No. Not this way."

Dawn shook his hand off. Crawling around Jason, she again made her way forward. As she went, her head screamed in furious hope. 'I can do this. I'll open the door and when I do it'll be all right. Michael will get out and we'll go home. All I need to do is open the fucking door.'

A comber swept in, drowning her. She grabbed the railing with both hands as the boat settled deeper. She looked toward the bow. Most of the wheelhouse was under water, the shattered outer door off its hinges. She had no choice but to turn back.

She found them where she had left them. She was determined not to cry, not in front of Jason. When she crouched at the porthole, she saw water up to Michael's chin and sobbed anyway. He reached out, cupping her face in his hand.

"Hey now, there's my girl. Oh, my brave, brave girl."

"Oh, Michael no. I can't."

"Oh, yes you can."

"No, I can't." She smiled through her tears at him.

"See? Yes, you can." He stroked her cheek, his eyes so steady. "God, I love you. I'd have had nothing if I hadn't found you."

She reached through the porthole and they clung to each other. The boat lurched hard and he pulled away.

"It's time," he ordered. "Do it, Dawn. Do it now. Go on, get out of here!"

"Not yet."

"Look at Jason." She turned, looking at her son's terrified face. "Do it for him, for God's sake!"

Dawn nodded. She pulled back, her arms reaching around her son's waist.

"Daddy!" Jason screamed. "I want my Daddy!"

Sobbing, Jason reached through the porthole, grasping his father's slicker with both hands. Another wave hit. The half-decker shuddered, listing more. The boat's red-painted belly, spotted white with barnacles, slipped above the sea. Dawn grabbed Jason, pulling him from his father. She looked once more into Michael's eyes as water surged over her. Then she leaped overboard, taking Jason with her. They fell into the fist of the maelstrom.

A cresting whitecap pushed her under. Spinning in the turbulence, Jason was torn from her grasp. She spun downward, thinking she would spin forever. Desperate, she stretched, kicking, pushing past the detritus of the sinking boat. Breaching the surface she twisted, unable to find her son within the confused whitewater.

"Jason!"

She heard the distant clamor of a bell, spotting the yellow buoy as it swung in heaving seas. Then the storm had her again, forcing her back under. She surfaced once more, coughing up the whole ocean. Through the raging crests she again saw the buoy. Jason clung to its side. She fought through the whipping crests and growing darkness, breathing hard between breakers. When she at last made the buoy she grabbed Jason by his belt, pulling him up. He grasped a steel handhold, leveraging himself into the church-steeple structure and its clanging bell. When she tried to haul herself up beating waves forced her off.

"Daddy!" Jason screamed.

She followed her son's eyes. The burning trawler sank, pincered between foaming swells. The wheelhouse had already submerged, the rising stern throwing up sheets of flame which lit the twilight. The winds grew stronger, the waves higher, beating her against the steel sides of the buoy.

Then, from across the whipping sea, she heard a cry.

The song was at first indistinguishable from the blowing gale. It floated in on the wind and, as it came closer, its voice multiplied as if one singer had been joined by a hundred more. Still clinging to the buoy Dawn twisted, searching the storm. A pod of dolphins streaked through the sea toward her, leaping over cresting waves. They turned as one, as if a hunting pack. Then they were past her, heading for the stricken boat. She caught sight of a white-faced dolphin bounding in front, leading the pod toward the flaming wreck. They leaped around the vessel, their images backlit by the fire.

The sea glimmered with light. She looked up. What she saw made no sense because the island was almost a mile away. Yet, it was here. Right here. Solas Mór reared from the raging whitewater. Its towering peak tore through the violent squall. Though it was still hours before dawn the sun rose behind it, lighting the ocean in a terrible beauty. Then the light contracted in upon itself, spinning into a pinwheel of gold as the song surged as solid as the sea from which it came.

Dawn shook herself from the waking dream. She found herself still lying on the cove's pier, gazing up at stars that flashed in a clear night sky. She touched tears on her cheeks and, as she did, remembered the song of her dream. She thought she could still hear it. The song drifted to her on the wind and she was certain she was insane. She turned to the sea, hunting for its source. It warbled like bird song searching for its mate. Her eyes roved to the shingled beach. In the tide, she saw the shadow of the beached dolphin. She jumped off the pier, running to it across the rocky shore.

Kneeling in the surging water, she examined the mammal. Gunshot had left deep wounds in its head and flanks, obliterating the right eye. The sea around it was thick with bright red blood. Its breath came in shallow sighs. She waded into the ocean, pressing her hands hard against the wounded flesh. It gasped in pain.

"You'll be all right," she whispered. "Please God, let me make it all right."

Grasping its great pectoral fin, she struggled to pull the dolphin into deeper water. The outgoing tide helped to ease the heavy body from the shingle. As she worked to push it on, the mammal's breathing became more labored. Blood oozed from its blowhole. She began to cry as her feet pressed hard against the pebbled bottom. Coming into deeper water, the sea was up to her chin, waves lapping on to her face.

"Don't die. Don't die and leave us all alone."

Its breathing slowed. It trilled quietly then did not breathe at all. She grabbed it by the dorsal fin, struggling to keep it afloat. A wave taller than the rest pulled it from her grasp and it disappeared beneath the surface.

"No!" she cried.

Her terror and defiance echoed off the hills. She gulped in air and dove to find it. The sea was deeper than she had thought because she could not see the bottom. She searched frantically, finally spotting the dolphin's white patch glimmering in the darkness. She swam to it, grasping the unmoving fin, struggling to pull it to the surface. When she couldn't move the massive body she swam to its beak, looking into its uninjured eye. She caressed its head, stroking the white face.

'Thank you,' she thought, wishing it could hear her. 'Thank you for what you tried to do for us.'

Almost out of breath she was forced to release it, watching as it settled into the dark emptiness beneath her. When it disappeared, she swam toward the surface. But then she heard the song again. She rotated underwater, peering down. Specks of light darted through the darkness like fireflies.

She shot to the surface, gasping. Treading water, she put her ears beneath the surface. Again, she heard the song. Distant singers seemed to join the single voice because the ocean echoed in a chorus of life. Dawn filled her lungs and dived, deeper this time. The white-faced dolphin still drifted lifelessly below her. Hearing the song again, she swung hard around. A dolphin streaked by, its flukes leaving behind a trail of foaming bubbles. Then another dolphin and another, and the sea was filled with their power. Hovering above them, her skin tingled as she watched the pod circle around the white-faced dolphin, as if forming a group at prayer. Their flukes thrashed as they swam faster and faster, dancing to the chorus of their melody. The water churned, sparkling white. Then the dance slowed and stopped. The white-faced dolphin still drifted, dead.

One of the mammals swung its flukes, tail-standing in the darkness. It trilled a distinctive five-note song, its voice resonating out to sea. Again, it sang. Then a third time. A distant call echoed in a five-note response. The ocean filled with an approaching rumble. Dawn swung her arms, back-peddling as the sea erupted. Dolphins of many species streaked by her, the water boiling from their passing. Risso's dolphins, striped, and spinners; spotted dolphins, white beaked and bottlenose. The other tribes joined the pod of Common dolphins, dancing in time to their song.

The circle formed a sphere, encompassing the white-faced dolphin in a globe of swimming bodies. They revolved faster, the ocean pulsing with their energy. As they spun facets of light as bright as diamonds struck her, filling the sea with phosphorescence. Her body vibrated, held by its rhythm. Then the song quieted. The dancing circle slowed, coming to rest. The living sphere split as the dolphins peeled away. They drifted on the current, waiting.

Dawn swam closer, peering down at the wonder beneath her.

The body of the dead dolphin shimmered like flashing embers. When its pectoral fins trembled Dawn pulled back, afraid. She watched as its body glowed gold in the darkness. The wounds on its flanks and face puckered and closed, glittering white then dark as the jagged edges fused. When both of its eyes opened, she swam to its beak, gazing into depthless wonder. Within the eye's unfathomable darkness, she saw a flash as bright as lightning. A chrysalis was born, hanging within clusters of glowing galaxies. It shattered. A butterfly unfurled wings of sparking gossamer and flew free. The sea shook as the dolphin vented. Bright bubbles soared above her. A curtain of ephemeral sealight filled the ocean. It twisted, sparkling silver. Glowing sparks danced behind it, coalescing, as solid as stars. A face took shape. A mouth. Torso, arms and legs. The image of a man floated before her, suspended within luminous glory.

His eyes opened, finding hers. A hand reached through the curtained sealight, beckoning. She stretched. Her fingers slipped into his as easy as an old song. She could feel his solid warmth and gripped harder. Peering at his strong arm, she followed it up behind the curtain of light. She shuddered in recognition.

Michael.

The ocean brimmed with blinding light. Michael's presence dissolved, dissipating into sparkling clusters. They burst, departing like a kaleidoscope of butterflies flying before a gentle breeze.

Dawn blinked. She found herself standing on the pier. Rain struck her face. The song in her heart died as her certainty turned to confusion. She searched the sea but found only darkness. Afraid, she turned and ran.

CHAPTER THIRTY-ONE

Father Danny found her outside the church shivering in the rain like a frightened dog.

"Dawn, what's wrong? Everyone's looking for you."

"Where's Margaret?"

"Still at the hospital." The priest reached out, taking her arm. "Come on. Let's get you inside."

He ushered her through the fine mist which hung near the door and, when they were inside, led her to the sacristy. He sat and watched her pace the shadowed room. She was soaked and agitated; a blanket thrown over her shoulders. Her eyes burned with confusion which he recognized as the chaos of her heart. He forced himself to silence as she strode back and forth, waiting for her to speak. At last, she spun to him.

"Father, what if I told you I was crazy?"

The priest studied her. Dawn's face was gaunt with worry and exhaustion. Wet hair straggled down her back, unkempt and knotted. Her wild eyes darted around the room, her breathing ragged. He reached for a cloth, brushing rain from his jacket.

"I'd say you're only as crazy as the next person."

"Even if I started seeing things?"

Father Danny shifted in his chair at the unexpected statement. He had misunderstood the purpose of her visit, thinking she had come to talk about Jason.

"Dawn, you've been under tremendous strain. What do you think you saw?"

"You promised me I'd see him again."

"See who? You mean Jason?"

"Not Jason. Don't you remember?"

He thought back, recalling the last conversation they had in this room. He looked away, hoping to hide his sudden fear for her.

"You're talking about Michael, aren't you? Dawn, you know that's not possible."

"But that's what you said. That's what you promised."

"As I recall, I said we will see our loved ones in Heaven, God willing."

"But what if we don't have to wait?"

"Don't have to wait? I don't understand."

She stepped toward him, throwing off the blanket. "Father, what if Heaven is here? Right here. Like on another plane or something. Maybe when someone dies, we can still be with them. Not later, but now. Right now." Seeing his reaction, she turned away. "You don't believe me. You think I'm nuts."

Her wild speech cautioned great care. He tapped the chair next to him.

"Dawn, come sit with me."

She sat, eyes fixed on the wall, her foot drumming a mad staccato on the floor. The priest had seen the same desperation in many others. His experience told him that those dealing with the agony of loss had their breaking point. He worried Dawn had found hers.

"My friend, I'm here to listen. Why don't you tell me what happened?"

"I told you. I saw him."

"Sometimes, we see what we long for most. You long for Michael."

"That's crap!" She stood, pacing again. "You told me you believe your family is right in this room. You talk to them, for Chris-sakes. You told me to jump, remember Father? You told me to take a leap of faith. Well, I jumped and I need you to catch me." She walked close, kneeling at his side. "I saw him, Father. I know I did. You guys talk about ghosts all the time. You believe in them."

"Ghosts?"

"You know, like during Mass. We say 'we believe in the seen and the unseen'. That's what we recite, isn't it?" He was forced to nod. "Then why can't you believe I've seen the unseen?"

He was trapped. He could not deny the beliefs of his Church nor could he deny her desperate need for hope. He looked for a way out.

"Dawn, as I told you when we talked before. I don't know all the answers."

"You don't know?" she said, standing again. "You people are supposed to know. You told me to find faith. Maybe I've found it, okay? For God-sakes, Father. If you don't believe me, who will?"

She sat again beside him. Her anger was gone now, replaced by a heavy despair which cloaked her in darkness. He did not want to leave it that way.

"Dawn," he said slowly, "you don't need my permission to define your faith. Let me ask you something. What do you want to believe?"

She grew thoughtful but he also sensed great fear. "Michael died. I know he did. I saw it happen. But then I saw…"

"Saw what? Exactly what did you see?"

"I saw —" She looked to the floor. "It's just, don't you understand? I love him so much. He's here, Father. Right here. I know he is." What she said next sounded even crazier. "Father Danny, I touched him. I held his hand. It was warm."

Not knowing how to respond, he waited in her silence. He sensed how she agonized over the next words, tears falling on her cheeks. "Father, if you love someone so much; if he loves you back the same way —" She finally looked at him. "Is it possible to love someone so completely they never die?"

"But Dawn, that's what the Church professes. We don't die."

"I'm not talking about our souls, Father."

The priest leaned back as he considered her proposition, believing an insensitive response could destroy her. He looked to the ceiling, hoping to find the answer written in the paint. Then he remembered how, on many days in this very room, he talked out-loud to his family as he prepared for Mass. They always seemed so alive to him. So real.

"Dawn, the answer to your question is not in the catechism of the Church, of course. You're asking me, 'What do I believe? What have I experienced?'" He raised an eyebrow. "Truthfully? Dawn, I only know what I don't know. The world is full of unexplained mysteries. You ask me if your deep love could keep Michael alive. While it is not a teaching of the Church, maybe great love can do just that." He laughed. "God knows my Bishop would never agree. He'd throw me out for blasphemy." He reached out, grasping her shoulder. "What I am certain of is this. Do you recall what I said about Paul Tillich? Even great thinkers like him can't prove their faith. If you find comfort in your conviction, if you truly believe it, then take that jump. Make that leap of faith. Hold on to it and never let go."

"You don't think I'm crazy, Father? You believe me?" She bent, her hair hiding her face. "I don't even know if I believe it myself."

"Confusion is a fundamental part of our search for faith. If you decide to believe it, then I do too. Dawn, I promise you this. If you take that leap, I'll be right there to catch you." When he considered his words, the priest couldn't help but chuckle.

"What?" she asked.

"You're lucky."

"Lucky? How could I possibly be lucky?"

"Because," the priest said, his smile deepening, "I don't know anyone whose love has greater courage than your own." Sensing they were finished he rose, escorting her to the door. "Is there anything else I can do?"

Her chin quivered. "They want me to take Jason back to Boston."

"Is that what you want?"

"I don't know. I don't know what to do."

"I do. You're in a church. I'd say it's a perfect place to ask for an answer." He took her hand. "Remembrance Day is in two days' time. I hope you can stay until then. You promised to talk about Michael, remember? Your words will be important not only to me but to all who listen. Can you do that?"

"I'll try." She worked hard to smile. "Thank you, Father."

When she walked out of the sacristy, he closed the door and phoned the hospital, leaving a message for Margaret that her daughter-in-law was safe.

Then he stood in the shadows, thoughtful. He hoped the troubled young American would find peace because every soul deserves such a gift. Sinking to his knees, he prayed for her and all those who struggled to find faith in the face of great loss.

In the main church, Dawn stood in thought at the sacristy door. Her eyes cast about the darkened building, fixing for a moment on the silhouettes of the tables near the altar and the stack of wreaths for Remembrance Day. She suddenly understood the reason behind the ceremony. "We remember because none of us can let them go," she whispered, and smiled at the conviction her words held.

She turned, walking down the center aisle. As she did, she could feel Michael's song swelling in her breast, the same song she had heard when finding him. Her footfalls echoed to its rhythm. At the alcove, she entered. Rows of burning candles lit the Saint in dancing shadows. She remembered Margaret's actions when she prayed before the statue. Dawn lit a candle. Kneeling, she looked up at the kind face.

"I'm sorry, but I don't know what words to say. Michael was the good Catholic, not me..." Her voice trailed off as she searched her heart. "Saint Anthony, you're supposed to be the saint of miracles. The saint of the lost. If you really are, then let me believe it's true. Let him be alive." She thought some more and, looking back toward the nave, her eyes searched the shadows.

"Michael? If you're really here, please help Jason. Show me what to do. Michael? Are you there?" The only response was the sputtering of candle flame. She took a deep breath, bowing her head. "Or maybe you're not there at all."

Dawn stood and left the church. Behind her, a candle sparked in the darkness. Its shadow beat against the Saint's folded hands like wings of glittering gossamer. In the darkness, mist rose into the silence. A gentle breath stirred the candle flame. It flickered, rising bright, lighting the Saint's face in a miracle of metamorphosis.

The butterfly rested for a moment upon the iron candle rack, gathering strength. It stretched, unfurling, then took flight. On glowing wings, it flew out an open window intent on answering Dawn's prayer.

At the hospital Margaret had waited while others searched for her daughter-in-law. She had spent the time worrying, either praying for news of Dawn or looking in on her sick grandchild. She had met the doctor who had advised her that the boy's condition remained unchanged and urged her to convince Dawn to transfer him back to Boston. When the ward nurse had hurried in with Father Danny's message that Dawn was safe, Margaret had allowed herself to relax a little. But at the back of her mind, she fretted at what she would say about Jason's transfer when her daughter-in-law returned.

As she sat in the waiting area, her eyes cast about the room. Jackie had slouched out after Dawn's departure and the crowd had thinned. Many, including Joan and Mary, had stopped by to see her before they left, promising to return later that night. Margaret glanced at a set of chairs. Carol had chosen to stay whether out of sheer obstinance or a sense of guilt, Margaret didn't know. The woman lolled in the chair with Lydia sleeping at her side. Margaret thought of waking her to apologize for the uncharacteristic words she had levelled earlier at the woman but she could not keep her eyes open and was soon asleep.

As Margaret slept the glowing butterfly soared through the open front door and into the room. It fluttered close to her head, brushing her face, then flew high as in her sleep she shooshed it away. Looping in flight, it sailed through the critical care wing, streaking like starlight to the child's room. It flitted to the observation window, resting on the glass, wings pulsing as it saw the boy's ashen face.

Within the glittering insect Michael's consciousness sensed that his transformation was complete. When the pod had resurrected him, they had left behind a piece of each of them. Combined with the gift his brother had already given him, he was aware of the power of many within his glowing psyche.

His mind stretched, reaching. From his shimmering wings, a curtain of sealight spun across the window lighting his boy's face in an eternal glow. He breathed out with his love. The sealight fell through the glass and into the room, the cup of water resting on the nightstand vibrating to his song. He saw his boy's monkey snuggled beneath the blankets and chuckled at the comical face. Then his light shimmered star-like and he stood naked, again as a human being. He leaned over his son. Studying the vacant face and unseeing eyes, he sang to the child's unconsciousness.

Jason blinked in the soft light. He reached for his monkey and, as he clutched it, looked up into his father's sparkling eyes. Jason's mouth worked as his mind searched for the familiar sound.

"Daddy?" he asked softly, testing it, and smiled at the simple word. "Daddy," he said again, but this time his voice held the strength of confirmation.

His father's strong arms lifted the boy and his monkey, nestling them both against his naked chest. Michael bent, kissing him.

"Come on, son. Let's get you home."

"Home?"

"Home." His father smiled down at his child. "But first we have a message to leave for your mother."

The sealight contracted, enfolding them in shining mist. It flashed once, rumbling with distant thunder. Then it glowed and they were gone in a streak of starlight.

Dawn stopped at the house only long enough to change out of her soaked jeans then jogged back to the hospital. As she entered the waiting area, she found her mother-in-law sleeping on a chair.

"Margaret?" she whispered, touching her shoulder. "Margaret?"

The older woman opened her eyes and smiled. "I must have fallen asleep. I was worried about you." She sat higher. "Dawn, did you talk to the doctor? She was looking for you again."

"She still wants me to take Jason back, doesn't she?" Her mother-in-law answered by gazing at the floor. "Margaret, what do you think I should do?"

"I'd rather he stay here. But the doctor believes it's for the best. I think you should follow her advice. She asked if you've talked to Jason's doctor in America."

Dawn shivered. Her prayer for Jason had been answered but not in the way she had hoped. At least she now understood the only way left to help her son. She looked up at a wall clock. Doctor Morrison was probably still at Children's Hospital.

"I'll see if they'll let me use a phone to call Boston. Did you see Jason?"

"He's the same," Margaret replied, and took her hand. "Dawn, I'm so sorry."

She squeezed back. "So am I. I'll look in on him first."

Walking to his room, Dawn discovered only an empty bed. She stepped out to the hallway, spotting a nurse.

"Where's Jason?"

"Isn't he in his room?" the nurse asked, looking through the window. "He's scheduled for a scan but I thought it was for tomorrow morning. Let me check."

Dawn waited while the man walked to a nurses' station. He flipped through some paperwork then made a call. When his smile dropped, she realized he didn't know where Jason was, either. He hurried back to her.

"Mrs. McCarthy, why don't you go back to the waiting area."

"You don't know where he is?"

"We'll find him," the nurse answered, and marched down the hall in the other direction. Dawn walked back to the waiting area unable to comprehend the disappearance.

It took an hour for staff to search the hospital. When they couldn't locate Jason, hospital security notified the local Gardaí. At the same time Margaret woke Carol, explaining.

"They can't find him?" Carol barked, still half-asleep. "He couldn't have walked out on his own. Margaret, do you think someone took him?"

"Oh, my good Lord," Margaret said, and burst into tears.

Carol rose, hugging her. She looked across the room. Dawn paced the floor with anxious steps. When she turned, she presented a face flushed with worry, eyes red-rimmed from crying. Studying the distraught woman, Carol realized for the first time that the American was only a loving mother who wanted to do the best for her child, just as she did. She thought back to the words she had used over the past few days and her opinion of the brash young woman. Reaching for her bag, Carol pulled out a phone.

"What are you doing?" Margaret asked.

"Making up for lost time."

Carol rang half the town despite the late hour. When she finished, she took Margaret's hand. "Can you watch Lydia? You and Dawn stay here in case someone brings back Jason. We'll find him." The woman grabbed her coat, marching out the door before Margaret could say a word.

Within minutes, town's people were out searching. Church women scanned the square and the local playground. Farmers prowled their fields. Carol, Mary and Joan hunted the main street and outside the closed shops, then searched the church. With Father Danny, they looked under every pew and in every corner. In his damaged trawler, Jackie shook off his weariness. Grabbing a spotlight he swept the shadowed pier, examining every boat tied up there.

As the hours passed Dawn found it impossible to wait at the hospital. She and Margaret went first to the house, searching it. Then they took the car to the cove, thinking her boy might have found his way there. Standing on the pier, she looked out to a sea glowing pink with the early morning light of dawn. As she called her son's name, she prayed again for Michael to answer. All she heard was the tide lapping across an empty beach and the distant cry of a shorebird.

CHAPTER THIRTY-TWO

"Dawn?"

She slept on the couch in Margaret's living room, waking in a fog of exhaustion. She looked up expecting to see her mother-in-law but instead found Carol.

"Did they find him?" Dawn asked.

"I'm sorry, Dawn. No, they haven't."

When Carol sat down Dawn found she couldn't look at her.

"Carol, I owe you an apology. I'm sorry for what I said to you in the hospital. You didn't hurt Jason. Margaret told me what you did last night, how hard you tried to find him. I was upset. I shouldn't have said it."

"I had it coming," Carol grunted. "I've said and done some stupid things in my life. Dawn, I caused this. I know I did. If I hadn't told Jackie to do something about that silly *crater*; if I'd only kept my big gob shut, none of this would have happened. I can be such a fool." With that, Carol burst in to tears.

Dawn couldn't process the woman's apology. Coming fully awake, she looked across the room. It was filled with people standing in the sunlight which streamed in through the wide front window. Two Gardaí in blue uniforms took notes as they talked with Margaret about her missing grandson. Joan and Mary stood with the church women discussing Jason in hushed voices. A group of fishermen huddled in a corner. Dawn could hear them in snatches and realized they were planning to drag the bottom of the harbor for her son.

"I can't do this anymore," she heard someone whisper and recognized the voice as her own. She rose and fled from the crowded room, retreating into the depths of the house.

She found herself in the studio, sitting on the big chair. She did not at first notice the warmth of the morning sun spilling in through the open window or the tugging screams of seagulls as they called from the harbor. She was too tired to even cry.

As she stared into space, a facet of light caressed her lips. It crossed her face again, higher this time. When it glittered into her eyes she blinked, focusing. She found herself peering at the easel and the unfinished painting of Solas Mór. She stood, taking a step toward it. Reaching out, she fingered a necklace which swung from the corner of the canvas, sparkling in the sunlight.

"Dawn?"

She turned, finding her mother-in-law at the door.

"Margaret, where did you find this?"

"But I didn't," Margaret said, peering at the necklace. "Did you lose it?"

"Yes, I mean not exactly, but…" Dawn faltered, and recalled how she had flung the dolphin necklace into the sea. Her eyes moved to the canvas. She reached out, touching it with a fingertip. She pulled it back smudged with wet paint.

"When did you finish it?"

"Finish what?" Margaret asked, stepping further into the room. "What are you talking about?"

Margaret stopped as the canvas came into view. Someone had painted in the blank space, completing the picture. The white-faced dolphin leaped high above the raging sea. A man sat astride its broad back. They headed toward the island of Solas Mór, its tall peak jutting from angry seas into the light of a rising sun.

"You said there was a legend," Dawn whispered. "The Legend of Solas Mór. Tell me the story."

"But why now? Dawn, people are outside waiting for us."

"Please, Margaret."

Margaret heard the haunting plea in her daughter-in-law's voice. She frowned at the exhaustion in Dawn's face then, perching on an arm of the chair, let her eyes settle on the painting's fantastic image.

"The Legend of Solas Mór is not so much a story as it is a prayer. Maybe what we face now makes it even more important." She settled back and, taking a breath, started.

"It is an ancient legend and though the Greeks started it the Irish embellished it and now it is ours. It is a long narrative and I can't remember all of it but back then, a hundred years ago and more, many believed that sailors, at least the lucky ones, didn't drown if they were shipwrecked. Instead, they started a new voyage. An evolution of discovery. Cast into desperate seas, without hope or solace, the song of the dolphin came to them. The seas churned with the hope of life and the beauty of salvation. Then the sun would rise and their world was filled with light. Though born as men, these lucky few rejoiced in rebirth. They became dolphins." She paused, lost in thought.

"What happened then?"

Margaret glanced at her daughter-in-law. Dawn stared at the painting, eyes as round as dinner plates.

"Dawn, let's go back to the others. It's too much right now."

"Please, Margaret. Finish it."

Walking to the painting, Margaret cleared her throat, letting the story draw her in.

"In the legend, renewed life was not the sailors' only gift for the ones who were saved were given many powers. Power to travel out of their bodies. Power to control water. Power to again walk the land on a mist as timeless as tomorrow. Power to journey back to the world on an ocean of joy to find those they had left behind. For you see, Dawn, the Legend of Solas Mór isn't only a prayer of hope and forgiveness. It is also a prayer of eternal love."

Dawn looked again at the painting. As she studied it, she recalled the mystery she had witnessed a year ago on the night of the accident, one which she had not been able to tell anyone, a memory which made her think she was crazy.

Again, she remembered the raging seas and Michael's burning boat. Again, she remembered the towering island which should not have been there and the rising sun though it was not yet dawn. And again, she remembered the song and the vision that still haunted her.

Her mind filled with the terrible beauty of that night: of how, clinging to the swinging buoy, she had seen the white-faced dolphin swim from the sinking trawler, leaping through towering seas. A man lay prostrate on its back; a man with dark curling hair and powerful shoulders. As they swept past, he had lifted an arm, beckoning to her.

Dawn again studied the painting. The white-faced dolphin swam to the island through raging seas. The man on its back beckoned to her with a raised arm as if wanting to pull her into the picture. His eyes were blue, his arms muscular, his hair a mop of dark curls.

She noticed the table. Jason's acrylics rested on it; the tubes open. His brush lay beside them, the bristles still damp. Saucers were smeared with paint as if they had just been used. She touched them. The paint was wet, the glass of water filled with dirty paint water. A circle of silver floated on its surface.

Dawn took down the necklace from where it hung. She spilled it into her palm, studying the golden dolphin dancing through its ring of silver. Placing it around her neck, she again studied the painting and the man who gazed back at her.

"I know where they are."

"Who? Do you mean Jason?"

"No," Dawn said, turning to Margaret. "I know where they both are."

Having listened to Dawn's wild hunch Margaret had no choice but to agree. It was either that or phone a psychiatrist. She decided to stay quiet and let her daughter-in-law try to prove her point. The worst possible outcome was that they would find nothing.

"I'm not crazy, Margaret," Dawn insisted as they left the house, descending the back steps.

"I know you're not," she replied, but continued to worry because her response was only a half-truth. When Margaret mentioned that the journey Dawn had in mind was too far for the punt, she hoped she would change her mind. But faced by her daughter-in-law's insistence, Margaret suggested asking Jackie for help.

"Not Jackie. Anyone but him."

"Dawn, I hate what Jackie did to Jason but I have to forgive him. Can't you try, too?"

"It's a big ask."

"When you see the young fool, it will be easy."

"When I see the young fool, I'll want to kill him."

But when they found Jackie standing on the stern of his fishing boat Dawn noted the suffering in the man's eyes, so much like her own. She remembered what Michael had said of him and the friendship they had once enjoyed. Seeing the women on the pier, Jackie leaped off his boat with a rush of words. As he talked, Dawn realized the tears in the fisherman's eyes weren't fake nor was his sorrow.

"Dawn, let me say again how sorry I am," he mumbled, taking off his cap. "I was a first-class eejit."

"So you were," Dawn replied. "But then so was I."

She extended a hand and he shook it. When he asked if Jason had been found, Margaret turned the conversation to the journey they wanted to make.

"The island?" he asked, scratching his head. "Why there? What about the lad?"

"No questions, Jackie," Margaret responded. "It's enough to know it's important."

"When do you want to go?"

"Right now," Dawn said. "Will you take us?"

When Jackie informed them that his trawler was dead in the water due to its busted shaft, he looked down the pier. Johnny stood on the deck of his boat smoking a rollup in the sunshine.

"Do you think he'll do it?" Dawn asked.

"Johnny's a good skin," Jackie replied. "Come with me and we'll find out."

When they climbed on to Johnny's boat and explained, the old man threw his butt into the sea.

"Solas Mór?" Johnny growled, studying the group. "Now why would you want to go to Solas Mór? What about the boy?"

"Ask no questions and the ladies will tell us no lies," Jackie replied. "Now will ya do it or not?"

"For you, no. But for the ladies, well —" The old fisherman motioned them toward the bow.

Johnny's boat motored out into Bantry Bay accompanied by a fine day and a freshening breeze. When the half-decker cleared Bere Island, Margaret walked into the wheelhouse to stand with Johnny and Jackie. This time when the men asked why they were steaming to the island, she told them.

"That's what she thinks? But Margaret, the lad can't be on the island and neither can his Da'," Jackie cautioned, and pursed his lips in a low whistle. He looked out the window. The American stood at the bow railing, the wind blowing through her hair. "Ah, the poor Gersha. God forgive me, I've driven her mad."

"What you did makes no difference now, Jackie," Margaret stated. "Dawn needs to look. It'll come to nothing, of course. If she grows upset when she can't find them, can you help me with her until we get home?"

"We can always lock her below decks, if it comes to it," Johnny suggested.

"It won't come to that. But promise you'll help. She's frantic for the lad and God knows how she yearns for Michael."

Jackie looked to Johnny and they both nodded.

At the bow, Dawn gripped the steel railing just as she had the first time Michael had taken her to the island. The wind whipped through her wheat-colored hair as it had on the day of the accident when they were all alive and happy. Just as on both trips, Dawn hunted the horizon. Seeing the island's rugged peak, she caught sight of the yellow buoy rocking in a gentle swell. When Johnny steered his boat alongside, Jackie snagged it with a boat hook, hauling them in close.

"There's where we hit," Dawn said, pointing out the scratched paint and dented metal at the waterline. "And that's where the *Margie M* sank." She turned, looking to a spot a quarter-mile distant.

"That's where you saw the dolphin with the man on its back," Margaret said, ignoring the impossible. "Just like the legend."

"It was Michael. The dolphin took him there," Dawn continued, gazing at the island dwarfing the horizon. "Solas Mór was closer that night. It was right on top of us."

"And you really think Jason is on the island."

"I know he's there. Both of them are." She turned to her mother-in-law. "I don't know what you think of me. Maybe I should be locked up. Maybe I'm no longer fit to be a mother. But I have to know."

"What you've experienced would disturb anyone," Margaret said, and placed a soft hand on Dawn's arm. "That's why we're here. To find out."

When they arrived offshore, Dawn asked to go in on her own. Jackie looked sideways at Margaret but said nothing as he and Johnny lowered the half-decker's small punt into the sea. Dawn climbed in and when the outboard started Jackie untied the painter and tossed it to her. He watched as she gunned the boat toward the island.

"Will she be all right?"

"I don't know, Jackie," Margaret said. "She's been through too much."

Jackie squinted into the sunlight, tracking the punt toward the island's pier. "She's almost there. When she's finished looking, we'll go home and keep searching for the lad." He put an arm around Margaret's shoulders. "We'll find him, God willing. That's a promise."

In the punt Dawn steered through the surf, making her way up to the old pier just as Michael had done years ago. She lashed the boat tight and clambered on to the island. Hearing the raucous cry of gulls, she looked up, studying the sheer sandstone peak thrusting into a cloudless sky. She noticed a cormorant perching on the rocks stretching its wings in the sunshine. A pair of puffins swept in over the breaking tide, coming to rest on a rocky outcrop. She walked closer to the sea, searching the rugged landscape.

"Jason! Michael!" she called.

Their names echoed in the stillness.

She climbed on to a small promontory, looking both ways across the island. All she could see were foaming waves curling against rocks the size of small houses. She felt dizzy, thinking her search was madness.

She breathed in, filling her lungs. Steadier, she jumped off the small peak, treading north up the coast. Her steps quickened as she searched the inland crags, then turned to the waterline. As she stepped over a scramble of rock, she tripped and almost fell. Looking back, she found the sheared-off end of a hawser which lay wedged in the rocks, coated in bright seaweed. Its length snaked across lichen-covered stones toward the sea. She followed it to where it passed over a cleft at the island's edge. Peering down she traced it, falling to the thrashing seas twenty feet below.

A smear of blue caught her attention. A two-foot length of shattered wood rested on an outcrop of rock just beneath her. She reached down, grabbing it, turning it in her hands. One side was scorched black and stank of diesel fuel. Turning it again, black lettering came into view:

MARG

The rest was eaten away by fire.

She stood, catching a glint of reflected sunlight coming from the far shoreline. She looked closer, making out the lines of the shattered wheelhouse and smashed hull of Michael's half-decker. The remains of the boat were hidden beneath a rocky escarpment at the island's edge. Water sluiced in from the sea, pouring through the rocks, beating hard against the wreckage. At last, she understood why the Coast Guard had never found the *Margie M.* She turned from it, gazing again across the island.

"Jason!" she called. "Michael!" But her voice was lost in the surging of the sea.

She fell to her knees, her mind spinning, realizing her search was over. She bent, retching. As she sobbed, she thought this time she would never stop.

The song drifted in on the breeze. She wiped her face, scanning the ocean. She turned toward the peak, listening as the song grew stronger, her eyes falling on a pile of stone. Jason's monkey sat at the top smiling its lopsided grin. She stumbled to it, thinking it could not be real. But when she grabbed it, it was as solid as the rocks she stood on. A fishing line was tied to its tail. The line led up across the rocks to a ledge high above her. She recalled the first time she had visited the island and the ledge Michael had led her to.

The fishing line went taut, tugging. The monkey's tail swung. She grasped the line, feeling its pull. She followed it. The walk up the path to the ledge was as easy as she remembered. Trudging up the trail, she recalled the weight of Jason inside her and Michael's hand on her back before he had shared the excitement of his secret. She followed the fishing line to its very end.

Dawn paused on top of the ledge. Looking down into deep shadows, she remembered how Michael had lifted her to the sand, below. This time he wasn't there. Instead, she jumped. She pulled off her boots and socks. Barefoot, she walked around a stone outcrop. When she stepped into the sunlight, she felt the warm sand beneath her feet. Her breathing deepened when she saw the lagoon. Its waters lapped against the beach as blue and as smooth as she remembered.

"Please, let it be real," she whispered, her eyes rising to the sunlit peak. "Please, Saint of miracles. Don't let me be crazy. Let them be here."

Her eyes fell on a group of dorsal fins slicing into the inlet. One broke away from the pod, crossing to the center of the lagoon. The white-faced dolphin rose. Tail-standing, it gazed at her from across the dappled water. Light flashed, blinding. When she opened her eyes again, she heard his call.

"Mom! Over here!"

Jason raced across the beach with a smile as wide as the sea. He threw himself at her and she held him fast while he talked and talked.

"Dad says first, you need to take us back to Nana. But then we're supposed to come back to the island. Can we do that? Please, Mom, can we please come back? It's so cool!"

"What else did he say?" she asked, hearing nothing else in all the world but the words coming from his moving lips.

"He said," Jason chattered, "'Tug and I'll always tug back.' But I don't get it. What does that mean?"

"Well, I get it," she replied, and looked to where the white-faced dolphin lay waiting in the quiet water.

She hugged her son again and as they embraced the sun rose higher, as bright as a child's plaything. She heard the song and looked once more across the lagoon. The dolphin had disappeared. Her eyes hunted to the other side of the sunlit pool. Michael stood tall on a rocky outcrop, his dark hair floating in the breeze. He raised both arms in greeting. Then the light grew even brighter as the miracle of metamorphosis again took place.

His body glowed as he contracted into the glowing sealight of legend. The light coalesced, spinning, and Dawn beheld the mystery of transformation. A symphony of song echoed off the cliffs. She blinked. When her vision cleared, she saw the white-faced dolphin swimming again in the lagoon. But this time its body glittered as bright as starlight.

"I almost forgot," Jason said, taking her hand. "Dad says he loves you."

"Oh, he does, does he?"

"He sure does. Watch what he can do."

The dolphin leaped, water cascading from its back. Droplets glinted in the sunlight. A veil of butterflies filled the sky, fluttering across the lagoon in a kaleidoscope of color. They burst like fireworks and, as if glowing comets, streaked overhead, dissipating across the horizon in golden trails of his love for her.

CODA

CHAPTER THIRTY-THREE

As Dawn packed, she thought back on the long journey they had taken together and with it the heartbreaking string of failures. She recalled how, months ago, Doctor Morrison had suggested the unattainable remedy that he believed would heal her son.

"He thinks his father is alive," she remembered Morrison saying. *"If Jason saw him, he would talk again. But, of course, that's impossible."*

"It wasn't impossible," Dawn whispered. "All it took was a miracle."

She glanced at her healthy son. He stood at his father's bureau, the drawers open as he emptied them. She walked to the bed, sorting through a pile of underwear.

"Mom, should we bring these, too?" Jason held up a pile of Michael's old T-Shirts.

"Let's ask Nana to give them to Jackie. He could use them."

"Can Nana come see us someday? She'll miss us."

"Don't you worry. Your father will take care of that, too. Finish up. We have to go soon."

As her son organized his backpack, she thought back to yesterday's conversation with Margaret. Having arrived home from the island, they had talked late into the night. Dawn had concluded there was now no reason to go back to Boston with its barren future and empty bank accounts. Everything she and Jason needed was here, right here. All they had to do was leap for it. As she explained her decision, Margaret's eyes had filled with doubt.

"You don't believe me, do you?" Dawn had asked. "Margaret, I'm not lying."

"Gersha, I know you're not. Whatever you saw today, it shook you. You believe Michael is alive which is why you want to go back. But I'm an old woman. I'd have to see him for myself." She had dropped her eyes, unable to look at her daughter-in-law. "I fear you'll both come home disappointed."

"Then how do you think Jason got to Solas Mór? Why do you think he's talking again?" Dawn had taken her mother-in-law's hand, squeezing hard. "You taught me to believe in miracles. If I can do it, can't you?"

"I'll try because you want me to," Margaret had replied without conviction. "Dawn, you've made that leap but can't you see? It might be too far for me."

They had changed the subject by discussing what to tell the town about Jason's sudden reappearance. They had agreed it would be best to say nothing. People would assume he had simply woken from his illness, walked out of the hospital and found his way home. And as to his sudden vocal recovery?

"They'll believe that his talking again is a miracle," Margaret had said.

"Well, isn't it?" Dawn had replied, grinning. "See? If the town can believe in miracles, so can you."

After that they had gone upstairs to bed. The had slept for a few hours, rising early because there was so much to do. Now almost finished, Dawn scanned the bedroom. The contents of Michael's bureau as well as their suitcases fit into a single crate which rested on the floor. Margaret had promised to sort through it, earmarking most of the clothing for charity, but had told Dawn she would store the crate in the attic for now. "You'll be back," she had said, "and when you do at least you'll have something to wear."

Jason placed his backpack at the door next to the box holding his father's Uilleann. That's all they would take. They didn't need anything else. With everything prepared, Dawn stood at the open window for the last time. She looked out on the harbor which sparkled with the promise of a new day. Her face warmed as she remembered the final journey that waited for them.

"Mom, I'm ready."

She turned, spreading her arms. Laughing, Jason leaped into them. "Good," Dawn said. "Church first, then we'll go find your dad."

The Church of All Saints was packed for Remembrance Day Mass. Congregants crowded into pews waiting for the service to begin. Standing near the altar Dawn studied them, wanting to embrace them all. She saw Joan and Carol sitting together looking anywhere but at each other. One pew over Mary looked up, catching Dawn's eye. The old shopkeep wore a quizzical smile because Margaret had shared Dawn's unimaginable decision with her. Behind Mary, Dawn saw the rest of the wreath-making women whispering to each other. Next to them Jackie sat with his son Peter while Johnny, George and other fishermen were seated in a pew beside them. Behind the fishermen, farmers waited with their wives and kids while more shopkeepers as well as publicans and a group of schoolchildren who would take up the Offering were jammed into other pews.

Dawn spotted Margaret. She sat beside Jason, listening as he chatted with Lydia. It seemed her mother-in-law's gaze recorded every word of his laughing voice.

Dawn turned to the ninety-four wreaths spread across the altar steps. Framed photos of the dead stood next to each one. She studied the faces of Tomás and Michael, noting the strong resemblance. She turned again as the pub's traditional musicians walked down the center aisle. After taking their places they played a quiet hymn.

Her eyes moved to Margaret's finished painting which stood tall near the altar. The island of Solas Mór soared through tumultuous clouds into a sunlit heaven. The white-faced dolphin rose from the sea with a man astride its back, his powerful arms outstretched as if in benediction. Dawn smiled, at last understanding the legend because she was choosing to live it.

The door to the sacristy opened. Father Danny stepped out dressed in purple robes for the celebration. At his entrance, the traditional group played

The Voyage and Dawn's pulse quickened. The priest stood at the lectern and the crowd hushed for his opening prayer.

"Welcome to you all, both local people and those from foreign lands who live with us," the priest began. "Welcome, too, to those honoring loved ones lost at sea, be they gone yesterday or a lifetime ago." His eyes swept across the crowd, settling on Jason. "Welcome also to the small ones thought lost but found again. We delight in these joyful miracles." The crowd clapped and Dawn saw Jackie's quick glance at her son. She had asked him to help her return to the island and, when Jackie had asked why the sudden trip back, she had told him. Bound to secrecy, the fisherman's expression was filled with the same doubt that Margaret's face still wore.

Dawn's eyes moved away from him as the priest finished his welcome in a simple prayer. "Now let us remember them, oh Lord, our hearts filled with gladness." Father Danny motioned for Dawn to join him. She climbed the steps to the lectern, looking out on the sea of people.

"Good morning," she said into the microphone. Her voice boomed across the nave and when she smiled with embarrassment the congregation smiled back. The priest lowered the volume and she began again.

"Good morning. I'll start by saying I promise to watch my tongue. No words like 'pissa'." The congregants laughed and she relaxed. "Father Danny asked me to talk about Michael. But then I remembered — you all know Michael because you raised him. You gave him his humor and love of life. You gave him the song in his heart. So, if it's okay with everyone, I don't want to talk just about Michael." She cleared her throat, leaning closer. "You see, you've taught me so much. I know now I'm not the only one to have lost someone and I'm sorry if I sometimes acted like it. Joan?" she said, finding the librarian in the crowd. "You lost your husband fifteen years ago. I hear he was a fine man. I wish I could have met him. And Carol?" she continued as the woman looked up. "You lost Paul when Lydia was just a toddler. I know it's been hard, but you're raising a fine daughter. We hit some bumps along the road and I'm sorry. I wish I could have listened to you better."

She looked for her mother-in-law. "Margaret, you lost not only your only son but also Tomás yet you kept on marching. That took so much courage. You taught me how." She scanned the crowd, realizing how important they were to her. "Each and every one of us has lost someone we love to the sea. For a long time, I couldn't cope with it. You all tried to help me but I didn't understand. My problem was, I wasn't sure what to believe or how to do it. I think I know now. If you can give me a minute, I'd like to explain."

When Mass was finished everyone collected their wreaths and, in the sunlight, processed to the pier. Father Danny blessed the town's fishing fleet, praying for all those who ventured out on to turbulent waters. Standing in the crowd, Margaret caught her daughter-in-law's eye. They exchanged smiles and, as they did, Margaret recalled the other words Dawn had spoken at Mass, ones which still sang in her heart.

"*Father Danny says finding faith is hard. I tell you what. It is hard. He told me to leap for it but I was too much of a coward. But as Carol says, we have to get out there. We have to face our grief. Carol, I wish I could have listened. It would have saved us all a lot of trouble.*"

Margaret watched her daughter-in-law step through the Remembrance Day crowd. She saw Joan's surprise as Dawn slipped the dolphin necklace over her head in thanks for the gift of friendship freely given. Then she turned to Mary, giving her a walking stick she'd held back from the tourist sales, hoping it would help with the old woman's rheumatism. As they talked, Margaret smiled to herself. Dawn had never learned that it was her mother-in-law who had contributed to her salary at the Seashell. That secret would stay safe because Mary would never share it with anyone.

Margaret watched as Dawn made her way to Carol. She saw the look of surprise on the woman's face as Dawn handed her the wreath she had made for Michael. As they talked, Margaret knew her daughter-in-law was asking a special favor. Because she could not go out on the lifeboat due to an unexpected appointment, she was hoping Carol would throw it into the sea on her behalf. When Dawn opened her arms, the pair embraced.

Near them, Margaret caught sight of Jason giving Lydia a shy hug. Dawn called to him and, taking his hand, they walked away from the crowd. Then Margaret joined her family and, together, the three strode up the pier.

When they came to Jackie's trawler Dawn and Jason climbed onboard. From the pier, Margaret watched her daughter-in-law give the fisherman an envelope. He looked inside, shaking his head in disbelief. Margaret knew it contained over fifteen-hundred euro, almost everything Dawn had earned at the Seashell. It would not be enough to fix the broken shaft but it was a start. Jackie strode into the wheelhouse, returning with the shotgun. He broke it and, making certain it was empty, handed the gun to Jason. The fisherman lifted him above the gunwale and the boy threw it into the sea. Then they all shook hands on a deal well made.

With peace fully restored, Jackie joined them on the pier and they all strolled over to Johnny's boat. Before her family boarded Margaret said her goodbyes, still convinced she would see them later in the day. When she was finished, she walked back up the pier to the lifeboat where her friends waited for her. At the RNLI station she paused to gaze out on the sun-swept harbor and, as she did, reflected on the other words Dawn had spoken.

"I finally understand what you were all trying to tell me. With your help, I recalled something I had always believed but I'd forgotten how to do it. You taught me to believe in the miracle of endless love."

A few hours later, when Margaret had returned home from the lifeboat trip and after they had thrown their wreaths into the sea, she stood in her studio in a pool of sunlight. She looked down on Jason's monkey which she held tight in her hands. Her grandson had given it to her as a gift, explaining it would keep her company until he could see her again.

She gazed at its lopsided grin then sat down in the old chair. Her eyes moved up to Jason's drawings which still covered the walls, and the dancing dolphins he had painted which were filled with his hopes and dreams. As she looked, she guessed that her family was almost to their destination. She imagined she was in the wheelhouse of Johnny's boat, again with the men.

Through the window, she would see Dawn and Jason at the bow, gazing to the western horizon with the wind in their hair.

Margaret still did not understand how Dawn could believe what she did and had no idea where to start if she wanted to believe it, too. But she realized that if she remembered her painting of Solas Mór, the legend itself might tell her. Though it was still at the church she could feel it in her soul. As she recalled the painting's details, in her mind's eye she could also see her family as they clutched the boat's railing, waiting for Solas Mór to rise in the distance.

Margaret looked up when light struck her face. She stood, stepping to the window. A butterfly rested on the outside of the glass, its blue and white wings pulsing in the sunlight. She reached out, touching the window with a careful finger. As she did, Margaret recalled Dawn's next words at Mass.

"But I wonder. Rather than wait to see them in Heaven, what would happen if they were here? Right here. As alive as any of us. What if we could hold their hand one more time or even longer than that? I think it would make all the difference in the world, don't you?"

The butterfly sparked like a firefly, lighting Margaret's face in a rainbow of color. As she watched, it streaked from the house as bright as a star, leaving a trial of blazing light as it flew toward the open sea. When it disappeared over the horizon Margaret bowed her head, thanking the Saint of miracles for again showing her the way.

Dawn gripped Jason's hand as Solas Mór grew tall against the horizon. After they dropped anchor Jackie and Johnny helped them into the punt, handing down the green box and the backpack. Jackie waited on the half-decker while Johnny ferried them in. The old fisherman returned a few minutes later, alone. After they secured the punt, Jackie looked to the island. On its shore he could make out his dead friend's wife and son walking up a pathway of rock. He shook his head at their misguided belief, convinced that within the hour he would see them waving to come get them again.

On the island Dawn and Jason made it to the top of the ledge, then jumped down into the shadows. She led her son into the light where they stood again on the soft sands of the lagoon. As they waited, Dawn recalled the final words she had spoken at Mass and to the people who had come to remember those they had lost.

"Father Danny asked me to find faith and I have. But here's the thing. I've come to believe we can be with them now. Right now. All we have to do is jump. Maybe that sounds nuts but that's how I see it. Someday, I hope you can see it that way, too. Finally, I just wanted to say this —"

She took Jason's hand when they saw the pod swimming up the inlet. As the white-faced dolphin swam closer, their faces lit with the power of his love. A curtain of sealight rose from the gentle waters in front of them. She was certain that just beyond its glittering surface he waited for them. All they had to do was leap.

"You ready?" she asked. She tightened her grip on Jason's hand as, with the other, she picked up the Uilleann box Michael would never be without again. "Okay, Jason. Here we go. Ready, set —" They leaned forward into his presence. "Jump!"

When they did, an explosion of light enveloped the island.

Out at sea, Jackie and Johnny were awed as the sun rose again over Solas Mór even though it was only mid-day. Lightning flashed and thunder rumbled. Jackie looked over the side. A small group of dolphins swam past the half-decker, two adults and their pup. The fisherman put out a hand and Johnny grasped it. They promised each other they'd never tell the tale to anyone because no one would believe it.

Swimming away from the island, the family of dolphins traveled through sunlit seas and into the depths of the true Atlantic. The boy trilled, saying he needed to go play because the brother who nestled beside him said he wanted to. But his father quieted him, singing that he would have to learn first. At his side the female of the family tested her new flukes then thought of her final words to the congregation and what she had come to believe.

"You see, I believe we can hold those we love even though we are told they are no longer with us. We can laugh with them. Share our joy with them. Live our lives with them. In a forever I'll never understand. After all, isn't that what love is all about? Forever?"

As the family swam west into a setting sun, Dawn realized it was not the end of her voyage.

It was the beginning.

CHURCH OF ALL SAINTS

DAY OF REMEMBRANCE

WE REMEMBER THEM OH LORD

PEG DARCY	'NAILER' SEAN O'NEILL
ROBERT CLARKE	STEPHEN COURTNEY
LUKE MAC GABHAN	DONAL CAUSKEY
JOHN WALL	ROBERT SMITH
MARY PETHTEL	AL VESLEY
MICHAEL MCCARTHY	DAVID STOLZOFF
TOMÁS MCCARTHY	JAN DUGGA
JOSIE GREVILLE	JOHN EAGLE
JACK HARRINGTON	JULIA MALIN
JOSEPH CHHAN	ROLLEN KNUTSON
TOMAS MURRAY	DONAL O'DRISCOLL
BILL BUOTE	TANK ZIELINSKI
MOSS O'BROIN	JAKE O'MURCHU
JOHNNY CORRIGAN	SEAMUS RYAN
FINBAR HARRINGTON	DONAL RYAN
MAIREAD WILLIAMS	SEAN O'CARROLL

DEATH IS NOT AN END
IT IS BUT A VOYAGE BEGUN

ACKNOWLEDGEMENTS

As I write these words the world continues to suffer as the Covid-19 Delta variant sweeps the globe. In Ireland, over five-thousand people have died. In the United Kingdom, 128,000. The United States, over 600,000. The EU/EEA, circa 740,000. Worldwide: over 4 million souls have perished. So many people have experienced unimaginable heartbreak and loss, including this writer.

A few months ago, I stepped back and thought again about *Dolphin Song*. I realized for the first time that while the novel is a fairytale it is also a prayer of sorts — one which seeks to give hope as we yearn for those we can't be with anymore. A story, perhaps, which resonates with these times. On some levels the story of *Dolphin Song* was given to me as a gift, one which I want to pass on. I pray that it provides a bit of comfort to those who suffer.

Many people contributed to, and supported, the creation of *Dolphin Song*. Thanks, first, to those who read the manuscript and gave feedback including Ann Tracey, Jane Souness, Mary Bradford, Will Arnold and Michelle Lesley. Special thanks to Annabel Konig who provided valuable criticism. Grateful thanks to editor Delia Malim-Robinson who helped me to navigate various iterations of this story and offered suggestions and advice.

Thanks, too, to the many people who contributed their knowledge, hope and encouragement: my children Kristin, Cathy and Jonathan, as well as my grandchildren; my sister Cindy and my father Bill; the members of the Church of the Sacred Heart Choir, (Castletownbere, County Cork) whose love of song echoes across these pages; writers' doctor Claire Dobbin who told me, bluntly, that I didn't know how to write, offered to teach me and informed me that the process would be a marathon, not a sprint. (You know what, Claire? You were right.) To Ellen Win Wendl, Chairman of eQuinoxe Germany, for giving me another chance; Tom Bromley and The Literacy Consultancy for offering tremendous suggestions on how to improve the manuscript; the RNLI (Castletownbere, County Cork) for letting me clamber around their lifeboat; local *Seanachaí* Mary Maddison for the inspiration leading to old Squint; skipper Brendan O'Driscoll for explaining the life of trawler fishermen and the challenges of making a living in deep waters; skipper Damian Healy for lessons on net fishing; the people of Eyeries and Castletownbere, County Cork, Ireland, who provided me with so much inspiration; and, of course, to Carmel Murray whose loving support was with me every step of the way.

Dolphin Song would never have come to life but not for my great friend, Liam O'Neill. Filmmaker, producer, director and writer, Liam had a treasure trove of special gifts. Like me, he is an American who has lived in Ireland for many years. Like me, he was born in Chicago and is a devout Cubs fan. Like me, he loves his family and his craft.

In May, 2020, Liam passed away from Covid-19. He was 64. Liam leaves behind his wife, Annabel, and children Ben and Ella. Not a day goes by that I don't think of Liam and his family.

Thank you for *Dolphin Song*, my dear friend. I could not have made this voyage without you.

Ar dheis Dé go raibh d'anam dílis.

Eyeries, County Cork, Ireland
Summer 2021

NOW AVAILABLE

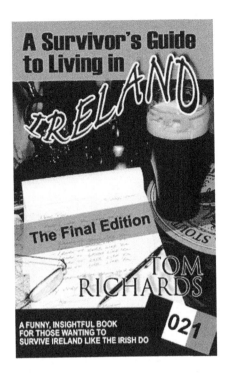

Come for a week and stay for a lifetime. That's the lure of Ireland.

In 1982, American Tom Richards took a four-week holiday to Ireland. He's been here ever since. If Ireland is the land of your dreams, this handy volume will help you to discover the magic of this glorious country for yourself. Learn to: laugh like the Irish, drink like the Irish, talk like the Irish and enjoy life just as the Irish do.

Witty, insightful, and loaded with tips on how to get a work permit, become a citizen and enjoy the general craic of living here, this 2021 edition is out now.

Google *A Survivor's Guide to Living in Ireland 2021* or go to: https://www.amazon.co.uk/Survivors-Guide-Living-Ireland-2021-ebook/dp/B08YRP3Z9N

Made in the USA
Coppell, TX
08 January 2022

71181813R00223